IT STARTED IN ROSWELL

A SCIENCE FICTION NOVEL

P. N. HABERMAN

RodaxLA Publishing

LOS ANGELES, CALIFORNIA

RodaxLA Publishing
P.O. Box 9982
Canoga Park, CA 91308
phaberman@earthlink.net

Publisher's Note: This is a work of fiction. Names, characters, places, and incidents are a product of the author's imagination. Locales and public names are sometimes used for atmospheric purposes. Any resemblance to actual people, living or dead, or to businesses, companies, events, institutions, or locales is completely coincidental.

It Started in Roswell / P.N. Haberman -- 1st ed.
ISBN 978-0-578-89602-1
Library of Congress Control Number 2021907897

Editor: Cary Editorial & Book Consulting
Book Layout © BookDesignTemplates.com
Cover Photo: Unsplash
Cover Designer: Fiverr / Cal5086

DEDICATION

Once upon a time a young man sat in a 7th grade study- hall doing what many youngsters were doing, avoiding anything to do with studying. An older boy in the same room reached over and handed the younger boy a book.

"Read this. I think you'll find it interesting."

The book was *Cycle of Fire* by Hal Clement. That older boy, David Paulo, lit my own fire. He later gifted me *Earthlight* by Arthur C. Clarke and *When Time Stood Still* by Ben Orkow. Those three paperback volumes still reside on my book shelves along with hundreds of other Science Fiction titles.

The truth was that I had devoured over a hundred books in my elementary school library but neither that school nor my middle school offered me what those three volumes did. Another truth was that finding a kindred soul who read SciFi literature was surpassed only by those that admitted to a liking for the genre by watching motion pictures at their neighborhood cinema and later on television.

Today I am encouraged to write by my inner muse. Isaac Asimov expressed it best; "I write for the same reason I breathe - because if I didn't, I would die." I probably wouldn't die but it might be a close call.

My family understands—I hope. They are part of my reading group and offer honest appraisals of my efforts. My fellow writers at IWOSC (Independent Writers of Southern California) also are supportive encouraging me to write more and "publish, damn it." Special thanks go to Sylvia Cary, my editor and creative director, of Cary Editorial & Book Consulting, who gave me the final push I needed to set this train in motion.

To all of you who take the time to read my stories I thank you. There's more to come.

"Two possibilities exist: either we are alone in the Universe or we are not. Both are equally terrifying."
— **Arthur C. Clarke**

PART I

IN THE BEGINNING

CHAPTER 1

IT WAS THREE A.M. ON a brutally slow Friday morning. No drunk drivers, no calls on my police radio, not even an inebriated Native American to break the monotony. I was sitting in the parking lot of Momma Tuckers Donut Shop, a half-eaten bear claw in my hand, when I wondered, not for the first time, "What the hell was I doing here?" Coming to Roswell, New Mexico, seemed like such a good idea considering the mess my life had become. I had given twelve years of my life to the U.S. Army, twenty more to the LAPD, thirty years to Lillian, my childhood sweetheart, and not enough time to work on my desire to be something...more. My thirty-year marriage came crashing down when Lillian decided she wanted a divorce and a chance to meet someone that more closely matched her intellectual ideal of a man. The fact that I never saw it coming, nor did I anticipate the moving company that showed up to remove all of her belongings, started me on a gradual slide that ended in Momma Tucker's parking lot in Roswell.

Alimony wasn't a concern since Lillian was a tenured professor of mathematics at UCLA earning far more in salary and perks than I ever did. I got along fine with income from renting out my former family home, a bonus that Lillian granted me, plus a modest pension from my tenure on the police department. What I thought I gained was the ability to finally write full time and amaze the world with my pending science fiction masterpiece. That was one of my reasons for relocating to Roswell, site of the infamous alien invasion and UFO crash landing. What better place for me to begin my new adventure than being surrounded by all that alien culture.

The bear claw hadn't moved an inch for several minutes while my imagination wandered when a tap on my car window followed by several more, each harder than the last, broke in to my self-absorbed contemplations.

"Officer Sands, are you all right in there?" Crazy Joe Farris, a senior citizen of undetermined age, self-cut gray hair streaming out from under his baseball cap, was crouched down from his over six-foot height, seemingly replacing the little gray alien on the billboard sign behind him advertising the upcoming Annual UFO Festival. He was staring in my patrol car looking like he thought I was the crazy one. "You ain't moved an inch in almost ten minutes. If you're not too busy I need to have a word."

Okay, I said I was in Roswell to write and that was my intention. Except to write you need inspiration and that seemed to be missing once I made it my primary occupation. But good old Mike Sands had always found a way to change direction and that is what I did after arriving in New Mexico just over a year ago. Several years before, Walter Boone, a partner of mine from LAPD, had taken the job as Chief of Police in Roswell. When he learned I was in town he offered me a chance to be a mentor to the many young officers on the force. The pay was shit compared to L.A. but once I had accepted his offer, I realized how much I missed being in uniform. An almost fifty-year-old Lieutenant Sands, Graveyard Watch Commander, was born.

"I ain't got all night, Officer. Get your ass out here."

He wasn't going to go away so I climbed out of the new Ford Explorer, four-wheel-drive, patrol cruiser that Walt had issued to me as an inducement to enlist. I faced Joe, took a final bite of the bear claw while waiting for him to finally tell me what was so important.

"You ever see anything that looks like this?" he said pushing a blue plant that resembled a succulent in my face. "I been studying things in this desert for nearly thirty years and ain't never seen another plant like this one."

"I'm not a botanist or a landscaper, Joe. Why is this so important?"

"I studied agriculture back when I was a student and I never saw a plant quite like this growing in nature."

"Damn, Joe, I can't picture you being a student. I thought you were born in the desert and raised by coyotes."

"You're not the only one needing a reason to move here, ex-LAPD Officer Mike Sands. I was born in Detroit, studied at the University of Michigan and worked for a major Ag firm before heading west. Now, if we have our personal lives out of the way can we have a discussion about this blue whatever it is?"

"Sorry, I was feeling sorry for myself when you interrupted my introspection. My question remains the same; why bring this to me?"

"No one takes me seriously in this town and that includes the idiots at Eastern New Mexico University. I've tried to talk to the teachers in the Ag Lab, but most of them aren't any brighter than a burned-out light bulb. They basically told me I would be arrested if I showed up on campus with one of my wild stories. Don't ask me why but I had a feeling you would at least listen to me."

"Man, you might have me wrong. Everyone thinks I'm an outsider and unable to understand the way things are done in a small city. Who am I supposed to take this plant to if you can't approach folks who have a similar background?"

"They got a new gal teaching Ag up at the school. I heard she was a hot shot botanist at Ohio State before coming here. Probably another lost soul like you and me but you might be able to get this thing to her for an opinion. I wouldn't ask none of the other shitheads on your Department because they would just as soon slap me in handcuffs and cart me off to the state hospital again."

"You just keep coming up with tidbits that encourage me to trust you, don't you Joe?"

"Here's another thing, Officer; we need to take a drive out to the hill country so I can show you where all of these plants are growing."

"You mean there are more of these things?"

"There are acres of them and even better, they weren't there two months ago."

"I'm definitely way out of my element on this. Okay, I'll try to get up to the college at the end of my shift and get some answers. Now go find a place to sleep off whatever you are on and let me finish my coffee."

Crazy Joe put the blue plant on the hood of my cruiser, smiled and jumped on his bicycle without saying thank you or anything else for that matter. It was still at least three hours before I could approach anyone at the college so I leaned back against my car and studied the plant. It was very smooth and oily feeling but nothing came off on my hands as I examined it. I wondered about a plant that could grow and spread so fast but not even a web search on my smart phone gave me any clues.

I finally looked up and realized that I was not alone. My graveyard partner, Lee Anne Hart, had pulled up next to me and was smiling, not exactly a happy smile but one like she was a hunter and I was the prey.

"I thought I caught you sleeping standing up, Lieutenant. Damn my surprise when I realized you were smart enough to use your phone for something other than making calls. Are you watching porn or kiddie cartoons?"

"Neither, actually," I remarked trying to regain control of the moment. "I was researching reasons why a good-looking Mescalero Apache woman wanted to be a cop in Roswell. Turns out there was no good reason."

We both laughed and I watched a very shapely thirty something officer as she walked over to get her cup of coffee. She seemed to be swaying her behind and making sure I noticed as she walked. It made me think that if I hadn't been the watch training officer…I stopped that thought before it grew legs and took me where it was dangerous to go. Besides, I wasn't sure I was ready for any kind of romantic involvement.

"So, you going to tell me why you have a cactus in your hands?" was the first thing Lee Anne said as she walked back stirring her mostly milk flavored coffee.

"Crazy Joe gave it to me. He said there was a lot of it growing in the hill country but he had never seen anything like it before. What does it look like to you?"

"I can't say I ever saw any plants that blue on the Res or anywhere else for that matter. What's Joe think it is?"

"That's the crazy part; Joe has an Ag background and he's just as puzzled as we are. He wants me to take it up to the college."

"Ah, it looks like you have a second job running errands for a crazy man."

"Except for arresting intoxicated Native Americans, it may be the most exciting thing I'll have done in weeks."

"If more local businesses were interested in hiring all the folks my people put through technical schools you wouldn't be arresting so many. Hey, I'm taking my coffee to the station, old man," Lee Anne quipped, giving me that sardonic smile again, "so don't go falling asleep, unless you call me first to tuck you in."

CHAPTER 2

T HE REST OF THE SHIFT was spent in a futile on-line search for a plant that resembled the one I held in my hand while also wondering why Lee Anne was acting so strangely. As seven o'clock approached I put my improper thoughts away and drove to the university. I was at the campus security office hoping the day shift wouldn't give me shit for being out of my jurisdiction.

"Well, if it ain't Mister LAPD come looking for some higher education," spewed out of the mouth of Lieutenant Abel Gomez. "What you need this time?"

Not a friendly greeting but at least he wasn't ordering me off the campus like he did almost every week. Gomez didn't mind my being on campus as long as I was out of uniform and showing up for a class but his blood ran hot every time he saw my new patrol car. His team was driving used cars donated by the Roswell PD and that seemed to be an insult to the proud officer.

"I got a problem that needs an opinion from the Ag Department, Lieutenant, and I heard you have a whiz bang instructor straight out of Ohio on staff." I was going to be as solicitous as possible to keep Gomez from going off on me for no reason.

"Yeah, she's a doozy all right. Her name's Alice Moore or Morrison or something like that. Her resume says she's a botanist, some kind of plant scientist, but she's teaching a biology class. You can find her in the Arts and Sciences Building on the south end of the campus." Figuring he had said it all, Gomez started to walk away but stopped.

"Don't park that shiny new car on my campus, Sands," he yelled over his shoulder. "There are plenty of spots on the city streets for you to use."

I fought a late arriving student for the last spot of street parking before making my way to the Science building. Alice Morrison was listed on the faculty roster, posted outside the main entry, as being in Room 235. I was not sure what I was expecting, maybe a gray-haired old harridan. I stood silently outside her open office door looking at a very attractive blond, probably near my own age, having an animated conversation with a very unhappy student. When he finally stopped ranting and bolted for the door I was still standing outside and looking in.

"Are you going to stand there all day, officer, or do I have to walk over and drag you inside?" She chuckled at her joke so I did too.

"Sorry, Ma'am, it's been a long night." I couldn't wipe the smile off of my face as I approached her desk. It suddenly felt like I was a school boy standing in front of his teacher.

"Well, what is it Officer?" she said impatiently as she stared at my uniform. "I have a class to teach in forty minutes."

"One of Roswell's old-time citizens found this plant out in the hill country," I said as I started to hand it across the desk. "He wanted to know what it was. He somehow coerced me into bringing it up here hoping to find some enlightenment."

As soon as she reached for the plant in my hand a mild discharge of energy, seemingly coming from the plant, caused both of us to jerk back letting the plant drop on her desk. I got a strange look of fear and anxiety from her as she rubbed her hand and turned her attention to the plant. She carefully rotated it every way it could be viewed, tested its texture and finally, figuring she wouldn't receive another shock, picked it up.

"I've never known of a plant to do that. Let's go next door to my lab so I can get a better look at its structure," she said coolly as she lifted the plant without waiting to see if I was going to follow. I had gone from surprised student to puppy dog as I trailed behind her.

"It's not much to look at," she muttered glancing around the room while she prepared a slide, "but it's all the school can afford."

"It reminds me of my old chemistry lab in high school," I offered lamely. "Is there anything I can do to help, Miss...?"

"Damn, how embarrassing, I never did introduce myself. I'm Alice Morrison and you are...?"

"Mike Sands, late of Los Angeles and relatively new to Roswell P.D."

"Why bring this curiosity to me, Officer Sands?" Alice stopped slicing thin pieces of the plant as she looked up at me.

"Like I said before, one of local desert rats, a man who claims to have some interest in Ag work, found a field of the stuff north of here and said you were the one best suited to examine it. He claims that he has never seen anything like it and wanted me to go with him to see the field so I wouldn't think he was crazy."

"Who is the desert rat? He was right when he said the plant is unique."

"An old guy named Farris; said he studied Ag in Michigan."

Alice stared at me as if I had just discovered the second unaccounted artifact in the space of one night.

"Was that Joe Farris?" Alice asked almost in a whisper. When I nodded yes, she yelled, "He's a fucking PhD from Michigan State. Oops, pardon my language. Folks around here aren't used to a woman swearing like a man. It freaked out my student just before you walked in. Are you sure the guy said he was Joe Farris? Everyone assumed he had died because he disappeared off of the face of the earth."

There was a pause as Alice thought over what I had said while viewing her specimen on the microscope.

"So, Doctor Farris is puzzled by this plant," she finally remarked. "Well, so am I. There is nothing on earth with this kind of structure, at least there wasn't until now. When can we go see the rest of it?"

"Whoa, slow down. I'm off duty, right about now actually, but I need a few hours of sleep before I go exploring. I'd need to find Crazy Joe so he can guide us in."

"I have classes until three and then I am free for the weekend. What's your schedule?"

Somehow, I was being roped in to making a crazy field trip and couldn't explain why it didn't bother me. What was worse was that I couldn't explain why I was willing to let her go with me. Miss Morrison was attractive, in an older sort of way, but I was trying hard not to be drawn to her.

"I don't have to be back at work until Monday night so, against my better judgement, I'll set aside some time to go exploring. All we need is our crazy guide."

"I hope you don't mind but my daughter Jeannie has to come along? She's a very precocious ten-year old but I can't leave her at home alone."

"Sure, why not add one more to our expedition? I remember taking neighborhood boys on camping trips back when they were young and I kind of miss the interactions."

"So, I guess you're married," Alice said oddly with a reduced level of enthusiasm.

It made me wonder if she was suddenly becoming reluctant to take a road trip with a married man, or any man for that matter.

"Divorced, like a lot of cops, but gradually getting over the shock of it."

It took a minute for her to make up her mind but she finally nodded.

"So, are we on for this afternoon, say around four?" she said as if she were taking charge. "I'll pack some sandwiches so we can hang around until the sun goes down. I want to see what happens to these guys when they don't have any sunlight."

Alice thought for a minute and then wrote out her address and phone number. She passed me the note as if she was doing something unpleasant. I looked at her note, smiled and then passed her my business card and cell number. She made me wonder why I was suddenly happy I had walked in her office. I gave her my stupid puppy dog look as I prepared to walk out. We shared a professional handshake and promised to see each other later that day.

Crazy Joe was definitely going to get an earful about sending me to the college. I didn't have long to wait as he was leaning on my car when I finally managed to make my way outside.

"What did you find out and don't say the botanist is good looking? You've been in there almost an hour. How long does it take to hear the plant is not of this planet?"

"Have you become my mother, you old fart? She agrees with you and also told me you are far more deceitful than I thought. Doctor Joe Farris, for god's sake? What the fuck are you doing out here in this wilderness?"

"That girl has a big mouth. I suppose she agreed to go with us, too. What did you set up?"

"Be at my place no later than three thirty and I'll drive to Alice's apartment to pick up her and her daughter. I assume you know where I live since you seem to show up wherever I am."

"I'd just as soon take Miss Botanist and leave you and the little girl here, except my vehicle's low on gas. Can I trust you to look after my bicycle?"

"Three thirty, doctor, and don't be late."

CHAPTER 3

M Y BED NEVER LOOKED SO good but sleep was a long time in coming. I kept having thoughts about being with Alice, thoughts that I was not in the mood to have. Finally dozing off I was pissed when the alarm on my phone went off at two forty-five. That gave me a half an hour to shower and get ready for Crazy Doctor Joe to arrive. I needn't have rushed as I found the good doctor asleep blocking the front door on my porch. I had to bang him with the screen door to wake him up.

"Damn you, Sands, I'm awake. No need to be so violent."

"I couldn't be sure since your snoring blocked out the noise of me opening the door. Do you plan on leaving your bicycle on my porch?"

"We need to take it along. My cabin is on the way back and you can drop me off."

"Great, now toss it in the back of my pickup so we can get going."

"You get a brand-new cruiser at work and at home you drive a dirty old Ford F150. What's up with that?"

"The truck was one of the most reliable things I had left after my wife walked out and I don't plan on letting it go. Are you afraid your bike is going to get dirtier riding in the bed? I could put you back there, too, if you like."

"At least you got seats for us scrawny folks to sit on."

"And four-wheel drive to bounce your skinny butt around."

"How far do we have to go to pick up your two girlfriends?"

"She's not too far from the college so about ten more minutes. And she's definitely not my girlfriend. I just met the woman and you know a damn sight more about her than I do."

13

Alice and Jeannie were waiting in front of a familiar looking apartment building which caused Joe to stop asking questions. I jumped out of the truck to help load the picnic hamper and small cooler in the bed while at the same time trying to hold a door open so Jeannie could climb in the back seat next to Joe. He had done the gracious thing and moved to the rear of the extended cab truck without my asking. Introductions were made all around. Joe seemed intimidated and was very quiet. Alice smiled and touched my arm, something that somehow felt out of place.

"This going to be so much fun," Alice said while buckling her seat belt. "Jeannie and I haven't had much time to do any wandering since we got here and who better to show us around than a renowned scientist and our very own security man."

This was a far different Alice Morrison than the woman I had met earlier that day.

Joe had pushed himself as far away from Jeannie as was polite on the narrow bench seat at the back of the cab. The little girl seemed as interested in the old desert rat as he was of the blue plants taking over his piece of the desert. She started throwing questions at Joe in a constant barrage until he finally had to answer her to get her to be quiet for a moment.

We drove north on U.S. 285 just out of town when Joe put his mouth next to my ear.

"State highway 246 is coming up there on your left and we gotta go that way for quite a bit, about sixty or seventy miles," Joe remarked as he pointed out the road and nearly poked my eye out.

"How in hell did you manage to go that far on a bicycle?" was the first thing I thought to say.

"I do drive once in a while. You just keep your eyes on the road and don't worry about how I get from place to place."

Alice had bounced to the middle of the front bench seat as we went over some rough road. She leaned further against my shoulder trying to see where Joe was pointing. I hoped she would stay right where she was and at the same time hoped she wouldn't. She didn't seem to want to move and smiled up at me.

"Are you okay with me being so close; I'm not crowding you, am I?"

"You can stay there forever," I thought inside my head. Aloud I said, "Whatever makes you comfortable." I hunched down and kept driving, afraid to look over to see if she was offended.

"Momma has been talking about you and this trip ever since she got home. She never says anything nice about the people she meets, at least not until now." Looking in the rear-view mirror all I could see of the little girl was a face wide smile and lots of teeth.

My part of the front seat seemed to get very warm for a bit while everyone drifted in to embarrassed silence. I zoned out and drove for an hour through the seemingly empty desert until Joe shouted in my ear.

"B001 is on the right just up ahead. You need to go about two miles and then I'll point out the dirt road. It meanders for a couple more miles until it goes between two hills. The growth will be right in front of you unless you want to drive in to a whole patch of it. You did say you have four-wheel drive on this rust bucket, didn't you?"

"Yes, old man, this rust bucket even has a heater and air conditioning if we need them."

"Here's another fact I hadn't mentioned; the ambient temperature around the blue growth is fifteen to twenty degrees warmer than the surrounding arid landscape. The bigger the patch gets the warmer the air. It's supposed to be in the low thirties tonight but it will be much toastier near our mystery plants."

The drive on this last dirt path was rough enough that I had to shift into four-wheel-drive, an action that caused Joe to whoop loudly.

"See, I told you you'd need it." Our old companion had become giddy and made Jeannie move as far from him as possible. "Jesus Christ, Sands, slow down...slow down. It wasn't near this far up the road when I saw it day before yesterday."

Braking hard on the downhill side of the pass, the front of the truck was embedded two feet in a short patch of blue plants. I backed up cautiously as I took in the field of blue in front of me. Some of the plants toward the center of the small valley we had just entered were seven or eight feet tall with sizes getting smaller the farther from the center you traveled. Alice and Jeannie were staring out of the windshield with a glazed and uncomprehending look. My first reaction was to turn around and get as far away from whatever was slowly creeping towards us.

"Ain't you gonna get out and check this stuff out," Crazy Joe said as he pushed my seat forward trying to get me to move.

I looked over and Alice was already out of the passenger door and heading for the nearest plant. Jeannie was right behind her and since I wasn't moving, Joe climbed over to the passenger side and out the door close behind the two ladies.

"It don't bite, as far as I know, Sands, so why not join us?" he needled as he walked away.

CHAPTER 4

HOLDING A PIECE OF THE PLANT in my hands seemed a lot different than looking at fifty acres of blue plant life stretching out in front of me. I knew there were cattle and sheep on nearby properties and a ranch or two within a few miles. This couldn't be good for any of them.

Once I decided to get out of my truck, I made a very cautious approach to the edge of the growth. The girls and Joe were ten feet inside the outer perimeter and looking closely at a stalk that was as tall as Jeannie.

"It seems to know we are nearby, Doctor Farris. Look at how the outer branches try to move away from my hand. Have you ever seen anything like it before? It's almost like they are sentient." Alice was in her element and seemed to be enjoying herself. She waved me over and looked amused when I was hesitant to walk among the plants.

"Tell me what you think from a lay person's point of view, Mike," she said using my given name for the first time. "Don't you find this intriguing?"

That was not a word I would have used. Something other worldly was happening and I couldn't explain what it was. I thought the plants were talking to me. Not talking, as in using words, but communicating by sending me simple images that said they were afraid of us. How was Alice going to feel about me if I seemed as crazy as Doctor Joe?

"Well, Mike, tell me what you think," Alice demanded, looking for all the world like she was back in her classroom.

"They're afraid of us, Alice, that's why they move away from your touch." Saying it didn't make it seem any more real but Alice's look of disbelief was definitely real.

"He's right, momma, they are afraid of us. I felt it too," Jeannie said to verify what I had sensed.

"What are you two talking about? These are plants and can't have more than a rudimentary set of nerve endings. Doctor Farris, did you hear what they just said?"

"If'n I had told you about the plants communicating before we got here would you have come out here with me? I only took that little piece of a plant because I knew it was allowed."

If I thought Joe was crazy, how was I going to explain the plants that were surrounding him and putting their branches against his body like they were caressing him? Alice seemed oblivious but Jeannie and I watched and felt the respect the doctor and the field of blue had for each other. Another mystery was how serene Joe had become as he wandered among the plants letting his hands trail over the branches. It took a will of iron to hold back from joining him.

"Let's have a bite to eat before the sun goes down," Alice suggested. "I want to be ready to see how the plants react to the cooler air."

Alice was all 'Miss Efficiency' as she walked back to the truck and tried to reach in to pull out the picnic hamper. Being around five feet tall made that too difficult as the raised bed of the truck was higher than she was. I rushed over took my time reaching over her to bring the basket to the ground. We stood, my front to her back, for almost a minute with me getting more embarrassed but neither of us trying to move.

"Maybe we should eat before we get stuck in this position," she said tersely as she pushed away. "We can discuss standing strategy later, if you like."

"I would like it if Jeannie doesn't mind," my unfettered mouth commented as my body cringed.

"You already made her a happy girl by allowing her to come along. But, maybe it's much too early for you to push your luck."

Grabbing the cooler, I walked to a flat spot where the plants hadn't made an appearance and spread out a blanket that I kept in the truck. Jeannie had grabbed Joe's hand and was pulling him through the plants, somewhat reluctantly, in our direction.

Bologna and cheese sandwiches were served and conversation seemed to be lagging for the moment. Both Joe and Jeannie had their eyes glued to the field of blue and a smile plastered to their faces. Joe was the first one to speak.

"Looks like the guardian is on his way over to greet us."

All I could see was the taller plants moving as if someone or something was moving through them and heading in our direction. Jumping up I remembered that my off-duty weapon was locked in the truck.

"No reason to panic, Sands. Those guys just make sure their garden is well kept."

"You sound like you have a relationship with whatever is coming our way."

"It does sound nuts, don't it? Somehow, they liked my way of looking at the strategy the plants are using as they move across the valley. The Guardians kinda look like us, but don't at the same time, so there's no reason to go off halfcocked and start shooting."

"I wasn't planning on shooting anyone, Doc, at least not until I think we are under attack."

My last words were not out of my mouth when something very human like walked out of the plants. It looked to be slightly taller than my six feet, had a human looking face perched on a long neck and a body that, if I had to give it a shape, looked slightly waspish. Its skin had a bluish hue, much lighter than the plants but in the general shade. The plants were treating the humanoid in the same manner as they had Crazy Joe, rubbing their branches across any part of its body they could reach. It stood still at the edge of the field and stared at me. I moved twice to see what it would do but its eyes never wavered from mine.

Jeannie came over to me and took my hand.

"It wants to talk to you, Mister Sands," she said as she began to lead me over to our visitor. "He won't hurt any of us; he just wants to introduce himself."

If I had thought Joe was the crazy one, I wondered what anyone watching this scenario would think of me. Jeannie was as calm as I was nervous but I followed her lead much as I had followed Alice when she led me to the lab at the college. I almost pulled back when the creature held both arms out as if to give me a hug. Instead, it took my forearms in his hands and got a strained look on his face. It took about thirty seconds before I began to receive images in my head that could have come from no one but our visitor.

By the time the last image was received Alice and Joe were standing behind me. Jeannie had wrapped an arm around my waist and kept her eyes on our visitor. She hadn't moved from the moment I was held by the gardener, not the guardian as Joe had claimed. I now had a story of how he, and four other gardeners, had been deposited in this valley by someone they called Master but not an explanation of why they chose this location to plant their crop.

The speech in my head became clearer and more like English the longer we were connected. The next comments were like a conversation.

"The blue plants are a primary food source and this particular variety requires a dry and heavily saline soil to grow properly. The Masters are searching for similar places on the planet and will return when this crop is ready to harvest. The field will not grow beyond the barriers we set up in the valley.

Somehow, I was able to respond. *"I think the plants might be sentient."*

The alien gave me what I thought of as a laugh.

"They just reacted to the emotions of the person closest to them. If they felt love they caress the giver. If no emotions are shown, the plants remain still. If fear or anger is present the plants will shy away or, if attacked, will do the same in return."

My entire conversation felt like it had gone on for hours but in reality, had lasted no more than two minutes. It took a second more to realize my arms were now free and Alice had begun pulling on one to get my attention. Jeannie now had both of her arms around my waist and was not letting go. When I finally came back to earth, I unconsciously pulled Alice in to a group hug with her daughter but still was not able to speak coherently.

Joe, however, was going crazy in the background.

"Did that big bug talk to you, Sands? Why you and not me? I was the first one to find this place and should have been the one to have the conversation. Hell, I was the first human the critter came up to weeks ago. Why aren't you talking to me, Sands?"

The truth was that my conversation, as Joe called it, had left me with a feeling of complete calm. The ability to communicate without having to speak aloud was so much simpler and precise. It was almost an effort to have to reply to Joe using actual speech.

"Give me a minute, Doc; I'm trying to collect my thoughts." Alice and Jeannie were still joined to me and for some reason I couldn't let them go.

"This is a garden," I finally managed to say, "and, according to my new friend, the blue plants are the food source for the gardeners and the Masters. It seems these plants like dry, salty, soil and only grow in a defined area. My friend, who didn't seem to have a name we could pronounce, didn't say when the crop would be ready to harvest but we can expect the Masters back to conduct that chore. Oh, and the plants are not sentient but they can be nasty if exposed to lots of emotion. I think they have been calming you down, Doc, so keep your temper in check."

The tranquility of the moment had me ready to zone out again when Alice mumbled, "I wish we could stay like this forever but my feet are getting sore and I need to pee. Can we take a break and come back to discuss this in a couple of minutes?"

"I'll keep your spot warm, Momma," Jeannie piped in. "I like being with Mister Sands."

The sudden warming of Alice to my embrace had me concerned. The change in attitude by both Alice and earlier Lee Anne seemed way too intimate for people who didn't really know me that well.

With Alice taking a minute behind some rocks I moved Jeannie back to the blanket and relieved the pressure on my own feet. Joe was still stomping around, upset that the gardener chose to speak to me, the least interested person where agriculture was the main topic.

Alice rejoined us and surprised me as she laid her head on my shoulder.

"You said earlier today that you were divorced. Is this too soon to ask what happened, Officer Sands? Did one of you cheat?"

I took some time to frame my answer wondering if this was some kind of a trap.

"There was no cheating by either one of us as far as I knew, just a gradual drift in interests and priorities. What about you?"

"Same thing about a change of priorities but my ex was a serial cheater and abuser so I thought it best to put some distance between him and Jeannie. Coming to Roswell probably saved me from a murder charge. Was it the same with you?"

"No, I thought we loved each other right up until the day she served me the divorce papers. Then everything about our relationship became a question mark."

"Wow, aren't we a pair of losers? Do you think you can deal with two lonely females on these trips to the wilderness?"

I began to shake my head as I felt things were moving way too fast. My head wasn't thinking but my body was responding in a very positive way.

"You should worry more about a lonely guy who speaks to aliens. I'm okay dealing with both of you so long as you are okay with me."

Crazy Joe finally stopped pacing and came to a stop directly in front of me.

"What are you going to do about all this craziness," he shouted. "If that bug is right, we have an alien invasion on our hands. Are you going to call out the National Guard or the State Police? Damn it, Sands, do something."

"You need to go stand around your friendly plants and get your attitude adjusted, Doc. You seemed much happier before I had my little conversation with Gardener." It dawned on me that I had just given the creature a name I could handle. "Besides, you were the one who seemed to be in love with the whole idea of the big blue garden."

"That was before I knew we were being invaded."

"Just for drill, what was out here that had so much value? Most of the scrub growth wouldn't interest the few cattle roaming around. Other than you, who comes out here or even knows about this stuff? These plants are a whole lot prettier than the crusty dirt and maybe they have nutrients that might be good for humans. I'm not a big brain like you but I am curious to see what the Master's look like. I'm sure we can wait a while."

"How about you Miss Fancy-Pants-botanist, do you think the same way as our layman city official?"

"Well, Doctor Farris, it seems like we are quite a ways out of the city. If Mike doesn't seem too worried about the aliens, then I would have to take his years of experience over your normal psychotic outbursts."

"Am I the only sane person out here?" Joe cried to the rapidly darkening sky.

My waspy friend came back in my head, this time without being close nor holding my arms.

"Is the old one feeling all right? He should come back in to the arms of his blue family."

"Thanks for the invite; I'll try to convince him he'll be safe back in the field."

"Joe, you have Gardener and all the plants worried about you. I think they are ready to talk to you if you go over there. I'll keep an eye out to make sure you stay safe but maybe you need to make sure our blue buddies don't get too aggressive."

"They want me to go back over there? What if it's a trick, Sands, did you think of that?"

"The one thing I felt when communicating with Gardener was that he was incapable of lying. Both his and my minds were like an open book. Maybe you can get him to tell you when the harvest is supposed to happen and if the plants are even safe for our people to eat. Can't hurt to try, Doc, you know, to act like an inquisitive human."

"Come on, Doctor Farris," Jeannie said while taking Joe's hand, "I'll walk you over."

Joe looked embarrassed but walked hesitantly behind the young girl. At the edge of the field Gardener reached out and took Joe's other hand and led Joe deep in to the growth.

"The gardener spoke to me, momma," Jeannie shrieked as she ran back to the blanket. "He thanked me for helping. He was really nice."

"So, everyone but me has had a conversation with our planetary guest," Alice griped. "I'm the botanist and I can't even get a word in. Why was he so eager to talk to you, I wonder."

"I think it was something to do with my curiosity about the alien lifestyle and my lack of aggression. Maybe you were too eager to find out about the plants and disregarded Gardener in the process. He, or it, is very protective of the crop and you may have felt too threatening."

"That's crazy; all I wanted to do was find out what the plants are and why they're here."

"How about I give you a proper introduction and see if that smooths things over?"

"I suddenly feel like the student and you're the teacher." Alice pulled her head off of my shoulder and nodded to agree to my suggestion.

CHAPTER 5

ARDENER WAS WAITING AT THE edge of the field when we walked over. Jeannie and Doc Joe were strolling through chest high plants that I'm sure were only waist high when we arrived. Gardener put his arms out and Alice raised hers, going in a mild trance as the two of them had a conversation. I was surprised when my right arm was pulled into Gardener's grip and I found myself part of a three-way conversation. Alice seemed shocked to be left so open to my mind and me to hers. It surprised me when I saw that she was developing a romantic interest in me. And, as reluctant as I had been to get involved, I felt the same way about her. Gardener was smiling, both mentally and visually, which took both Alice and me by surprise. Both of us seemed embarrassed by the revelation causing us to try to think of other things.

Alice asked our new friend, *"What kind of value do the plants have?"* and was surprised at Gardeners answer.

"The plants give complete nutritional and medicinal value to my people, the Jinn, to the Master's and all other species on our vessels. I can see no reason the same would not be true for the humanoids on this planet."

Gardener refused to say any more claiming he had not the authority to speak for his superior's. He pulled away and walked towards the deeper growth where I now saw four other Gardeners standing and staring disapprovingly at our new acquaintance.

"What if he got himself in trouble talking to us?" Alice pondered. "I would hate to think that we caused him a problem when he has been so forthcoming."

"Did you get the feeling he was just reciting something he had been ordered to say? Friendliness aside, he appears to be doing a

25

very menial job when I get the sense he is very intelligent." Staring across the field at all five of the gardeners I found I could receive their conversation and none of it was hostile.

"Can you hear them from that far away?" Alice asked.

"It's like I was standing next to them and they know I'm listening. They're surprised but not upset. They think we are like the Master's, but superior, and are to be listened to. I took the opportunity to ask about the harvest and they said it would be in the next week or so when the Master's return. I guess we have a date for another visit."

"I assume you mean for Jeannie and me, as well," Alice said, lightly holding my arm. "Was what I saw in your mind about me true, Michael Sands?"

My stomach did a flip and I was at a loss for words. I swallowed hard and then answered.

"Look, it's Mike and not Michael. My mother was in such a hurry to get out of the hospital when I was born, she put as little info on the birth certificate as she could. No long name, no father and no close parental connection. I wasn't lying before when I said that the open mind can't lie. I really thought it wasn't the right thing to get close too soon. With my family history I was sure I'd scare you off if I said or did anything. I mean, we've only known each other for a day."

"I learned more about you in one mental visit than I did after years of being with my ex-husband. You don't frighten me, Officer Sands; quite the opposite."

"Is your daughter going to be quite that accepting?"

"She's like an open book without having a mental picture to look at. There is no duplicity in that child. You will be surprised what comes out of her mouth without a filter of any kind."

"We have to leave," Jeannie was shouting as she ran towards us. "The plants are going to expand and we are right in the way."

Joe was puffing as he ran to keep up with the little girl and trying to talk at the same time.

"The plants may not be sentient but you can feel when they are about to do something, like expand or strike out at someone.

Damn things pushed the two of us out of the field, gentle as can be but very authoritatively."

"Did they tell you about the harvest," I asked.

"No, they can't talk, you idiot, but they sure are decent at making a person feel good. What do you know about a harvest?"

"We have at least a week to find out if the blue plants are safe for human consumption before getting to meet with the Master's. Of course, they don't know we already planned a meeting so it might get interesting. I assume you are free to make a return trip."

"I am and hope you plan to bring the girls with you. I've grown quite fond of the little one. You can have the mother."

It was during this brief repartee that I saw movement at the edge of the field. Gardener had returned and was holding something in his hands. Almost immediately I received an image of me eating and Gardener holding out a platter of what looked like pastries. Knowing he couldn't lie I assumed he was telling me his offering was safe for me to eat. Jeannie seemed to be receiving the same message because she began pulling me towards the field.

"Where are you two going, now?" Alice was running to catch up and reaching for her daughter at the same time.

I pulled up short of Gardener's offering allowing Alice to join our little group. Joe was still on the blanket and shaking his head as if he thought we were the crazy ones and not him.

"Why do you think that what's on the plate is safe for us?" I asked my little companion.

"I can't explain it, Mister Sands, but I know he wouldn't try to hurt us. Can I just try a little bit, momma, a little tiny taste."

Alice looked at her daughter and then at me, not able to make a decision. She knew it was dangerous to try an unproven food. Jeannie broke free from my grasp and made the decision on her own. She took a small square from the dish and shoved the entire thing in her mouth.

"So much for caution and a week to see if this stuff is edible," I thought as Alice ran to try to clear the food from her daughter's mouth. Jeannie had already swallowed and had a wondrous look on her face.

"That was so good, momma, you need to try some. My friend says it will give me extra energy and make my thoughts clearer. You should try some, too, Mister Sands."

My hand was half way to the plate when I realized what I was doing and jerked my hand back. There was an immediate sense of disappointment emanating from Gardener that almost made me reach again. I was surprised to see Jeannie pushing a piece of the pastry in Alice's mouth and even more surprised when Alice chewed and swallowed. Alice, Jeannie and Gardener all turned towards me as if to say it was my turn.

"I'm not sure what this stuff is supposed to do for me but it sure tastes wonderful," Alice enthused. "I don't think it has any toxic properties but if I die in the next few minutes you have to promise to take care of my little poisoner," she finished with a laugh as she hugged her daughter.

Sensing a challenge, I took a larger piece and scarfed it down, getting a look of amazement from the girls. I also received images that I took for satisfaction from Gardener along with one that felt like I should appreciate the results in a short while. Not feeling any ill effects, I took the offered platter and walked back to the blanket.

"I ain't touching any of that stuff, Sands," Joe snarled, "so you can put it in the cooler for Miss Morrison to take back to her lab. I still can't believe all of you ate some of that shit before testing it first. Don't come complaining to me if your skin turns blue or you start looking like a bug."

Remembering that we were in the next expansion zone, and that we had a week to wait for the harvest, we packed up our gear and began the drive back to Roswell. The first thing I noticed was how clear the road seemed. I reached up to adjust my glasses and realized they were still in my pocket. It had been years since I could drive at night without eyewear and my first thought was about the otherworld pastry. Both Alice and Jeannie had dozed off the minute the truck started to move and I didn't want to wake them to ask if they had noticed any physical changes.

Most of the way back to Roswell Joe had me turn off on another dirt track on the way to his house. Completing a night of surprises, Joe's home was a pleasant looking ranch style house with proper vegetation in the yard, solar panels, a windmill and a late model Chevy dual cab pickup parked at the side.

"Do you want to tell me why you ride your bike everywhere when you had a pickup a lot newer than mine parked next to your house?"

"Damn thing is a gas hog and it's cheaper and healthier to ride my bicycle for my local errands. Besides, I knew you wouldn't trust Crazy Joe to drive you three out in the middle of nowhere. It seems you got the better of the deal if that little lady with her head on your shoulder means anything."

Joe was still laughing as he unloaded his bike and walked to his front door.

The drive back to the highway and then to Alice's apartment was way too short. I was enjoying the close feeling of a woman nestling next to me and would have parked in front of the building all night if Alice hadn't sat up.

"Can you grab the stuff in the back while I wrestle my daughter inside?"

Dutifully, I went to the bed of the truck and realized the lid of the cooler had come loose. It was apparent that it hadn't done so on its own as half of the remaining pastries were missing. "Joe must have had a change of heart about trying them," I thought as I lugged the two containers towards Alice's apartment.

"Can you stay for a little while?" Alice whispered as she put Jeannie in her bed, a small cot next to Alice's single.

We walked to the kitchen and sat at a small folding table pushed against the wall.

"This has been the best day, Mike Sands, and the most surprising for more than one reason. I wish you could stay over but that would not be right considering the limited space we would have and the need for us to have a serious conversation."

"It is probably presumptuous but my house is larger and has two bedrooms if our conversation ends up taking a long time."

"Is that an offer for me to visit or to move in?"

The smile she gave me had more than a little hint of playfulness that caused my heart to race and my face to flush bright red.

"Either would be fine," my traitorous mouth mumbled.

"You move pretty fast for an older cop, Mister Sands, especially one who seemed so reluctant a little while ago. Besides, I haven't had an offer like that since my early thirties. I think I like it. When would be a good time?"

Now I was on the spot. "Do you have anything planned for tomorrow?" came out of my mouth, once again my brain failing to engage before speaking.

"Can we wait until after we meet the Masters? It'll give me time to talk to Jeannie about it so we can make a more practical decision. It also gives me more time to do a thorough examination to the plant in the lab...and the pastries."

"Speaking of pastries, the cooler lid was partially off after I dropped Joe at his house and half our supply was missing. Either he has changed his mind about snacking or he plans to do some testing in his own lab."

"Speaking of testing, do you feel any different since eating that huge piece?"

"Yeah, my night vision has gone from blurry with halos around everything to crystal clear. And, I should be tired but I'm full of energy. How are you feeling?"

"Energized, like I need to get to the lab and put in some hours on our project."

"Do you want me to stay and babysit?"

"No, I need you to leave before I change my mind about waiting for a week. I'll call you tomorrow, if that's okay?"

"I'm going to leave under protest. If you need me to watch Jeannie tomorrow you just have to call."

Alice reached up and pulled me close so she could give me a quick kiss on the lips.

"I promise, when the time is right, there is more of that to come," she said as she ushered me out of the apartment.

CHAPTER 6

THE FOLLOWING MORNING MY PHONE began ringing bringing me out of a deep sleep. My first thought was that Alice wanted to talk about yesterday but I knew she was probably buried in an examination of the blue plant. Almost in the same breath I figured it was the station needing me for something but my bigger surprise came when I finally opened my eyes and looked at the screen. The caller was my almost ex-wife, Lillian. It shouldn't have been a surprise since we each made a call about once every two weeks just to check up on each other. As depressed as I had been over her walking out, at least until this past Friday, we were still on good terms and shared what was going on in our lives.

"Hey, Lill, what's cooking?"

"I was about to hang up, baby, or leave a message or something. You sound like you just woke up. That would be totally unlike you."

"Well, I had a late night and didn't realize it was almost ten o'clock. Is something the matter?"

"No, we hadn't talked for a while and I still like to hear your voice."

"Right, so long as it's on the phone and not while standing, or lying, next to you."

"I never minded you being close to me, quite the opposite, especially in bed. You know damn well it was me that had the problem in my head, it was never you."

"I'm glad we got that out of the way."

"So, was it work related or did you finally go out and have some fun."

"If you mean last night, it was definitely fun. I was surprised I remembered how to do anything fun."

"Oh, that means you finally must have gotten laid. How was it?"

"That was too soon, Lillian, and no, I didn't get laid, at least not yet."

The line got quiet for several seconds, with breathing sounds coming through the receiver, as if my almost ex was upset that I may have found someone. I knew she had had several lovers over the three plus years of our separation but in all that time she never encouraged me to find someone new.

"Are you still there, Lill, or did you hang up on me?"

"I'm still here, Mike, just kind of surprised. You never mentioned having met someone in any of our calls."

"It's a recent thing but we're both on the same page, kind of like we're in each other's heads. Are you still with that snake, Rex, the financial baron?"

"His name is Roy and he works for an investment firm. We are still seeing each other and that is partly why I wanted to call."

"Are you asking my permission to keep seeing the guy?"

"No, dumb shit, I'm calling to see if you signed the divorce papers and sent them to my attorney."

I looked at the unopened manila envelope that had been sitting on top of my dresser for months and wondered why I hadn't completed the paperwork. It was my turn to be embarrassed and go silent for a few seconds.

"You haven't mentioned it for some time, are you desperate to have it done now, all of a sudden?"

"Just the opposite, I need you to hold off for a while.

"Why the change of heart, are you thinking of trying to get us back together?"

"I can't say I haven't been thinking about it but, no, that's not the reason. Roy keeps pressuring me to marry him. The divorce papers are the only excuse I can use to fend him off, other than not loving the guy and really not wanting to be married to anyone. So, do you still have them?"

"I have them but as of this past week I am seriously considering getting them off to your shark of a lawyer."

"I fought Thelma tooth and nail to make sure you got more than a fair division of our community property, including you getting all the real estate, except for my townhouse."

"She was still nasty to me when I was willing to bend over backwards to make the separation as pleasant as possible. Look, that's all done with and we are still hospitable to each other. That's the important thing, isn't it?"

"You have been very generous and I appreciate it. Let's not get so feisty that we don't get to talk to each other, baby, I would hate that. I've got to run so you work on that new relationship. I'll call again for an update in a week or so. Bye."

The line was dead and, like most of our conversations, I felt like I had just gone ten rounds in a prize fight, except I never got the decision. I moved my ass out of bed and grabbed the manila envelope, opened it and pulled out the papers. The damn forms had an aroma that smelled sickening sweet like Thelma Grimm, Lil's lawyer. It gave me a shiver.

Putting the paper back in the envelope I had a sudden urge to sign them and put them in the mail. A quick shower woke me up and black coffee kept me there. I called Edith Murray, my local real estate broker, to see if she was available to notarize my signature, received an okay and headed out of the door. I was happy to see that Joe wasn't asleep on my porch.

Forty-five minutes later I was at the post office just before noon closing time completing the registered mail request and finally waving goodbye to my marriage. As conflicted as those forms made me feel, I was almost jubilant to see them go. Lillian was going to be pissed.

"You know Monday's a Post Office holiday, don't you, so it's gonna be a day or two late in delivery?" the clerk said as I stood at the counter.

"It can be several days late for all I care," I responded a little too glibly.

"I can make that happen, if that's what you want."

A smile and a nod was all I offered and got the same response from the clerk. I had my receipt so was not worried about when the Shark would get the papers. Maybe it was the satisfaction I felt but my mind was suddenly jolted back to reality when I ran this morning's conversation with Lillian through my mental filters and recalled one very short phrase. It was when I said, *'Are you thinking of trying to get us back together?'* and Lillian responded, *'I can't say I haven't thought of it.'* Cold shivers ran down my back as I tried to figure out what was on her mind. The comment bugged me all afternoon.

Alice phoned at four o'clock, making me forget about Lillian. She was home and making dinner, something special for me she said. I was ordered to get to her place immediately. An extremely happy ten-year old greeted me at the door to unit sixteen, pulled me inside and pushed me onto the couch. Jeannie climbed on my lap and gave me a hug that she refused to relinquish. I was torn between allowing it and gently pushing her. Alice was standing in the doorway to the kitchen and laughing.

"Isn't it you who should be giving me a hug?" I threw at her, immediately feeling embarrassed for being so aggressive. She responded by sitting next to me and wrapping her arms around both me and her daughter.

"Jeannie hasn't been this happy for a long time. She was the one who wanted you to come for dinner. I may have to get jealous if she steals your heart away before I can close escrow on it."

"It feels like my heart already belongs to you but it's like a duplex, room enough for the two of you." That earned me a kiss on the cheek and another quick one on my lips.

"You better believe you are going to stay around for a while after Jeannie goes to bed, mister. We might even get some time to discuss what I learned about blue plants." She was laughing again as she walked back to the kitchen.

Dinner was not rushed, all of us crowded around the small table talking about things we liked, Jeannie drinking her grape juice, making toasts every two minutes, and Alice and I killing a bottle of a good cabernet that blended nicely with the pasta. All three of us cleared the table and washed the dishes, something that felt so natural that I wondered why it hadn't been a ritual in my previous life. After the kitchen had been made spotless, we all returned to the couch and resumed our previous positions. I was sure that Jeannie had gained ten pounds over dinner.

We continued to talk but it felt like we were inside each other's minds, almost like we had been when talking to Gardener.

Jokingly, I asked, "Did you put some of that blue plant in the pasta, Alice?"

"As a matter of fact, I did. My examination today made me believe that stuff is a miracle plant. Not only is it nontoxic, it has a list of properties that are good for a host of troublesome issues plaguing the human condition. Has it made you ill or uncomfortable?"

"God, no, I feel very alive and ready to do wondrous things. And seeing as your daughter has fallen asleep on my chest, I might want to do some of those things after we put her in bed."

"I'll get her in her PJ's and you can give her a kiss goodnight. Then you can kiss me properly."

Five minutes later we were back on the couch, lights turned off except for a small light in the kitchen and I received the first of the promised kisses.

"I wish we had more privacy," Alice whispered between kisses sometime later in the evening.

"What if there was?" I said, saying before thinking.

"Do you want to explain what you have in mind, Mister Sands? Might it be an indecent proposition?"

"It might have felt like I was joking yesterday when I said that my house has two bedrooms and the master is almost as large as this whole apartment. I'm still suggesting that the two of you could move in with me."

Alice pulled back and stared at me.

"That had better be a serious offer because if we move in, we are never going to move out."

My face had flushed again and I could feel a bead of sweat rolling down my sides. My gut said it was the right decision but my mind was roiling, not believing I had made that kind of an offer so soon after meeting Alice and Jeannie.

"I'm positive and would like nothing better than to make us one family." I wasn't sure if it was me talking or whatever was in the blue plants Alice had put in the pasta.

"Just to be sure, I'm still going to give you more time to think about it. Jeannie has to finish the semester in her school and I don't want to disrupt her so close to the end of the year. Besides, I'd have to give notice to the landlord and my lease isn't up for another three months."

"I'll deal with the landlord and I'm sure he will let you out early."

"Tommy, the on-site manager, said the owner was a hard ass and difficult to deal with. I don't want you to get in any trouble."

"I'm on a first name basis with the owner and I promise there won't be any trouble."

"How can you be so sure? I can't take another hit on my credit."

"Because, Miss Morrison, I bought this property six months ago when it went through foreclosure. Everyone living here is protected, especially the folks in unit sixteen."

"Is this the only property you own?"

"I own my humble abode and one house on each side plus a ten-acre parcel right behind my cottage. It was my retirement savings put to good use. The lot would make an excellent site for a rather grand family home if I can find a reason to stay in Roswell."

The sudden fist to my chest was unexpected as was the stern look on Alice's face.

"Aren't we enough reason to stay?"

"You are fairly convincing but striking an officer of the law could get you confined for a life sentence," was my reply as I pulled Alice to my injured chest and kissed the top of her head.

"I thought we had already agreed on that but can I get two life sentences if I hit you again?" she mumbled in to my chest.

I felt her give me a hard squeeze that went on forever until I heard sounds that told me Alice had fallen asleep. I gave her the entire couch and got ready to leave. I was staring at what was beginning to feel like my new life partner when the light from the kitchen threw a shadow across her skin, a shadow or was it a slight hint of blue. Turning on the lamp in the front room would surely wake her so I convinced myself that it was in fact just a shadow.

All the way back to my house I kept staring in my rear-view mirror trying to see if I was turning blue, but street lamps and head-lights made me look more yellow or amber. Light traffic kept me from endangering any oncoming cars until I finally decided my coloring was just my normal shade of graveyard pallor.

CHAPTER 7

SUNDAY STARTED WITH ME BEING back to my normal schedule for my days off, up early and ready to complete errands and house work. Things were normal until my phone went off. I assumed at first it was Alice calling to check up on me but quickly discarded that notion. Next, I thought maybe Lillian wanted to continue our discussion from yesterday but the number displayed was wrong and her name didn't appear. Out of curiosity I answered, something I rarely did with just a phone number and no name on the display. It was my boss, Chief Boone.

"Took you long enough to answer. Did I catch you still in bed?"

"Not this time, Walt. I actually thought you might be someone else."

"Fuck me, Sands; there was a rumor of you finally meeting someone and taking her on a drive out to the desert. I hope it was someone of the opposite sex, or maybe you prefer someone of the same sex this time around?"

"Why are you calling me on my day off, Chief? I don't have time for chitchat. That will have to wait until I'm on duty."

"You need to be in my office tomorrow at one P.M. Before you start spouting off, that is a direct order and not to be confused with any other thing you may have planned. Are we understood?"

Walter Boone never gave me direct orders because he knew I would piss in his Cheerios' if I didn't like what he had to say. Before I could acknowledge the order to appear the line went dead. I got it that Walter was deadly serious.

That evening, over dinner with Alice and Jeannie, I mentioned having to see the Chief, and how unusual that was. My

38

concern was that I done something wrong on the job but there was nothing dire enough that came to mind to demand an audience. Then I worried that Abel Gomez had complained about me being on campus but he had seemed okay with my visit, that time at least. I couldn't conceive that my associating with Alice or Crazy Joe was the reason since I hadn't used my police cruiser to go to the hill country. It was going to have to wait until the next day.

Alice tried hard to allay my anxiety especially after Jeannie went to bed.

Monday seemed to drag but it was finally time to see the Chief. Walt had an office that was all glass on one wall but his privacy curtain was wide open. That had to be a good sign. I had already built a defense for each alleged infraction and was ready to begin explaining when Walt closed the door to his office and began to smile.

"I'll bet you thought I was calling you in to chew your ass," the Chief said around his chuckles. "For once you're off the hook. I've got two things to talk about, my old friend, one good and one you may not like as well. Shall I begin or do you need a moment to forget whatever shit you were going to spout at me?"

I took a deep breath and realized that Walt was in a very good mood, something you didn't see too often.

"I'm good so let's have it."

"The mayor had the sudden urge to resign, something to do with inappropriate behavior and misuse of his office and city funds. His resignation was effective immediately. You may wonder how that affects you and me, my old chum."

Sometimes it took a long while for Walter Boone to get to the point and I hoped this was not one of those times.

"I've been asked to complete the unexpired term of Mayor John Fender. That means for the next three years I am going to head the City council. Doesn't that just frost your ass, me being the mayor of anything?"

Walt kind of expected me to jump up and pound his back but I was as surprised as he was to get that kind of offer.

"And do you know what the best part of the whole deal is, Lieutenant Mike Sands?"

This was the part where I was supposed to guess what was next. Instead, I just looked stupefied.

"The Council agreed to appoint you as interim Chief of Police."

When I remained silent, Walt poked me in the chest and laughed. When I still didn't respond he began to look worried.

"Didn't you hear what I just said, Sands, Chief of Police?"

"You can't be fucking serious, Walt. You know how I hate authority. It's hard enough being a lieutenant on this job and now you want me to be Chief. What about all the guys with a ton more seniority and experience in this two-bit town? They are going to ambush me and store my decomposing body in some out of the way mineshaft."

"Suck it up, brother, this is a done deal. Out of five city wards only one Councilperson objected and that was resolved when I agreed that the title would be interim Chief. If a better solution comes along, you can go back to being a uniform drone on the graveyard shift. How's that suit you?"

"How about if I just resign and head back to LA? That solution isn't good either but at least I can be my own boss."

"What's your new sweetheart going to say if you bail out now? Yeah, I heard about your college professor and I'm glad for the two of you but I really need you to help me out on this. You're not the only one looked on as an outsider but I want, no, make that need, an ally on the PD. This is short term at the best and slightly longer at the worst. Besides, there is a very nice bump in pay, just for being agreeable."

I walked out of the Chief's office holding instructions for my swearing in ceremony and almost ran over Lee Anne Hart, my graveyard partner.

"What did the asshole do to you this time, Sands? You look crushed."

"It was the worst thing ever, Apache Girl. He just told me he had been appointed mayor."

"You mean we get rid of the carpetbagger? What's bad about that?"

"He just appointed me Chief, that's what. It's like the department went from bad to worse."

"He made you chief? That is so hot. The guys are all going to love that bit of news. I hope you have fire proof undies, old man."

Staring at the almost hysterically laughing woman I had a sudden inspiration.

"How's this for a way to shake up the troops, Lee Anne? I'm going to make you the lieutenant to fill my spot." Laughter turned to a look of panic. "You'll be the first Apache in your family and first on the Department to reach management."

Lee Anne was still standing in front of the Chief's office as I walked out of the building, got in my truck and began to drive. An hour later I was parked in front of Alice's apartment building wondering how I could extricate myself from this mess. A text to her phone got me a less than promising response. Alice was going to be working until five due to a late student appointment. I began to drive again, this time ending up at Crazy Joe's house. His truck was gone and there was no answer to my pounding on his door. At that point I wasn't sure what I would have said to the man.

At five, I was back at Alice's place, sitting on the steps outside her apartment.

"What the hell, Mike, why are you sitting out here? I thought the owner would have a spare key."

"I just needed a place to sit and think, babe. Every other place I went didn't seem appropriate. This was the least intrusive place that was still close to you."

"It's nice you feel that way but you are acting rather strange. Let's go inside before my neighbors wonder what new craziness I'm up to."

"Where's Jeannie? I thought she would be with you."

"She's at a play date and dinner at one of her friends. The mother is going to drop her off about seven thirty. Wow, isn't that convenient, Mister Sands?"

Walking inside the apartment I was assaulted by a frenzied woman, only remembering to close the front door before being pushed down on the couch.

"Whatever is bothering you will have to wait until we conclude some unfinished business." Alice whispered as she began unbuttoning my shirt.

The unfinished business took longer to complete than I anticipated.

Later, over leftover Italian we finally had calmed down enough to talk.

"Chief Boone is leaving the Department to become Mayor of Roswell," I said and then ran out of steam.

"Is that a good thing or bad?" Alice asked, not knowing where the conversation was going.

"It's good for him but he is making me his replacement."

I was staring down at the table when I heard a loud whoop and then felt a pair of arms around my neck.

"That is so fantastic, Mike, getting a promotion like that. I know Jeannie will get a real kick knowing her favorite guy is the Chief."

"You definitely seem happy for me, babe. It does sound like a good deal, doesn't it," came out with not much enthusiasm.

"That didn't sound too impressive coming from the new boss of the Department"

"Who's the new boss of what Department?" came from a small voice standing in the kitchen doorway.

"Mister Sands was made Chief of Police today."

An impetuous ten-year-old gave me another of her fantastic hugs and suddenly my worries seem to go away.

"If you can get off of work at two tomorrow afternoon I'd like both of you to be at City Hall to watch the swearing in ceremony. That is if you want to watch a fairly boring ritual. Perhaps the new mayor will allow you to assist in pinning my new rank on my uniform."

"We will be there, Chief Sands," cried both of my favorite women.

The promotion and pinning ceremony was brief with Boone commanding the stage and me being decoration. When the ritual was over, I watched Alice and Jeannie leave for home while I was taken back to my new office by the newly promoted mayor. The next three hours were spent going over my new duties, signing forms and becoming acquainted with my staff. Memory never being my long suit I was amazed that every detail seemed to fall into a well-organized file cabinet in my head. When Boone had bombarded me with as much as he could that afternoon he stopped and gave me a hard look.

"A week ago, I wouldn't have thought you could handle this daily minutia but you surprise me, Sands. You're grasping things faster than I did. I am concerned that you look a little blue tinged peaked, like I might have been putting too much on your plate. It can't all be from working in the dark all the time, could it?"

My head snapped around when he said it looked like my skin was a little blue but put it off to the harsh lighting in the office. I put a note down on my calendar to have the tubes changed to give the office a softer look.

With Boone off to see to his new duties I was left to stare out at the people in the outer office and wondered if they were staring back at me. Realizing it was well after six I tried to make a hasty exit but was stopped numerous times for some positive congratulations and some not so generous. At the last I was dragged off to the officer's favorite watering hole for the express purpose of buying drinks and bankrupting my credit card. It was almost eleven that night when I finally made it to my house having been escorted by several of my more concerned staff.

CHAPTER 8

WEDNESDAY MORNING CAME WAY TOO soon but I was still up and showered by seven. I was heading out to grab a cup of coffee and a bear claw at Momma Tucker's when I almost tripped over Crazy Joe sitting on the front step of my porch.

"I got security video of you pounding on my door on Monday. What was that all about, Sands?"

"Strange as it might seem, Joe, I was in some kind of a mood and wanted someone to talk to. Alice was my first choice but you ran a close second."

"You should have left me a message. I know I gave you my cell number but, if you recall, I said that I didn't check it too often. Anyways, now I need to talk to you, too. Do you have time?"

"Toss your bike in the back of my truck and you can talk while I get us some coffee."

Joe was quiet for the first part of the ride and then couldn't stop talking.

"I was back out at the valley yesterday and all the plants are well over eight feet tall. It took me over an hour to locate the bugs but they seemed happy to see me. They all wanted to know what you had planned for them to do once the harvest was completed. I had no idea you had anything planned and had to put them off until we met with the Master's. You made some kind of impression on them critters."

"I have no idea what they were talking about, Joe. I kept getting the impression they thought we were all related. Could that be a possibility, I wonder?"

"Maybe more than you realize. Plant DNA and humans are vastly different but there are always some common elements. I had some of my own blood samples that I took some time ago. I checked them against a sample I took after we had ingested some of that blue plant pastry."

My expression must have shown my surprise.

"Yeah, I know I said I wouldn't try it but I did. My newest sample showed a change in my DNA. Instead of the normal twenty-three chromosomal pairs, two new and previously unidentified pairs have been added. The two pairs are almost indistinguishable from two pairs in the plant genome. They weren't in my earlier sample and could only have come from the plant. Can you explain that? Hell no, you can't, you're not a scientist."

"It might not make a difference," I explained, "but my body has made some changes since we had the pastry. My vision is almost perfect, especially at night, and my arthritis seems to have disappeared. I don't take any meds, except for an occasional aspirin, so tell me why else I would suddenly feel and look years younger."

"I'm not so concerned that we seem to be getting healthier, my young friend, it's the why we have been selected and what is the end game for the Masters?"

Joe had nothing more he wanted to tell me. He rode off on his bike as I stared into my coffee. Nothing was making any sense to me at that moment, not the plants, the Masters, Lillian's call and my sudden promotion. Well, Alice and Jeannie made sense so my thoughts weren't all dark.

What jolted me out of my daily introspection was an image message from Gardener. I don't know how he was able to put such drama in his communications over such a long distance but this message, telling me the Masters were going to be back in three planetary rotations, which happened to be on Saturday, was delivered with enough emphasis to make me think I was being commanded to appear. The others on my team were optional but still invited.

A phone call to Alice was answered with Alice saying she was hurrying to her next class.

"Did you get a mental message from Gardener about Saturday?" I managed to squeeze in. I could hear Alice stop running but she said nothing.

"When did you get a message?" Alice sounded upset about not being included.

"Not more than five minutes ago," was all I could say.

"Are you the only one who was contacted?" she finally asked.

"I haven't tried to call Joe and I assumed Jeannie would be in school. You were my first choice to call."

"Are we invited or is this a command performance for you alone?" Alice was sounding petulant so I eased her mind.

"All of us are invited but I was given a command to appear. It's kind of harsh to boss around the Chief of Police, don't you think? I mean the Masters aren't the Mayor or City Council."

Alice's smile came through the phone. "What time is our invitation on Saturday?"

"Gardener didn't say. I assume we should be there early so we don't piss anybody off. If we want to be there by eight, we should be on the road by six. Maybe you and Jeannie ought to spend the night at my place."

"Very clever strategy, Mister Sands, but you make a good point. Just don't ask Crazy Joe to spend the night with us. I've gotta run as I'm already late. Will I see you tonight?"

"You'd see me every night if I can make you move in."

"I'm working on it. Bye."

Joe didn't pick up so I left a brief message. My feeling was that he would make another mysterious appearance rather than phoning. Finishing my coffee, I made my way to my new office and tried to put thoughts of the Masters out of my head. That worked so long as I had nothing else important in front of me and then it was all I could think of.

The rest of the week passed with no further communications from Gardener. Friday evening was spent with Alice and Jeannie at my house, having a pleasant dinner and then sitting, talking and watching a movie. All was warm and fuzzy until Jeannie asked me a question.

"Is it all right if I call you something besides Mister Sands?"

"Sure, you can. What did you have in mind?"

"Can I call you Poppa? Momma said it was up to you but she didn't mind."

My infamous flush turned my face red and it was difficult to breathe for a moment. I pulled Jeannie to me and wrapped her up in a hug.

"You always surprise me with the things you say. Of course, you can and it would make me so very happy if we could make that for real. That's another decision your Momma has to make."

It was Alice's turn to have her face go red as she punched me, again.

"You need to ask me properly and then I'll decide."

Jeannie was in bed early, in the spare bedroom, and we followed shortly after. It seemed like no time had passed when I heard a thump at the front of the house. The clock by the bed read four thirty. I crept to the front window which looked out on the porch and saw Joe sprawled out on my wicker couch. His bike was leaning haphazardly against the front handrail. Trust Crazy Joe to make his presence known even before the sun was up. Since he hadn't answered my call, I wasn't sure he would appear. I should have known better.

I was back in bed and asleep in mere seconds but was awakened at five thirty by Jeannie jumping on the bed.

"Momma says she has breakfast almost done and you need to get up and shower. She already woke Mister Farris and he's ready to eat."

Jeannie ran out of the room and I ran to the bathroom. Ten minutes later I was seated at the head of my small table surrounded by what was turning out to be my new family. It also included what every family needed, a crazy uncle. At six, we were loaded in my truck and starting the now familiar drive out to the valley in the hill country. Alice was leaning against my shoulder and Jeannie was asleep with her head nestled against Joe's leg. Doctor Joe looked uncomfortable but kept his hands folded on his lap and didn't move her.

The drive north seemed to take less time each visit so I was surprised when the turn off for the valley appeared dead ahead. Cresting the hill, the field of blue stood at least ten feet tall and masked any evidence of the area where we had picnicked the week before. My friend, Gardener, was waiting at the edge of the field and waving before I had time to shut off the engine.

"Master, it's good to see you again," came in to my head like a lightning bolt. How was it that I was now considered a Master to anyone? I also realized Gardener had not spoken to my companions.

"It appears that our arrival was anticipated," Joe grumbled. "Are we going to sit here all day or go see when the big reveal is supposed to happen?"

Joe's comments put me back in to action mode but I was still reluctant to get out of the truck. Jeannie made a dash to Gardener and grabbed his arms. The rest of us were not so quick to approach.

"The Master's will be here shortly to determine when the field will be ready to harvest," Gardener said before I could ask.

"Are you talking to the bug without us hearing?" Joe wanted to know.

"Well, he's talking to me but I haven't said a thing to him yet. He says the Masters will be here soon."

CHAPTER 9

THERE WAS NO NOTICE OF THE Master's arriving, just a quiet whoosh and then the appearance of a large spaceship hovering over the middle of the field. Stories told in Roswell about a sleek ship that hovered soundlessly were only correct about the lack of sound. What I saw was a battle-scarred hulk, pitted and dented, as if it had gone through a lot of wars or bounced off a lot of asteroids. Looking back towards the ship caused Gardener to rush off leaving me with the feeling that he was not very happy to see whoever was in the ship and anxious at the same time.

Twenty minutes later Joe was pacing around like a mad man and Alice and Jeannie had settled on some flat rocks to wait. I was staring at the ship and marveling at how silent it had been in its approach when the plants seemed to be parting to get out of the way of something distasteful. Gardener and his four cohorts were rushing towards me and insisting that I follow them through the field. When we were directly under the middle of the ship we were met by a very human looking man, dressed in a military styled jumpsuit. The man seemed agitated but I wasn't sure who it was directed at. When he came closer to me his eyes seemed to bulge. All of the Gardeners resembled five creatures waiting for an inquisition to start.

My friend Gardener was the first to approach and trembled as he took my arm.

"Master is disappointed because we allowed local inhabitants to witness us taking care of our crops. He became more distressed when I said you were also a Master."

Looking dumbfounded was not how I needed to appear so I answered, *"Did he expect the entire world to ignore a non-native plant that mysteriously appeared? Why doesn't he address me himself if he has questions?"*

"I needed to allow my translator time to adjust to your local dialect," the man answered having heard the mind conversation. "The Jinn says you are the person in charge and the one most like us."

Before I could respond another whoosh played through my head and I was suddenly standing in what I assumed was the deck of the man's vessel. My host was smiling now at my obvious confusion and discomfort at the change of location. We both took time to study each other. The alien was shorter than me but otherwise seemed to be as close to human as anyone else I had seen who came from outer space. His accent was strange but so is mine when I go to Tennessee to visit friends. I was finally able to answer the man's question.

"I suppose I am somewhat in charge but there might be some dispute about it among my colleagues. My name is Mike Sands, an officer of the law in the nearby city. May I ask why you are so angry?"

"I am more confused than angry. I thought you might be humanoid but I had not expected you to be so like us. The team that found this place said there were no bipeds close enough to discover our field yet here you are and not alone either."

"Humans are located all over this region so it was inevitable that you would be discovered at some point. Do you have a name or do I call you Master?"

"My civility is lacking, I am afraid. Welcome to my vessel. You are my guest and my name is Doren, Keeper of the fields of Dora, the product growing beneath us. The Jinn you call Gardener tells me that you have been courteous to him and his fellow caretakers. May I ask if he offered you some refreshments when you visited previously?"

"Yes, he did, some type of pastry, which was actually very good. He said it was made from the plants in this field."

"Dora is the main product that sustains our community. We use it in everything. It is unfortunate that we do not have the room or ability to grow this much needed plant on our vessel and must rely on local resources to grow enough to feed our people."

My view of the size of Doren's ship and the quantity of blue plants filling the valley below must have registered in Doren's mind.

"This ship is not used for harvesting, Mike Sands. We are at least seven planetary revolutions away from that occasion. This is a scout vessel and much smaller than the next vessel that will appear," Doren explained. He took a moment before deciding to continue speaking. "I hope the pastry you were offered was pleasant and had no ill effect on you or your companions."

"It was easy on the eye and our stomachs. It produced some interesting results, though, something you might explain."

"You must mean an improvement in your health. That is one of the benefits of this organism. I am both surprised and happy that you saw the same results my people enjoy. Dora was engineered by some far distant ancestors, something we no longer have the expertise to replicate. None of those on board our mother ship is an engineer, scientist or advanced technician. Part of our mission, other than to feed ourselves, is to seek out advanced species to see if they can…sorry, I have been saying too much."

"Why would a species able to travel through space need to find other advanced people? I would think you would have all you need on board your vessel."

"We have been traveling for a very long time and passed through many systems before we arrived here. An unfortunate result of that much time in space was an exposure to radiation. The lack of adequate shielding on our vessels has resulted in a somewhat diminished ability to understand the documents left to us by our ancestors. If we find other species on our journey that have a scientific or mechanical aptitude, we invite them to join our family of adventurers. A more serious problem as a result of the solar radiation exposure is the inability to reproduce viable offspring. Those of us that do conceive fail to carry a child until birth. Unfortunately, most of the species we encounter are like the Jinn, farmers or lesser skilled workers and incompatible to mate with our crew. My people remain the brightest and long lived but we are failing. The Dora keeps us at a level that lets us operate our equipment but not comprehend how they work. Sorry, I did not mean to be so long winded or expose our problems to you."

"I'm kind of confused, Doren. Is it your desire to find places to grow your crops or to seek a species you can mate with? Or are you only looking for beings smart enough to comprehend something your ancestors wrote a long time ago? Wouldn't you fear that those of my people bright enough to interact with what your ancestors left might also be strong enough to take charge of your entire civilization?"

"Your point is valid but the Jinn feel you and your companions might well be the ones we seek. The one you call Gardener gleaned that you have long had an interest in meeting an alien race so that you might document the event and see how that meeting could impact your society. He also said that the others, except for the smallest one, were scientists and already studying our food source. I would offer to allow you to study us further."

"That almost seems to be an invitation for you to study us. How do we know it isn't an attempt to abduct us?"

"We are not so different, Mike Sands," was suddenly spoken in my head. *"The Jinn claim that when they first encountered you there was little to differentiate your species from mine. They have the ability to determine the genetic coding of anything they can touch. It seems your genetic code has changed slightly since ingesting the pastries and now may be identical to that of my people."*

My mind was confused, wondering what part of Doren's conversation was aloud and what had been conveyed mind to mind. I must have been thinking loud enough that Doren began to laugh.

"It is another benefit of the Dora, the ability to communicate in our minds so long as one of the Jinn is nearby. You have that ability which proves how like us you are. My invitation does not obligate you to remain with us. We have been studying your world from a great distance for many years. It was only recently that we discovered that there were patches of soil able to successfully grow our crops."

"Our similarities raise another issue, Doren, the probability that our species are the same. Would your documents also give us knowledge of how two people from different areas of space can be so much alike?"

"You would have access to all that you need to discover if there is any truth to that possibility. But now, I must leave and prepare for the harvest. You have several more planet rotations to think about my offer. In the meantime, I will confer with my council to get their agreement. Until that time…"

The next thing I knew I was back on the ground surrounded by a very enthusiastic group of Jinn.

"None have ever been taken on board the Master's vessel, Mike Sands, who were allowed to return. We knew you were one of the Masters. Our status will rise since we were the ones to discover you."

"I believe it was us that discovered you and your Dora, but I'll concede the point. You will contact me when it is time for the harvest, won't you?"

"You will be notified before I contact Doren."

Five minutes later I was back at the edge of the field and surrounded by my new family.

"You've been gone for a long time, Sands, what were you doing in there?" Crazy Joe was grabbing at me as if his actions were likely to make me speak sooner.

"I've been on board the Master's ship and met with what I assume was the Captain. He never said that's what he was and I never asked. He is very interested in us and wants us to come onboard to review everything his people have recorded from time immemorial, however far back that goes."

"What does come on board mean?" Alice demanded. "Is that an invitation or does he have something else in mind. There have been too many things in the newspapers and on television about alien abduction to believe it's something completely innocent."

"Those same thoughts crossed my mind after Doren sent me back. He seemed to think we would be able to leave any time we wanted but there were some inconsistencies in what he told me."

"Well, why should that surprise you, Sands?' Joe snorted. "How could they expect to keep such a large crop invisible when the blue color can probably be seen from the space station or any plane flying overhead?"

"Compound that with his comment that they had been studying earth for a long time and only recently discovered intelligent bipeds lived on this planet. The guy was very courteous but my nerves were on edge the whole time I was on his ship."

"Well, here's another question for you. How are they supposed to put this entire field of blue in that small ship? It makes me think there is a much larger ship somewhere." Joe was beginning to pace again and point his finger at me as if I was the one he thought was suspicious.

"Doren said the same thing but I got the impression there was more than one ship. Gardener had already told me there were a lot more than one species involved. Doren mentioned a larger vessel was coming to conduct the harvest in a few days and we had until then to decide what we wanted to do."

"You said we, Mike, does that mean he wants all of us? What about Jeannie, was she included?"

"I'm not completely sure who he meant or if he wanted us to recruit other people as well. He said no one on the ship was able to do more than operate what they had. They have lost the ability to decipher old documents or engineer fixes for escalating mechanical issues. And yet, they managed to move across galaxies to get here. It does not seem logical and the more I hear myself talk it just feels wrong."

"About time your layman's mind figured that out. So, what do we do, wait for a week and then tell him to piss off?"

Alice had put her hands over Jeannie's ears thinking that Joe was about to explode in a torrent of profanity. Jeannie wiggled free and stared at each of us.

"Why don't you ask the Gardener what he thinks? He likes us a whole lot and would never want us to be unhappy."

I looked at Jeannie and smiled, thinking that would have been the easiest solution, if I thought the Jinn would tell us the truth.

"Can you still read their minds like you did last week?" I hoped she would say no so we could put the discussion off for a while.

"They've been listening to you guys shouting at each other since you came back, Poppa," Jeannie said, smiling as she used her new word for me for the first time, "and they are worried. Gardener says you might be right. He said something about bad intentions. What does that mean?"

"It means we have to be careful no matter what we decide. I'm all for heading home. Can we discuss this tomorrow?"

Alice and Jeannie moved in to my arms and began pushing me towards the truck. It took Joe another minute to decide he had better come along or get left behind. My conversation with Gardener would have to wait.

CHAPTER 10

SUNDAY WAS SPENT DOING ERRANDS and cleaning house. I wanted everything to be ready when, and if, Alice decided it was time for her and Jeannie to move in. My old vacuum cleaner was growling and groaning making it hard for me to hear the pounding on my front door. Eventually I realized it was not the vacuum and hoped it wasn't Joe coming over for another round of heated discussion, much as he did almost all the way home yesterday. The man at the front door was not someone I had seen before. "You're Mike Sands, aren't you?" was the first thing out of the man's mouth.

He was very Mediterranean in appearance, dark hair and eyes, shorter than me but seemed very fit, in a greasy kind of way. I thought he might be a process server but I knew I hadn't done anything vile enough to warrant a law suit since arriving in Roswell.

"May I ask who's asking?" It was too soon to get angry about the discourteous way he had asked so I waited for the guy to speak again.

"My name is Roy Morano and I don't like the way you have been treating my girlfriend."

The name meant nothing to me. The first thought I had was that he was Alice's ex but she had described him as a weight lifter and this guy certainly wasn't.

"Which girlfriend are we talking about?" I was hoping to make him think I had several lying around the house.

"You know damn well I'm talking about Lillian, you asshole."

He got my attention that time.

"You must be the latest grease-ball in her erection collection. You realize you're interrupting a very important house cleaning so why don't you get around to saying whatever it is you need to say."

My lack of enthusiasm must have irritated Roy because he began to get red in the face.

"You know," I added, "I am often told my face gets that same shade of red when I get angry or embarrassed. Which one are you, angry or just stupid?"

Speaking calmly didn't seem to be helping so I decided to remain silent. It took a moment for Roy to calm himself enough to speak, although his voice seemed a little tight.

"I've been asking Lillian to marry me for the last month but she keeps refusing claiming you haven't signed the fucking divorce papers. I'm here right now to make you sign the damn things so I can take them to her attorney for processing."

It seemed my smile wasn't what Roy wanted to see, either, so I decided to give him the good news.

"The divorce papers were signed, notarized and dispatched after Lillian called last week and asked me to hold on to them for a while longer. What do you think she meant by that, hold on to them, I mean?"

Roy took a step back and looked at me as if I was one of Roswell's resident space aliens.

"She said that, hold on to them? She never told me…All she said was she wasn't able to get married again. I thought it was because of you being a dick."

"Well, I was being a dick but decided to man up and kiss the bitch goodbye. It seems I might have been too hasty. Did Lill happen to mention anything about wanting to get back together with me?"

Roy turned a darker shade of red and I began to worry about him stroking out. It was time to put my charade to bed.

"Look, Roy, the divorce is done and the two of you need to work out where your relationship is going. To ease your mind, Lillian is never going to move to Roswell and I sure as hell am not going back to Los Angeles. So, if you two can't work it out, try moving on. Do you have anything else you wanted to discuss, like local real estate or job opportunities?"

"I drove all the way out here for nothing," Roy whined as his head fell down to his chest. "Do you mind if I sit on your porch for a while until my head clears?"

"Be my guest but you may have to share. I have a rather obnoxious friend who drops in unexpectedly every day or two who especially likes to recline on the wicker couch. In the meantime, I am going back to my chores."

A couple of hours must have gone by before I had a chance to look out at the porch. Roy was gone but Joe was asleep on the couch. I moved back to the second bedroom and continued getting it ready for Jeannie.

My second beer was getting warm in my hands when Joe walked in my kitchen.

"It's courteous to knock when coming in the door, old man."

"Kind of like you were courteous to that jackoff at your front door a while ago?"

"I didn't think anyone was around to hear the conversation. How long did he stay on the porch?"

"Not long; he tried to whine to me and I told him to fuck off. He left a couple of minutes later mumbling something about the bad natured people in New Mexico. I waved at him but he got in his car and drove off. He must be a pretty resourceful guy to drive such a big Mercedes. Is he your ex's boyfriend?"

"He's the latest of several and probably the next to hit the highway."

We both had a chuckle since that was exactly where old Roy was right now. Joe decided to change the subject in the middle of my happy thoughts.

"We need to inform some official somebody about the blue stuff in the valley and that there may be some visitors gonna be there in a few days. Seeing as you are the new Chief it ought to be you breaking the news."

"You have some kind of imagination, Doctor Joe. This is Roswell, for God's sake, and every crackpot in the nation thinks Aliens, with a capital A, are going to turn up here. You are better able to get things rolling if you come out of retirement and approach some of the eggheads in Albuquerque or some other big city with a university. I know this whole scenario is true and I still think it's crazy."

"So, what do you want to do, take a vacation on an alien space ship?"

"Seeing as we are all crazy, the idea does have me interested. But, like you keep telling me, I'm just a layman and not trained in any scientific or engineering protocols. I'd be no better than the other residents on Doren's ship who lack essential skills. And what if he's lying and getting us on board is just a ruse. Better yet, I'm damn well not letting Alice go up there."

"You're sounding suspiciously like me now, Chief Sands. Do you have any other thoughts on the matter?"

"What if the Dora could feed the world's hungry people? What if you or some other crack scientist could figure a way to grow the stuff in something other than a salt marsh? What if the changes that have happened to us are just a starting point and we have no idea how to reverse the effects? What if we become another species like the Jinn? There are too many variables, Joe, and I have no idea how to address any of them."

"You're sounding more like a scientist than you realize, Mister Sands. Most of that has been running through my head since we first decided to put some of the Dora in our bodies. Alice said the same thing when we talked this morning. By the way, she is worried about you and hopes you aren't thinking of leaving town."

"Where would I go? Oh, she means on Doren's ship, doesn't she? I'll call her in a little while. I'm having another beer first. Do you want one?"

"Nope, I'm riding home and don't need to be stopped for riding my bicycle while DWI even if I'm only a little bit inebriated. Your girlfriend, Officer Hart, has her Apache heart set on putting me in handcuffs. I don't think she means to take me to jail, though. Maybe you should read her in on our secret and let her get the Mescalero Apache Nation involved."

That took a moment to sink in but it brightened my day.

"You are a genius Doctor Farris. That might be exactly what we need, a Native American intervention, something to get the attention of the media and the government. We could always refer to it as another Apache uprising. Lee Anne Hart may be the perfect person to engineer a solution."

"You've really gone off your rocker, Sands. Why use the Apaches?"

"They have a lot of students in the local college and a bunch more who have received technical training but can't find a job. Plus, we can feed an entire tribe with a small part of what's grown in that valley. They could become self-sufficient. What if they become the agents for Doren's people and we act as the liaison? This could end up being very interesting."

"It might be interesting, so long as the feds or state suits leave us alone. How do we keep them out of the picture or do we even want to?"

Before I could think of an answer my cell phone began to buzz. I hoped it was Alice but looking at the screen I saw it was Lillian. I was tempted to push her to voicemail but knew she would keep calling until I answered.

"Hey, Lill, what's up?"

"You son-of-a-bitch, you sent the papers in after I specifically asked you not to. I ought to send Roy out there to knock some sense in your head."

"It wouldn't look good having your boyfriend arrested for assaulting the Chief of Police and besides, he was just here trying to get me to sign the damn things."

"Roy was there? He just called me from his car and said he was on the way back from a business meeting. You mean that asshole was in Roswell and not Salt Lake City? What did he say exactly? No, forget that; what did you say to him?"

"He told me he wanted to marry you but you kept putting him off because of me. I told him what you said about not wanting to get married and he became rather upset. One of my friends was close enough to hear our conversation and thought Roy was going to explode. My last comment was for him to work things out with you or move on. I thought he was going to cry but he didn't."

"You didn't hit him, did you? You can be kind of touchy at times."

"We talked, Lillian, like you and I used to, with you shouting and me listening calmly."

"You always were good about listening, Mike. Wait a minute; did you say something about being a Chief of Police? When did that happen?"

"They made Walter Boone the interim mayor and he appointed me the Chief. It was all very sudden and totally unexpected. In fact, Boone gave me no choice in the matter. Why is that important to you?"

"Everything you do is important, baby. I ought to come out to help you celebrate."

"I already have someone to celebrate with and you have Roy."

"Are you afraid I might want to stay? You do have two bedrooms in your house, don't you, not that we would need two?"

"I do and both are spoken for; Alice in mine and Jeannie in the other."

"Wow; that was fast, especially for you. You've only known each other for a couple of weeks and now she's moved in? I'm not sure which one of you is the faster worker, you, which I doubt, or your new hussy."

"This conversation has taken an unexpected and unpleasant turn and it's time to say goodbye." And for once I was the first one to disconnect the call.

"How big a stable of ladies do you have, Sands?" Joe had a silly smile on his face.

"Being discrete is not big on your list, is it old man? You could have moved to the other room while I spoke to my ex."

"You could have done the same thing if you wanted some privacy. Besides, I like a little gossip now and again. Do you think she was serious about coming out here?"

"Are you hoping I'll fix you up with her? She can be like a piranha, Joe; she'd eat you up."

"She left some meat on your bones and you seem to have weathered her attack fairly well."

"Dealing with Lillian, you still feel beaten up, win or lose with that woman. I am always surprised we were together for thirty years. Things didn't get uncomfortable until I started talking about retirement; correction, uncomfortable for Lillian. I was completely oblivious until the minute she walked out. Do I want her back in my life or closer than a couple of states away, hell no? I'd rather join Doren's crew first."

"Your idea of the Mescalero Res taking part is probably the better idea. Besides, you're the first person I've spoken to that doesn't try to get me tossed in the looney bin."

"It's not because you and sane fit in the same sentence but you are very entertaining. Even Jeannie seems to have a liking for you but I'm not sure about Alice."

"Alice is okay in my book, just wound a little too tight. That must sound crazy coming from me but who better to see someone with a like mind. The two of you balance each other out so don't let her get away."

That ended our conversation so I kicked the old geezer out after he rejected an opportunity to help me clean the rest of my house. The balance of the afternoon was spent thinking of ways for Lee Anne Hart to bring the Tribal Council in on our project.

CHAPTER 11

L EE ANNE WAS ON DUTY when I finally reached her. She had no problem, in fact was enthusiastic, about coming to my house for dinner. She never did question why I wanted her to come over. To be on the safe side I made sure Alice and Jeannie would be there, as well, still thinking about Joe's comment of me having a stable of ladies.

If Lee Anne was disappointed to see Alice, she made up for it when she and Jeannie hit it off. Dinner was a running commentary between the two until Alice and I decided to sit back and be entertained by the two younger women, even with their age difference, talking about things they had in common. It definitely made me feel old and Alice appeared to feel the same way.

Alice didn't inform Lee Anne that she had consumed a meal that was made with a generous portion of Dora until after dinner was over. Lee Anne was skeptical that such a plant existed and that Alice and I were trying to poison her. She couldn't explain how she was feeling more energetic especially after having such a large meal. I pointed out she had held a piece of Dora in her hands at Momma Tucker's the same morning Joe had brought it to me. To bring Lee Anne up to date we sent Jeannie to her new room to sort out some of the things we had brought over from the apartment. I began to explain how we got in touch with the Jinn minding the field and my interaction with the Masters who were responsible for putting the crop in that valley. By the time I got to the part of my plan for the field of Dora and of involving the Mescalero's, Lee Anne was ready to call a special meeting of the Council.

Alice, however, was starting to raise all kinds of questions.

"How are we going to make sure Doren and the Masters buy in to your solution," she queried without offering an answer.

That was the one part of the equation that I hadn't figured out. If Doren needed tech savvy people, the solution was right in front of him. It needed to be a tradeoff and I wasn't sure how good of a negotiator either the Apache's or the Masters were. The first challenge was calling a meeting of the Council and getting their buy-in. Lee Anne departed that night with a head of steam I hoped she could maintain.

Two days later, thankful that Gardener had not contacted me, Lee Anne notified me that the Council would hear my proposition the next day. Alice was ready but Joe was having second thoughts. Not long after I left him a message, he was at the police station arguing with the desk sergeant who was refusing to let him see me. I made no friends when I overrode my desk supervisor and walked Joe back to my office.

"I'm worried about all this, Sands. What if we do all the negotiating and the damn Masters refuse to play ball? What's our backup plan going to be?"

"I guess at that point we have to notify the feds that we have alien guests on our planet. That might piss off both the Masters and the Mescalero if one or both get cut out of the equation."

I finally cut Joe short and walked him back out to the lobby.

The Tribal Council meeting was scheduled for six in the evening to accommodate those members holding paying jobs. Alice arranged for a sitter for a very disappointed Jeannie but I saw no benefit in dragging her to the meeting. Lee Anne Hart met us at the Tribal offices on Central Mescalero Avenue and gave me a sour look as I drove up in my Roswell Police cruiser. She shook her head positively as she realized I had left my uniform at the station and had put on a business suit. She made me shed the tie before we walked inside.

"The members of the Council barely tolerate law enforcement from on or off the Res so try not to act like you do at the station." Lee Anne was giving all of us a quick once over, making sure we didn't have anything on our persons that might offend the members. She led us in the chambers, actually a multipurpose auditorium, like she was the mother duck leading her ducklings. We sat waiting to be called upon.

The Council was made up of eight members, all sitting at a long table like many small city councils. All had a name plate in from of them but only one person looked ready to jump over the table, the Chairman of the Council, Abraham Torrez. He kept a wary eye on all of us but was very intent on everything Lee Anne said or did.

"So, Mister Sands, or should I call you Chief Sands, what brings you here in such urgency? Actually, on the Res, I am the Chief and you are just a guest. I hope you have something to say that is worth the time of this Council."

Lee Anne was ready to jump up and complain but I grabbed her arm to calm her down and make sure she didn't interrupt.

"Well, Chief Torrez," I said making sure I emphasized the word Chief, "a couple of weeks ago Doctor Farris, seated to my left and a well-known agronomist, located a field of very unusual plants growing in a valley about eighty miles northeast of here. He brought me a sample of the plant and I, in turn, took it to Doctor Alice Morrison, a botanist working at the University in Roswell. She is seated to my right next to Lee Anne Hart. We all determined that the plant was not native to this planet but had no toxic chemicals or agents that could harm humans. A subsequent visit to the valley revealed the entire area was covered in the plants."

I took a minute to remove a sample from a case wheeled in by Alice. I put the two-foot royal blue growth on the table in front of Torrez and stepped back. Torrez pushed away from the table and made no effort to examine the Dora.

"The sample on the desk is a small piece from plants that are at least ten feet tall. I had a conversation with the caretakers, a race of people called Jinn, who said the plant, something they called Dora, could be used in almost any combination of food items and was extremely nutritious. He offered us some pastries made from the Dora and they were in fact delicious. We learned the Dora was extremely wholesome and had many natural health benefits. I bring that up because a small portion of the crop in the valley would feed every member of the Mescalero family on the Res. In fact, if handled properly, Dora could become a money crop that could support the farmers and merchants on the Res."

"Do you expect me to believe that a cactus can feed all of my people?" Torrez shouted while the rest of the Council smiled or laughed.

Lee Anne jumped to her feet before I could stop her.

"I've eaten food prepared with this plant and I haven't felt this good in years. Whatever it is, my people need its curative properties and its ability to provide nutrition to all the children who now go hungry."

Lee Anne reached for Alice's case and removed a bag of pastries and a pile of paper plates. She doled out one for each council member as well as plates for the four of us. She was the first to take a big bite of the confection, smiling as the sweet taste filled her mouth. She stared at Torrez as if daring him to follow her lead. Torrez growled but angrily grabbed the pastry and stuffed it in his mouth. The rest of the Council watched until they were sure Torrez was not going to die and then every one of them ate a pastry.

I leaned over to Lee Anne, who by then had retaken her seat.

"Why was Torrez so angry and then gobbled the pastry?"

"He was not going to be shown up by his daughter in front of the Council. He still has issues because I took a man's job off of the Res. He's also a little sensitive I took my mother's name instead of his at the naming ceremony."

"You never said Torrez was your father."

"Would it have made any difference to you if you had known? This way family and politics can be kept separate."

"It seems you didn't try to kill us so maybe this plant, 'Dora' you called it, may be good for our people. What do we have to do?" Chief Torrez was starting to come around.

"Find a salt marsh on the Res, plant the Dora and watch it grow. I will need to get the starter plants and instructions from the caretakers but the rest should be easy," I hope, I said to myself.

"How soon can this be done?"

"We need to communicate with the Jinn and then I can set a date. However, the Dora is not the only thing I want to discuss."

"You are asking a lot of this Council, Chief Sands. What else do you have for us?"

"Lee Anne and I have had many conversations about the lack of opportunity in the job market for your unemployed members. What if there was a chance for some of them to use their technical training working for the aliens who brought the Dora to this planet?"

"Are you falling in to the same trap as all of the people who come to this area looking for lost space ships? I gave you more credit than that." Chief Sanchez must have thought sarcasm was called for.

"The proof will be in the valley where the Dora will be harvested. Put together an advisory group and send them with us when we return for the harvest. I'll make the introduction and then we will see how things transpire. The most you lose is time away from the Res by some of your unemployed members."

"I'm still confused as to why we want to send people other than farmers to meet with the supposed aliens."

"I have been told that the aliens have lost the ability to understand and work with the scientific and engineering issues on their vessels. You have some bright people who could benefit from the experience of identifying those issues. The main reason is that buried in the ship's memory are many advanced systems that we could download, patent and market for additional income. Feeding the hungry is nice but making a ton of money due to scientific programs is much better."

"Do you believe the aliens are going to let us walk away with their technology without some kind of compensation?"

"It's a tradeoff, our giving them access to lost tech and paying us with Dora and use of the tech on earth. By my reasoning it's a win-win but we still have to negotiate with the aliens."

"Lee Anne, what is your thought on this proposition brought to us by Chief Sands? Can he be trusted or is he just another greedy white man?"

The last statement had the Council murmuring among themselves. Lee Anne was quiet for a moment as she studied her father, trying to gauge his intent.

"Mike Sands is an honorable man and always tries to do the right thing. He brought this proposition to you instead of going to the local or federal authorities because if he did that, he knew we would see nothing of the rewards that could be obtained from dealing with the aliens. It would be foolish to throw away a chance to better our people and honor the man who brought this to us."

"That was very eloquent, my daughter. You have learned well. Take our guests to the lounge while the Council discusses the situation. You may return in case we need more information."

CHAPTER 12

THE LOUNGE WAS AT THE far end of the building and completely out of range to overhear anything that went on in the Council Meeting Hall. Joe had been silent for the entire proceeding but was looking very smug. After Lee Anne returned to the meeting I huddled with the old scientist.

"What's up with you, Joe? There has never been a time, no matter what was going on, that you didn't have a comment or argument."

"You don't get it, do you Chief Sands. This whole charade was so your little Apache girlfriend could make a big splash with her Indian chums. If this isn't a big waste of time…"

"You were the first human to find Dora and did as much research on the stuff as Alice. I'll bet you have a more sophisticated lab at your house than she does at the college. You could have spoken up about the benefits of Dora instead of sitting mute."

"You were doing just fine, for what it's worth." Joe slouched down in his chair and refused to say anything more.

A look over to Alice wasn't much better. She was looking glum, as if our trip to the Res had been a waste of time.

Twenty minutes had gone by when Lee Anne came back to the lounge.

"The Council wants Chief Sands to return for some additional conversation." Her disposition was so bland that I couldn't tell if she was bringing us good news or bad.

Joe and Alice stood up ready to accompany me when Lee Anne held up her hand.

"This conversation is between the Council and Chief Sands. You two have to remain here."

Lee Anne started to walk out and stopped when I failed to move with her. She looked over her shoulder and gave me a hard look that made me think she was the one in charge and not me. I followed as she walked briskly back towards the meeting room. Before we got to the door she stopped and turned to me.

"You made a good impression in there, especially with my father. Keep calm and especially don't show any emotion at anything the members may say. This is very important if you want to impress the Mescalero Apaches. Can you do that, Mike?"

All I could do was nod my assent and wonder what in hell was going to happen next. I walked in and looked at the stoic faces of eight Council members, none of them showing a sign that reflected they were in favor of my earlier appearance.

"Chief Sands," Torrez began, "it is not every day that the White Man brings us opportunities to make our life better without attaching numerous conditions. What are yours?"

That little speech made me think back to what Lee Anne had said to me so I stifled my anger about the Council thinking I was out for my own greed. Each face seemed to be interested in the manner of my answer not the content.

"Did you assume I was doing this solely to become rich at your expense? I could have done that without coming here at all. Do I wish to receive something of value out of this exercise? Of course, I do but it will be whatever you wish me to have. I will set no worth on my contribution but will leave it up to you. There is enough greed in the world without me adding to it."

"That's very much what Lee Anne predicted you would say. However, in order for you to share in any part of this you would need to be connected to the Mescalero in some way. The Council has decided to grant you status as a member of our family. If you accept you will be listed on our rolls as an honorary Apache with all the rights of a full member except that you may not vote in our elections. All other benefits will be yours including an equal share in any profits derived from this business enterprise. As part of this ceremonial position, you must choose a spirit animal so that we may use it during your indoctrination. Do you accept these terms?"

Stunned would be too mild a statement as to how I felt. Looking at each of the faces in front of me I could see a sense of amusement at my reaction. It wasn't until Lee Anne punched me in the shoulder that I came alive. She was laughing at me as I turned to look at her.

"A golden eagle," I shouted, "that has always been my spirit animal, ever since I was a child."

"A very noble choice," Chief Torrez replied, "and spoken very firmly. You shall be known as Mike 'Golden Eagle' Sands on our books. There is one more matter to attend to. Lee Anne Hart will be your mentor as she is the one who recommended your application for membership. All things Apache must be through her, is that understood?"

"That is acceptable and more than okay with me."

"Well then, brother, you are now one of us."

The entire Council came off of the dais and each gave me a full body hug and a pound on the chest. There had to be something in the air in this part of New Mexico that required me to receive a pounding from everyone I got close to. Chief Torrez took me aside when all the others had given me their congratulations.

"This is a rare honor we are bestowing on you, Sands, so don't fuck it up. And make sure you treat my daughter with respect throughout the training and indoctrination. Just because you were recommended does not mean you will be able to pass all the tests a warrior must face, especially at your age. Do the best that you can and in a valiant manner. If you are brave, we may have reason to remove the honorary label and vote you in as a full member. That would be an even rarer feat."

The Chief gave me another thump on the chest and then walked to meet with the rest of the Council

Lee Anne was still smiling as I walked over to her.

"What was all that about? Why would you even think to make me a member of your tribe?"

"I have my reasons, Golden Eagle, but you are going to have to wait to learn what they are. In the meantime, Alice and Joe's hall pass on the Res is about to expire so we have to get them back to Roswell. Go bring the car up to the door while I fetch your two compadres. Oh, and since I didn't want my police cruiser vandalized while on the res, you get to give me a ride back to the city."

Lee Anne was taking this mentoring thing a little far but as long as we were on her turf, I let it slide.

The ride back to Roswell was completed with Alice going crazy over acceptance of the project and my becoming an honorary Apache.

"Jeannie is going to go ape shit, Mike, completely over the moon." Turning to look to the back seat she saw Joe trying to stay as far from Lee Anne as possible while Lee Anne kept trying to poke the old man in the ribs. "How did you manage to pull this off, Lee Anne? It didn't look that good to me when they kicked us out of the meeting."

"Mike is a very convincing speaker and had already gained approval before you left the room. The Apache are prone to bargain before accepting any deal and this was done the same way. Mike responded like an Apache when he was given the conditions and everyone was happy, especially me."

Alice turned back around and slumped in her seat, all of her enthusiasm seemingly gone.

"What's that all about, babe? Are you okay?"

"Why shouldn't I be fine? Are you sure you haven't bitten off more than you can handle?" she said as she glanced over her shoulder to the rear seat.

The rest of the ride was completed in silence, the only sounds coming from Joe, grunting as he tried to avoid Lee Anne's probing finger. Lee Anne was dropped off at the police station and then we headed to my house.

"I don't understand, Alice, did I do something wrong?" I was at a loss as to why things had gotten so cold in the car.

"Wrong," Joe cried out, "how much did it cost to give your balls to that little Apache girl?"

"What the fuck are you talking about? I didn't give up anything. They offered me membership because of what we can bring them. What does Lee Anne have to do with that? She's not on the Council, for God's sake."

"She kind of sounded like you belonged to her, now," Alice piped in, "her being your mentor and you having to follow her rules."

"That's just business, Alice. I'm a one-woman man and you are that woman."

It was comical the way both Joe and Alice said, "You are so naïve," almost in unison.

"Well, maybe I'm not as smart as I thought I was," came out weakly.

A snort from Joe and a sarcastic chuckle from Alice was all I got out of them the rest of the ride home. Joe rode off on his bicycle which he had left parked on my porch declining to stay for dinner. Alice decided to stay even though she still wasn't answering my questions on why she felt I was being naïve.

Jeannie was dropped off soon after we got home. She broke the somber mood when she heard I was now an honorary Apache which caused Alice to thaw a little.

"Can you remember when Lee Anne began to pay more attention to you than to any of the other cops?" was the first question that addressed her concerns.

"I guess it was when I didn't give her a lot of shit about being a woman doing a man's job. We had a lot of female officers in LA and I treated her the same way I did with my old partners."

"Does she joke around with you, maybe flirt and make vague references that can be construed as sexual in nature?"

"My god, Alice, she's fifteen years younger than me. I just didn't think of her actions that way. Maybe I am naïve but it was fun bantering with her. Neither one of us had been treated like we belonged on the Department so it was like we kind of bonded. Does that mean she took more meaning from it than I did?"

"Bingo, you genius, you are finally getting it."

"It makes more sense now what Abraham Torrez said when the meeting concluded and he took me aside."

"Wait, he spoke to you in private?"

"He said I had to treat his daughter with respect while I was being evaluated and after that Lee Anne said there was more to come. She does think she has a chance with me, doesn't she? What do I do now? Before I met you it had been over thirty years between serious flirting and now I'm confused."

"Poor baby, let me give you a hug while you try to reason it out."

By the time we went to bed the mood had definitely gone from cool to warm but hot was not on the menu. I was almost afraid of the conversation I would have to have with Lee Anne to try to make things right.

CHAPTER 13

BEFORE I COULD HAVE THAT conversation with my new mentor I had a mental message from Gardener telling me the Master would be at the field in two revolutions. My attention was drawn to ensuring the Apache delegation would be ready to make the journey to the valley in two days which put Lee Anne to the back of my mind.

A phone call to Abraham Torrez later in the day verified his team would be ready. Six of the brightest people on the Res would meet us at the intersection of State 246 and Highway B001 at seven o'clock. Hopefully Doren would find the change in his offer to his satisfaction.

For the next two days I tried to stay as far from Lee Anne as work issues would allow. Fortunately, she was still on the graveyard shift and not around headquarters during the day. On the morning of our return to the valley she signed off of work early and made sure to be waiting at my house next to the truck when Alice, Jeannie and I came outside. I felt Alice tense up until I put my arm around her and kissed her cheek. Lee Anne smiled as if it was the most natural thing to do and climbed in the back of the cab. I was confused, expecting some kind of a reaction from my Apache mentor.

Joe was waiting on the edge of the highway at route 246 and smirked when he saw Jeannie and Lee Anne in the back seat. Everyone was convivial on the way to meet the Apache's, almost as if everything was normal.

The Apache team was in a new passenger van making my old truck look even shabbier. Ten minutes later we were at the hill at the top of the valley and could go no further due to the thick growth of Dora. Most of the stalks were as thick as a man's thigh and rose ten feet in the air. Lee Anne and her tribesmen were frozen staring at the strange plants until Alice led the way up to the edge of the field.

Gardener did not show up until I finally got out of my truck and joined the group gawping at the field of royal blue plants. It appeared as if the taller the Dora grew the more brilliant the color became. Gardener came to the edge of the field and held his arms out for me. I joined in the embrace and heard the Apache's gasp and step back.

"You have brought many friends with you, Mike Sands. Is Master aware of this development or will he be surprised?"

"Doren asked for my help but never limited how many people it would take to be successful. This was my decision."

"They are different from you and those who were here before. Master might not be happy."

"I will deal with Doren and come to an accommodation. When is he going to arrive?"

"He is on the way and will be here in his own time. Can I provide some refreshments for your people while they wait?"

"That would be appreciated. Would you also like to know each of the new members before Doren arrives?"

"I am not sure, Mike Sands."

"That was not something up for debate, Gardener. I will have each of them introduce themselves."

Stepping to the side I gestured for Lee Anne to come to me. I placed her right arm on Gardener's left and stood back. The shock on her face was enough to let me know she was having a conversation with my alien friend. What surprised me was when Gardener included me even though we were not touching each other. Lee Anne's reaction about meeting an alien and her thoughts about me came through clearly making me turn red again. Interestingly, Gardener kept my thoughts private, something I was very grateful for.

When each of the tribe members, four men and two women, had been introduced, Gardener disappeared for a few minutes returning with a platter of pastries. Alice and Joe eagerly grabbed one while Lee Anne's team was hesitant.

"Lee Anne has already eaten some of the Dora," Alice piped in, "when she ate dinner with us and at the Council Meeting where we all shared some. It would set a nice example for our hosts if you all took a bite and swallowed."

Lee Anne took a pastry from Gardener and took a big bite, smirking at Alice each time she chewed. Her actions and the knowledge that the Council had also tried the pastry encouraged the two women to take one. The men, so as not to be outdone, made a bigger production of taking a piece and chewing it slowly. All of them had smiles on their faces as the last of the pastry was consumed. Gardener was beaming as he returned to the blue forest.

It was almost two hours later when I felt the sudden change in air pressure that announced the arrival of the alien ship. I was prepared to see Doren appear but this time he was not alone. Two other members of his crew stood with him as the plants parted announcing his arrival. It seemed the plants weren't too happy to see any of them.

"I expected only to see you and your two companions, Mike Sands. Who do you have with you?" Doren did not seem pleased that I had a small army with me.

"You made it clear that you needed technicians to unravel what was lost to you over generations. I brought a solution to make that happen. Did you have a different resolution in mind?"

Doren turned to confer with his two companions, speaking mind to mind, forgetting that I could hear every word. Doren was trying to convince the other two of my good intentions but was running up against some serious apprehension. I decided it was time to interject myself but to do it verbally.

"Is there a problem, Doren? You seem to be having trouble with your companions. Tell me if I'm wrong but I sense that they might not trust us."

"We have been treated poorly on other worlds we have visited and our crops destroyed. These two think you might have the same intentions."

"Do they understand what we are saying or will you have to translate for them?"

"They are conversant in your language because of the universal translators. You may interject if there is a question not understood."

"Good, what we wish to negotiate is a trade of services. Your Dora appears to be compatible with humans on this planet and grows fast enough to feed not only your people but many of the unfed folks on this world. My team is ready to plant Dora on their lands to feed their tribal members. They will ensure there is always enough for your needs as well. Any surplus will be sold in an attempt to recoup expenses. Can you understand my offer?" was said to Doren's two companions. I got the impression that the other two were members of the Ship's Council Doren had to report to.

The taller of the two pushed Doren out of the way proving my point as he faced me.

"My people call me Torgon and I am the head of our council. You are the strongest of those present and I assume you are the leader, no matter what Doren has said. Why should we grant you permission to take our crop when we need every bit of it to maintain ourselves? What else do you offer?"

Doren was looking pleadingly at me as if saying he had no choice in bringing his superiors to meet with us.

"Doren told me you were solely dependent on Dora to feed your people. We have a wealth of food products that might vary your diets. In order to pay for those products and to correct your inability to use the data stored on your vessel I propose that my team be allowed to analyze your systems. If we can gain access to the information, we will gladly train the brightest of your people to properly use it so long as we can freely take information to improve our own standard of living."

"You ask a lot for a backward civilization."

"None of the people on this world have had any of their abilities reduced due to exposure to large amounts of radiation. We are bright and resilient, Torgon, but wish to forge a partnership, not an adversarial relationship. You can gain knowledge and the ability to chart your own course, so to speak. Why would you want to do otherwise?"

"You sound much like another member of the Consortium. I find your terms acceptable but must put them to the others that make up the Consortium. You have only met the Jinn, who may be the mildest of the species, and may have to confront others not so agreeable.

"The members of my team, those not seen before today, are from a proud, warrior, society. They will give you the best that they can but be warned, they will not suffer being disrespected without consequences. You need to put that information to your, what was you called it, your Consortium."

"We are not fighters, Mike Sands, we are travelers. Those with us are other travelers we have encountered while moving from world to world. Yours is the first place where anyone has offered to bargain with us. Most other places want us gone or to steal what we have. How can I be sure you are not like the others?"

"Had I been like the others I would have brought government officials instead of representatives from a small impoverished community. I might ask the same of you. How do I know my people will be safe while in your custody? It's a matter of trust."

Torgon stepped back and had another conversation with his companions. This time there was no antagonism in their voices. I listened patiently while the three aliens convinced themselves that our offer was in everyone's best interest. They also wanted to think how to take advantage of the situation,

Realizing that I had been ignoring the rest of my team I turned to find Joe and the Apaches in conversation on how best to approach solving the riddle of the information locked on board the alien ship. They were obviously not interested in me so I looked for Alice and Lee Anne.

The two of them were huddled together about forty feet away and seemed to be getting on with each other much better than I thought they had a right to, especially after the event in the Apache Council meeting. Both of them looked over to me and giggled making me worry that I was in for some additional trauma. When I walked over to them, they stopped talking and just smiled.

"Why do I get the impression I was the subject of your conversation? Should I be worried?"

"You have no idea how worried you should be," Alice said while trying not to laugh. "You'll figure it out when you report back to Lee Anne's father. It will be up to him to talk to you about it."

"You don't seem to be too upset about whatever was being discussed so I guess I shouldn't worry too much."

"That's open to interpretation," Lee Anne added. "Alice and I have come to an understanding, if that was what worried you."

My head swiveled back and forth between the two women but got no further comment from either.

About that time Torgon called me over.

"We have decided to agree to give conditional approval to your proposal. Our harvest must come first and then a shuttle will arrive to pick up your technicians. We are disappointed that you are not one of those who would come with us and would suggest you rethink your decision. In your absence it will require the presence of the old one, the one the caretaker called Crazy Joe. Is that a name of fondness?"

It was my turn to laugh.

"He is a well-respected scientist but can be somewhat difficult in how he approaches things. He is a personal friend of mine and must be treated as such." I had decided to act as pompous as Torgon, assuming that was what he respected. It seemed to work.

CHAPTER 14

M Y GROUP WAS ASKED TO move to the highest point in the pass to the valley as the vessel doing the harvest might not know that we were not a part of the crop. Standing at the summit the size of the craft caused all of us to gape. It was also pitted and well worn, judging by the look of the hull, much like the smaller shuttle. Something about the way Torgon spoke began to worry me. The safety of my team was of the utmost importance.

The story of the ship's crew being subjected to space related radiation coupled with the look of the ship's hull made me pull Joe aside for a conference.

"Does the damage to the hull of the harvester worry you? I mean I think Torgon was pretty honest regarding the radiation problems and I don't want you or the Apaches to get over-exposed."

"If we are not any further up than the space station, we should be fine. I'll make sure we are all equipped with radiation badges and get us back to earth at the first sign of trouble, assuming we are allowed to return."

"I'm more concerned about Torgon's comment about their inability to reproduce. We are sending a very healthy and virile group to be among folks who need some fresh blood in their lineage, not counting you, of course."

"Why not me, God damn it? I might be ready to share my genius even if you want to keep yours parked on earth."

"What are you two arguing about?" Alice asked pushing in between Joe and me. "You've got your pal, Gardener, all worked up. He wants you to come over to him for a talk of some kind, Mike. Do you know why he's so excited?"

"Why doesn't he talk to me from there? He's done that before, even called to me when I was in Roswell."

"He was talking with Jeannie, not me, but she said it was important. This whole thing has gotten me very nervous and I can't figure out why."

"Keep that feeling, babe, it may be the best indicator of something to watch out for. Joe, why don't you follow me just in case I need some backup assistance?"

Gardener was jumping from one skinny leg to the other until I walked to the edge of the field. The harvester was on the far side of the valley and working slowly our way. I was surprised when Gardener grabbed my arms and held on tightly.

"Master has ordered me not to talk to you, Mike Sands. If we speak while connected to each other none of them are able to hear us. You should be very wary of those beings. I sense you have your own reservations and that is very wise. The Masters have long held the belief that they are the only ones of our association that have adequate intelligence to navigate space. Our Queen allows that misinformation so that she can gather enough data to gain our independence. She believes your people are the first she has encountered that may be superior to the Masters but does not wish you to suffer at their hands. I am the one responsible for providing that opinion to my Queen and feel a responsibility to ensure the safety of you and your people. Remember this; a lack of ability to gain access to the history stored on the ship has not prevented any of us from traversing vast distances and subjugating numerous species. Some of us may claim to be peaceful but do not be deceived by everything you hear."

That had to be the longest and most illuminating speech a Jinn had uttered and caused me to revise my opinion of their level of intelligence. Gardener obviously heard me think because he smiled brightly enough to light up the area surrounding the two of us.

"What do you suggest we do? Should I refuse to send my people as I promised?"

"Send them, Mike Sands, and my people will ensure their safety. As payment, you and your people will provide us a place

to stay until we can make needed repairs to our ship. You may not have realized that the Masters claimed to have captured many space going species and connected their resources to their own. Ours is one of the last added to the Consortium and can be freed with little effort. Can you promise us a refuge?"

"I may have a place for you if you can promise to help us grow more of the Dora. Answer me this, my friend, why did you not come to me on the hill?"

"You should have realized by now that the Dora and my people are somewhat symbiotic. We protect each other however the Dora do not favor the Masters. During the harvest the upper portion of the stalks are removed but the important part that gives them life lies beneath the ground. The Masters were close to extinction before they made us a part of their Consortium. Our vessel produced enough Dora to support my people but not enough to keep all of the others the Masters had added fed and healthy. Healthy is an overstatement. None of us are healthy, just alive would be closer to a good description. You are aware that the Masters, much like the other species exposed to radiation, are unable to procreate? Your species is compatible and I fear they may be used for that purpose."

"You verified my suspicions, my friend. Can I assume you and your Queen are not as devious as the Master's and plan no harm to us? If we are to fear one, shouldn't we fear all who come to visit us?"

"Was it not you who mentioned trust in an earlier conversation? We gain nothing if you refuse our help. While the Masters deny being aggressive, you have seen how that may not be true. Instead, the Jinn have treated you well and allowed you to see in to our minds. Have you seen a lie or deception?"

"Does the mere statement by you make it true or a hope I will believe everything you say? You should realize that humans are not only devious but can become extremely aggressive with very little provocation. If you can live with that threat, I guess we will have to live with the unknowns presented by the Jinn."

"My Queen accepts that offer, Mike Sands, and can't wait to have a personal audience. You have impressed her and that gives me status in her eyes."

Gardener turned and made his way back through the field. I turned to go back to my team and found Alice, Joe and Jeannie standing open mouthed right behind me.

"That was awesome," Jeannie cried as she grabbed my arm. "Did you know that Gardener let us hear your conversation?"

"He did what? I was so wrapped up in his level of intelligence I never thought to see if anyone else could hear us. It is very interesting that he blocked the Masters but included you guys. He must think as much of you as I do. So, what do we do now, keep to our original plan, assuming we update the Chief of our new information, or just forget about everything?"

"The Dora is too important to lose now, even if it means helping the Jinn to break away. The information stored on the space ship would be nice to have but in time we will have the same kind of knowledge without becoming Torgon's Guinea pigs," Alice offered.

"The bug said he and his folks would protect us, didn't he? If he can show me how that would work," Joe offered, "I'd still like to take a look at the ship. Did your Gardener ever mention if the ship doing the harvest was their main vessel?"

"I got the impression there is a really big collection of ships sitting out there so, no, I don't think this is the big one. Are you sure you want to do this, old man? I have to imagine it might be taxing on your old body."

"If I can stand living in the middle of the desert when the temperature rises to one hundred and twenty degrees, playing with some aliens should be a breeze. Just make sure them Apaches don't think the old white man is the enemy when we get on the space ship."

"Damn if you don't have a sense of humor when faced with the biggest challenge of your life. I'll make sure your companions treat you with respect. Just make sure you keep your eyes open and your opinions to yourself."

It suddenly dawned on me that Lee Anne wasn't part of our little confab nor were our Mescalero technicians.

"Where did the rest of our group disappear to? Lee Anne should be part of this discussion."

"She took her people back to the Res," Alice said as if there was something more she wanted to say. "You are supposed to brief Chief Torrez when we get back and arrange the time to get the techs on board the ship."

"Was she pissed off about something? Did it have to do with the conversation I saw the two of you having?"

Alice smiled and shrugged her shoulders refusing to say anything more.

The ride back was made in relative quiet. Joe was contemplating what he would need to do while he was a guest of the Masters. Jeannie had her head, complete with ear buds, buried in her cell phone. Alice was nestled against my shoulder but not saying anything. I was trying to figure out what mischief the ladies in my life were contemplating and how I was going to be involved.

The forty-five-mile trip back to Mescalero City seemed to take forever with no one communicating but eventually I pulled up to the Recreation Hall. Lee Anne was standing outside.

"My father is waiting in the lounge and seems uneasy about this project. The techs were excited though and wouldn't shut up all the way back to the Res. I'm sorry we left without talking to you but you were really deep in a conversation with the alien looking thing. Is that actually one of the species that live on the space ship? I showed my father one of the videos I shot and he couldn't believe the thing was real."

"The Jinn are real and very intelligent but Torgon and his folks don't seem to know that, at least I don't think they do. Why is your father getting upset? Is he thinking about trashing the project?"

"Go talk to him and you'll find out. Keep reminding yourself that he is the Chief of all the Mescalero's first and then my father second.

Lee Anne kept the rest of my passengers outside while I made the lonely walk through the empty building to the lounge. Chief Torrez was stretched out on the couch, feet up on the coffee table with the television blaring Judge Judy or some other court live action bullshit. That stuff never was as realistic as the real thing but most people never see a real courtroom.

"Lee Anne says you need to see me, Chief. I was on my way in with an update so I guess we can handle both issues. Which do we do first?"

"Are you trying to pull a fast one on me, Sands? That thing on my daughter's video, that's a joke, right?"

"Is that what Lee Anne said or is that something you determined by looking at her video? It was a damn sight more real than that shit up on the TV. It's as real as the sample of the plant pastry you ate or the fucking space ship that was harvesting the Dora. If you are so doubtful of the reality of the situation you need to come out to the valley and see for yourself."

"Calm down, Mike, I was only trying to find your strength of conviction in this whole thing. By the way, Lee Anne was totally convinced it was all a sham before she went out there and now she has completely changed her mind. She was an advocate for you before and now she has increased her belief in you. That brings me to my next topic, Lee Anne."

"Whoa, Chief, I thought we had already had a discussion on Lee Anne mentoring me in tribal ritual and stuff. Are you changing the rules?"

"Yes, Chief Sands, I am adding a little something to the equation. No man has ever gotten my daughters attention like you have and I want her to maintain that presence of mind. I would like you to consider taking my daughter as a wife. Stop, before you scream your objections and let me finish. I understand from Lee Anne that you and the female botanist are a committed couple and that you have given Lee Anne no reason to believe you and her could be together. It is the Apache custom for the father to choose the mate for his daughter, whether she is the first wife, second or third. Taking Lee Anne as a wife would bring you in to the tribe as a full member as well as any children you might have. Don't say anything until you have some kind of a solution to this space monster fantasy. I would like to know we have invested wisely and that there is not an underlying threat that we have not seen."

"You have expressed my feelings about the situation, Chief. More is happening here than has been offered by any of the aliens. That includes the Jinn wishing for a place of refuge so they can get away from the Masters and the Consortium. I want to be able to either pull the plug or overcome any actions any of our visitors might take. As to the subject of Lee Anne, is this her idea or yours?"

"It's totally mine but I did mention it to her the other day. She thought I was crazy and that it would probably be a problem with your woman. She did promise to discuss the situation with her. You should discuss this with the both of them."

The Chief went back to his TV program and I got the impression I was dismissed. By the time I got back to my truck I was steaming. Both Alice and Lee Anne were looking like they were ready to run away.

"Does someone want to tell what the fuck is going on? I suppose the two of you having a private conversation had something to do with the one I just had with the Chief. Anyone care to fill me in?"

"It's not totally Lee Anne's fault, Mike. She was looking upset the other day after talking to her father and I had to see what the problem was. I guess part of the reason was that she had hopes you would pay more attention to her and had been giving you subtle hints for months. She was devastated when we got together but fell in love with Jeannie so tried to put her feelings aside. I told her I wouldn't stand in the way if you preferred her."

My jaw must have hit the ground and bounced back up causing my teeth to grind when my mouth closed. I had gone almost three years without being in a steady relationship with a woman and now three, two in Roswell and one in Los Angeles, were making noises about being with me. I didn't know whether to be appalled or ecstatic at my sudden popularity.

"What if I left it up to both of you to choose," I remarked very snidely and watched as they both had shocked looks on their faces. "Did you doubt what I said when I asked you to move in with me?" I addressed to Alice. "And you," I said turning to Lee Anne, "why didn't you say something to me straight out instead of waiting so long? Why don't I do what your father wants and marry the two of you?"

Both women broke out in the hottest smiles I had ever seen.

"I told you he would go for it," Alice proclaimed as she threw her arms around me.

"How could you tell, Alice? He's always been so conservative," Lee Anne added.

"You had this planned, didn't you?" I tried to say as Lee Anne wrapped her arms around my neck.

"It was kind of spontaneous but it felt right," Alice mumbled into my shirt.

There was nothing I could do but return hugs and the occasional kiss. Jeannie and Joe were watching this unfold from the front seat of the truck, Joe looking confused and Jeannie smiling as brightly as her mother.

My euphoria was short lived as I received a mental message from Gardener.

"The Masters are planning something, Mike Sands, and it would be helpful if you could return to the field while the Masters are involved in the harvest."

"Why now and not tomorrow? I am involved in a family matter at the moment."

"I waited until you reached a compromise before interrupting. There are things I need to explain and the sooner the better. The Masters will suspend harvesting during darkness so it is a perfect time for us to meet. Bring your mates, if you like, they may offer suggestions. Please hurry."

My head cleared and Alice and Lee Anne were staring at me as if they had been hit with a Taser.

"Why, after all this time, did your Gardener friend decide to include me in that kind of a conversation?" Alice cried.

"You mean I wasn't going crazy, that that creature was actually talking to us? We are forty-five miles away from them and we didn't even have to use a phone," marveled Lee Anne. "And you have been communicating with them like that for weeks? We are so going with you, Mister Sands, if not out of curiosity, then to protect your sorry white ass."

"Someone needs to take Joe and Jeannie back to his place," I proclaimed. "There isn't enough time to drop them off and then run back to the valley. Joe, do you mind watching Jeannie for a while?"

"You actually trust me with the little darlin'? I'll treat her like she was my own granddaughter. How do I get home or are you expecting me to stay here?"

Lee Anne got one of her sinister smiles on her face. "It would seem appropriate that my father get to meet his future granddaughter, assuming, that is, that we are going to be a married polyamorous family."

"Let's introduce them," Alice said with her own nasty smile. "Jeannie, and you too, Joe, let's go see the Chief."

CHAPTER 15

TWENTY MINUTES LATER, WITH a full tank of gas in my truck, we were on a return route heading towards the valley. While I worried about the Jinn throwing another monkey wrench in my plans, Alice and Lee Anne were preparing some kind of marriage ceremony. Trying not to listen was a chore but I did manage to keep the truck on the roadway in the growing darkness.

We were met at the edge of the field by Gardener and his four companions. They were all holding on to each other by an arm and waited until we approached to extend an arm to each of us.

"Thank you for being prompt," Gardener started as Alice, Lee Anne and I were offered an arm. "Our Queen has requested an audience and this is the time when the Masters require rest. If you have no reasons to refuse, we will transport all three of you to the Queen's chamber."

Gardener was so serious in his request that my hackles rose. My new ability to sense what he was thinking was blocked but my curiosity was hammering at me to go along on this journey. Both Alice and Lee Anne were waiting for me to make the decision for them, a new wrinkle in our relationship.

"I have some reservations but I am going to accept. You need to remember what we discussed about trust. I am offering ours for the moment."

Nothing more was said but in the next breath the now familiar "whoosh" had us standing in an area of a ship that was much smaller than I expected.

"Don't look so concerned, Mike Sands," the Gardener said with a strange smile. *"This is merely one of our shuttles. We will be in the Queen's ship after a short time."*

Never hearing the sound of an engine or rocket ten minutes later I assumed we were leaving Earth's atmosphere. I was shocked when I felt another 'whoosh' and found we were in a space much different than where Doren had taken me. This room had strange items of furniture, chairs that were more suited to the physical characteristics of the Jinn, but tapestries that lined the walls defined a rich culture and history. Alice and Lee Anne were turning and staring at the walls in awe, obviously as impressed with our surrounding as I was.

"The Masters are never allowed on this part of the ship so you may consider yourselves honored guests. My Queen is waiting in the next room and is eager to meet you. Please follow my lead and do nothing to embarrass me or yourselves. Refrain from speaking until she allows it and all will be well."

This was a new Gardener, someone of power and responsibility, and a person who would not entertain disloyalty. I was duly impressed.

"We will behave in a courteous manner, my friend. I thank you for all of us for arranging the meeting. I have to say I was not expecting such a lavish habitation after my visit to the ship with Doren."

"He merely took you to a cargo hold on a transport which perfectly explains his opinion of your people, an opinion that is shared by his supervisor, the one called Torgon, and his Council. I am afraid they greatly underestimate you and your people. We may discuss this further but first you must meet the Queen."

Gardener led us through a short hall to a large chamber. I was expecting to see the sort of Queen usually seen in documentaries where insects are surrounded by workers that fluff and pamper her huge child bearing belly. This Queen was nothing like that. She was tall, even taller than me, svelte, and if you were to disregard the slightly waspish behind, one of the most beautiful women I had ever seen. She was staring at me with such intensity that I felt cowed but drawn to her as much as I was to Alice. Then Queen broke out in a silent laugh that warmed the entire room.

"Your descriptions are so colorful, Mike Sands, and so refreshing. None of my people, and certainly none of the other species on this group of vessels, would think to voice such perfect truths. It is what my Minister of State likes about you, your inability to hide your true feelings when you communicate. Welcome to my chamber and feel free to sit or stand. I may roam about the room as we talk and you may join me or not. You may wait in the other room, Minister, and I will call for you later."

Gardener, or Minister, smiled, took the Queen's hand and seemed to have a quick conversation that we were not privy to before walking out.

"Is there any part of our conversation that you wish to keep from your companions? If so, they can wait with the Minister," the Queen asked politely.

"They are my equals, Queen, and can and must be included in all our discussions."

"I am glad your females are held in such high regard. None of the other species surrounding us allow their females to hold any position of responsibility. I am sure that is the doing of the Council."

That last comment was said with such disdain that I wondered about their relationship.

"You are so open, Mike Sands, and so intuitive. You are correct that the Council and the Jinn have had many disagreements and it was only due to dire necessity that we accepted their offer to join their Consortium. The number of our vessels was rapidly depleting our fuel reserves and we had no other option but to share what we had. They, on the other hand, were starving and gladly accepted a portion of our Dora as a tradeoff. We had decided to remain with them until such time as we could locate a new source of fuel and a place to process more of our basic version of the Dora."

Queen took a moment to roam the room looking as if she was organizing her thoughts.

"You have questions about the Dora, I see. This may lead to another area I wish to discuss. Any of you may ask me about anything. I may answer or defer answering until another time."

"The Dora has many properties that are unique and not found on our planet," Alice said eagerly. *"I get the feeling that you provided the Dora and yet the Masters claim it was a gift of their ancestors."*

"You are one of the scientists, aren't you, the one called Alice Morrison. Your people have such strange names. We merely have titles and our names are attached to our thoughts. All are unique and never repeated, at least by us. Unlike you, the others species in the Consortium cannot tell us apart and so never learn who we are. Well, Mike Sands is also unique because he can see us as individuals although our names are difficult for him. To answer your question, the Dora comes from our home world, a place no longer available to us. We have room enough on this vessel to produce Dora for the needs of my people and a little more to be used in an emergency. The Masters, however, are collectors, a species that takes what it wants, such as the Dora, and claims it as their own. The untranslated information that they want you to decipher was not from their ancestors as they claim but from a derelict ship discovered by the Jinn on a barren planet," the last spoken with some anger.

"Why do you expect my team to translate something that no one else has been able to?" Lee Anne threw out with a lot of attitude.

The Queen smiled and turned to face my Apache fiancée.

"Your spirit is what I value about your people, Lee Anne Hart. It is the Council who wishes the information. They had my people remove the boxes containing the information from the Ancient's vessel and bring it to a meeting of the Consortium. They found they were unable to connect it successfully nor make it work. They only know the boxes contain information because we told them so."

"Then what are we supposed to do if there is no way to access the files?" Lee Anne was frustrated and did nothing to hide it from the Queen.

"I said the Masters were unable to access the information, not that the Jinn were unable."

That shut up everyone. I was about to say something when the Queen held up her hand to keep me quiet.

"It is my decision, not the Council's, that you have access to the Ancient texts. Besides being incompetent they would add you to

their complement as soon as you provided them the infor-mation. We deciphered the process needed to gain access to the boxes but have had no success in reading the script. You should know that part of the reason for planting Dora on your world was to entice some of the curious to find it. We can actually grow Dora anywhere, not only in the valley where the old sci-entist found it. We also alter the components so that not all who receive it are gifted with all of the benefits it can provide. My Minister needed to see if any of your people would share the same genetic similarity as my own. That was why on the day you were first at the valley he fed you the same variety of tasty treats that we consume and not the pap we provide to the oth-ers."

At this point Queen was standing in front of me and direct-ing her dialogue at me. I had no option but to listen intently as I knew there was important meaning in her words.

"We are all of a similar genetic background, Mike Sands, but as strange as it might seem, you are closer to the Jinn than you are to the Masters. I have no idea what the old ones saved on the machines but I trust your diligence and curiosity will do what none on board this Consortium of vessels has been able. I will give you access if you promise me one thing."

"Why give us the information?" As duplicitous as I found the Masters something here was still not being said. *"My world is made up of belligerent clans who would go to war with each other if they thought they had a serious advantage. If what's contained in the boxes is so significant and potentially danger-ous, why expose it at all?"*

"Your concerns are why I chose you to receive it, Mike Sands, not a representative of the government. It was happen-stance that the crazy old one took the piece of Dora to you but it was good fortune that you agreed to help him. Like I said earlier, you and your people see us as individuals and respect our intelligence when others in this Consortium do not. The promise I require is that those Jinn holding the data are kept safe and not exposed to the belligerent clans you claim popu-late your world. Perhaps if you can feed Dora to enough of your

people, they will grow more peaceful, especially if the Dora reacts with them as it has with you."

"We will do our best to keep the information safe but your last comment brings up another issue. Alice, you want to jump in here regarding the new genetic pairs?"

"Queen, when Joe, the old scientist, sampled the Dora in his lab he discovered that the genetic material in the Dora's makeup had two pairs of code that matched something that was now in our code but was not there before we were given samples to eat by Gardener, oh, I mean Minister. Have we been altered in any way that can be considered harmful?"

"For the most part the plant is benign but it does heal those carrying the genetic anomaly you speak of. It also enhances the mental processes. Only some of the species we have encountered on our travels have experienced the new genetic material after eating Dora but none of those are members of the Consortium. Again, your people are unique, a word I hate to keep using. We may all come from a common ancestor but not all of us act alike or have the same goals. I would hope that we are enough alike to be able to work together."

Queen again turned to me.

"Are you ready to receive the information?"

Alice and Lee Anne were looking at me as if I had the fate of the entire world in my hands and maybe I did.

"How are we supposed to transport the information to our planet? There are only the three of us"

"Most of it is already on the surface and the Minister has the last of it."

I must have looked incredulous because the Queen began laughing again. I was surprised, as were my companions, but the tension that had been building has diminished.

"I find you so amusing, Mike Sands. I wish I could keep you with me."

Her comment caused both Alice and Lee Anne to groan and burst out laughing.

"May I inquire why that is so amusing?" Queen was definitely looking confused.

"Mike has been accused of having the ability to attract and accumulate many females and he has no idea why we believe that way. When it comes to females, he is very naïve," Alice remarked with a smile on her face.

"In my world," Queen responded, *"we collect males. Females are always considered a threat. My people are always confused when I destroy the egg of a female and future Queen but it is very self-serving. I assume that is not the case on your planet?"*

"I sometimes wish we could eliminate some of the males," Lee Anne added with some heat, *"but not Mike. He is one of the rare ones that treats everyone equally."*

"I agree," Queen remarked, *"he is very much like the Jinn and would make an excellent addition to my staff, especially as my mate. If you ever tire of him, please let me know."*

The last comment was supposed to be directed only to Alice and Lee Anne and not to me. I was surprised that I heard every word.

"You do realize that your comments about me were very clear. Was I not supposed to hear what you said?"

"You were most definitely not supposed to hear what was said."

Queen got serious and addressed all three of us.

"Your abilities, Mike Sands, are more reason for me to trust you with this mission. As I said most of the information is on the planet. It is contained in the genetic material of those you call the gardeners. My Minister has the means to transfer the coded material to another medium which you can then work with at your convenience. Do not, under any circumstances, allow any members of the Council to have access to whatever you find. We do demand that you share anything you discover with us. This goes to the matter of trust you have expressed several times. Are we in agreement on this?"

Present now was a sense of danger that exuded from the Queen. Not looking particularly ominous when we first entered her chamber we were now faced with a very fierce looking female. Alice and Lee Anne had taken a couple of steps back but I held my ground.

"Do you require me to swear an oath or is my word good enough?"

The tension in the room vanished when the Queen began laughing again, pulling me to her chest.

"You are both valiant and amusing, Mike Sands. I hope you can visit me again when you can stay for a while, assuming your two mates will not mind?"

That was the end of our interview. Minister was at the door waiting to escort us out and as soon as we were all standing together the now familiar "whoosh" found us back on the shuttle.

"So, what now Minister? I guess we need you to transfer all the data."

Minister grabbed my arms and held me close, ensuring what we said would not be heard by the Masters.

"My team will need to go with you once the harvest is completed, which should be in another rotation and a half. You must transport us to a safe location and provide us with whatever equipment is necessary to transfer and store the information. I, for one, will be glad to have it out of my body. It was good the Queen chose you, Mike Sands, and your females of course, to be the ones to do this. I will notify you when it is time to come back."

"Won't the Masters miss you if you leave?"

"They can't tell one of us from the other. Queen will send five to take our place and we will wait for you outside the valley."

"I thought you said you couldn't leave the Dora?"

"Not until after the harvest. We are needed to keep it calm. Besides, we will be bringing seedlings of the same version of Dora we gave the old one that you can use for planting wherever you situate us. You did say you wished a crop to feed Lee Anne's people, did you not?"

"We will await your call, Minister. Stay safe until then."

CHAPTER 16

THE DRIVE BACK TO THE Res was made with me filling Alice and Lee Anne in on my last conversation with Minister and on finding a location to house him and his team. Lee Anne's father was going to have a part in any decisions since it was obvious I was not going to be able to house the Jinn in alien crazy Roswell.

Chief Torrez, Joe and Jeannie were all curled up asleep on couches in the lounge with another of the Chief's court shows blaring on the TV. They all looked so comfortable I hated to wake them but Lee Anne had no such reservation. She turned the TV off and then kicked Joe's couch causing it to move and squeal as the feet moved across the tile floor. All three of them jumped as if shot causing Lee Anne to laugh long and hard. Alice and I stood with arms around each other watching Lee have fun, a break from the tension from our visit to the Jinn Queen.

The Chief was excited about the Jinn being so cooperative.

"The perfect place for them is the unused basement in this building. All it has in it are a bunch of old chairs and desks. We can run cable down to it for computers, if that's what you are going to need, and secure anything else the alien things might need. I am glad we won't have to send anyone up to those space ships."

"The alien beings we are going to work with are called the Jinn and they are the ones who will be in the basement," I cautioned. "I promised their Queen that they would be safe and, trust me, I would advise against doing anything that could jeopardize that promise. Secondly, we need a plot of ground to plant some of the Dora. A perimeter will be set up so it only grows in a specified place but it gets very grumpy if people with bad intentions come close."

"You mean the Jinn get grumpy?"

"No, the plants have an attitude if they sense bad vibes."

"Kinda like a bright blue Venus Flytrap, I suppose."

"Don't test it Chief. You've got a lot of vacant land on the Res so pick a spot for us."

"There are a lot of valleys around Black Mountain. Too far north and you run in to the Apache Ski Club. Too far east and there is the casino. Around Black Mountain may be the best place until we can market the Dora as a new food source. Do you really think we can make money on this?"

"In order to do that we need the Jinn to help us with the crop. They and the plants are sort of like symbionts and help the Dora grow. Hopefully, some of your people can do the same."

"Wait, you want my people to become whatever those Jinn are?"

"Jesus, Abraham, we only want to establish a link to help the plants not mate with the Jinn. Look, Alice and Joe will take care of the crop and Lee Anne and I will work with your techs to try to understand what we are dealing with on the ancient data. Remember, we all have day jobs so don't expect us to be here ever day at your beck and call."

It was decided that Lee Anne would drive Joe home so Alice and I could get Jeannie to bed. Before we all split up Lee Anne pulled me aside.

"I've already told Alice but I want to come by your house tonight so we can put some kind of a game plan together. I know you would rather crawl in bed with one of us but I want you to put on your thinking cap so we know we aren't making any mistakes that could get us all messed up."

"Are you talking about the Jinn or something else?"

"Damn you, Mike Sands, you know I'm talking about the four of us and my father's decision. You already know how I feel but we need to discuss logistics."

We departed on that note. Alice was not ready to discuss things until Lee Anne was with us so the ride home was very quiet. My take away from this situation was that I felt strongly about both women and had no idea what would happen if one or the other decided not to go through with our multiple marriage. I did know that we needed to think about moving to a bigger house.

Half way home my phone buzzed. Alice had been holding it since my truck did not have Blue Tooth capability. Without thinking she answered it, put it on speaker and held it up to my face. It was the last person I expected to hear.

"Mike, honey, are you there?" Lillian was at her sickeningly, sweetest best.

"It's kind of late for a call, Lill. What's so important?"

"I kicked him out, baby, and I thought you should know."

"Are we talking about the financial genius and, if so, why should I care?"

"You were right about him. You are always so right."

"Look, Lill, I'm driving and on the way home, so can we put off this conversation until tomorrow?"

Alice was rolling her eyes the entire time I was on the phone and trying not to laugh.

"I never knew it, baby, but I really miss you. Can I come and visit, please?"

"Now is not a good time. In fact, never would be better."

"Well, think about it and maybe I'll surprise you."

When Lillian disconnected Alice began laughing in earnest and I was afraid she would wake Jeannie who was sprawled out on the rear seat.

The rest of the drive I was mumbling to myself about the constant emotional damage my ex-wife kept inflicting on me and Alice kept making snide comments about my being so attractive to women.

We finally made it to the house but before we could park my phone went off again. It was another unexpected call.

"Hey, Walt, it's kind of late to be calling, isn't it?

"Where the hell are you and what the fuck is going on with Lillian?" Walt was not sober and was very pissed off. "She called me crying about you not loving her anymore. You two are divorced, aren't you?"

"Yes, Walt, we are officially divorced. How did she get hold of your number? I thought like all good cops your number was unlisted."

"I want to know why she didn't call you, you son-of-a-bitch. You're supposed to be on call all the time."

"I was out on the Mescalero Reservation, Walt, having a business meeting with the Chief, Abraham Torrez." I was telling Walt a version of the truth he would want to hear.

"Why would you be dealing with the Chief? That's the prevue of the mayor and city council."

"He's related to Lee Ann Hart and complained to her about a lack of job opportunities in Roswell. He said no one from your office would return his calls so I went out to smooth things over for you. So, back to our primary reason for this call, what did you say to Lillian when you two spoke? Didn't you remember that I moved to Roswell to get away from her?"

"How the fuck do I know what any woman can do? You'd think I'd have figured it out after three divorces. She was your wife not mine. Anyway, she cried and screamed wanting your address so I gave it to, her. Sorry, but she got me so flustered I wanted her off of the phone. I just wanted to warn you, is all. We'll talk more during the week." He hung up.

By the time we got Jeannie in bed Alice was over her hysterical laughing and was collapsed on the couch. I was downing my first beer and watching my almost wife when the doorbell rang. Hoping it was Lee Anne I swung the door open only to find Lillian standing there.

"Oh my god, what are you doing here?"

"I told you I might come for a visit. Aren't you going to invite me inside?"

Thinking too late about slamming the door in her face Lillian stepped past me and walked in. I hadn't heard Alice get up but as I stepped back, I realized that she was right next to me with her arm around my waist. Lillian stopped and shot daggers at Alice but, as tense as she felt, I looked down to see my petite fiancée smiling at Lillian as if she was greeting an old friend.

"Who's this, Mike?" Lillian was not smiling. "She seems kind of possessive."

"Lillian, meet Alice Morrison, my fiancée. Alice, this is Lillian, the ex-wife I keep complaining about. Why don't we all take a seat so I can finally close this door?"

Lillian sat on the couch, assuming I would sit next to her, but I sat in my easy chair with Alice sitting on the arm, practically on my lap, keeping her arm across my shoulders.

If I thought things were tense it got worse as Lee Anne walked in through the front door. The tension escalated as she sat on my other side and joined her arm with Alice's. I thought Lillian's eyes would bug out. It took a few minutes of utter silence before Lillian erupted.

"And who is this one, Mike, another conquest?"

"This is Lee Anne Hart, my other fiancée."

Lillian shut up and stared at all six feet of Lee Anne who had stood up by that point, ready to protect my honor.

"You've really turned in to some kind of sex fiend, and discourteous to boot," she began to shout.

"Can you tone it down, lady, my daughter is asleep back there," she said pointing to the hallway.

Lillian's jaw fell open and she dropped back on the couch. It was the quietest she had been since she walked in.

"Why are you doing this to me, baby? I thought we might be getting back together, like we talked about on the phone."

"Back together, are you nuts? Think back, Lillian, to what we were together, thirty years ago. Two young, immature kids who fell in lust and got married by a Justice of the Peace. I was a corporal in the army and you were starting out at Cal State. Do you remember who paid for your college education? I kept on supporting you even when we had to move due to my reassignments but you kept on studying and not paying any attention to me. And what about encouraging me to leave the military so you could utilize the scholarship at UCLA. It's a good thing LAPD was hiring but, again, you couldn't even make it to my graduation. Are you sensing a theme here, Lillian? But wait, I'm not done. Besides making a home for us, I watched you rise through the ranks when you were offered a teaching position at UCLA but you didn't offer me the same courtesy during my time on the Department. In fact, watching you and your obsessed desire to succeed made me leery of trying to promote, something that would put two of us in that same rat race. Don't speak yet, there's more. Did you know that while I watched you climb the academic ladder, I was taking classes at UCLA as a dependent of an employee? I earned a Bachelor's degree in Public Administration and was two units shy of my Master's in Cultural Anthropology when you walked out. I'll bet you never knew any of those things. Only a few friends came to the commencement for my Bachelor's and were always there to help me study, but you weren't. The truth was I loved you and was willing to let all of that go, right up until you put that manila envelope in my hand. So, do I want to get back together when I have two very supportive women who value all, well most, of the things I do, I think not. Whew, that was a long speech. Who wants a beer?"

Lillian had sagged back on the couch and looked defeated. I knew that was only momentary so I made my way to the kitchen.

"Do you have something I can eat?" was the only thing she had to say. "I haven't eaten since yesterday because I was driving all day and night."

"We have some really good pasta that should perk you up and some delicious pastries if you want some dessert?" Alice said with a wicked smile on her face.

Lee Ann looked over to me and her eyes got really wide. We both looked at Alice who was on her way to the kitchen.

As she passed me, I whispered, "Is that the pasta you made with the Dora?"

All I got was one of those sinister smiles that she shared with Lee Anne. I moved out of the way and hoped the end result was going to be worth improving Lillian's attitude.

Lillian slept on the couch that night too tired to look for a hotel room or maybe it was the Dora. She decided to stay in town for a few days so we got her set up at the Fairfield Inn and went back to work. She took in the tourist sights and then, without a word, went back to LA.

CHAPTER 17

I T WAS ACTUALLY THREE DAYS before the Jinn called and demanded we arrive well after dark. They said the Masters and the other crew, like any other farming community, were celebrating the completion of the harvest. They believed the revelry would probably go on for some time. Fortunately, they were celebrating in their ship, well above the atmosphere, and would not notice an exchange of Jinn on the ground.

Lee Anne drove the Res school bus out to the field, now a dusty and empty expanse. Minister and his four companions were waiting with bags of seedlings and cases with their personal possessions. When everything was loaded the return-trip was made with no interference from the Masters. I met the bus at the rear of the Mescalero Hall and, along with the six Apache techs, got the Jinn set up in the basement. Before I could leave Minister pulled me aside.

"Mike Sands, we will need your help during this process. Until our Apache friends have consumed a significantly bigger portion of Dora and are able to communicate with the ease that you are able, we will need you to act as a conduit to your machines. Is that convenient or should we explore other options?"

"I have to work, Minister, and won't have much time. How about using Doctor Joe instead?"

"His mind is always in turmoil. You are normally clear and concise and therefore much easier to work with. This is very important work, as well. Once we develop a proper methodology the actual transfer can be done while you are at rest."

"If I'm the conduit, will I retain any of the material that passes through me?"

"You may and it may also enhance your cognitive abilities. A difference in our composition allows the Jinn to eliminate unnecessary memories when they are no longer needed while you retain almost everything. It must be very cumbersome."

"Yeah, I can think of several things I wish I could purge from my memory. All right, I'll be your conduit but I want Alice and Doctor Joe present while the transfer is taking place. The first sign of trouble and we yank off any connection. Can you live with that?"

"As you wish, Mike Sands. Were you aware that the Queen has designated you as the most important person in our culture and that songs about you were already being sung?"

"I never knew you guys could sing. Why sing about me when I haven't done anything yet."

"You entertained the Queen and were able to leave with your two females. That is unheard of in our culture."

The Jinn, with Chief Torrez's help, put together a combination cot room and technology lab so both the Jinn and I could relax when the transfer of data was being accomplished. Trying to sleep in a room next to Minister and his companions making noise was difficult enough but having Alice or Joe hanging around my head all night was just as disturbing. It reminded me of the sleep apnea examination I had taken before I left Los Angeles and trying to sleep with wires and connections all over my body.

The data transfer proved easier than I had anticipated and was over in four days. I didn't seem any smarter, as far as I knew, but I had no reason to utilize any of the Ancient's knowledge. We still hadn't begun to find the key to translating what we were looking at. To be on the safe side I had Joe draw more of my blood for another DNA test to see if any other changes had occurred. Joe had to run the test three times because while the tests looked normal, well, the new normal, one or two genes showed a slightly different positioning on the new chromosome pairs.

With their work in the lab done Minister and his crew were taken to a high valley south of Black Mountain. The seedlings were planted and the same barriers used in the first planting were placed around the perimeter of the new fields. Minister said to expect the new crop to be slower in growth as they needed to establish a root system. Additionally, there was no need for the kind of pressure to grow issued by the Council. Minister and Gardener's Two, Three, Four and Five, I had given each of them names, were content to relax and assist Joe and Alice in the lab and in the new field.

My time on the Res was limited because Walt, the mayor, had decided to punish me by piling new projects on my desk, including one to find employment for as many Native Americans as there were jobs available. It was subtle but my speed in handling my new workload increased to the point that the Mayor felt I was short changing the process. Proving my work was complete and thorough did not change his mind, since he was convinced I was as lackadaisical as when he hired me. I just ignored him.

Things came to a head a week after the crop was planted when I was contacted by Torgon. It probably surprised him that I was able to hear him as he tried to mentally message me from his ship. I had to assume he had one of the Jinn with him to act as a signal booster.

"Mike Sands, why haven't the promised technicians arrived to decode the Ancient's texts?" Torgon was definitely in a sour mood and I could feel the Jinn laughing in the subtext of the message.

"There has been a hitch in our plan. The technicians I had selected have assumed a different assignment, one that pays them enough to care for their families. None of the other members of this tribe were willing to take on your project. That is just the way of things on this planet. If it pays more, people have no hesitation in jumping to the new position."

"This is unacceptable and there may be consequences. Aren't you aware of our strength?"

"Would your strength be dependent on the Jinn by any chance?"

"What do you know of the Jinn? Have you been in contact with any of them, one of higher rank in particular?"

"I warned you and Doren that my people were devious and prone to warring with anyone perceived as an enemy. Did you expect we would simply accept what you had to say? You should be very careful of any threats you might make, Torgon."

The consequences might be harsher than if you just flew away. You have your harvest and to this point we are not enemies. We have a saying on this world; "Don't poke the sleeping lion." A lion, by the way, is a ferocious feline who is considered a king of the animals. My people are much like that lion."

"Your people can barely get off of your planet, human, so why should we fear you?"

"You need not fear us if we remain cordial. Consider how long you have been flying through space searching for someone to do your dirty work. Thousands of our years, I would guess? In far less time than that we will be in space and then we would hunt you down. It would not take us long to take what you have and make you our chattel, much as you have done with those in your Consortium. If you do not believe me ask the Jinn who is handling this transmission."

The sudden silence seemed to coincide with the inspiration, totally unaccounted for, on how to improve our race to space. That lasted until Torgon finally spoke.

"The Jinn speak highly of you, Mike Sands, almost as if you were a god. My Consortium will think on what you have told me and give you our decision on how to proceed."

Sudden cessation of communications, both from those in space and our friends on the ground was becoming all to frequent. I was shaking my head wondering where I had gotten technical information that only an advanced degreed engineer would have in his brain. My destination had been the new field of Dora growing slowly at Black Mountain but I changed direction and headed for the Mescalero Hall. Alice was at the computer with one of the techs when I barged in.

"Can I have a look at one of the original screens?" I demanded pushing the tech to the side. I wasn't about to push Alice for fear of having her punch me again.

For a minute the screen looked like a jumble of unconnected images. The next minute the images began to take shape and I began scribbling notes on how to translate what I was seeing. The funny thing was I could read what was on the screen but I had almost no clue what any of it meant. It was the screaming behind me that finally broke my concentration and made me look up.

The entire team was looking at me as if I had two heads and the realization of what I had done made my infamous red blush appear once again. My translation gave the team the key to opening the files. Thankfully, I had no further inspirations and was content to let the team do its work. Most of what was found was a history of a people long dead who stretched themselves too far from home and then could not find their way back. There was some technical data but not what the Jinn or the Council was hoping to find.

My one epiphany on space travel was passed on to a guy I had met in LA and he began working on plans to move people off of our planet. Based on what was on the Ancient's texts I cautioned him about moving too far too fast.

With most of the work done by the end of summer, Alice returned to her classes at the college and Lee Anne and I to our work on the Roswell Police Department. Doctor Joe Farrell decided he had been blessed with enough excitement and returned to his wanderings in the desert. He does stop by occasionally but it's to see Jeannie, or as he describes her, his adopted granddaughter. A house was built on the ten acres behind my cottage and I moved in with my three women. Abraham Torrez performed a legal marriage ceremony on the Res and, according to Apache custom, Golden Eagle was now the husband of two Native American wives. Yes, they accepted both Alice and me as full members and made all three of us, Lee Anne included, perform a tribal initiation.

On occasion I receive a mental message from the Queen of the Jinn giving me an update on how far from Earth the Consortium had fled. She had decided to remain with the Consortium as an antagonistic source of inspiration to the Council but promised to return to Earth if ever I decided to be her mate.

By the following spring the Dora was full grown. Chief Torrez made an impassioned speech to his people and was finally able to recruit a team of Res farmers to complete the Harvest. Once over the shock of meeting the Jinn all of the harvesters were fed large amounts of the Jinn pastry ensuring they would be able to feel the emotions of the plants they were culling. That summer the entire Res was well fed and thriving.

The Ancient's texts did serve a purpose other than provide a warning to the unwary traveler. It was the inspiration for the first volume of my great American science fiction novel and it practically wrote itself.

PART II

AFTERMATH

CHAPTER 18

I WAS POUNDING MY FIST on the steering wheel of my rental car as traffic came to a stop on the San Diego Freeway heading north out of Culver City. It had been forty-five minutes since leaving the company that was publishing my Science Fiction best seller and, stuck in emotion crushing bumper-to-bumper, middle of summer, freeway chaos, I was no closer to reaching my appointment with my engineering partner, Lawrence Davis, who was waiting in the calmness of the Antelope Valley, fifty miles away. Alice and Jeannie were on their way to Universal Studios with a tour group and all I wanted at that moment was to abandon my car and run screaming to a local bar. Three years in New Mexico and I was no longer capable of handling L.A. traffic.

Two years had gone by since the Jinn had given us the gift of Dora, a plant whose properties included a near miraculous ability to improve the health of those that were privileged enough to include it in their diet. The fact was my partners, the Mescalero Apaches, on a reservation near Roswell, New Mexico, had franchised the plant, with the aid of five Jinn who remained on Earth. They had made a fortune selling starter plants cheaply to other Native American tribes, most of them on the low end of the financial spectrum. The Native American's were fed and found their mental abilities greatly improved, meaning more jobs and less dependence on welfare.

The other gift from the Jinn was a wealth of information obtained from a derelict ship left abandoned on a remote planet. Neither the Jinn, nor any of the members of their space going collective claimed to be able to decipher the ancient script but after numerous helpings of Dora infused foods, I, the least computer literate of our group, found the key to translating the remarkable history of an amazing race. Among the stories was a treasure trove of engineering files that described, in detail, how to manufacture and maintain an advanced space going propulsion system. With my friend Lawrence's help, we formed our own consortium of aerospace companies dedicated to the building of a prototype space going ship at a secret development center in the far reaches of Los Angeles County. That had been my intended destination now delayed by the crush of smoke belching vehicles.

When my cell phone went off, I had to look around to make sure there wasn't a highway patrolman close by, not that he would be able to reach me in this traffic snarl. The number was unfamiliar but so were the numbers of most of Lawrence's people who had been phoning me lately. I answered the phone wishing I had my wireless headset with me.

"Mike Sands here, can I help you?"

"Mister Sands, please hold for the President."

My mind went crazy wondering if this was some kind of a joke. I didn't have long to wait as a very distinctive voice came over my phone.

"Chief Sands, this is John Phillips. Are you on a secure line?"

"I'm locked in my car stuck in traffic in Los Angeles if that counts as secure. Sorry, I didn't mean to be so flippant. How can I help you Mister President?"

"The thing I'm about to say is so far beyond the realm of reason it will sound insane."

"That sounds a lot like my life recently, Sir."

"What do you know about a person who goes by the name of Queen?"

My mind went on defense as soon as he mentioned the Jinn Queen.

"Can you be more specific?"

"Don't fuck with me, Sands; I don't have the patience or the time. Do you know who I'm talking about?"

"I believe I do, Mister President."

"Can she talk to you in your head, like mental telepathy or some kind of shit?"

"If it's the same Queen I know, then yes she can."

"Where exactly are you and I mean you need to be very specific?"

"I'm northbound on the 405 just past the intersection of Interstate Ten."

The President was a Los Angeles native so I was sure he knew exactly where I was.

"How soon can you get off the freeway and make it to Beverly Hills?"

"Not anytime soon, Sir. We haven't moved five feet in the last half hour and according to the navigation system in the car the highway is going to be blocked until they can get a crew in to clean up a chemical spill."

"Are you under an overpass or is it clear over your car?"

"There is nothing above me except smog, Mister President."

"Please don't leave your car, Sands. My people have tracked the GPS on your phone and will be there shortly. I am on my way to L.A. and want to meet with you as soon as we can get together. I have a lot of questions and not many answers so be ready to talk to me."

The line went dead and I found that I had broken out in a cold sweat, even with the air conditioning on maximum. It wasn't five minutes later that I saw some of the people who had gotten out of their cars pointing up and shouting. Opening my car window, I looked in amazement as two helicopters hovered above my car and three people began repelling down to the freeway. All three converged on my car as I saw a multitude of other drivers and passengers with their cell phone cameras aimed in my direction.

"Mister Sands, I'm Agent Cortez and we need you to come with us."

"Are you nuts, Cortez? What about my car?"

"Another agent will take your place and as soon as traffic clears it will be brought to you. Time is short, Mister Sands, and we need to move."

This felt like some kind of an action movie and I was now the Tom Cruise character. Cortez reached across me and unbuckled my seatbelt, assuming I was moving too slowly, so I grabbed my briefcase, slung the strap around my neck and crawled out of the car. Standing in the middle of traffic reminded me of doing much the same thing as a patrolman during my time on LAPD. I was in a fog as one of the agents placed me in a harness while Cortez strapped himself in. We were both lifted to the closest helicopter. Once onboard I was pushed down on a seat.

"Strap in, Mister Sands, the ride will be fairly brief."

We rose up as soon as Cortez and I were seated. The chopper headed towards Bel Air, an area of large homes and many vast residential properties. Minutes later we were landing behind a plush estate on a dedicated helipad and ordered off the helicopter. Cortez led me in to the home through what appeared to be the servants' entrance and then to an unoccupied room on the ground floor.

I could hear the helicopter taking off as Cortez and one other agent turned me around and frisked me.

"I could have done a better job of searching if you'd like me to give you a demonstration," I said as my temper cooled after the physical intrusion.

"It's merely protocol, Mister Sands. Be glad we didn't insist on a strip search."

"Yeah, I got it. Just for your information, it's Chief Sands, not mister."

"Look, Chief Sands, you're about to meet the President and I will do anything I need to do to ensure his safety. What would you do in my shoes?"

"Point taken, Agent Cortez, it's just everything happened a little suddenly and it got me agitated. Do you have any idea what the President wants with me?"

"You know that better than anyone, I imagine. We guard the man but he doesn't always include us in the why of what he does. Can I get you anything while you wait? His plane won't be landing at LAX for another twenty minutes."

Two hours later the sounds of an arriving entourage filtered in from outside. Moments after that I was confronted by four secret service agents who burst in the room and gave it a very thorough inspection, me included. When the President,

John Phillips, walked in I was surprised at his appearance. On television he always seemed so tall and dynamic. The man who walked in was shorter than my six feet and looked like one of my neighbors or anyone you might meet in your neighborhood beer bar. His smile though was as genuine as on any one I had ever met.

"Glad you could meet with me, Chief Sands. I'm on a tight schedule so I hope we can get this meeting done in record time. What can you tell me about this Queen character?"

"Are you ready to suspend belief in a lot of things, Mister President, or are you a sceptic?"

"I had a person who said she was a Queen talk to me in my own fucking head, Sands, so my belief is already suspended. Start telling me things I don't know and if I like what I hear I will tell you what she said to me. How's that for my skepticism?"

"Sorry, Sir, but things have been strange ever since I moved to Roswell."

"Christ, this isn't another alien invasion story, is it? I got that impression from Queen."

"That's all news to me but it fits with what has already happened."

I spent the next twenty minutes filling in the Commander in Chief on my meeting with the Jinn, the miracle of Dora and its benefits, the discovery of the Ancient's data including the discovery of plans for the advanced rocket engine and my interview with the Jinn Queen. The President was sitting by the time I finished speaking.

"Fuck me, Sands, all this is incredible. Who in my office knew about any of this?"

"No one, as far as I know. Everything from the Dora to the rocket development was on a very secret, need to know basis. How does any of this have to do with Queen contacting you and not me?"

"If you knew an enemy alien fleet was on the way to Earth and that their intent was to subjugate us, what would you be able to do, except tuck your head in your ass and pray?"

"I suppose I could try to contact someone in government, anyone who could get word to you."

"And who in their right mind would believe a police officer from the capitol of alien invasion folderol, a place where people go to see pictures of little grey spacemen who mysteriously crashed a spaceship just outside of town. A theory never proven by the way."

"You made your point, Mister President. What is it you want from me?"

"The Queen said I should contact you because you were our best hope for preventing a disaster. You don't appear to have made any kind of an impression outside of Roswell so why should I think you are our savior?"

"Perhaps you shouldn't because I have tried to keep as low a profile as I could."

"A low profile, you say? You wrote a best-selling novel talking about a lot of what the Queen told me. Now you tell me you have a miracle plant feeding Middle America. And you top it off with the development of a new rocket engine that could take us to outer space. How low key is any of that and why didn't I hear about any of it from you?"

The fire in the Presidents eyes had me reluctant to speak. It became evident by his demeanor that I wasn't going to get off by being silent.

"My intention was to elevate my indigenous family from near destitution and under employment while generating some income for myself and the tribes I was helping. If I had made a big deal out of our discoveries big business would have gotten involved and squeezed all the little guys out. None of the tribes wanted government participation or intervention because of their lack of trust in you. There have been a lot of broken promises going back more than a hundred years. I don't suppose that's what you wanted to hear."

"My family is one sixteenth Osage, Sands, so I might have been very interested in what you were trying to do. My question now is whether your prototype, and yes I know about it, will prove to be the progenitor of a fleet of ships that can save our asses."

"I was on my way to see the prototype when traffic and your people waylaid me. May I ask how you became aware of what we were doing?"

"Did you not patent your engine and isn't the Patent Office a part of my government? Furthermore, don't many of your aerospace partners have government contracts? At this point you are going to need a lot of government money to get your space ship in production. What have you done about weapons and armor on the ship? You can make it fly but I can guarantee that it has the latest equipment our labs have developed, most of it never mentioned in the press. Are we on the same page yet, Sands?"

"I was never expecting an invasion and didn't think we needed those things. Did the Queen tell you how long we had to get ready?"

"That's where you come in, Sands. She said all further communications would be through you as she trusted you more than anyone else. I wish to god she had never contacted me but I do wish I knew how she had done it. Can you give me some help on that?"

"Usually, the Jinn transmit and we receive. For us to transmit first you'll have to have eaten some of the Dora. I can't explain it any better than that. Is there any chance you were given some in a pastry, the most common use, or as part of another meal?"

"My family attends a lot of Native American celebrations and brings some local food favorites to me on occasion. Is it possible whatever you called it, Dora, was part of the recipe?"

"You need to check with your family for that answer. My question is what happens to me when this conversation is over?"

"You go to your meeting but take one of my agents with you. Tighter security will be installed and you will update me every day on the progress of the program. Just for laughs, I've ordered the program to be called the Roswell Project and you are now designated as the Director. Welcome to my staff, Chief. I hope your tenure is successful."

CHAPTER 19

THE PRESIDENT WAS ON HIS way shortly after he notified me that I was on the Federal payroll. Ten minutes after that I was escorted back to my car, now parked on the long circular driveway in the front of the mansion. My surprise at meeting with the President was duplicated as Agent Cortez climbed in the passenger side and buckled up.

"The President assigned me to be your right hand, Chief. Just so we can get along, my first name is Carlos and I would like it if I could call you by your first name. It will seem as if we are a lot closer that way if you get my meaning."

"Since I don't seem to have a choice, my first name is Mike. You don't have to follow me to the bathroom or when I need some private time with my wife or daughter, or do you?"

His laugh was quiet and warm as he turned towards me.

"I'm not an enemy, Mike. I just need to make sure you remain safe and able to let my boss know what's going on. I promise to be as unobtrusive as possible. If what the President says is true, we need you to keep all of us safe. I have a family and kids, too, and your success is important to me, as well. A handshake will guarantee I will look after you and your extended family."

"You have a deal, Carlos, and I will hold you to it."

Taking Sepulveda instead of the freeway, which was still bottled up and made me wonder how they got my car off of the highway, we made it to an open on ramp beyond the spill and rejoined the 405 traffic heading north. I advised Lawrence about my delay but left out my diversion to talk with the

President. That would come later as would the appearance of my new partner, Carlos Cortez.

The entrance to the engineering complex now had new security precautions, an addition mandated by President Phillips. I was handed my new identification card at the gate and had my fingerprints taken by a portable scanner. I was now bagged and tagged like the cattle that roamed the vast areas near my New Mexico home. Cortez merely flashed his ID and we were waved through. The new procedure was going to cause my partners some consternation but it had to be done to ensure security.

Lawrence and the rest of the team were seated around a conference table looking bored until I walked in accompanied by Carlos Cortez.

"Where the fuck have you been, Mike? This is a rather high-priced delay of time," Lawrence said as he swept his arm around the room.

"It's nice seeing you, too, Lawrence. This is my new friend, Carlos Cortez. He works for the President as do I as of an hour ago. It seems like there has been some loose talk that made its way to Washington and the President has decided this project is now being sponsored by the government. Welcome to Project Roswell. To those of you who want no government intervention, all I can say is tough shit. There are going to be some additions to our plans that will need to be implemented but first we need to make sure this puppy will fly. I know you all have questions so take your best shots. What I can't or won't answer will be thrown over to Carlos. So, gentleman, fire away."

The next hour was spent letting all the players vent and come to their own conclusion that they had no choice but to follow the new guidelines. Another eruption occurred when Carlos explained the new security precautions and then it was off to the construction floor.

The prototype sat on the hanger deck looking like no other flying machine in any country's arsenal. It was both sleek and boxy, the thickest portion being the area that housed the alien designed engines. Thruster ports lined the top, sides and bottom of the fuselage, explaining how the ship would be able to navigate and change directions in a void. I had to learn that thrust, not resistance, was the way to fly and stop this baby. The neatest feature, at least in my mind, was the antigravity unit that pushed the rocket powered machine skyward without using a propulsion unit until it was at sufficient height to fire off the rocket engine. At least in theory that was what was supposed to happen.

Lawrence had been an Air Force fighter pilot and had volunteered, no, make that demanded, to be the first one to fly the Beast. That was the name the assembly crew had given the ship and we all thought it was as good a name as any. Quickly suited up, Lawrence climbed in through the belly hatch and was soon seen sitting in the cockpit, thirty feet above us, with a humongous grin on his face. His arms were moving all over the place and soon a loud hum and accompanying vibration announced the Beast lifting off of the cement floor. The expectation was that the ship would fly but the realization that it was hovering fifteen feet in the air with no engine sounds was astonishing.

After staying aloft for fifteen minutes Lawrence gently dropped the ship to its cradle and shut down all the systems. He dropped out of the hatch and was bouncing around like he had jumping beans in his pockets.

"Did you fucking see that thing lift up?" he cried as he ran around in circles.

The chatter on the floor grew louder as everyone realized what had been accomplished. Now all we had to do was make sure the rocket propulsion system would take us out of our atmosphere.

"When do we take the Beast out for a trial run?" I shouted above the tumult. "I want to be the co-pilot on that first flight."

Once again, my mouth spouted something my brain was not ready for. Everyone stopped talking and stared at me as if I had lost my mind. Cries of, "You're not qualified," You're the boss," "That's insane," and a lot of variations on that theme came back to me.

"The President is not going to like that decision, Mike," Carlos offered in my ear.

"The President put me in charge and if I want to take a ride in my space ship that is exactly what I plan to do."

Lawrence was smiling as he walked up to me and grabbed my hand.

"I knew you had an adventurer's soul, Chief Sands. I'd love for you to be my co-pilot."

"So, when can we do this, fly the Beast, I mean?"

One of the engineers, a guy from Lockheed, said, "We need to do some final testing on the thrusters and the gyros. It wouldn't do for you to fly all over the place and then not be able to change direction. The last piece is the internal artificial gravity mechanism that needs to be installed. Two weeks, maximum, and it should be ready."

Carlos grabbed my briefcase and dragged me out of the building before I could commit myself to any further dangerous exploits. Taking my car keys, he pushed me in the passenger side and began the trip back towards the city.

"You amaze me, Chief," Carlos claimed. "All the reports said you were very low key and non-confrontational, a stand-up guy who led by strength of character. Did you know your troops would jump in front of a moving train to protect you and keep you from mussing your uniform? I wonder if they would be surprised to know how big of a risk taker you really were."

"You probably would get a better answer from my wife and my Apache family."

"You mean wives, don't you? At last count there are three of them, correct?"

"Two who are actually part of my immediate family and the third is an ex-wife who has been on a pilgrimage to return to the fold. I've held her off for the last couple of years but Alice and Lee Anne want me to give Lillian another chance. I understand what we are doing with design and construction of a space ship but I have little or no clue on what goes on in the minds of my wives. Doing the test flight may be an easier exercise than trying to out think two aggressive women."

The thoughts going on in my head were interrupted by my phone going off.

"What is with all of the security, Mike? Why do we have two Secret Service agents sticking to us like glue? Everyone is staring at us like we were Middle Eastern royalty or something. Is this your fault because if it is I'm not sure I like it?"

"Slow down, Alice, and let me get some answers." Looking at Carlos, he was trying to appear disinterested. "Carlos, is this another order from your boss?"

"From the moment he hired you to be the Director of Project Roswell you became a valuable government asset and that included your family. When I say family, it means all of them, including your ex."

"When I joked about you following me to the bathroom it wasn't really a joke, was it?"

"Who are you talking to, Mike and what was that about bathrooms?"

"Sorry, Alice, I was in conversation with a new business associate. Are you guys still at Universal or on your way back to the hotel?"

"We're pulling in to the parking deck at the Hilton. Jeannie wants to try out her new bikini and take a swim. Are you coming to join us...please?"

"Yeah, Carlos and I will be there in about twenty minutes."

"Carlos?"

"You've got your security team and I've got mine. I'll see you soon."

CHAPTER 20

ARLOS AND THE TWO AGENTS assigned to Alice and Jeannie stood close but not too close in the steamy confines of the indoor pool at the hotel. Jeannie was surrounded by a group of young people, surprisingly mostly male, while Alice and I reclined on lounge chairs off to the side.

"So, tell me again about getting airlifted off the freeway and meeting with the President. That doesn't happen to regular people like us, does it?"

"It obviously does and did happen. Getting air lifted off of a freeway was the most nerve-wracking event in my life, at least up until my next adventure."

"What is that supposed to mean, hot shot, your next adventure?"

"You've seen the prototype, at least the version that sits on the ground and does nothing. The latest version can float using antigravity technology and next it will be flying out to space."

"What does that have to do with an adventure? Are you planning to fly the thing?" Alice stopped talking and stared at me. "That's it, isn't it? You plan to be on board when it goes up for the test flight. Are you out of your fucking mind?"

The last was said loud enough for our detail to look our way and take a step in our direction. Almost everyone else in the pool area merely stared.

"Being out of my mind has been normal ever since Joe brought us the crazy blue miracle plant that started all of this. You know how my mouth makes noise before my brain engages? Well, that's what happened today. As soon as I said I wanted to be on the maiden flight I went in to a panic about making another stupid decision and then realized it was what I truly wanted to do. The last three years have been one decision after another that took me further and further out of my comfort zone, especially the part where you and I got together. Don't tell me you feel different because we both had no reason to want to be with each other. Only one day and we were connected like we had not been with anyone else, ever. I wouldn't change any of it and I won't change my mind about going on the maiden flight." Alice's mouth was hanging open and she had one of those 'what are you talking about' looks on her face. "You can close your mouth now, babe, I'm done talking."

"You know I love you, don't you, you big stupid oaf? Queen told me while we were on her ship that you would be back in space at some point but I thought it would be to see her again. For whatever reason the Queen never felt like a threat and I never got jealous when she wanted you to become her consort. I knew she would send you home eventually. Your rocket ship, however, is making me a little jealous because I don't know if you will survive your adventure. Does any of that make sense?"

"If you insist I stay behind you know that's what I'll do. My family is more important than anything but this is something I have wanted to do since I was a kid. Being in the Master's or Queen's ships wasn't the same because we never had the sense of being in space. This is something I helped design, or at least sat with the engineers who actually deciphered the drawings I pulled out of the Ancient's records. Each record is still in my head, Alice, and I need to see how…"

"I get it, honey, I really do. Maybe it's because you have always had to react to things in your life instead of being the one who creates. Lillian said much the same thing when we met for lunch the other day. It's the new you that she finds intriguing much as Lee Anne and I like who you are. You know you are going to make Joe Farris very upset that he isn't going to go with you, don't you?"

Ignoring the comment about Joe Farris I stared at my wife.

"You had lunch with Lillian? When were you going to tell me that little tidbit? I am not interested in getting back with her no matter how much you think I should talk to her."

"Holy crap, husband, I was not trying to reunite you two. She is a brilliant mathematician and had some ideas on your project. She called me before you got here and wanted to know why she had a security team lurking about her office. I guess someone had given her a briefing on the reason and she intuited a whole lot more, parsing part of it from having read the not so fictional accounts in your novel."

"She read my story? Did she say she liked it?"

"Are you even listening to me? She said she can help you. There was a contract with one of the space agencies she claimed to have worked on that dealt with exit speeds and trajectories. I understood about five percent of what she was talking about but you need to give her a call so she can explain it better. Make up your own mind afterwards."

Jeannie wandered back towards us as I stewed over getting my ex involved in the project. Glancing up I realized that the almost thirteen-year-old was well on her way to becoming a very attractive woman as evidenced by how she looked in her bikini and the four young boys following her. It reminded me of how I followed Alice to her lab on the day we met.

"Are you okay, baby, you kind of spaced out there for a minute?"

"I'm fine, Alice. I'm going to our room so I can call Lillian. The team will have to agree to have her come on board but I'll hear her out. Thanks for keeping me grounded."

It turned out that aeronautical math was Lillian's specialty, something I had never bothered to learn while we were married. It was another instance of two people living parallel lives that, except for sex, had caused our own interests to push us farther and farther apart. I finally understood why Lillian had walked out but wondered why neither of us had tried to close the gap.

My engineering team was excited when I mentioned Lillian's interest in the program. Her reputation in her field earned her immediate acceptance and me kudos for bringing her to their attention. It was one more thing that I never knew about my ex that made me ashamed. When I told Carlos about Lillian, he took the initiative to have her clearance updated and ID cards issued.

"Were you aware that Lillian's security clearance is higher than yours?" Carlos mentioned as we were on the way to the Antelope Valley the next day.

"It's not something she ever mentioned and I never thought to ask."

"Damn, Sands, she is one of the most brilliant people in her field. Do you know why she never finished her PhD?"

"I might have partly been the cause of it. She had her dissertation completed but we separated about the time she had to schedule her oral presentation. I think it threw her off kilter. I have no idea why she hasn't followed up since then."

"The President was excited when I briefed him last night and was even happier after he had Lillian vetted. He wants you to encourage her to finish her degree. He thinks she will be a good addition to the project."

"Have either of you been talking to Alice about this because I can sense her hand in it?"

"She and I had a little chat while you made another trip to the bathroom last evening. She felt having Lillian around was a good thing." Carlos stared off in to space for a second before asking, "How is it you seem to have so many women wanting to look out for you. I know we had a brief discussion about it the other day but, damn, Mike, three women and an alien Queen? You're not that great looking."

"It's only two women, Carlos; the rest are wanna-bes."

"Not the way I hear it, old buddy. I am going to keep an eye on you."

Over the next week I watched Lillian interact with the engineering staff, marveling at how she turned a sometimes surly group in to a team. She was the junior member but soon elevated herself to the leader, sometimes cajoling, other times flirting and always working harder and longer than the others. It was the first time I had seen this side of my ex and I felt my attitude towards her softening.

Each night Alice would ask how things had gone that day and I knew she was fishing for news about Lillian. My almost daily call to Lee Anne started with how she was handling her position as Acting Chief of Police but always seemed to devolve to a discussion about me and Lillian.

Getting off of the phone I snapped at Alice.

"Why do both you and Lee Anne want me to like Lillian so much? I admit that she's a hell of a worker and has the team farther ahead than I thought they would be but it's all business."

"As much as you deny it you are still carrying a torch for her and have never gotten over the way she walked out. So, in order to figure out how you really feel both Lee Anne and I want you to get together with Lillian and have the talk you both put off before she left you."

"I'm not going to have any say in this, am I?" The constant prodding had me irritated but at the same time I was looking forward to spending a little private time with the woman I had spent thirty years with.

"No, you're not. As a matter of fact, you are going to have dinner with her tonight and spend as much time as you need to iron things out." Alice added a little smirk as she seemed to visualize what might happen during our meeting.

CHAPTER 21

CARLOS DROVE ME TO LILLIAN'S townhouse in Encino. I looked for every opportunity to jump out of the car and run away but a look from my bodyguard kept me rooted to my seat. As we pulled up in front of the building Carlos looked over and smiled.

"Alice catered the meal from Maggiano's, claiming it was Lillian's favorite restaurant. I'll be parked close by but if you decide to spend the night just shoot me a text."

"Did Alice cater that too, a night of sex with my ex? What else can I expect?"

"You do realize there is a good chance you might die when you take that test flight? I'd want to make sure all my issues had been cleared up before that happened. All I can tell you is that I will be close by if you need me but I'd rather you didn't."

There was no reason for me to feel nervous as I walked up to Lillian's front door but I had more butterflies than I did meeting my date's parents on the night of my junior prom. Lillian opened the door looking like she did most nights that we spent together which relaxed me more than if she had dressed to the nines.

"Are you going to stand out there all night or do I have to drag you in?" Lillian was smiling and acted like this was like any other day of the week.

The aromas of our favorite dishes, Linguini di Mare and Rigatoni "D", wafted out to me as Lillian grabbed my arm and pulled me inside.

"The food just arrived so we need to eat before it gets cold," she said as she led me to the dining room.

We sat across from each other as she stared at an unopened bottle of cabernet, willing me to open the damn thing. I never got used to Lillian's ability to send messages straight to my head but, after dealing with the Jinn and their Queen, mental messages seemed normal. The wine was opened and poured and, as was usual, we shared each other's plates, commenting on how the food was good but not as good as we remembered. Lillian was surprised when I helped clean up after eating, a chore I had assumed when I got together with Alice.

"This is nice, Mike. I never knew you could be so domestic."

"It must be something I picked up when I was living alone."

"Or something you learned living with Alice and Jeannie."

"Is that something you failed to come to grips with or are we going to have to discuss that first?"

"I have had several long lunches with Alice. Once she realized I was not going to try to steal you back, unless it was something you wanted to happen, she and I got along famously. She is a very smart woman and had to remind me that you have your own talents, as well. Is it true you finally received your Master's?"

"You should have known how close to my degree I was when you walked out. That set me back a few years but Alice got me back on track. But my education is not why we are here tonight, is it? Both Alice and Lee Anne insisted I do this and now I want to know if there was some ulterior reason."

"Okay, here it is. Both Alice and Lee Anne want me to be a part of your polyamorous whatever it is you three have going and I can't understand why they want me. I did all kinds of spiteful things even when you tried to be a friend to me after I walked out. You have always been the most honest thing in my life and two of the most different women I have ever met still find me worthy."

Lillian's tears were now flowing and I was not sure if I wanted to say something to make her feel better. I was in shock that my two wives would go behind my back.

"The truth is I would jump in your arms if you said it was okay but not if you have even the slightest doubts. Damn it, I thought I could do this without becoming a soap opera bitch. I love you and always have. I forgot I did for a while but remembered when you and Alice got together. What do you say to that?"

"Alice always said I still carried a torch for you but I kept denying it. We spent thirty years together, Lillian, not always happy years, but good enough that I thought we would die in each other's arms. Do I want to go back to that limited kind of relationship, fuck no? I'm not sure what Alice and Lee Anne have in mind but there would have to be a lot of changes before their plan could work."

"Can we see where things go when our project slows down? I mean, you're already different than what I remembered and I know I can change, too. If Alice and Lee Anne think I can be part of the family, can you, at least, give it some thought?"

Now I was at a loss for something to say. If I said no, I was contradicting what Alice and Lee Anne had proposed to Lillian. If I said yes and things didn't work out, I would look like a lecherous old man who was just what Carlos had suggested.

"All right, let's give this some time. Meanwhile, I'm going to call Carlos and have him take me back to the hotel. I'm sure whatever I tell Alice will get back to Lee Anne and you, if you continue your clandestine lunches. Believe me when I say I am not going to make any promises, even if we do get along like old lovers. I'll see you at work tomorrow and we can begin working towards whatever this is."

I gave Lillian a kiss on the cheek as I stepped outside and made the call to my chaperone.

CHAPTER 22

T HE RIDE BACK TO THE hotel was made in silence, even
with Carlos trying to get me talking about my evening. He
finally shut up and let me think. Things didn't get any better
when I arrived at our suite and Alice took up where Carlos had left
off. My report was brief and to the point, ending when I told Alice
to give Lillian a call since they were now like sisters.

Trying to get a clear head I stepped out on the balcony staring
at the city in which I had worked and loved for so many years, wishing we were back in Roswell. Alice had taken me at my word and
was on the phone. I closed the sliding door to avoid hearing something I was not prepared for when something else I was not prepared
for happened.

"Mike Sands, my love, are you ready to join me on my vessel?"

"Queen, are you so close that I can escape for a little while?"

*"Soon, Mike Sands, but not for some weeks, yet. We are in your
system but the bigger worry is if your President managed to impress
upon you the danger your world is in."*

*"You managed to shake him badly enough that he not only kid-
napped me but put me in charge of a mission to help protect our
world. Why is this needed so quickly?"*

*"This will be a horror story. We stayed with the Consortium so
that we could guide them as far from your Earth as possible before
we left them. Before we had a chance to do that another race of
beings, something called Marauders, appeared and boarded the
Master's vessel. We managed to separate our ship, along with about
a dozen other smaller vessels that are still nearby, and watched
from a distance while the Masters were subjugated. Before we left,
we were able to disable the Master ship's drives and took the*

majority of the Dora. The Marauders had a large vessel but not much power. They needed the Master's faster ship to continue their raids. We could not see what the Marauders were thinking but knew the Consortium was bargaining for better terms by exposing your planet. We have been traveling for many lunar turns of your planet and know that at some point the Marauders will be following that same path. Once they make their repairs, they will still be several of your years behind us. Please tell me you are well on your way to creating a defense against those animals."

"You sound frightened, my Queen, something I never expected to hear."

"This is bad, Mike Sands, one of the worst things my people have encountered in all the years we have spent traveling between worlds. Yours is the friendliest of the worlds we have visited and I do not wish to see it destroyed."

"This is a long way from using our planet to grow crops of Dora, Queen. I worried then that we would have to defend ourselves against the Consortium not the assholes who defeated them. But to answer your question, if all goes according to our plans, our test ship should be in space before you arrive. We may be able to rendezvous with you during our test flight. We can exchange greetings and information at that time."

"Does that mean you will finally be close enough to seduce, my Chief?"

"You have no idea how agreeable that sounds right now."

"Stay vigilant, Mike Sands, and tell my sisters, Alice and Lee Anne, that they are welcome to visit me as soon as I am close to your world."

A moment later my head felt empty. The railing was the only thing that kept me from falling over until my sense of balance returned. My stumbling around obviously caught Alice's attention because she was out on the balcony before I managed to stand upright.

"What just happened, Mike? You looked like you were a million miles away and ready to pass out."

"The Queen just called and I guess the length of the conversation took more energy than I thought. She sends her greetings, by-the-way."

"What length are you talking about? You've only been out here for a couple of minutes."

"It felt like an hour or more and most of the news wasn't good."

Pulling my wife close to me I related the entirety of the Queen's warning and some of the personal greeting, getting small nods against my chest as Alice reflected on what I was saying.

"Did she ask you to be her consort again, is that why you got woozy?" Alice turned her head up to me and laughed. "Maybe you can see her when you take your rocket ship on its test flight. You could kill two birds with one stone that way. I'm sure that Lawrence won't mind a little side trip."

"Between all of the conniving women in my life I am going to be worn down to a stump. When did I become so attractive to so many women? My life used to be so simple before the Jinn and Queen. Before I go totally crazy will you please take me to bed?"

The following morning, I made my daily report to the President, apologizing first for my failure to report in the previous night.

"Damn it, Sands, you need to get your people working faster. We are going to need a fleet of your ships and it might take a year to get production to a level where we can protect our planet. Did your Queen give any idea how far behind those Marauders might be?"

"Unless something has changed, we have a couple of years at the worst, or a couple more if what she told me slowed them down. Whichever way, when they arrive, we still need to be ready."

"When will your project get off of the ground and I don't mean that as a joke."

I had to pull the phone away from my ear to save my eardrums.

"We should fly in the next couple of days. We are still waiting for your munitions guys to hand over plans and test units for the weapons packages you promised. Our test bird is unarmed and I want every future version to be ready to be deadlier than what we are about to face."

"You'll have an answer today, Sands. What about the Queen's ship, does she have any fire power on board?"

"I don't know and she never mentioned anything."

"That worries me, Chief. Any chance she is playing us?"

"It is impossible to lie when talking to the Jinn, at least that's been my experience. My gut tells me she likes us and wants to be as big a help as possible. Get me my armament and I'll do like President Reagan always said; 'Trust but verify."

"Yeah, and I trust you realize I have an election coming up in two years and you will want me to be around to keep your project on track. You fuck this up and both of our asses get burned. Thanks for the report, Sands."

The call terminated and I was left staring at a dead phone.

"I assume you were talking to the boss," Carlos said as I realized he had probably been close enough to hear the conversation.

"Could you hear his side as he shouted at me?"

"That was his normal talking voice. You'd be able to hear him in the next building if he really started shouting. For what it's worth, the man likes you, Mike. That may not save your ass, as the man said, but I think he will do anything he can to protect you. Just don't die when you take the test flight."

The drive out to Edwards was unusually quiet. Carlos took me at my word and avoided asking about my dinner meeting with Lillian the previous evening. Even getting an early start we were the last ones to arrive. Lawrence ran over as soon as he saw me walk in to the hanger.

"We are good to go tomorrow, Mike. They need to get us outfitted with some flight gear and run you through the bare bones tutorial I put together. God help us if I need you to fly the Monster but it pays to be prepared."

The team had assembled a variety of this generation's NASA space wear. None of them looked like the bulky suits you saw when the space station crew was doing their space walks.

"These are the suits the astronauts wear during takeoff and reentry, Mike. You're looking a little skeptical but these function just fine. NASA even provided a box of space diapers since we will probably want to fly around for a while."

"About that, Lawrence, what would you say to trying to meet up with my friend the Queen? It's a long shot but we may be close enough to her ship for a visit and I would like to see firsthand if the lady has some guns we could employ."

"Didn't you tell me she wants you in her bed or whatever they use when they mate? Are you sure guns are what you are looking for?"

"Jesus, you sounded like Alice for a second. That is a separate topic and I do not want to go there, at least not yet. For the moment can we concentrate on getting a suit that fits, including a properly sized diaper? I suddenly feel like my grandfather."

"You'll be glad to have one if you lose your water on reentry, old pal. Don't be ashamed because I know I won't be. Be glad we don't have to use a catheter."

One of the NASA technicians finally showed up to assist us in our fittings and within two hours we were suited up for our attempt at climbing in the cockpit. Our first problem was a need to do a redesign on the hatch entry as it was almost too small for my larger frame to squeeze inside. Almost was the by-word because I was not going to delay the first flight. There was also a top hatch that could connect to an access way to a space station or another vessel.

The pilot was seated in the front and the copilot, me, behind him, like in some of the Navy jets I had seen. The pilot's controls were all facing him but mine were on consoles at both sides of the seat except for the digital display that dropped down when it was called for. Lawrence went through the flight training operations several times until he felt I was not going to crash and kill anyone, meaning him. I was sweating and felt like I was in a steam bath before our lessons were done. I couldn't wait to get out of the cockpit.

"You look like a drowned puppy, Sands. Did I forget to plug in the ventilation on your suit? Remind me not to forget tomorrow."

CHAPTER 23

ALF OF THE NIGHT BEFORE the test flight was spent in the infirmary at the Lockheed Martin facility where our group had been working. The Monster, all one hundred and fifty feet of it, was moved overnight from its hanger and prepared for flight. At the same time Lawrence and I were poked, prodded and examined to ensure we would not die when taking our first flight to space. When we were finally released and allowed to rest, I found Alice, Lee Anne and Jeannie sprawled on the bed in my newly assigned quarters. The noise of my clumsy entry woke all three.

"You didn't think we would be here to see you off, did you?" Lee Anne said while hugging me.

She was part of the group hug with Jeannie taking up more room than she had such a short time ago.

"I am really glad to see all of you but I have to lie down. Being tortured by doctors before a flight is going to make what I go through on board the Beast feel like a vacation. I thought I was supposed to be in isolation, like the astronauts? How did you guys manage to get in here?"

"According to Lillian, we are still on the preferred visitor's list," Lee Anne answered. "She stuck us in here while she checks to make sure your mechanical Golden Eagle is flight ready. It is funny that you get to emulate your spirit animal, husband. My father will be very jealous."

As I started to drift off to sleep, surrounded by my family, my mind wasn't on our test flight, nor on the pending arrival of the Marauders, but on the sight of a Golden Eagle flying over the desert outside of Roswell. When this mission was done, I was going...home. Lillian could run things with Lawrence but I was through being a hero.

The knock on my door came way too soon. Everyone in the room was grumbling about a lack of sleep but I was hustled out to the pilot preparation area to get ready for my first flight in a space ship. I was told to clear my bowels since the confined space of a ship was no place for an accident. Emptied, cleaned and dressed in several layers of insulated under garments, including the space going Pampers, I was finally stuffed into the flight suit and taken to the standby area. As nervous and filled with anxiety as I was, Lawrence was almost bubbling over with anticipation of our upcoming flight.

"Come on, Mike, get in the proper mood. This is going to be the chance of a lifetime. No one is ever going to have the opportunity to be first in flying a ship like this. It's historic my old pal so put a smile on that ugly puss."

Lawrence's enthusiasm was infectious, causing the entire crew to laugh along with him. I tried to be happy. I had volunteered for this and was not about to back out now but I was scared shitless.

The team escorted us to the ship which had been moved to the launch pad. The name on the side of the ship had been changed from The Beast to Golden Eagle, the name of my spirit animal. Lee Anne's influence was all over that change. I followed Lawrence up the ladder, maneuvering through the hatch which still needed to be enlarged. My copilot's seat seemed smaller today but Lawrence's lively chatter, still on full throttle, kept my mind on other things. The sound of the hatch being sealed raised my anxiety level another notch.

"Starting the antigravity engine, Sands. Are you all strapped in?"

"Strapped and glad I took a shit before we dressed. How long before we lift off?"

"Look outside, Chief. We are already at about one hundred feet up and still rising. Wow, this thing is so smooth. Another couple hundred feet and I'll start the rocket. Damn, I am so pumped."

Those were the last words I remember hearing because the rocket thrust pushed me back in my seat so hard I think I blacked out. I know Lawrence was talking a mile a minute but it took me some time to hear what sounded like normal speech.

"We're about to blast through the mesosphere. Things might get little warm, pardner. This baby is super-fast. I knew it was going to be powerful but I am really impressed. Are you doing okay in the back seat?"

"I'm just dandy, pardner, just dandy. I can't tell if I wished the windows back here were bigger or a lot smaller."

"Those are called ports and once we get through the thermosphere your view will seem pretty dark. Can you believe we are passing thirty thousand miles an hour and still accelerating? The fastest manned flight before us was only twenty-five thousand miles an hour. How fast do you think your Queen's ship can travel?"

"I have no idea but the Jinn travel between planetary systems so it must be fast."

"Passing forty thousand miles an hour and still climbing. Can I tell you that I was never confident that the information you downloaded from those ancient files was accurate? I now stand corrected. Fuck, this bird is so smooth. Forty-five thousand and still accelerating. We are already hitting the exosphere. This is outer space, Mike, the new frontier."

"How long are we scheduled to stay up here, Lawrence?"

"Are you that eager to go back? We are good for at least one day and up to six. It depends on what happens during this shakedown cruise. Personally, I am hoping we stay for six. Drop your overhead screen down and take a look at the tasks you have been assigned. They'll keep you occupied and help the time pass."

Once we determined that the Eagle was air tight and the internal temperature in the cabin was designed for humans, we were able to remove our helmets and store them close by. I tapped the digital readout, not believing what it read, that said our speed was now fifty-five thousand miles an hour and still accelerating. I finally obeyed the pilot and dropped my screen down and started doing useful things.

That was how the first two days went by. The rocket had shut off during the end of day one but we still kept gaining speed. At the end of day two Lawrence became very excited.

"How big do you think the Jinn ship is, Sands?"

"Damned if I know. I was on the ground and then I was in the ship. It was kinda like Star Trek with their transporter beam. Why do you ask?"

"Well, something a lot bigger than the Empire State Building, surrounded by a bunch of smaller buildings, is dead ahead of us according to our sensors. I need to hit the reverse thrusters if we want to stop and visit."

"Is it visible out of the ports?"

"Nope, it's still too far away but we are closing fast. We should see it in a couple of hours, longer if we slow way down."

Not wanting to wait I tried contacting the Queen.

"Queen, is that your ship in front of us?"

"Mike Sands, I thought we would get to your planet first and surprise you. You have, instead, surprised me. Do you wish to dock with my ship and come on board?"

"I don't know if we can, Queen. This is our maiden voyage and we haven't worked things out on how to connect with another vessel."

"You needn't worry. When you are close, we will pull you in to the docking bay. We can accommodate almost any type of vessel. My engineer says we should be at optimum distance in approximately four of your hours. Will you need assistance departing from your vessel?"

"It's a tight fit but we should be okay. We will need some sanitary accommodations before we actually meet."

"Yes, cleanliness is always important. You will have quarters waiting for both you and the other I sense being in the vessel. Does he know about us?"

"He knows in general but has not met the other Jinn who decided to remain on the Apache Reservation. It should be interesting watching him connect with you. I've been feeding him pastries made with Dora so you should be able to communicate."

"I will be anxious until you come on board my ship."

The communication was over as fast as it began.

"Are you okay back there, Sands? You seemed to fade away for a bit."

"Yeah, just talking to Queen and getting her okay to meet up. It should be interesting seeing the two of you together."

"You never said much about your Queen. Am I going to be disgusted when I see her?"

"Everything will be okay, Lawrence, so just let things happen at their own pace."

CHAPTER 24

THE NEXT HOURS DRAGGED AS we reduced speed and the Queen's ship came in view. It grew so large that it eclipsed the entire view outside of our small ship. When we were side by side, next to what I originally took to be a small man door, a hatch large enough to handle a battleship opened and began to draw our ship inside. There were no grappling hooks or any mechanical equipment just the pull of some magnetic source.

Fifteen minutes later we were inside a docking bay that our monitors said was filled with an earth like atmosphere. The landing gear had deployed automatically but with our bottom hatch open we were still thirty feet above the deck. We had shed our flight suits after day one so getting through the hatch was not a problem but dropping thirty feet was going to be.

Standing around the hatch I felt the same as the first time I was transported to the Master's ship and later to the Jinn's. One second we were inside our ship and the next we were in a corridor being led to our quarters by two of the Queen's people. Lawrence was beginning to be aware of where he was and started to panic. His flailing arms nearly knocked me down as I wrapped him in a bear hug.

"There's someone in my head, Sands. Am I going crazy?"

"That's probably the Queen. It's how the Jinn communicate. I told you about that weeks ago. Quit fighting it and let her in."

"Is that what you're doing when you kind of space out?"

"She won't harm you, for God's sake. The first time is the most traumatic, kind of like when we just transported to her ship. You did get all your body parts back, didn't you?"

"Oh, fuck, does that happen, losing body parts, I mean?"

"For a guy who just flew a guided missile to outer space, you're acting like a little kid. Reach down and make sure your balls are still there, Lawrence."

We continued walking until our guides pushed us in rooms across the hall from one another. The rooms were Spartan but had everything we needed including toiletries. The shower in the attached lavatory activated the moment I stood in front of the shower head, spraying me with water, then a cleansing agent of some kind and then a quick rinse. Warm air blew from all sides drying me almost instantly. The entire process took less than three minutes.

Returning to the bedroom my jumpsuit and undergarments had vanished only to be replaced by a clean set of clothes, duplicates of the type worn by the Queen's attendants. The material was very stretchy which relieved my thinking that the rear end would be as baggy as the big bottomed Jinn. I had just finished dressing when Queen spoke to me.

"I hope the quarters meet with your approval. Most of my people share large dormitories. Your rooms were originally designed for the Masters on the rare occasions when they were asked to stay. Has your companion relaxed, Mike Sands? Do you think he is able to hold a conversation or should I wait until the both of you are together?"

"I was surprised Lawrence reacted so bizarrely, Queen, but it might be better if I was close by the next time you make contact."

"I would like both of you to join me for a meal. My security team will be at your rooms very shortly to provide an escort. Please make sure your companion is prepared."

"His name is Lawrence Davis, Queen, and he is usually a very brave man. Speak to both of us next time. It should make his anxiety lessen."

The walk to the Queen's chambers, the same one I had visited with Alice and Lee Anne, took over half an hour. We were obviously walking through a small part of the length of the ship, a trip that did nothing to lessen Lawrence's anxiety. I was looking forward to meeting our host but was conflicted about what would transpire. The low mood lighting, cushions spread on the floor and trays of food scattered about the room gave me a good idea what Queen had in mind.

"It is so good to see you again, Mike Sands," she said as she walked over and gave me a kiss that was more than one reserved for a friend. *"And this must be your companion, Lawrence Davis. He is quite acceptable as a consort. Thank you for bringing him to me."*

It was obvious that Queen was sharing the conversation because Lawrence turned bright red. He couldn't hide his thoughts, a byproduct of consuming food laced with Dora, as he had conflicting emotions running through his head. He was admiring Queen and at the same time was concerned about her slightly waspish figure. There was also the thought about how two different species would be able to mate.

It was almost a tie as to who laughed first, Queen or me. She addressed one concern by giving Lawrence a kiss that made her earlier effort with me seem tame.

"My physiology is the same as your Earth females, Lawrence Davis, but unlike them I have no qualms about who I mate with as long as the male is virile. Do you meet that qualification?"

Lawrence began to turn a darker shade of red as the Queen made quick work of removing his jumpsuit and dropping her gown. I was completely ignored as Queen proved to my friend that they were compatible. I had a moment of jealousy as I realized he was doing something I had dreamed of but never allowed to happen. Instead, I settled on a cushion and began to nibble on the delicious treats.

"You realize, Mike Sands, that my next generation will be more like your people than my current one" Queen remarked when she and Lawrence finally reclined. *"Your companion is going to be the father of this new race, something you could have been. Are your wives going to be upset that it is not going to be you?"*

"My wives have kept me busy enough that I had not thought of it until I saw you with Lawrence. He is a good friend and deserves the honor."

"While he recovers and prepares for another consummation can we discuss the advent of the Marauders following me to your planet?"

"It was something I hoped to do. How much time do we have and what will it take to defeat them?"

"They are very crafty and took over the entire Consortium with little effort. Of course, none of the other species were very good at defending themselves. They usually relied on the Jinn to take care of security. As I told you before, the attack proved to be a perfect time to break our alliance and resume our own journey. The fact that several other members of our Consortium decided to join us was an asset. As to the amount of time it will take for the Masters to repair their engines and begin the excursion to your planet, I would estimate at least eight cycles of your planet around your star. The Marauders may be slow and lack talent but they are very persistent."

"One thing we never addressed was whether you have weapons that would aid us in protecting Earth. None of the diagrams we recovered had weapon designs."

"Our ship does have a weapons array but be warned that they consume a great deal of energy. We discovered on our last visit to your world that you have nothing that is comparable to our weapons systems. But perhaps we can execute another trade for services that would make it worthwhile for both of our people."

The sense that the Jinn were a benevolent race began to fade. My ability to see what the Jinn were thinking caught a glimpse of a much darker side of the Queen, one who was not against taking what she wanted if an advantageous trade could not be reached. Lawrence, worn out from his initial tryst, had no idea what was going on around him.

"Perhaps, Mike Sands, you should take some of the treats and return to your quarters. We can discuss terms when I have had my fill of your companion. That may take a while and will require some additional time for him to recover. Think about your best offer and whether your president will agree to it. Be aware that nothing the Jinn do is without cost."

CHAPTER 25

R ATHER THAN STAY AND WATCH as Lawrence got rav-
ished, I loaded a napkin full of treats and began a walk back
through the ship. A guard was at my side almost instantly
making sure I kept on my way and did not try to go on a sightseeing
tour. I believe he was totally unaware that I was reading his thoughts
and musings about the crazy humanoids from Earth.

Several hours had gone by when I heard a scraping at the door
to my quarters and assumed it was someone requesting to enter. Before I could get off of the bed Queen walked in. She had not
bothered to put on her gown and had a very bedraggled Lawrence
behind her being held up by two of Queen's security team. Lawrence was led to his quarters as Queen closed the door and sat next
to me.

*"Quit worrying, Mike, I have had my fun for the time being. I'm
here to discuss an arrangement."*

*"I guess that means I am not to be the next donor to an im-
proved race of Jinn?"*

*"The Jinn traits will always be included but we hope to em-
brace the aggressive nature of your people. The Jinn lost that
attribute during one of our previous generations. Perhaps I should
explain my comments about our future generation being more like
your humans. The Jinn are like the Masters in many ways. We are
a far older race and have been in space much longer than most other
species we have encountered. Most of them are incompatible with
us but occasionally we encounter a race that, after consuming Dora,
develops attributes we can incorporate in our genome. It also gives
them the ability to mate with us, or me specifically. The Masters
came to our aid, as I told you in a previous meeting, but genetically,*

147

they are not compatible. Your race is the closest to what we were long ago before several new generations had been incorporated in to our being. Have I made myself clear?"

"If I understand you, the Jinn take elements of another race which changes you genetically and physically but you really want to return to your original form. You've already bred with Lawrence so what else can we offer?"

"Part of my mating with Lawrence was the fact that the human genome contains both male and female characteristics. I plan to give birth to both male and female offspring, a radical change from our long history. The females will not be Queens but will be attendants. The males will become warriors taking on the human aggressiveness and ability to seek retribution. Those were qualities we had lost. But that is only part of my solution. To continue the process of becoming more human I will wish my new generation to mate with humans. Your President must agree to provide suitable candidates when my new born have matured."

"Two questions, Queen; first, how many of your new generation are we talking about and second, what do we get in return?"

"My normal group of hatchlings, delivered thirty at a time, approaches three hundred when the total clutch is finally out. My fertilized eggs are transferred to our nursery where they mature. Once they are free of their confinement, they grow to maturity in one to two cycles of your planet around your star. They should be ready to mate one further cycle later. As to your reward, we will give you all the schematics for our weapons array. I believe you get the better end of the deal. You will also get access to the files we neglected to give you that contain information on weapons the Ancient's possessed."

"Why were you holding out on us? Are there any more surprises or is everything in the open?"

"There are always surprises my young friend. When you spend as much of your lives trying to find a friendly haven as we have, you learn to be cautious. I will assume you haven't told me all of what you found in the Ancient's files. I sense that

is very true. You are learning to hide your thoughts, much like the Jinn. That confirms that we are very much alike."

Thoughts of what I needed to know to fly the Eagle, what other shit Queen was going to throw my way and how to best get the President's approval to provide sex slaves to the Jinn rattled around in my head.

"I need to get back to Earth so I can relay your request to the President."

"You will have to travel alone, I'm afraid, as Lawrence will be remaining with me."

"That's crazy Queen. I'm not a pilot and will probably kill myself trying to fly back through Earth's atmosphere."

"You will fly your Eagle with Lawrence's help. His ability to communicate may be weak but I will transfer his instructions. I will make sure he hears your cries for help and answers you properly. Your ship has been refueled and made ready so take some time to rest. We have continued towards your planet so your return journey will be much shorter. I am counting on you to convince your President of our demands."

Queen was done talking so she patted my leg and went across the hall to Lawrence's room. I tried to rest but knowing I was going to be in the pilot's seat had my nerves rubbed raw. Somehow, without realizing it, sleep came. I had no idea how much time had passed but my security team was standing by my bed when I awoke. My cleaned and refreshed underclothes and jumpsuit were on the bed. To my great surprise they had even cleaned the diaper.

Dressed and ready I was escorted through the ship to the stern docking bay and was instantly transported back to the flight cabin. Regaining my equilibrium, I locked everything down and clumsily climbed in my flight suit, hoping I had connected everything as they were designed. Sitting in the pilot's seat I had a momentary jolt of absolute fear, freezing me for several minutes. Once I regained control, I began to get excited as the Eagle was pushed out of the bay in to space.

Lawrence began giving me instructions that allowed me to charge the engines and start my voyage home. Our two ships had covered most of the distance to Earth which meant my descent was about to begin.

If you asked me how I managed to land without dying, I would be unable to answer. It was as if Lawrence and Queen had taken control of my brain and directed everything from inside my head. That was something I had never experienced with any of the Jinn with whom I had been in contact. It had to be something only the Queen was able to do. My first clear recollection was hitting the runway in Palmdale and realizing it was the middle of the night. The control tower was going crazy as I made my way to our hanger and put the Eagle to bed.

As I unclasped the safety harness and made my way to the bottom hatch, I stood by for the transporter to activate before realizing I had to wait for the ladder to be rolled over to the ship. Disobeying protocol I stripped out of the flight suit and donned my jumpsuit before climbing to the ground. Maybe I was expecting a welcoming committee or a big band to celebrate my return but all I got were the two puzzled crewmen who wheeled the ladder to my ship.

Stumbling to the office I was met by Lillian who looked like she hadn't slept for a long time. She wrapped me in a hug that almost took my breath away. I was too tired to shake her off so I hung on to keep from falling.

"You were supposed to let us know you were on the way back, you jerk. And where is Lawrence? Is he still in the ship?"

"I'm so tired, Babe, can we take this conversation back to my room?"

Lillian walked with me, never letting go of her near stranglehold. Lee Anne was sleeping in my bunk but Alice and Jeannie were gone.

"We've been taking turns manning the radios waiting for you. Do you realize it has been over two weeks since you took off?"

"Two weeks; how is that possible? By my calculations we were gone for four days."

"Didn't Lawrence keep an eye on the chronometer? Where is he, by the way? Is he planning on staying on the ship?" Lillian was definitely getting excited but not the kind I was ready for.

"He's still on the Jinn ship. It's part of a problem I need to address with the President. I flew the Eagle back on my own, sort of."

"You're not a damn pilot, Mike Sands. How could you do that and not crash?"

Lillian's shouting finally woke Lee Anne causing her to jump out of bed ready to have a fight. Realizing I was in the room she launched herself at me and knocked me over, landing on top of me as we fell to the bed.

"Not quite the greeting I was expecting but it will have to do," I said as I was buried under kisses from my Apache bride.

"What was Lillian saying about you flying the Eagle? That has to be the craziest thing I have ever heard."

"It is my spirit animal and I was flying, just like in my dreams when I was a kid. Talk about dreams coming true. Aren't you glad I was able to land safely?"

"Wait until I tell Alice what you did. She will kick your ass. What was Lawrence doing while you were flying?"

"He was becoming the new royal consort to the Jinn Queen and father to their new generation of little Jinn's."

"Get out of here. I thought we had arranged for you to have that honor?"

"It seems my reservations about cheating on you and Alice..."

"You better include Lillian in this story."

"...and Lillian...may have been a little too obvious for Queen. Besides, Lawrence's adventurous nature was more of what she was after. It's the generation after that concerns me."

"Does she plan on keeping Lawrence until all her eggs are hatched? He could be up there for years."

"That's the crazy part. She wants the President to authorize human mates for her new, I guess I can call them children, so that her people become more human than Jinn. And, she thinks it might be less than three years before they are mature enough to bear offspring."

As if on cue my cell phone, still in my backpack, went off. Surprised it still had a charge I stared at the President's private number.

"How does he know I am back? I never spoke to the tower before landing and you are the first person who knows me that I have seen...except for the guy pushing the rolling ladder."

I hit the talk button before the sixth and last ring expecting to get a tongue lashing for failing to check in. Instead, the President was as excited as I had been on takeoff.

"Mister President, what are you doing up so early? It's barely past five in Washington."

"I'm always up at this hour getting a start on my day. I was extremely surprised when my agent at the airfield called to let me know you had landed, Sands, and I wanted to be the first one to hear all about your voyage. And I want to know why you were the only one on the ship when you got back."

It took less than five minutes to update the President and thirty more to answer all his questions, especially when it came to Lawrence remaining with the Queen.

"Why does that Queen want to have her people become more like us? Is she planning some kind of an invasion? She got us all hot and bothered by the Marauders coming to Earth and now I feel like she is planning her own invasion. What's your take on this?"

"The same as you, Mister President."

"Christ, Mike, in moments when you and I are in private conversation you gotta call me John. If you get too official, we are never going to figure this shit out. So, what's the bottom line?"

"We give her some folks who are unadulterated by space radiation and she gives us plans for weapons arrays that can defeat the Marauders. I think I told you before that I can tell when there is subterfuge in our mental conversations, and lord knows Queen tries to hide things from me. I may not know what the truth is but I can tell when a lie is present. I don't believe she knows how well I can read her."

"So, what do we do, draft some horny guys who don't mind some alien pussy?"

"You're not getting the point, John, she wants both men and women because her new generation, the one Lawrence is helping to spawn, will include equal numbers of females. I get the horny guys but how do we justify the horny women being drafted?"

Lee Anne, listening to both ends of the conversation poked me hard in the ribs, whispering, "There are just as many horny women, maybe more, than men, you misogynist."

"Volunteers are not the problem. Making sure we get the weapon's plans is my primary concern. So, how do we handle this? Are you up to making another trip to her ship or are we going to handle this with a mental conference call?"

"There is one other matter. I counted four days as the length of my first space voyage but Lee Anne claims I was gone for two weeks. I was too busy to check the chronometer and can't account for the missing time. I wish I knew if the Queen has some other items on her agenda that will screw up our strategies. She put Lawrence in my head so I could fly the Eagle home and that is something she had never done before. If she passes that talent over to the new generation, she could declare a coup and we might never know it."

"If the Marauders get here, it might not make any difference. Let's arrange for the weapons and then figure out the rest. Get some sleep Mike and we can talk some more later. Nice work by the way. Give Lee Anne a kiss and tell her not to breathe so heavy when she is listening to our conversations."

CHAPTER 26

IF LEE ANNE HAD OTHER ideas on what to do once I was in bed, she had to be disappointed because I was asleep as soon as my head hit the pillow. I was awakened five hours later, just before nine, by three crazy females climbing in next to me, hugging and kissing me awake. A fourth stood in the doorway looking like she wished she could join them. I was actually tempted to see if Lillian could find room on the already crowded bed.

"The President wanted you awake and back on the job," Lillian remarked wistfully from her position at the door. "He said if he could get by on five hours sleep so could you." She gave a glance over at the pile up on the bed and disappeared down the hall.

Pushing through the gaggle of females telling me I didn't have to go yet was an exercise in perseverance as I had torn feelings about wanting to stay in bed or needing to get up. The moment was settled when Alice pushed Lee Anne and Jeannie out of the room and led me to the shower. Alice made getting ready for work a lot more difficult.

The questions in the hanger from the team were centered on why Lawrence did not return with me and how in hell I was able to fly the Eagle when I had practically no experience as a pilot. I responded to the best of my ability but it left a lot of unanswered questions. The rest of the day went by with the Eagle being examined stem to stern and me trying to explain what Lawrence and I had done on the maiden flight. Everyone got excited when I related being taken in to the Jinn ship by a tractor beam and wanting to know if I had negotiated for that technology. Our lack of science was exposed each time I gave some new bit of information on something the Jinn had that we did not.

Every few hours I got a call from the President wanting updates. It dawned on me that my bodyguard, Carlos, had been missing since before I boarded the Eagle. Just before six that evening I received my last call from the President.

"Mister President, you have to give me some space. My team is working like crazy and we should have an answer to your questions by tomorrow or the next day at the latest."

"This is really hard on me, Sands. I want to be able to notify my party and Congress that we have a plan. I guess what I really want is to be one of those guys who makes the trip to the Jinn ship. That's not going to happen unless we have room for a whole team of Secret Service agents."

"Speaking of agents, what has happened to my bodyguard? He hasn't been around since I got back."

"He used the time you were gone to spend with his wife and kids. I keep him away from them too much and owed him the break. He'll be with you tomorrow, I promise. It sounds like the two of you are getting along so I'll put off having any rotation of personnel authorized."

"Yeah, I'm surprised at how well we mesh. It must be all the police experiences we share."

"By the way, I've received preliminary approvals on the Queen's demands, Mike. No one likes what she wants but everyone is eager to see what weapons she is going to provide."

Talking about the weapons triggered something in my head. The missing days came flooding back along with schematics for a dozen different weapons packages. I remembered being on my bed in the Jinn ship nibbling on the various sweets I had taken from the Queen's quarters and then there was a blank. That lifted as I sat in a lab with leads stuck to my head. Several techs were repeating what was done in the basement of the Apache meeting hall and extracting my new information. Queen was showing an act of faith that I would deliver on her proposals. All I had needed was for the President to say that he would agree to the terms.

"Fuck me, John, I already have all the plans in my head," I commented on my next call. "She had me loaded like I was some kind of hard drive during the missing days. She must really be worried about the Marauders to give us the tech before we even send...shit, she already has Lawrence and her next generation. She's a couple steps ahead of us and keeps giving us tidbits so we can negotiate for more tech."

"This may be difficult to answer but do you trust that she will stand by us? I mean she ran when the Marauders attacked, what were they called, the Masters? How reliable can she be?"

"The Masters were not warriors and neither are the Jinn according to the Queen. She once told me she wanted that warrior spirit infused in her people, which is where Lawrence comes in, so they could better stand up for themselves. I guess we are going to see if that actually happens."

"And this all started because the Jinn needed a planet on which to grow their damned product. God help where this is going to take us."

"It's going to take us to outer space. The question remains if we are going to stay there very long."

Reviewing all the data on the Eagle's systems took longer than the one or two days I had promised. It was in the second week after my return that I had another call from the Queen.

"I hope you have recovered from your first space voyage, Mike Sands. Did you manage to find the files I left for you?"

The amusement in Queen's voice made me realize that she was toying with me and I was not amused.

"You stole two weeks of my life that I can't get back. We all appreciate the plans for the weapons but I thought we had an understanding to be honest with each other."

"Was there any deceit in what I gave you or in how you interpreted the manner of the giving? We are not the same, you and I, and you have not tried hard enough to understand how my people think. Develop your weapons and contact me if you have any questions."

Queen was gone from my head and I was left wondering what brought on her change of attitude.

As confused as I was my team was thrilled with the designs I dredged out of my head. Our weapons production partners, the same people that provided aerospace scientists and engineers to our team, had prototypes ready for testing within a month. In all that time Queen had not contacted me nor the President.

That changed the day when the energy burst from our first prototype cannon obliterated a tank on the military weapons testing range in western Utah. Nothing was left of the target but small pieces of twisted metal. The President, who had insisted on being at the site, was ecstatic and couldn't stop pounding me on my back even though I tried to pass off all the praise to my team. We were on a military transport on the way back to our base in Palmdale when I heard from Queen.

"Congratulations on a successful demonstration. My scientists could never get that design to work, continually blowing up the cannon instead of a target. Hopefully you will have as much luck with the more powerful weapons."

"Can I assume you have had us under some type of observation since I returned?"

"You and your people have been observed for far longer than that."

"Why did you wait so long to make contact?"

"I told you we were not always joined with the Masters. That association was advantageous to both our peoples and was never intended to be long term. They served their purpose and we were always ready to go our own way. Had the Marauders not returned we might have used them longer."

"Are they any closer to Earth? Do we have time enough to develop all the weapons we will need?"

"They are still far out of your galaxy, Mike Sands. We left sensors along our path that will let us know when the danger gets close."

"Can't they use the sensors to track you, Queen, or are they not intelligent enough?"

"You always bring up such salient points. No, the Marauders are not bright enough but the Masters are. Be pleased that they have very slow vessels. Speaking of that, I am sending Lawrence Davis home in one of my armored shuttles. Lawrence will be accompanied by one of my pilots who will remain with you to advise you on how

you can improve your space craft. Treat them well, Mike Sands, and keep your eyes to the sky."

It had been almost two months since our initial trip to the Jinn ship and I hadn't heard from Lawrence the entire time since my return. So, it came as a surprise when he made mental contact with me two days after our return to Palmdale.

"Sands, can you hear me? I'm still not comfortable talking this way but this shuttle has no radios."

"You're sounding very clear, Lawrence. I hope you are on your way home."

"We left the Jinn ship an hour ago or however you reckon time up here and should arrive in Palmdale sometime after dark. This shuttle is more like a sleek race car and is so very cool to fly. My pilot let me take the controls once we left the shuttle bay and I never want to let them go. I need you to be on hand when we land along with your pal, Carlos, if you get my drift. I have a lot to tell you."

"I'll be there, Lawrence and welcome back."

"'You have no idea how good it will be to stand on the ground on Earth, old pal. Talk to you soon."

CHAPTER 27

WHEN NEWS OF LAWRENCE'S IMPENDING arrival spread through the team, not one of them wanted to be left out of greeting him on his return. Alice, Jeannie and Lee Anne had returned to Roswell, Lee Anne to assume her duties as the interim chief and Alice and Jeannie because the new school year was about to begin. The person happiest about their departure and Lawrence's arrival was Lillian, my new Chief of Staff.

The Jinn shuttle landed and was so quiet it was a moment or two before anyone realized it was taxiing to the hanger. Longer and much lower to the ground than the Eagle, the Jinn ship looked like it was speeding even when standing still. I expected Lawrence to be swept away as the side hatch swung inside and a ramp pushed to the ground. What I was not expecting was the human female who preceded Lawrence and the Jinn pilot following him.

While everyone gawped at the ship, I went quickly to the ramp to greet my friend.

"Before you say anything or ask any questions, Sands, tell me what day it is and how long I've been gone."

Lawrence looked haggard and seemed to have aged since we were split up.

"It's been two months and the date is September first."

"Fuck me, Sands, it can't have been that long. I mean other than breeding with Queen, sleeping and eating, I don't feel like it's been more than a couple weeks."

"I lost two weeks that felt like four days and had my head pumped full of weapons data. Maybe she did the same thing to you."

My eyes kept moving over to the female now standing be-hind Lawrence and trying to become invisible. She was dressed in a lightweight flight suit but was carrying a very ugly purple purse.

"Where did you find your new friend? She couldn't have been hitchhiking out there, or could she?"

"This is Cassie, pal, and no, she wasn't hitchhiking. She was one of about two dozen earth females on board the Jinn ship. It seems Queen forgot to mention they had been to Earth before. She managed to abduct the girls to try to breed them with her security guards but it wouldn't take. She wants to re-patriate them in exchange for some new favor or other. I snuck Cassie on board the shuttle so she could give you her story first hand."

"She seems rather taken with you the way she's holding on to your shirt. She's rather quiet, Lawrence, doesn't she speak?"

"She was ill treated by the security guards, the same as the other girls, when she spoke out loud. She does whisper real well."

"Very close to your ear, I suppose."

"Look, Mike, this whole trip and arrangement with the Jinn may be something other than what we've seen. The attitude on the ship after you left was making me feel like a third-class cit-izen. Yeah, I got all the alien pussy I wanted, and lots of food, but when I was not with Queen I was moved to a dormitory and locked in with the Earth girls. Most, no, all but Cassie were afraid to talk or get close to me thinking they would be beaten. There is some evil shit going on up there that we need to find out about."

"I can tell you some of what's happening," Cassie said as she looked around Lawrence but never giving up her hold on his shirt.

"Okay, I'm ready to listen but we need to get you and Law-rence inside for a medical evaluation. Besides there are a lot of folks who want to say hello and welcome him back. While they are doing that is there anyone I can call or let you call to say you are safe?"

"My mom might care but there is nobody else. Lawrence said I could trust you, Mister Sands. Was he telling the truth?"

"A great many people have given me reason to believe I'm trustworthy so I'll have to believe them. Sometimes I have doubts but I guess that's normal. Will you walk with me back to our quarters?"

Cassie dropped her hand from Lawrence's shirt and grabbed my arm. Lawrence looked lost for a minute as I started to walk away with his friend but was quickly surrounded by our team. I did not try to talk to Cassie until we were safely away from the crowd, even signaling to Carlos to stay behind so as not to frighten the young girl.

We walked to the lunch room where Cassie looked longingly at the array of food.

"Can I get you something, Cassie, a drink or something to eat?"

She nodded her head and pointed to several items, looking like a very young child as she grabbed a sweet roll and a banana in one hand and a cup of hot chocolate in the other. I watched her eat and smiled at how much like my Jeannie she seemed. After another sweet roll she finally sat back and smiled.

"How is it you have a purse? That doesn't seem like part of a standard ship's uniform."

"The Jinn let us keep all of our personal possessions after they determined we had no weapons or contraband. It was the only thing I took with me when Lawrence said it was time to leave."

"How long do you think you were on the Jinn ship?"

"Not as long as the other girls. It's hard to tell time when the lights never go out and there are no clocks around. I know it was at least several months because I had my monthly cycle a bunch of times, if you know what I mean. That was the only way I could tell how much time had gone by."

"Do you mind my asking how old you are and how old the other girls were?"

"I'm twenty-two but I've always been small for my age. The youngest girl said she was seventeen when she was taken but all of the others are in their twenties. Some of them had been on the ship for a couple of years, I think."

"So, you said you could tell us something about the Jinn's intentions. Do you want to tell me now or wait until you make your phone call?"

"It's too late to call my mom," she said as she stared at the wall clock reading two ten in the morning. "Can I talk to you and not anyone else?"

"If that's what you want."

"And I don't want anyone else to be with us, just you and me."

"What about Lawrence, don't you trust him?"

"He was fucking the Queen and everyone knew she said he was special. He's nice but I don't trust him like I do you."

"You just met me, Cassie, how do you know I can be trusted?"

"Because Queen was afraid of you. That's why she chose Lawrence because she could control him."

The Queen being afraid of me was a revelation. I was always the one who was concerned she would take offense to something I said and throw me out of a hatch.

"That surprises me because she never gave me that feeling but she was good at deception. So, it's you and me talking. Can I record what you say? I will need to report back to my boss and it would help if I had an accurate record."

Cassie shrugged her shoulders and smiled. I took out my smart phone and set it up to record.

"Can we do this in some other place? I keep thinking others are going to want to come in here."

"My quarters are down the hall and no one should bother us there."

The smile Cassie had on her face should have warned me to be more careful where I took people but Carlos was not there to warn me, again, of my capacity for finding females who liked me. Everyone was still in the hanger with the new shuttle and Lawrence so we walked to my rooms, unseen. Cassie sat on the bed and I was on the chair at my desk when she started talking. For someone used to whispering she sounded very confident and clear of voice.

"Lawrence told me you first met the Jinn who were guarding the Dora field and then met the Masters. I hadn't been on the Jinn ship very long when I learned about how the Queen had made contact with the Masters. I'm not sure when that was but I know they were not together very long. You were told the Masters found lone ships they could capture and then stole their technology but it is actually the Jinn who do that. The Masters are amateurs compared to the Jinn. The Queen seduced the Masters by getting them committed to Dora as a food source and then used it to coerce them for favors. I overheard some of the security people talking after they had, you know, serviced us. They were saying that the Marauders were getting close and it was time to break away from the Masters so the Marauders could do their part. Later I heard some other security guys talking about how the Marauders were all part of Queen's army. We had left the Consortium before I could see any of the Marauders but I know their next target was Earth."

"Queen has been giving us all kinds of technology to defend against the Marauders. Why would she do that if they weren't the enemy?"

"Have you improved on the technology or merely used the plans she gave you?"

"Improved on it, most certainly. Do I get the impression Queen wants to use the tech against us after we give her the improved models?"

"Queen is always complaining that her scientists are stupid. When she found out humans are smarter than her people, she wanted to see firsthand if that was true. It's why she abducted us and is using Lawrence to birth a new, smarter generation. We had all been to college and she hoped she could breed more intelligent members by using us as brood mares. Her males couldn't make babies so she was stuck with us...until she found you. I don't know why she thought you would be a better stud than her own males but you were a subject of conversation for quite some time. You were supposed to breed her and then us. When she chose Lawrence all of us girls were disappointed."

"So, what's next, Cassie, what does she have on her mind?"

"She wants to keep you occupied with a continuing stream of technology until the Marauders get here. I don't think it's going to be as long as Queen said. They are a long way off but we heard that they move fairly quickly."

I was so concentrated on writing notes and keeping an eye on the recording that it was a shock when I realized Cassie had taken off the top to her flight suit. I was ready to throw a blanket over her when there was a knock on the door and Lillian walked in.

"Oh my, what do we have here," Lillian exclaimed and then smiled. "That was fast work, even for you, baby."

"Thank god you're here. I would not normally be happy to see you in my room but you arrived in the nick of time."

"All I came to tell you was that Cassie needs to go see the doctor for her examination. Did you plan on giving her one first?"

Lillian's grin was enough to cause my perpetual blush to resurface and cause her to start laughing.

"I'll save you this one time but you owe me and I do plan on collecting."

Lillian got Cassie's shirt back on her and led her to the clinic. It left me to wonder what might have happened had she not knocked on my door.

CHAPTER 28

MY CALL TO THE PRESIDENT did not go well. He had not had a good night's sleep and erupted in a scathing list of oaths on the deceptive nature exhibited by the Jinn Queen. He must have ranted for fifteen minutes while I listened with the phone away from my ear and tried not to fall asleep from exhaustion. He finally wore down and was quiet for some time.

"Well, what are you going to do about this problem, Sands? This is your project and I hope you have something positive to present."

"I learned about this just before calling you, Mister President, and haven't had time to process all the ramifications. If what Cassie says is true, we need to keep our secrets to ourselves. On the other hand, both Cassie and Lawrence had missing time while on the Jinn vessel and could have been loaded with who knows what much as I was in my missing four days. I need to study both of them as well as the pilot who came with the shuttle. All or none of them might be enemy agents and not know it."

"Consider yourself on lockdown, Sands, at least until you can verify the good intentions of all three of the shuttle passengers. And you can add yourself to that list since you can't completely account for your missing time. Keep up your regular updates and, by God, no more conversations with that Jinn Queen. Are we understood?"

"You are loud and clear, sir. If you don't mind, I am going to sign off and get some sleep. I'll be in touch."

At ten o'clock I woke to find I was not alone in my bed. I rolled over to see Lillian sleeping, breathing lightly like I had seen her do for so many years. Watching her sleep and look so peaceful used to be one of my early morning pleasures. It was one habit I had hated to lose. As always happened when we were married, she opened her eyes and smiled. And like always we never said a word, just stared. Lillian broke the silence.

"We went on lockdown early this morning and since I had never been issued quarters, I didn't think you would mind sharing a bed for a while. I am fully clothed and on top of the covers so I guess it didn't really count as having slept with you. I did like our early morning staring contest, though I wish it could have been done under the sheets."

My mind was swirling thinking that maybe Alice and Lee Anne were right and I should give Lillian a new chance. Before I could express an opinion, another annoying knock on my door broke the mood.

"Sands, are you awake?" It was Lawrence. "We need to have a meeting with the entire team. Any idea where Lillian is holed up?"

"I'm awake, Lawrence, and I have a pretty good idea where Lillian is. We'll be in the conference room in twenty minutes."

I heard his footsteps moving down the hallway and saw Lillian with her face covered with a pillow trying to stifle a laugh.

"Do we have time for a quick shower together?" she asked while still smiling. "You could really do with a wash and I could scrub your back. Do Alice or Lee Anne do that as well as I do?"

My heart was beating faster as Lillian quickly stripped down and stood at the door to the bathroom.

"You better get in here or Lawrence is going to come searching for you."

The last of my resolve disappeared as I headed for the bathroom and a long overdue reunion.

The crew was assembled when we made our way to the meeting forty-five minutes later. My first order of business was to dissect the Jinn shuttle to see what superior technology we could use. The ship's computer had a complete set of schematics for the vessel that the pilot seemed unable to comprehend or explain, confirming that my team was worlds ahead of the

Jinn in understanding technology. My chore now was to keep any of our findings away from the pilot so he could not send anything we found back to the Queen. That meant keeping the pilot on a short leash and away from our research.

Getting inside Lawrence and Cassie's head was also important but the President out maneuvered me that same day by sending in a cognitive psychologist to help uncover their missing memories. Doctor Adam Glass was a tenured teaching psychologist at Stanford University whose specialty was memory disorders. He looked the part of a cartoon character with a scraggly beard and Alfred Einstein hair but a quick computer search showed him to be one of the most preeminent men in his field. I turned him lose on Lawrence since his time on the Jinn ship was finite. I needed to know if there was additional technical data placed in his head by the Queen or her people, things that could be a danger to the team and Earth.

Cassie was another story. There seemed to be more to her than she had allowed Lawrence to see. Her act of coming on to me in our interview had me concerned so I enlisted Lillian to sit in with me during another interview.

With the conference room free until our next team meeting, I had Cassie meet us. She had changed her clothing and was now wearing a tank top and loose-fitting shorts instead of the ship's clothing the Queen had issued to her. She smiled at Lillian and sat down.

"Are you and Mister Sands together?" she asked before we could start the interview.

"Why do you ask?" Lillian replied with a smile of her own. "Are you interested in him?"

"The Queen promised me I would get a chance to mate with him. The rules are different on Earth than on the ship so I thought I'd ask."

"We were married once but since then he has become more of a free agent. If he wanted me back, though, I'd be more than willing to consider it."

"This conversation is better suited for some time when business does not need to be discussed, so, if you ladies don't mind…"

"You need to see something…" Cassie interrupted as she reached in her ever-present purse. She handed me a clear glass bottle containing a very dark blue liquid that I instinctively knew was a liquid form of Dora. "This is what all the girls and Lawrence were told to drink before we had sex with the Jinn. It allowed us to do anything that we were asked to do and made us sleep after we were finished. We never knew how we got back to our beds or how long we slept. I saw Lawrence brought back by the Queen's guards and sleep for long periods after his time with Queen. I kept this sample to give to Lawrence when I heard he was going to be released but when he told me I was going with him I kept it for you instead. Do you think it's important?"

I stared at the bottle and wished Alice was here to give me a botanist's opinion of what I held in my hand.

"Do you have any idea what's in the bottle?"

"The guards were very talkative after sex and one told me it was a concentrated form of Dora. He said that Queen used it to promote better relations with her subjects, especially since they seemed to get addicted to it. That wasn't true for the girls who just liked it for the extra sensations it provided. We don't know if it affected Lawrence the same way."

"Do you have any idea whether any of the Jinn conducted experiments or testing on you or the other girls while you were asleep?"

"What kind of tests? The guards were very physical during sex so I'm not sure if we could have noticed anything else going on afterwards."

Cassie was turning out to be very intuitive. She looked from Lillian to me more than once and finally sat back in her seat.

"I want to call my mom now if that's okay," she said rather abruptly while taking a cell phone from her purse. "We can talk again another time."

It never dawned on me until later that Cassie was about to use a cell phone that could not have been active since she hadn't been able to pay her cellular company during all the months she had been gone.

CHAPTER 29

I WALKED OUT OF THE CONFERENCE room and was immediately joined by Carlos and a large female, Helen, Lillian's security agent. Carlos looked concerned and seemed anxious to say something.

"Are you okay, Mike? Helen and I listened in on your interview, on orders from the boss, by the way, and it seemed like you were being led by Cassie. She sounds really sharp."

"Oh, something is definitely not right and I hope we can figure out what it is before the Jinn get too much closer. Did the psychologist come up with anything or is that a closely held secret?"

"Cassie's really hard to read. We wish she was like the Queen so we could read her mind."

It suddenly made too much sense. The Queen allowed Cassie to escape so that I would do exactly that, read the mind of someone who had a lot more to tell me or, even worse, cause me to do something that could derail our efforts to protect Earth.

"It's what she wants, Carlos. I'm supposed to communicate with Cassie like I do with the Queen. What the fuck does she want? She gives us food, then tech, then even more advanced tech while all the while planning to invade us. What's even crazier is that she has been to our planet who knows how many times before when she was kidnapping the girls and never gave us anything in exchange. She has to know that we're not going to give her our improved specs on the weapons nor anything else we developed that's been improved."

"Is that all you think?" Carlos said while starting to laugh. "Seems like you have given this some serious thought. What do you want us to do?"

"Find out who Cassie called on a cell phone that should not have been active and get some of this concentrated Dora to my wife and Joe Farris for a thorough chemical analysis. It's not that I don't trust your government scientists, but..."

"I get it, Mike. You want your personal team looking at things. As to Cassie's phone call, every cell call made on the property gets intercepted and the recipient of the call scrutinized. It's all part of the protocol. What's your plan for Cassie?"

"Simple, I'm going to see if I can communicate with her mind-to-mind. Just make sure you have Doctor Glass close by in case things go sideways."

"You don't have to do this," Carlos cautioned. "We have staff that might be able to break her down...eventually."

"I don't doubt that but I think this is the way the Queen wants this to play out. She does love to play her games and I am betting that this is another one. She hasn't tried to hurt me, yet, and I don't think she intends to now. I'll keep Lillian with me but everyone else needs to stay out of sight. Can you make that happen, Carlos?"

"Reluctantly, yes, but I am going to be right behind Doctor Glass just in case."

I asked Lillian to step out so I could bring her up to date and ask if she could hear any of Cassie's conversation with her mother.

"It sounded like any conversation I would have with my mother after being missing for a very long time. The strange thing is there was no shouting or crying on either end, almost as if it wasn't the first time Cassie had gone missing."

"Stranger and stranger," Carlos remarked. "I'm going to make sure we vet whoever was on the other end of that call. I'll say it again; you better watch your ass in there. I trust that girl less and less each time I hear something about her."

"I'm not going to let anything happen to him,' Lillian proclaimed. "We've just got to an understanding and I'm not letting that slip away again."

Damn woman had this knack that caused me to start blushing again. Turning away from the group I took Lillian's hand and went back to my meeting with Cassie.

"So, how long did you think it would take for me to catch on," I sent to the young woman.

Cassie looked shocked when I addressed her in her mind and, for the first time, seemed afraid.

"You must have been told that Queen and I have had extensive conversations and my nonverbal communication skills were probably equal to hers. The fact you are reacting to me tells me you have some of those same skills."

"Queen never said how strong you were, just that you had some ability. She thought I could influence you in some way but always laughed when I asked her how I could do that. Her only direction was to get you to impregnate me and then return to her ship. I really don't want to go back there. Can I stay here with you?"

Without warning her I began to probe the young woman's mind hoping to find something the Queen might have implanted. I retrieved directives that were to become active when Cassie and I performed sexually and others when it was determined I had earned her trust. No new schematics or documents were found.

When I pulled back, I realized that Cassie had been crying and looked to be about twelve years old.

I began to speak to her aloud.

"Was that really your mother on the phone a little while ago?"

"Yeah, she was not too happy to hear from me. When I disappeared, she stopped receiving my rent money so she had to find a way to pay for our cell bill and her other pleasures. I usually stay with her since my name is on the lease of the townhouse. At least I did up until I got kidnapped."

"I take it your mother didn't believe your story about being on a space ship?"

Cassie began to laugh and grabbed my arm. "Would you believe a story like that? Part time actress gets abducted to be used as a sex slave by aliens." Her laughter was verging on hysteria. "I'd be in a looney bin if you weren't the one who I came to see. Can you even begin to imagine what it was like being locked in a room with all those freaks? Ask your friend Lawrence about it if you don't believe me." Her laughter turned to loud sobs causing Lillian to move over and hold the young woman in her arms.

Cassie's comment about Lawrence made me jump and run out of the room.

"We need to locate Lawrence and put him under surveillance. I was worried about Cassie and he was the one who was spending all that time with the Queen. Damn, I hope we didn't miss something last night. Make sure the same security is placed on the pilot."

Carlos didn't bother to ask me why but ran off to see to my demands. I directed Helen to watch over Lillian and Cassie and then ran after Carlos. My problem was that I was so befuddled after my time with Cassie that I didn't know where I was running. I ended up in the hanger staring at the shuttle that had brought my friend back from the Queen's ship.

Something was drawing me inside the sleek vessel and I had a hunch it was the next installment in the Queen's treasure hunt. Standing in the open hatch I marveled at the clean lines of the interior and the commodious layout of the flight crews seating. What struck me as obvious was that nothing on this ship was designed or crafted by the Queen or her people. I wished Lawrence was with me so he could point out how things worked. More importantly, point out what didn't belong. I put a call out to him.

"Lawrence, are you hearing me?"

"Damn, Mike, yours is the first friendly voice I've heard. Why are they treating me like I'm some kind of an alien agent?"

"Partly my fault and partly because you arrived here in one of your consorts shuttles escorting someone who in fact could be an alien agent. We need to determine what went on during your missing days, partner, but I'm not really concerned about it at the moment."

"That doesn't sound too reassuring. If not the missing time, what then?"

"I'm in the Jinn shuttle and something about it doesn't feel right. You know I'm not a pilot or an engineer so I need your expert opinion. What am I missing?"

"I know what you're feeling but never got the chance to look around. The Jinn pilot put me in the driver's seat before my curiosity went too wild so I had to concentrate on flying. Do you think that was the plan?"

"Queen knew you liked to fly but it certainly was convenient, wasn't it. Look, I'm going to have Carlos convince your security guy to bring you out here. Maybe with two sets of eyes the anomaly will jump out at us."

I kept scanning, looking for I didn't know what until the sound of shoes scuffing across the concrete floor got my attention. A moment later Lawrence was standing next to me with his hand on my shoulder.

"Thanks for getting me out of that room. It almost felt like I was a captive on Queen's ship again and I was about to crack up."

"Not a problem. Sorry you were the one who got sucked in to that bitch's trap. She had me all primed for the honor. I almost felt jealous when she chose you instead and then I didn't. So, what's wrong with this picture? It has to be obvious but I've looked at everything in this cabin, inch by inch, and it still won't come to me."

The two of us spent the next ten minutes asking each other about one element or another while I expressed my opinion about who might have designed and built this ship. I kept talking until Lawrence got very quiet and put a hand on my arm.

"The panel next to the copilot's seat, does it look odd?"

"It's just an inspection panel, hiding some internal controls, I guess."

"It's the only item not perfectly flush to the interior surface. That has to be it."

Neither of us wanted to be the first one to go over to the panel so we remained staring at it for several minutes.

"Do you think we should call one of the engineers out here to examine it before we blow all of us up?" I asked.

That must have motivated Lawrence, my telling him that an engineer might be more qualified than him. He walked over to the panel and one smooth move later the panel slid wide open. Both of us stood open mouthed as we saw vial after vial of liquid Dora stored in the cabinet.

"Who was all of that supposed to be for?" I wanted to know.

Lawrence was physically shaking as he looked at the vials. "What's the matter, partner? Why are you so upset?"

"I hoped I would never see another bottle of that shit. The fucking Queen would make me drink one each time she fucked me, telling me it would enhance my performance. By the time she was done with me and I had been dragged back to the dormitory I couldn't tell you the time or what day it was or how long I had been with her. I didn't even have enough energy to look at all the naked women in the room. That blue poison is some nasty shit, Mike, and just for kicks it is very addictive. Right now, I don't know which one of the three of us that came here on the shuttle was supposed to do something with this stuff. God help me, I hope it isn't me."

Lawrence slammed the panel shut and walked back to the hatch looking like a man who was trying to find an easy escape.

"Do you suppose Cassie has an idea about the Dora?" I asked. "You know she gave me a vial of it a little while ago. Pulled it out of her purse like it was another part of her makeup or something. Did you think it was strange that she was carrying a purse after being a prisoner for such a long time?"

"What do you mean she had a purse? I don't recall seeing one in the dormitory or as we were making our way to the shuttle. Are you positive she had a purse?"

"Oh yeah, I'm sure. It's an ugly shade of purple and she had the strap around her neck. It was on her when all three of you came out of the shuttle. I don't know how you could miss it."

"It seems I've missed quite a lot, partner. I'm not sure what's going on in my head but someone needs to help me figure it out before I do something crazy."

CHAPTER 30

AN HOUR LATER I WAS sitting with Doctor Adam Glass trying to figure a way for him to be present in Lawrence's head while I probed around. Lawrence had begged me to help him recover whatever time he had lost and had the feeling I could do that much the same as the Queen had. I never told him that I had already done the same thing with Cassie. In fact, it had surprised me that I was able to pull that off. Perhaps that was another gift from Queen. In the end, Doctor Glass was going to have to monitor both Lawrence and me.

I wasn't sure what Queen had done to my friend, other than the obvious in her boudoir, but the inside of his mind was as crazy as a carnival fun house. Thoughts were careening around with few of them having anything to do with the one that came after. I could pick up a word or phrase but nothing made sense. My biggest surprise was when I said 'Knock it off' and was able to stop all the uncontrolled motion and reorganize the patterns so that everything was logical. Just when I was starting to see a pattern to his thoughts Lawrence kicked me out.

"What the fuck did you just do, Sands? It felt like I had an earthquake happening in my head and then my mind went completely clear. Was any of that the Queen's doing?"

"You tell me. I was about to find out when you decided to evict me. What do you remember?"

"It wasn't just Queen in there. Something she called a Marauder was pushing her to change some things in my head. I felt like that thing was the one in charge and Queen was laughing as it told her to follow its directions. What's a Marauder, anyway?"

"The Marauders are the militant arm of Queen's colony. But, based on what you just said, what if the Queen and her people are actually the front for the Marauders? She claims they act on her orders but it sounded as if her role is to soften the next target by gaining their confidence and assistance leaving the way clear for the brigands to sweep in. If that's true, why did Queen give us the schematics for weapons more powerful than any we could develop? I got the sense that she was really impressed with our demonstration some time ago and couldn't wait to see the weapons used in a real fight. Does that suggest anything to you?"

Lawrence seemed to be in a daze and held up a hand to make me shut up. I waited while he reorganized his memories and then began to smile.

"Queen did leave me with something. It's actually a message for you. Do you want me to tell you what it says or would you like to dive in my head again?"

"Tell me what she said and lose the sarcasm."

"This is the first time I've seen this so give me a moment to make sure I've got it right. Okay, here goes. She's thanking you again for not objecting when she chose me instead of you for the insemination ritual. Yeah, well I wish it had been you instead of me, brother. Anyway, continuing. Her reason was to keep you mentally clear for what was to come. She could not relay that message in person because she was being monitored by the leader of the Marauders. She was being truthful about the Marauders following behind the Jinn and taking control of any other species with whom she came in contact. The Masters were a bonus but only useful due to their superior ships and navigational abilities. Her hope is that you will use the information she has given you to defeat the Marauders and set her free. The pilot who is assigned to transport your people has additional schematics waiting for you to download which should make your ability to defend yourself much easier. She only wishes her people were capable of using that information but is confident you will be able to do so. Please hurry as the Marauders might be much closer than she implied. This part is to me.

Tell Lawrence that I enjoyed his company immensely and will welcome him back whenever he chooses."

By the time Lawrence was done relaying Queen's message I was sitting with my head in my hands wishing I had never met her. Each time after having one of her mental conversations I was ready for a long nap and now, two conversations and one message later, I was exhausted.

"Does it strike you as strange," I offered, "that outside of the Jinn I am the only human able to initiate a mental conversation? Somehow, I've been given the ability to read minds and transfer data from the Jinn to my head and then download it to a fucking computer. What does it all mean, Lawrence? What did I get the two of us in to?"

"Right now, you dumb shit, it means Queen is giving us the means to protect ourselves. You need to get whatever the Queen's pilot has to offer and then negotiate some terms that get all the women Queen has kidnapped back to their families. But what about all of the liquid Dora in the shuttle? What do we do about that?"

"Maybe the pilot has the answer. I'm going to take an hour nap and then see what he has to say."

One hour became four and would have been longer if Lillian hadn't begun to massage my neck.

"I keep finding you in bed, Chief Sands. Shouldn't you be up and about saving the world?"

"No one ever told me that being a super hero was going to be such an exhausting occupation. I should never have gotten out of my police car that night to talk to Joe Farris."

"That would mean you'd never have met Alice and Jeannie and learned how to be a human being. You need to get moving, Mike. Lawrence told me about your conversation and I agree the pilot may hold the key to your questions. Would you like me to be your witness?"

"You can sit in if you want to but all the questions and answers are going to be inside the pilot's head. My head, too, I guess."

When Lillian and I entered the pilot's room he leapt out of bed and practically genuflected. I was ready to back out of the room when his voice was all over the inside of my head, shouting a lot like Lawrence had, not much of it making sense. I finally managed to get his mind to quiet down.

"Why are you so excited to see me now when you weren't that excited when you landed?"

"It was all so new, Chief Sands, and everyone was crowding in on me. My Queen had spoken so highly of you that I was afraid. You know that among the Queen's attendants you are almost a God, the only being that the Queen appears to fear. Not even the Marauders cause her to do that."

"Is that why you were chosen to pilot the shuttle, because she knows you're afraid of me?"

"My Queen gave me messages and demanded that I deliver them to only you. She said you would know how to retrieve them from my mind, as you did with the information she claims were found on the alien ships. She also said more information is carried in the minds of Lawrence and the girl."

"Wait, the Queen knew the girl was going to be on the shuttle? I thought that was Lawrence's decision."

"I begged for Cassie to be allowed to come. She and I have bonded which is something unusual in my culture. Then the Queen laughed and said it would create a larger puzzle for you to solve. All three of us have pieces of the information but I am the only one who knows that."

Everything I needed to pull information and transfer it to a server was located on the Apache Reservation outside of Roswell. Thinking about what I needed to do, all of which would have to be done in New Mexico, made me feel like a weight was being lifted. All I had to do was convince my project team, security and the President of my need to go back home in order to solve the mystery.

"We are going to make a journey and follow the Queen's clues. Did she assign a name to you?"

"She said I was to be called Roz and that you would understand why that was chosen."

"Your Queen has a sense of humor, Roz. Of course, she would name you Roz since she knew that was where we needed to go to pull the data. So, one last question; why did you bring all of the liquid Dora?"

"I'm glad you found it," he said with relief. *"Queen was afraid the Marauders would get to it first. It is the last of the highly concentrated liquid made from the Earth harvest. A very small amount in the vials is given to the workers and the captive females although Cassie and I refused to drink it. Queen also uses it to bend the members of her confederation to her will. Also, all of my science team was told to use it when we try to solve a difficult problem."*

"Besides being the pilot you're also a scientist? Do you have any other secrets to tell me, Roz?"

"Won't you see all of them when we travel to your home? There is one more thing. The shuttle has a vast amount of information stored in its systems that should aid you in upgrading your fleet. Not even the Queen knows about that."

I had almost forgotten that the Jinn workers had almost no guile and took everything at face value when asked to divulge information.

It was time to make my arrangements. Lillian and I walked back to the team office so I could brief them regarding my session with Roz.

Reminded by Carlos, my next move was to call the President to get his approval to travel to Roswell. He was busy dealing with another world crisis so I was told he would call me when he had a few free seconds. Lillian was not happy with my decision to go but knew I would eventually provide the team with far more data. She was also unhappy about my leaving since we had just managed to rekindle an emotional connection with each other. But, knowing she would have total leadership of the team, it eased her pain.

Security was another matter. Carlos was adamant that going to Roswell was a bad idea. He tried to cite the many reasons how I could be compromised but, after an extended argument, ended up agreeing but only if he was able to enhance my security. That was when I surprised him with the information that Lawrence and Cassie were also going along and that we were taking the Jinn shuttle.

Everyone went to crisis mode, screaming that I was upsetting the many plans the team had in motion. All I could do was smile and sit back to wait for the call from Washington.

President Phillips was not amused by my request and spent five minutes telling me so in a very profane outburst. When he wound down, I was finally able to get a word in.

"This is all to our benefit, Mister President," I started to say when I was cut off by two more minutes of verbal abuse.

"Damn it, Sands, every time I hear from you it costs the government more time and money. Are you certain that the information you are going to recover will be worth going to New Mexico? Can't you do something to retrieve it at Edwards?"

"The equipment and my Jinn support team are on the Apache Reservation. Plus there will be fewer interruptions while I am hooked up to the machines needed to make the data transfer. You are more than welcome to send a support team to make sure the downloaded data gets back to Edwards for analysis."

"Why thank you very much for your considered opinion on what I can do, Chief Sands. All I can say is that you better come back with some shit that will knock those bastard Marauders right out of my fucking sky. If you are going to be all wired up I want Carlos to give me hourly updates on your progress and that, my friend, is a Presidential Order."

"So I guess the answer is that I can go home?"

"Fuck you Sands, yes, you can go home."

CHAPTER 31

FROM THE GROUND I AM told the Jinn shuttle looks like any one of the swept wing attack fighters now in use by the military so it didn't attract too much attention until it made a vertical landing on the Res. Lee Ann, Alice and Jeannie were waiting at the foot of the ramp when my small army of passengers deplaned, or rather de-shuttled. Carlos and Lawrence got hugs from the girls while Cassie, Roz and the new security members gathered around waiting for introductions.

I hadn't gone two steps when Abraham Torrez, the Apache Chief, came barreling out of the Council Building and wrapped me in a hug. Every security person went to high alert until I could calm the situation and make an introduction. Following right behind the Chief were my Jinn companions. Surprising me was my friend, the Minister, or Gardener as I first knew him. He was smiling and began to pump my hand in a most earthlike manner.

"How did you get here, Minister? I'm surprised that Queen could afford to let you go."

"Did not the pilot tell you he brought me here before continuing on to your base? The Queen's hand is evident, once again. Queen wanted me to witness the data transfer but did not say why. Did she say anything to you, Mike Sands?"

"I'm solving mysteries, Minister. Perhaps when I retrieve the files I'll have an answer for you."

Turning to Alice and after receiving another hug it seemed someone was missing.

"Didn't anyone contact Joe Farris? I had hoped he would bring his gnarly ass out here. I missed his daily insults while we were back in L.A."

"Joe said he would see us later today," Alice admitted. "He thought you might need some time with us before he created a scene. He did say he had some news about the sample you sent us."

"Speaking of samples, Lawrence and I found a shit load of very highly concentrated Dora in the shuttle. It would be interesting to see how that matched up to the sample Joe is working on."

"Why would the Jinn need such a concentrated formula?" Alice mused.

"The Queen controls her subjects by keeping them dependent, Alice Sands," I heard the Minister tell my wife.

Alice jumped when the voice entered her mind, having forgotten how the Jinn communicated. She was just as surprised when she felt me listening in. Both Minister and I got a dirty look as a result.

"Tomorrow, first thing, I need all of the equipment ready for my descent in the mind of Roz. Depending on how I feel, Lawrence and then Cassie will get their turns. For now, Roz is going to stay with Minister and his people and Lawrence and Cassie go home with my family. Does anyone have an objection?"

It seemed as if everyone was okay with me making all of the decisions but Roz looked somewhat disappointed.

"Chief Sanchez, I need you to find some camouflage to cover the shuttle. I know you have questions for me but it's going to have to wait until tomorrow. Alice, Lee Anne, please take me home."

Lee Anne began herding people to cars, with Lawrence and Cassie in hers, and we all made our way back to Roswell. The five-bedroom house I had built on the hill behind my old cottage had seemed way too large when it was only Alice, Jeannie and me but Lee Anne had managed to occupy some of the space and I assumed my women had plans for Lillian to occupy some more of it when she was in Roswell. Now with Lawrence and Cassie, plus the assorted and mandatory security personnel on hand, the house definitely felt crowded.

"The Boss approved us bringing in a couple of motor homes," Carlos announced at six thirty the next morning. "Ten of us trying to occupy the last bedroom or your bonus room just doesn't cut it, Mike, especially when we have agents continually changing shifts. My orders are to have someone close to you, Lawrence and Cassie at all times. I understand Alice and Jeannie's agents already have their own camper at the house so that's one spot we don't need to mess with."

"Am I going to have to contend with my own cavalcade of security cars each time I need to go someplace?" Carlos looked at me as if the question was stupid. "Isn't that going to attract a little too much attention? You have to remember how many conspiracy theorists live or visit here every week. I can see the online pundits having a field day with that picture or don't you agree?"

"Short of moving to the Mescalero Reservation, Chief Sands, what do you suggest?"

"The Apache are not going to be happy having a bunch of Feds running around their sacred grounds which is why I opted to stay here at my house. You have to realize that all of us tromping around the Res is going to put a lot of pressure on my father-in-law especially when all of us descend on his headquarters for as long as it takes to retrieve whatever the Queen stored in the heads of my three house guests." I was beginning to get agitated. "This house is my sanctuary, Carlos, my only respite. I have already done far more than I intended when this whole experience started out in the desert and now I need to rest."

"I don't think the President is going to have much sympathy with any of that, Mike, not when the threat of an alien invasion still looms over us. The reality of all this is that you and Doctor Farris started this carnival and you, at least, are expected to see it through." Carlos was working hard to make things work and finally said, "How's this for a solution? You and whoever you are mind-fucking that day will travel to the Res in one vehicle with whoever is that day's security team. Everyone else stays here with the remainder of the security team. Alice and Jeannie can go about their normal routine with their own security personnel. That way we keep the traffic to the Res to a minimum and you don't have to worry about keeping an eye on Lawrence and Cassie. Does that work for you?"

"Do I really have a choice, Carlos? Set it all up but you get to be my bodyguard, just as you have been, and I don't want to hear any gripes about being overworked."

Carlos's smile was all the answer I was going to get.

Finishing my second cup of coffee I realized I needed to get moving. Alice and Jeannie had departed for school an hour ago and the empty kitchen table was making me glum. I kicked myself in the butt and contacted Minister to let him know we were on the way.

"Minister, I will be with you in thirty minutes. Make sure Roz is hooked up and ready to go. How is he feeling this morning, is he up to all this?"

"The Pilot is ready but apprehensive. We await your arrival, Mike Sands."

I pissed off one of the security team by sitting in the front seat of the government Suburban while he had to sit behind me next to a smiling Carlos. Trying to remember all I had to do when I retrieved the ancient materials that jump started our space project reminded me that the entire process was going to be uncomfortable, both for me and whoever my daily subject was going to be.

I hadn't paid much attention to the drive home last evening but the morning revealed a lot of changes to the Res. There were new houses and pickup trucks, the result of increased tribal revenue due to the sale of Dora and technical information retrieved from the Ancient's alien records. I was feeling much happier as we pulled up behind the Tribal headquarters. The Chief was waiting by the rear door as I got out of the SUV.

"I'm glad you didn't bring an army of people, my boy. There were some of my people who thought I was being too generous to allow so many of the Whites to be here."

"You should know by now that I wouldn't allow that to happen. Lee Anne would be all over me with a tomahawk if I disrupted things too much. Your daughter has a very strong set of principles, as you should know."

"Am I allowed to know what you have planned? The Council needs to be appeased and I figured you would be too busy to speak to them."

"Tell them as little as possible, Abraham. Just tell them that all I am doing will eventually benefit the Tribe. I will say to you in confidence that our world is in a shit load of danger and the work we do here is meant to save all of us."

"What you say has never been far from the truth and I will pass that along to my people. By the way, I am glad you are back among us. Lee Anne is not the only one who has missed you."

The Chief left me standing outside as he disappeared inside the building. I followed as far as the stairs and went to the basement to meet my fate. The room no longer looked like a haphazard collection of tables and chairs. Somebody had obviously spent some money buying proper desks and chairs and had upgraded the equipment needed to download the data. It looked like a proper sound lab.

My entire Jinn technical staff, plus Minister, was practically standing at attention as I walked in the room. Roz was wearing a cap with a long cable on the side that was attached to a second cap that I assumed was for me. A second cable ran from my cap to a series of work stations.

"That looks pretty impressive," I remarked to the team. *"Who's responsible for all of the upgrades?"*

The entire team looked embarrassed and I knew it was a team effort.

"Okay, boys, let's get going. Someone hook me up."

One of the team made sure my cap was on properly and all the cables were positioned correctly while another verified that the connection to the workstations were in working order.

"Do you require some Dora before you start?" Minister inquired.

He was holding a vial of the concentrated Dora, presumable a vial taken from the shuttle.

"I don't think that's going to happen, Minister. If Roz requires some so that I can access his memories then give him a small amount. I'm sure I can do my job without it."

I waited for the drug given to Roz to take affect and then dove right in. Things in the Pilot's mind were a lot calmer than yesterday. There was practically a bunch of road signs directing my way to the stored files. The number of them seemed to be unending so I began the arduous task of transferring them through me to the server.

Time seemed suspended until I felt the hand of the Minister on my shoulder. I looked up to see him holding a glass of something that I knew was not Dora and gladly took a long swallow of whatever was in the glass. In seconds I felt energized and immediately turned back to my task. Two or three more times I was disturbed to find Minister offering me a liquid refreshment or food of some sort. I ate but never stopped working.

Sometime after dark all of the files had been downloaded. Roz appeared to be asleep in his chair and I knew I was not very far behind him. The Jinn removed his cap and took him to a cot at the side of the room. Minister was not in the room but Lee Anne was, looking worried as I struggled to stand.

"Don't you dare kill yourself getting all of that stuff out of their heads," she ordered before putting her arms around me. I think she was as much holding me up as giving me a hug.

I was too tired to talk so just held on as my Apache wife led me outside. The air was brisk and seemed to revive me so I included a kiss with the hug and watched Lee Anne smile.

"Do you have any idea what Minister was feeding me all day? It sure seemed to perk me up and keep me going."

"It was some of my father's secret Apache recipes. I'll let him know how much you appreciated it. Now, can I get your security team to take us home? I promised Warren he could return to his position in the front seat."

"And where are we going to sit?"

"We get the middle row all to ourselves. Carlos is going to drive and one of the other agents is getting the privilege of driving the Chief of Police's Explorer."

Putting my head on Lee Anne's shoulder I never made it out of the parking lot before I was asleep.

CHAPTER 32

THE FOLLOWING MORNING I AWOKE lying between two of my favorite women. I had no desire to move or get out of bed. The pressure in my bladder made the decision for me. By the time my morning necessities were complete, Lee Anne was waiting for me to continue my ablutions in the shower. Alice was ready to take our place as soon as Lee Anne and I got out making me wish I had built a bigger bathroom. I thought that maybe I should do that after I had finished saving the world.

Breakfast was almost over before Lawrence and Cassie, holding hands, made it to the kitchen both of them looking slightly embarrassed. My first thought was about Cassie's supposed commitment to Roz, the pilot. Alice, Jeannie and Lee Anne had all gone to work or school so I was on my own with that observation. I buried my head reading the morning news on my tablet and tried not to acknowledge what could end up being a difficult situation.

"So, are you finished with Roz or is there more data stored in his head?" Lawrence asked brightly, trying to start a conversation.

Taking time to look up it was obvious that Lawrence was trying to be the same unassuming rascal he had always been but with a bit more stress showing on his face.

"I've finished with Roz for now," I remarked dryly, "but with the Queen's usual ability to fuck with me he may still have more secrets buried. I guess it depends on what you and Cassie have waiting for me. Cassie is next on my schedule, at least according to the clue Queen left in Roz's head. All of this treading through people's minds is more difficult than I thought. I'm really not ready to do another download yet but maybe we can get it done this afternoon."

"Are we going to go out to the Reservation before then?" Cassie asked. She looked like she would prefer going any place but there knowing I was soon to be running around in her head again.

"Is there some reason for not going early so we can get prepared?" I replied with a little bit of rancor, looking at both Cassie and Lawrence.

"You seem upset that Cassie and I spent the night together," Lawrence declared hotly. "We spent a lot of time together on Queen's ship, partner."

"Roz said much the same thing about him and Cassie, only adding that he and Cassie had bonded over their relationship. Does that mean something different to the Jinn than to humans?"

"It's all a matter of survival, Mike. Cassie and I are both back on Earth and not being held hostage any longer. Roz will have to adjust to this new dynamic," Lawrence asserted.

"Just so we are clear, all three of you have information that might help in creating a defense against the Queen or her Marauders. I don't want a war to develop before I have all of it locked up in one of the servers. Perhaps you three can create something positive out of your relationships much as my wives and I have done but please don't fuck things up before my work is done."

I didn't wait for a response. I grabbed my tablet and retreated to the back patio where I joined a group of agents who were enjoying coffee and the morning sunshine.

At two o'clock I grabbed Cassie and our security team and made our way to the Reservation. I left Lawrence at the house with orders to his security team to keep him there. Arriving at the Council offices it didn't come as a surprise to find two dozen members of the tribe gathered outside to see what I was up to. Some of them had gone so far as to look under the camouflage to get a peek at the shuttle. Everyone made room as I stepped out of the Suburban so that Cassie and I could make our way in to the building. We were greeted at the door by my father-in-law.

"Sorry about the welcoming committee," Abraham said. "Someone on the Council must have opened his mouth and you know how the Apache communication system works. Tell one person and ten instantly know what was said. Anything I can get you, my boy, other than the Apache snacks I provided yesterday?"

"That was well received, Chief, and will be again, if you don't mind. When all this is over, I will give you a brief heads up so you can calm any frayed nerves on the Council."

Squeezing the older man's shoulder, I escorted Cassie to the basement.

Minister smiled when we walked in and immediately took charge of Cassie by getting her cap in place. I was happy to see that Roz was nowhere close by. My attendants got me hooked up and before Cassie could think about what was going to happen I entered her head. The clue that I had found in Roz's head led me directly to the hidden files in Cassie's mind, saving me much time and fruitless searches. Even having transferred Roz's data, much like my earlier explorations, I always managed to retain a lot of the technical material.

The information in Cassie's mind fitted seamlessly with Roz's and gave me a general understanding of the next generation of weapons that needed to be developed. I was also given the last clue to locate the information held in Lawrence's head. As a bonus, Queen had left a clue to more files hidden in my own head, not to be located or opened until after I had finished with Lawrence.

When I became aware of my surroundings, I was surprised to find that only two hours had passed. Cassie had been disconnected and was asleep on a cot but, unlike yesterday, I felt invigorated. It surprised me to find three members of my Edward's engineering team standing behind me as I was unwired, all of them appearing awed.

Reggie Ward, the Chief Engineer under Lillian, and a former collegiate basketball player, bent down to review what was appearing on the monitor on the table.

"Do you understand all the gobble de gook that's on the screen?" he asked.

"A program I developed a couple of years ago will do a rough translation, enough that you should be able to fill in the blanks. By the time all the information has been retrieved and downloaded you should have learned most of a new language, one that is not spoken by any culture on Earth. My Jinn team can help you through it."

"I thought I was surprised that a small-town police chief could be at the head of a project this large but you have surprised me again, Mike," Reggie remarked to the unspoken agreement of his two colleagues. "It makes me wonder what you have up your sleeve for a follow up."

"Depending on what we need to do to keep the world safe, my follow up is to retire and let everyone else do all the heavy lifting."

"Yeah, and I think Lillian has some plans for that, as well. So, what can we do while all the information is being digested?"

"The data still needs the last piece from Lawrence to complete the schematics. You have to realize that Queen has no one who can decipher any of this data and no way to build any of the weapons. She is showing a lot of trust that we won't use them against her after any confrontation with the Marauders. At the same time, she is making me work for the designs. Queen believes in trading favors so we have to be wary of what she might want from us in return."

Getting up from the desk I started to walk out of the room, stopping at the doorway.

"You can take all the time you need to review what's on the screen but remember that we are guests of the Mescalero Apache nation. I will be conferring with the Tribal Council if you need me."

Abraham was waiting for me at the lab doorway.

"How could you know that the Council wanted answers about all the government people on our lands and want them immediately? Are you able to read our minds like those of the aliens?"

"You made me one of you, Chief Sanchez, and I would have wanted answers just as they do having seen all of the agents climbing off of the shuttle. Let's go ease their minds and then have a drink. We both might need one by then."

The Council actually took it easy on me only needing reassurances that the men in suits were not going to interfere with the Tribe's way of life. My guarantee was all they needed and sooner than I expected the Council joined the Chief and me for that drink. Questions about my relationship with the President occupied most of the conversation. That's where I learned they liked John Phillip's outspoken way of delivering a message. It didn't hurt when I told them that he was a member of the Osage Nation and often fought for Native American Rights.

Two hours of conversation coupled with my afternoon with Cassie had used up most of my energy. I begged off any further questioning and made my way downstairs to get Cassie ready for the drive home. She was sitting on the cot with Roz sitting next to her and not looking too happy. Unconsciously using one of my new gifts I found myself listening to their conversation, hoping it was not going to be acrimonious.

"I don't know what you want me to say, Roz," Cassie was trying to explain. *"We were on your ship and I had little or no say in what I was allowed to do. I appreciate that you protected me but now we are on my world not yours. Here I am a free person and can do what I want."*

"Doesn't the bonding we agreed to matter to you?"

Roz was becoming angry; the first time I had observed a Jinn about to lose his temper.

"I broke an oath to my Queen when we bonded, an oath that I would only be true to her. What do I do now, answer me that?"

"You can do whatever you want on this planet. There is nothing that says you need to go back to the Queen's ship."

"So, I stay here and who do I stay with? My brothers all live together much as they do on the ship but I learned a different way to live being with you. There are no female Jinn available to me, other than the Queen, and now she has Lawrence. Do you plan to share him? And if you do, why can't you share time with Lawrence and me?"

That last statement seemed to take both Roz and Cassie by surprise. If taken to its logical conclusion, things might work out for the three of them so long as Lawrence could buy in to a polyamorous arrangement.

Cassie seemed to have stopped talking so I took her arm and led her to our car. She was quiet the entire ride home which suited me fine. All of the data I'd received from Roz and Cassie was fighting with the old information already in my head leading me to believe I was going to get a major surprise when Lawrence's data was recovered and my final piece was released.

Later that evening Alice and Lee Anne dragged me away for a quiet dinner, as quiet as two talkative wives can be when they haven't seen much of their husband.

"You seem so quiet tonight," Alice said when she and Lee Anne took time from their conversation to actually speak to me.

"Sorry, but my head is so full of facts and diagrams that normal conversation is almost like a foreign language. I still have to follow Queen's clues and get more information from Lawrence. I don't know why I was so taken with her but she has to be the worst and most devious thing to have come in to my life."

"And yet," Lee Anne added with a smile, "she and her Jinn brought all of us together and made you a household name in the Science Fiction world. How many other people do you know who can claim they have the President of the United States on speed dial or have flown a space ship in outer space? So all in all I'd say you were pretty lucky and a very special man. Don't you agree, Alice?"

There was a certain sense of irony in what Lee Anne said but I could also see that both women were going to tease me unmercifully until I joined in the joking. Their attitude had the desired result and we spent the rest of the meal laughing at all of the weird things that made our lives so eventful.

The following morning it was Lawrence's turn. He and Cassie made their way to the table holding hands but neither of them was smiling.

"I'm not going to ask what's bothering you two. Just keep things under control until Lawrence and I are done today. Are you ready to go, Lawrence, or do you need more time?"

"Let's get this over with, Mike. When we're done, maybe you can explain how my life got so complicated."

CHAPTER 33

OW IS IT THE QUEEN can hide shit in our heads but you need all of this equipment to get stuff out?" Lawrence asked as he was being fitted with his cap.

"Were you aware of any equipment on the Jinn ship or were you unconscious while they worked on you?" I quipped. "Personally, I have no memory of anything during those days except for you and Queen rutting. My biggest memory is of eating a bunch of delicious treats I had taken to my quarters and then waking up in my bed after what I thought was some four days later. How the Jinn do their mind trick is still a mystery. All I know is that I can remove what she has put in and right now that is what I am going to do."

As with Cassie, Queen's clue took me to a treasure trove of files; more than Cassie had stored in her head but less than Roz's.

During the morning and afternoon I recalled being offered food and drink but there was no memory of taking a break. In the middle of the download one of the files was addressed to me. It was another note from Queen. I opened it with some trepidation.

"You are doing well, Mike Sands, better than I expected if you have gotten this far. You now have almost all of the files recovered from the Ancient's memories and must do what the Jinn have not been able to do...make sense of them. There is one more piece of information that is not in the minds of your three companions. You will need to look deep inside of yourself to find my last message. It is the piece that is most important to me and the Jinn. It is not to be downloaded, merely read and acted upon. You will need the full-strength Dora to go that far in your mind but I now have every confidence you can do it. The Jinn are depending on you."

The message ended on that dire warning and I was back downloading Lawrence's files.

It was close to six o'clock when I felt a soft cheek press against mine and Alice's tangy smelling perfume invaded my senses.

"We just put Lawrence on the cot, baby, and you look like you could do with a nap yourself."

One of the techs was removing my cap as Alice helped me stand.

"It appears that I have one more mind to search to complete this mission, Alice, and I'm not sure I want to go there."

"So, why don't you stop? Can't we get by on everything you've gotten so far?"

"The engineer's maybe but not me. Queen left me a personal challenge and it seemed to be as important as the rest of the files we've already recovered. But it's going to have to wait for another day. Actually, I'm afraid to see what she wants of me. Somehow, I know it's going to be painful, no matter what she says."

"Try not to worry about it until tomorrow. Right now, Carlos is going to drive us home so I can help you take a long soak in the hot tub. Lee Anne and Jeannie will probably be joining us so no hanky panky, buster."

Sometime later in the evening it dawned on me what Queen had said. Her message was for me alone and it required liquid Dora. If it didn't need to be stored in a server, I could retrieve the file from anywhere. There was no need to go to the lab. All I needed was one vial of the drug and someone to stand by to make sure I didn't flame out. I decided I wanted that person to be the one who got me in this mess. I made a call to Joe Farris.

"I wondered if you were still talking to me, Chief."

"No matter what else that has happened my life has definitely changed since we met, Doctor Farris. I'm sorry if I've not taken more time to check on you but I have passed along most of what we've learned so you could stay current."

"That I can agree on. I just didn't want our relationship to only be built on a blue field in the desert."

"It's a lot more than that, old man, and because it is I need a special favor."

"Oh, so now it's me granting favors, is it? You've got this whole thing by the balls and you need my help? Talk to me and let me know how else I can be of service."

"Queen stuck something in my head and I don't want to retrieve it by myself. If I go ballistic, I don't want Alice or Lee Anne to get caught in the inferno but I know you could handle it. It's a lot to ask but would you be willing to do this for me?"

Joe was silent for a long time and finally gave a loud sigh.

"You just need to tell me where and when, Mike, and I'll be there."

"I would like to do this at your place, Joe. You've got all the lab facilities in case there is an emergency. I need to go to the reservation first to grab a bottle of Dora and then I'll go directly to your house. Is that agreeable?"

"What's the Dora got to do with this? I've got some misgivings about that shit. It has so many strange properties in the concentrated liquid form it makes me wonder what it's really used for. But yeah, use my house if you want. Just don't expect me to clean it for you."

By the time I crawled in bed that night I was afraid the anticipation of what I needed to do would keep me awake. I didn't tell anyone about my plans for the next day and that included Carlos. When I woke at five, I realized I had not had any trouble falling asleep. I snuck out of the bedroom carrying my clothes and dressed in the kitchen.

I decided to forego breakfast and stopped at my favorite donut shop, Mamma Tucker's, for coffee and a bear claw. This is where it had all begun when Crazy Joe approached me at three in the morning over three years before. That thought was bouncing around in my head the entire trip out to the Reservation. The roads had been free of traffic as was the Council parking lot when I pulled up next to the Jinn shuttle. I expected there to be security around the ship but no one was guarding the alien vessel.

The hatch was closed and the ramp retracted when I walked up making me wonder how I was going to get inside. As I was running my hands on the ship's skin trying to find a hatch release the skin seemed to shiver, the hatch opened and the ramp deployed. I could sense the ship in my head and knew it was reacting to some-thing else the Queen had left inside me. The compartment holding the Dora was closed but, as if anticipating my ap-proach, the door next to the co-pilot's chair slid open. Several bottles of Dora were missing making me wonder who else had been at the stores of the concentrate. I grabbed one bottle of Dora and retraced my way outside as the storage door slid shut.

I was half way down the ramp when Carlos stepped out of the shadows.

"Kind of early to be out and about, isn't it?" Carlos said with a smile

"Is there any way I can do anything on my own around here, Carlos?"

"I don't suppose this is one of those times you need some privacy, like going to the bathroom?"

"Am I going to get that privacy or are you going to insist on standing next to me all day?"

"Alice was worried about you, Chief. She said you were acting kind of weird last night and wanted me to keep a close eye on you. She thought you were going to retrieve a message of some kind and thought I could be of some help. Are you going to let me do that?"

"Fuck, I didn't want to get so many people involved in this."

"Would I be one too many or perhaps just enough? Alice thought she heard you on the phone to Doctor Farris so I'm going to assume he is part of this."

"Look, Carlos, I'm on the way to Crazy Joe's house so that he can monitor me while I follow Queen's instructions. I'll trust you to come along but no one else is to know anything until it's over. Can you agree to my terms?"

"Spoken very much like John Phillips without the salty language. The President would be proud. So, I'll drive and you direct me to the elusive Doctor Farris's abode. He won't try to shoot me when we get close, will he?"

I began to laugh, as much for the picture of Joe with a gun in his hands as to the humor of the situation. I was as stress-free after that as I had been in days. The drive back towards Roswell with the bottle of Dora resting in my hands seemed to take no time and we were soon pulling up next to Joe's home and lab.

"Have you met Joe, Carlos?"

He shook his head and was staring at the tall, thin, man standing on the porch.

"This should be fun," I remarked as I climbed out of the Suburban.

"You didn't say anything about bringing a god damn suit with you," Joe shouted.

"He's my god damn body guard, you old fart. The President said I had to have him with me wherever I go. You never can tell when an assassin might pop up, even out here in the wilderness. He's good people, Joe, and a friend."

"Well, it's on you if he turns out to be the assassin. Come on in so we can get this foolish thing done."

Joe turned and went inside. He never looked back to see if we were following him.

The last time I was in the house it looked more like a laboratory than a residence. Nothing had changed. There was a couch in a corner and a fairly new forty-inch flat screen television across from it but those were the only creature comforts visible.

"I want a small sample of what's in your bottle to compare it to what Alice gave me and the raw Dora I got stashed away. What are you going to need me and Rambo to do while you're in dreamland?"

"If everything is like it's been so far downloading all the data nothing other than making me drink some fluids if I've been under for a couple hours or more. If I'd thought about it, I would have gotten some of that Mescalero shit that Chief Torrez fed me. Otherwise, don't let me kill anyone, especially myself."

Joe poured off a little of the Dora from my bottle and placed it in the lab. I closed my eyes and downed the rest of the blue fluid, finding that the taste was somehow familiar but not unpleasant. It could have used a little sugar. Everything in the room was immediately brighter and I found myself numb and falling on the couch. If this was how Lawrence felt after receiving a dose of Dora before fucking the Queen, I didn't know how he managed to get an erection.

All that I could sense being active was my brain. It was like I was on a toboggan run and I was picking up speed every second. In front of me was a bright light, a light that got hotter the faster I approached it. Suddenly, my toboggan was off of the run and floating inside the light. Three files came roaring out of the brightest part and filled my head. One file had diagrams for one of the deadliest space weapons I had seen up to that date, much more powerful than anything I had downloaded. The second file had complete schematics for the Ancient's space ship, a sophisticated marvel with engines that could approach light speed or maybe transcend it. The last was the personal message Queen said was waiting.

'*Mike Sands, my potential consort, you must be surprised at the contents of what I've given you. Everything you have received prior to these files will be enough to defeat the Marauders and set us free. By us, I mean both of our worlds, yours on Earth and mine in space with my Consortium. I believe the weapon in the first of these new files may be more powerful than anything I have ever come across. Once the Marauders are defeated you will become a hero to many space going races. You will also become a marked man. There are worse things in space than those you will have defeated, many who will want to claim your death as a measure of their strength. This new weapon and the ship I've given you, combined with the fuel extracted from the Dora concentrate, will make you and all humans nearly invincible once you truly become a space going race. They are my gift for ensuring the Jinn are set free. As a bonus, the humans on my ship are now on their way back to your planet. Take good care of them as they carry precious cargo. I still have hope that one day you and I might mate and produce a superior breed of Jinn. Until then, Mike Sands, enjoy the gifts I have given you.*'

My eyes flew open just as Joe and Carlos grabbed an arm each and kept me from landing on my face as I leapt from the couch. The numbness had gone from my body leaving every nerve ending buzzing as if I had an electric cord attached to every one of them.

"Was that what you meant by us keeping you from killing yourself, Chief," Joe was saying as he struggled to keep my limbs from flying all over the place. "Committing Hari Kari by jumping off of a sofa isn't very effective."

Fighting to focus on Joe I finally smiled and calmed down, going from completely wired to a damp dishrag in seconds. I remembered Lawrence saying he had nothing left after a bout with Queen and now I knew why.

"I think I'm okay guys, just a little limp. Drop me back on the couch and let me rest for a minute."

"Did you get what you needed, Mike?" a very worried looking Carlos asked.

"More than what I expected and some I wish I hadn't. Joe, Queen said the concentrate is the basis for a powerful fuel. I'm going to let you develop it and see if Queen is telling us the truth. We need to find out how such an outstanding food source can also be such a powerful biofuel, all at the same time. For now, we need to get ready for another shuttle and the returning captives. But first, I need to get back to my family. That's your job, Rambo, to get me home. Don't mind me if I sleep all the way to Roswell.

CHAPTER 34

AND SLEEP I DID, DEEP enough that Carlos had to call on several of the security agents to hoist my limp body and carry me inside. Cassie and Lawrence were hovering over me when I was unceremoniously dumped on the couch.

"You look like shit, partner, what the fuck did you do?" Lawrence was like a mother hen as he got me a pillow and a glass of water. "You look like I did after a bout with Queen."

"You would know, wouldn't you? But to answer your question, I was told there was more data locked in my head and the only way to get it was to drink some of the concentrated Dora. I hope Queen doesn't have any more of those surprises waiting for me."

"You're doing a lot better than me. I wouldn't be awake for hours after taking a dose."

"Did Queen say anything about my sisters?" Cassie managed to ask by pushing Lawrence out of her way.

"She did. She said they were on their way back to Earth. Damn, I need to get back to the Reservation and I need Alice and Lee Anne to be there with me. You and Lawrence also need to be there."

"Why us, Mike, what can we do?"

Lawrence seemed to be nervous about something to do with the arrival of the shuttle but he refused to say why.

"Lawrence doesn't want to see any of the other women," Cassie said and smirked. "He didn't have enough energy to service any of them after fucking Queenie and me and that made them angry. It wasn't Lawrence's fault but you know how catty some women can be."

Truthfully, I didn't know since all the women I had associated with, even my ex-wife, were logical and mostly understanding. Maybe I was lucky but then I never made promises I was unable to keep nor did I denigrate any of them for their perceived failures.

"Look, there are twenty something women. . ."

"Twenty-four," Cassie interjected.

"Okay, twenty-four women coming back to a strange place on an Earth that may now seem even stranger to them. You two are the only ones they'll know who will not seem strange to them and might be able to ease their way back to Earth normal. Can you do that for them or at least for me?"

Cassie put an elbow in Lawrence's side before he nodded his agreement. He and Cassie were acting more and more like a couple no matter the short time they had known each other. Roz was going to be another matter.

Alice was at lunch when I called but was enthusiastic about being at the Council building when the Jinn shuttle arrived. She made me promise to wait at home until she picked Jeannie up from school so that we could all make the trip together.

Lee Anne had an appointment with Mayor Walter Boone about making her Acting Chief a permanent position but said she would be on the Reservation as soon as she could. I was still technically the Chief but hadn't sat in that office for months. Lee Anne had been a good fit in that position and deserved the job.

My next call was to my father-in-law, Chief Torrez, to give him a heads up about another shuttle on its way to Earth. I could sense him shaking his head on his end of the phone.

My last call was to the President's private number.

"Phillips here, what do you have for me Sands?"

"New, more powerful, weapons data has been received and is now being decoded. And, we have another Jinn shuttle on the way to Earth carrying the female captives. I'm on my way to the Reservation to meet it when it lands."

"Now listen to me Sands and don't give me any of your shit. I want every agent assigned out there with you when that ship lands. I know you think you know what's best when dealing with the Jinn and that fucking Queen but I know what's best for the country. Do not defy me on this."

"I had no intention of doing that, John, and was going to tell you I planned on all the agents being with us. Queen claims to be a captive of the Marauders and wants to give us everything we need to knock them out of the sky, so to speak. She could also be playing all sides against the middle in her little game and I do not want to be the loser in that contest. You've been a very patient boss so far and I appreciate the latitude you've given me. I think we are near the end game so bear with me a little longer."

"You make sure you're right, Sands. I want more good news on your next report."

I was still staring at my phone, concerned that the President had not lambasted me with five minutes of profane abuse, when Alice and Jeannie walked in the house. She must have busted every speed zone on her way to pick up Jeannie and then get here in time to join us for the ride to the Reservation. Jeannie was so excited about seeing an alien shuttle she could hardly stay still in her seat. Our caravan of official cars made its way along the dusty road to the Apache Council offices picking up a following of Apache residents wondering what was going on. By the time we arrived behind the offices there were over thirty trucks and cars behind us.

Abraham and the rest of the Council members had set up a couple of banquet tables and chairs so the entire Council Membership could be outside to witness the landing. Since there was no indication when the ship would arrive, the members had arranged for food and beverages to be available for anyone hoping to be a witness. It had the air of a carnival and we were going to be the side show.

Abraham had made sure that my family had seats in the shade and a steady supply of Apache snacks and drinks. I needed the energy the snacks provided, especially since they were enriched with Dora, but declined every offer of a beer.

The warm air had me dozing and Lee Anne, who had arrived while I napped, had taken over as my watchdog, making sure no one woke me up. It had to be a couple of hours after we had arrived that the tenor of the noise changed from raucous to a quiet buzz. The change woke me up in time to see the shuttle off in the distance making a silent descent to our location. Watching the ship float above us and then settle much like a feather on the wind, had the entire audience spellbound and quiet.

This ship was twice the size of the first shuttle and sported gun ports both front and aft. It looked like a thoroughbred next to its smaller, sleeker, cousin. For seconds the only sound was that of the metal surface of the ship crackling as it lost the heat it had gained as it made its way through our atmosphere. As soon as the side hatch opened and the ramp deployed our apache audience backed away as if demons might pour out and attack them.

Lawrence, Cassie and I walked to the foot of the ramp as the first of the women, mid-twenties and very pale, came outside and stopped, looking like she was about to panic. She seemed to gain her equilibrium when she spied Cassie and Lawrence so it was a surprise when first she and then the remainder of the women ran down the ramp and surrounded me, pushing Lawrence and Cassie aside. It was eerie when none of the women made any noise so, on a hunch, I tried to listen to them much as a Jinn would. All I got at first was a cacophony of sounds, all of it seeming to express their happiness at being home.

"Ladies, you have to quiet down. I can't understand what you're saying. Have you forgotten how to speak aloud?"

In the ensuing quiet the first of the women who exited the shuttle smiled.

"My name is Chrystal and we kind of forgot for a minute. Queen said we would be very pleased when we saw you, Mister Sands, but she understated things, as usual. I know the rest of the girls want to say their own hellos but first I need to give you a message from Queen."

"Sure, Chrystal, what does she have to say this time?"

"She said it was extremely important and that you would know where to look. She also said that I should do whatever you said. Do you know what she meant by that?"

Alice and Lee Anne had made their way to my sides, concerned that so many women were vying for my attention and that one of them had it. Truthfully, it made me a little nervous, too.

"Chrystal, I need to look inside your head for the message. Do you mind if I do that?"

"I guess that's what Queen meant when she said you would be able to see through me if I acted foolish. Am I foolish?"

"No, not foolish, just a messenger."

Not waiting to explain more I dove right in. The message was in the forefront of Chrystal's brain and ready to be read.

"Mike Sands, this is the last part of my negotiation. It is an explanation as well as a plea. You are aware that the Jinn do not give gifts without receiving something of equal or greater value in return. All of the files were of no real value to me because no other race, mine included, could decipher what was written or use any of the information. They do have value to you and that is what's important to the Jinn. Failure to use what I've given you will result in the destruction of both our races so I implore you to be diligent in completing the manufacture of the weapons. You should know that you have already satisfied the need for payment for all I have given you. First, both you and Lawrence have provided the seeds for the next generation of Jinn. I apologize for the deception but the time you thought was missing was used to take your seed and fertilize a new crop of my eggs. Both you and Lawrence are the fathers of the new Jinn and will be celebrated. Secondly, the women who surround you have also been inseminated with your seed, seed that has been enhanced with my genetic material. Each woman will have a multiple birth although not nearly so many as I can produce. Human limitations make two or three optimal. All of the children will be yours, Mike Sands, a hybrid Human/Jinn. I will meet with you again, if only to see how our children are doing. I still find you the most interesting human I have met.'

"Chrystal, are you aware that you are pregnant?"

"Of course, we all know that and we also know that you are the father of our babies, Cassie's, too."

The gasp I heard came from everyone standing beside or behind me, the loudest coming from Lawrence and Cassie. Alice and Lee Anne grabbed my arms and held on.

"Queen said you would be surprised but that you would make sure that we were well taken care of."

I could hear Carlos in the background saying to one of the other agents, "Boy oh boy, the President is really going to love this information."

Lee Anne jumped in to rescue me. "Do any of you have families that we can contact? I'm sure many of you must have parents or partners who would be relieved to know you are alive and safe."

The returnees began to look panicked and I noticed they all began whispering to one another. Finally Chrystal turned back to me.

"We were under the assumption that we could stay with you, at least that's what Queen said. You are the father and should be near your children."

The closest Apache to overhear that part of the conversation put the information on the Indian grapevine. Within minutes the carnival had become an instant baby shower with locals offering food and drink to the pregnant newcomers. I stole away with Alice and Lee Anne, making a beeline for the Council lounge and tried to explain about the Jinn genetic infusion.

Alice looked sympathetic but Lee Anne was laughing.

"I hope you two have some idea what we are going to do with twenty-five pregnant women?" I wasn't seeing the humor in the situation.

Alice began to smile. "What if there were twenty-seven women who were pregnant?"

I began to tremble and looked crazy thinking about Queen's last message about enhanced genetic stock.

"Ease up, Chief," Lee Anne chided. "We were pregnant before you made the trip to the Jinn ship. It never seemed the right time to tell you with all the shit going on. Why does that seem to bother you?"

"You have no idea what just went through my mind. When Queen stole my sperm she added some of her own DNA before impregnating the girls. I never slept with that devious woman but I still got fucked."

"And all those women out there could say the same," Alice remarked. "How do you think they are going to feel if you abandoned them? Look, there's a partially empty dorm at the college. Get your pal, the President, to apply some pressure on the Dean to designate that part of the building as a government research and test facility.

The Dean will love the possibility of some extra government funding. We'll move the ladies in and provide them with medical care until we can find a more permanent solution."

"Are you saying you are okay with having that many women carrying my offspring so close to where you teach?"

"I'll get Crazy Joe Farris involved and we'll conduct some experiments so we can track the fetal development. Maybe we'll be able to write a paper on what we find. It'll be fine, Mike. Our team will make it fine."

"Just think of all the siblings our children will have to play with," Lee Anne added between guffaws.

During my call to the President, he laughed louder and longer than Lee Anne but agreed to have the Department of Education intercede with the college dean on our behalf. All twenty-five women would be given private rooms, unless they preferred to share, on two floors of the dorm. They would receive meals, medical care, an allowance for clothing and the ability to contact their families. In a not so big surprise, when told of the new arrangements, none of the women opted to leave Roswell.

Alice and Joe were left in charge of the returnees. Lawrence and I commandeered the Jinn pilots and the shuttles and flew them back to Edwards. We had ships to build and weaponize and a war to contemplate. Looking at what I left in Roswell for Alice and Lee Anne to handle I think I got the better of that deal.

PART III

PREPARING FOR THE END GAME

CHAPTER 35

MY ENGINEERING TEAM COULDN'T CONTAIN their excitement when given the opportunity to examine the second shuttle. They quickly found numerous ways they could enhance the onboard weapons package. Joe Farris's research on the concentrated Dora revealed the Jinn secret for a long burning fuel that was one hundred times more powerful than anything used by rockets on Earth. Joe theorized that power could be optimized to over one thousand times the current strength which could, theoretically, power the new ships to travel at near light speed. However, none of the current Earth planes or rockets could use the super fuel, outside of the two Jinn shuttles and the Golden Eagle, making the completion of the new Space Force a priority.

There was still no word on the location of the Marauder fleet. Queen sent a periodic message letting me know that our sector of space was still clear. She never said more than that and would not respond to my requests for a conversation.

Six months had gone by since the Queen and the Jinn had supposedly left our solar system. Every long-range telescope on the Earth's surface and in space did a constant sweep searching for signs of the Marauders, or the Jinn, but the skies remained free of an invading force. Still working on the fear that Earth was a target the governments of most major countries had formed an alliance to build a space going force using the plans the Jinn had provided. A bonus came with the additional plans and specs found in the second shuttle's memory.

I was holding back on the last set of plans given to me by Queen in the hopes the massive ship and powerful weapon would never be required. If they were needed, the ship, due to its enormous size, could never be built on the planet's surface. It was a ship for another time, a time when we had a massive space station with manufacturing capabilities outside Earth's orbit.

During the week Lawrence and I worked long hours at Edwards with me having become the translation specialist for the Ancient's files. Working with the documents I found I had become as grounded in the new engineering science as any of the people assigned to my Project Roswell team. It made my more frequent theoretical discussions with Lillian both illuminating and somehow erotic. Along the way we had decided to share my quarters at Edwards which caused Alice and Lee Anne to chide me over my long hesitation to even speak to my ex-wife. Lillian occasionally joined Lawrence and me on our weekend trips back to Roswell just so she could check up on her pregnant sister wives. I truly believe she joined us so she could spend time with Alice and Jeannie, both of whom she had come to adore. Lee Anne and Lillian had a more complicated relationship; more to do with which one of them was now senior in the relationship.

Alice also insisted that I spend time at the university dorm, getting to know the women released by Queen all of whom were bearing my children. Chrystal had continued as the spokesperson for all twenty-four and made frequent comments about how I was going to father all of her future children once this clutch was born. That conversation usually caused me to make an early exit to my visit. Cassie and Lawrence were smarter and avoided contact with the other women, preferring each other's company, and spending a lot of time in their room at my family home.

Each visit to the dorm was nerve wracking to me but seemed to be appreciated by all of the women. I kept going because each visit caused some new bits of information related to my relationship with Queen to come unstuck from one or another of the women's head. It was the last trip that released a file, again I couldn't say from where or which of us it had originated, that changed everything, one more time.

I was still obligated to have a daily call with the President and this one was going to be different.

"Good morning, John, did I catch you at a good time?"

"Your calls break up lot of tedious shit I have to deal with, Mike. Please tell me you have something that will titillate my senses. I never knew being President could be so fucking frustrating. By the way, how's your growing family doing? You have no idea how happy I am that it's you and not me in that situation."

"Well, somehow my next bit of information will probably keep you interested for a little while longer. Another message surfaced today but I can't explain where it came from. It contains a little more history, if you want to call it that."

"Get on with it, Sands. I might need a break but I don't have all day."

"Why do we assume that there are Marauders waiting at our doorstep to attack us?"

"It's what that bitch Queen said was going to happen. She told me in my fucking head."

"Yeah, she told everyone but never once provided any proof there were any Marauders out there. Neither Lawrence nor I saw any evidence of them and like you, it was all hearsay. Here's my new supposition. There are no Marauders, at least not yet. Queen said from the first time we met that she wanted her Jinn to be more aggressive, much more like humans. What if she was goading us to become even more aggressive than we are by giving us plans for powerful weapons and ships that her people couldn't understand or build all so we could use them in defense of her people? Perhaps it was in the hopes that to prevent raids by an unknown enemy we would go to space to intercept them."

"I assume you have a point to make somewhere in this narrative? Tick tock, tick tock."

"Mister President, Queen wants us to become the Marauders."

"That has to be the most far-fetched theory you have thrown my way, Mike Sands. How in hell did you come up with that?"

"Here are a couple more points that recently came to light. Doctor Farris found that the version of Dora that was originally given to us has a diminishing level of strength if left in the fields where they are now grown. Queen must believe that if we became totally dependent on the Dora for food, medicinal properties or fuel and run out of suitable terrain in which to grow it we would be forced to return to a time of greater starvation and fewer health benefits, things that could make us more dependent on the Jinn. Queen's usual option was to go to new planets and find fresh fields. That was her original intention when she came here. But Farris has found a way to enhance the growth of the Dora and enrich the soil of the current fields eliminating our need for Jinn assistance. Second point; as you are well aware we now have females on this planet that are pregnant with babies who contain Jinn DNA. Queen has hundreds more maturing eggs on her ship that have human DNA. She wants to see how our female's babies are progressing in comparison to her eggs or which batch is going to be the most aggressive. Conversely, I have many on my team who want to see what kinds of hybrids are going to be hatched on the Jinn ship. Queen is still close by, John, close enough to monitor our space going progress and to see which version of the hybrid humans will be most successful. Things aren't over with the Jinn; they might just be starting."

"You weren't drinking when all of this came to you, I hope. Do you have any proof, Mike, or are we going to go on your gut feeling again?"

"Each of the damn snippets came from the minds of the women at the dorm. Each is kind of like breadcrumbs that when collected and put together make an entire loaf of bread. Queen loves to play games and, to her, this is a game of strategy. She keeps poking at the human bees nest, but she doesn't realize that it is a whole hive of killer bees waiting to pounce. Here's the deal; we've improved on the design of every weapon that came from the Ancients, increased the power potential of the Dora biofuel, and actually found a way to avoid Dora crops failing so why would Queen run away from all that. She needs us much more than we need her."

"So, how much of all that do you think Queen knows and what do you suggest we do?"

"I've told her about a few small improvements. The only thing she's witnessed was one test fire of the first cannon that we developed. She has no idea what the latest fusion weapons are capable of. We could blow her out of the sky but she now has hundreds of humans on her ship and I won't risk their lives. I say we wait her out and see how far she wants to go in whatever games she's playing. I'm willing to bet that if challenged, there are a hell of a lot more tactical gamers in our arsenal that can outsmart one Jinn sitting in space."

"And you're willing to risk Earth on that hypothesis? God help you if you're wrong."

"We can wait for the mysterious Marauders to appear, John, or we can become them. Either way we end up the Jinn's masters. Better yet, it gives us the potential to become explorers of a vast new universe."

The silence on the Presidents end of the line stretched out for more than a minute.

"What have we become, Mike? Did the receipt of some new technology begin a process that is robbing us of our humanity? You're definitely not the same man I met not so long ago and I have to share the blame for putting you in that position. Reach back to who you used to be, my friend, to a time before that crazy alien forced her way in to our lives."

It was my turn to be silent.

"I don't know if that's possible, John, not with all the shit Queen loaded in my head. There's even more evidence of her meddling sitting in a dormitory on the college campus. That doesn't even address the potential babies in the nurseries on the Jinn ship. I used to be a passive cop and now I'm a half angry, middle aged, citizen who flies around in space ships and is about to become a father many times over. Thankfully, my family support system understands my dilemma. There's no way to reverse the course we are on, Mister President. Isn't it an old military axiom that we must 'Soldier On'?"

"I don't think I ever told you one other thing Queen said at the end of our conversation back before I had you kidnapped."

"What thing was that, John?"

"Before she got out of my head, she said that I needed to be wary because someday in the not too distant future Mike Sands was going to become the most powerful and most dangerous man in our universe. I thought she was trying to build up your credentials. Now I worry that she may have been right."

"Those are just words, John, meant to scare both of us. I'll try to be more human but I will do anything I can to protect our people and our planet. I hope you will continue to support me on this."

"I will, so long as you don't do anything to derail my reelection. We are a team after all."

CHAPTER 36

A M I A BETTER OR A WORSE person than when we first met?" I threw that out at Alice the morning after my conversation with the President.

"What do you mean better or worse? You've been given a great deal of responsibility and seem to be handling it. I mean there is definitely a wish on my part that you could be spending more time with your family here in Roswell but all of us, Jeannie, Lee Anne and myself understand what needs to be done. Is this about something the President said to you when you told him your theory about the Marauders?"

It was almost as if I didn't hear Alice as I started rambling.

"Do you remember when just the word science caused me to have a brain freeze, kind of like when I dropped that first piece of Dora on your desk while looking for an explanation? I had the same reaction to math problems in high school and college. Now I have technical discussions with the brightest minds in the country and offer suggestions that they find not only new but relevant. That is not the old me, Alice. That old me would love to read fiction about space travel and now I am engineering designs for a space station that will be used to manufacture the ships needed to make interstellar space travel a reality. Do you understand how scary it is when I try to understand how I got here?"

"Would you rather quit and watch everyone else get credit for all that you've accomplished? I don't think the new and improved Mike Sands would be able to accept that or retire. In fact, I don't think it would be allowed, if not by the President then by the Jinn Queen. You won't admit it but you're as much of a game-player as your adversary. If you don't believe me, ask Lee Anne or Lillian for their opinion. All I'm saying is we loved the man you were and all of us love the man you have become."

Alice followed up with a hug and a kiss as she made her way out of the house on her way to work. Still not feeling satisfied I evaded observation by Carlos and drove to the Reservation. I rounded up Roz, practically dragging him out to the large Jinn shuttle sitting in the rear parking lot. He was not happy about me making him fly the shuttle on a flight to an unknown location.

"I'm feeling unsettled, Roz, so I think we need to take a trip." That was all I would tell the Jinn.

"What of the marauders, Mike? Shouldn't we stay close to home until we have sufficient protection or some idea where they might be?"

"I'm not very concerned about Marauders, pirates, space bandits or a revengeful Queen. I want to be free of everything for a little while and you are going to help me get there."

"Is there such a place? My Queen frequently told us that there is always a consequence to what we do. What if we fly to a place where we encounter some unexpected event?"

"I am hoping that is the case, Roz. Does that make you afraid?"

"I have flown in space and that has never made me afraid. You are becoming so much like Queen, except you are prone to more drastic actions. That makes me afraid. Am I right to be afraid like that?"

"Queen wanted her people to be more aggressive, Roz, more like humans. If I frighten you think of what a whole world or ship full of half Human Jinn are probably going to be like. Who is going to be safe then?"

"That sounds a lot like Queen describing the Marauders. Is that what you believe is going to happen?"

"Just fly the shuttle, Roz. Take me someplace where I can think without any interference."

We flew to a point where the moon was on the opposite side of the Earth and far enough out that the International Space Station wasn't able to see us. I made sure that the upgraded weapons package that had been installed on the shuttle was armed and ready to fire before relaxing in my co-pilot's seat. I had come to believe there were no Marauders out here but I wasn't about to take a chance that I was wrong.

At some point, an hour or two or three later, Roz handed me a headset. One of the chores I had assigned to him was to dig out any old files left in the ship's memory that I might find interesting. Roz had been given a general knowledge of symbols to look for. As I was one of the few who could read and understand the Ancient's language, I usually had the first opportunity to read stories of a forgotten way of life. The Ancient's, I had discovered, were a lot like todays humans, full of secular hostilities and feuds, often resulting in internecine warfare.

The file that Roz had located and wanted me to read turned out to be a rare visual ships log, graphically presented by a medical officer. I was able to decipher nine words in ten but that was enough to gather the gist of the narrative even with the strange phrasing and syntax. The Ancient's ship that the Jinn had located had been disabled by one of a number of warring factions but was able to limp away to the asteroid where it landed and was later found. All of those onboard had decided to commit a ritual suicide in an honor death rather than surrender to their enemy. The log displayed a mostly clear picture of the medical officer, a picture that turned me cold. Separated by thousands of years was a picture of a being that looked more human than Jinn. To my eye the officer was most definitely a male. The strange thing was that the name Jinn was not found on any of the documents located on this vessel or the derelict found on the asteroid. If the log described the warring factions as technically savvy why were their descendants, the Jinn, so inept?

I had half an eye on Roz who had another set of headphones on. He could see the video but could not understand what was being said. His eyes were locked on the photo of the person speaking, a being much like himself. Roz turned to me with questions burning to be answered. I stopped the video and looked at my pilot.

"I know you have something to say, Roz. Spit it out."

"If that is a Jinn on the screen, is he my ancestor?"

"Nothing on the video identifies that person as being a Jinn. In fact, none of the files that you have recovered in the shuttle's memory identify any of the warring factions as being Jinn. This guy

seems to be a more highly developed version of your people but something must have happened to rob the Jinn of their technical abilities. Keep looking for more files, Roz. Maybe one of them will tell us some of the history we are looking for."

That was just what I needed, more reasons to wonder about Queen and her games. Now I had to wonder if she had any knowledge of her ancestors or their level of intelligence. Another thing that struck me as odd was that there was no mention of a Queen anywhere in the old video. You would have thought, had the old ones had one, the Queen would have issued the decree to commit suicide. She should have been the one recording the last message, not a medical officer.

Roz was unable to find any further video files but located a treasure trove of schematics for various pieces of equipment used on the shuttle. Being unable to read any of the technical information he kept placing the files in a folder on a jury-rigged thumb drive that I could access later and pass on to my team. That was how we passed the next few hours, Roz digging and saving and me reading. We would have stayed out in the darkness longer except that both of us had neglected to bring any nourishment with us.

The Council House was a hub of frantic activity, all of it directed to the fact that Roz, the shuttle and I had been missing for most of a day. Lee Anne was fuming as I stepped down the ramp.

"A call, a text message, or a fucking note about where you were going would have eliminated all this chaos you dumb shit." Lee Anne stopped herself one second from throwing a punch at me. "You had all of us worried when you didn't answer our calls. We thought the Marauders had finally arrived and took you."

The time away had wiped away most of the stress that had been building over the previous months letting my wife's anger roll off of me. I took her in my arms, albeit with a bit of a struggle, and let her cool down knowing I understood her concern.

"I'm sorry to have had everyone so upset but I needed the time away. Was Alice as worried as you?"

"Probably more, you doofus." Lee Anne threw a weak punch to my back. "She's inside on the couch. We had to give her a sedative." Another punch. "Jeannie is with her. You probably should go inside and calm her down."

"What about you, are you coming inside with me?"

"Not on your life. You get to handle the explosion all by yourself."

I stopped to grab some Dora laced pastry on my way, hoping the plant would give me some additional energy. Before I could take more than one step in the lounge Jeannie was wrapped around me like a soft blanket, crying her eyes out. That's when I felt sorry for neglecting to let my family know where I had gone and why.

Jeannie pulled me over to the couch where her mother was sitting and pushed me down next to her. Alice refused to look over at me, a sure indication she was upset.

"Sorry, babe, it was stupid and thoughtless of me. My only excuse was that I needed to get away from all the shit. I never wanted you to worry."

"It's bad enough that I worry every time you fly to and from Edwards in that alien shuttle but to disappear like that was too much, Mike. Never mind your family, look at all the turmoil you caused. I thought Carlos was going to have a heart attack. Was it really worth it to you to go where ever you went?"

"Yes, it was. If we can get out of here, I'll show you a file that changes everything. I'll have to translate but I would like your opinion and thoughts. Are you up to leaving?"

Everyone had questions about where I had gone but I ignored all but Lee Anne and Carlos, when he finally found me. There was a trail of vehicles behind my SUV as we left the Reservation, probably driven by people who wanted to make sure I didn't disappear again. Once at our house I made sure that Lawrence and Carlos were in the room as I loaded the thumb drive in my laptop.

As the video of the medical officer played, I did my best to translate and then asked everyone for their opinion on what they had observed.

"Was that truly a Jinn?" Lawrence wanted to know. "I know what you translated but there is something off about the guy. He's definitely a male but why is he so...so...?"

"Independent and in charge," I said. "Is that what you're thinking?"

"Yeah, none of the Jinn on the ship we were on, other than Queen, had anywhere near that guys independence. How old did you say this was?"

"Everything we know points to the derelict as being at least a couple of thousand years old."

"The physical features of the man on the video looked more human than Jinn," Alice added, "but there were stark differences. First, he was actually speaking and not doing the mind-to-mind thing. Physically, at least from what I could see, he doesn't have as much of a posterior as the current version of the Jinn. I'd like to say he looks more like us just different. Is that too crazy?"

"I can tell you," Cassie said from the back of the room, "There are definitely no Jinn on the Queen's ship that look like that. I don't know if you guys noticed but there are no photos, drawings or any depictions of any Jinn that I saw on that ship. It was like no one but the current generation existed."

"So, are you going to tell the President," Carlos asked, "that the Jinn may not be who they purport to be and there may be another, more intelligent, more warlike, version of them out there?"

"Isn't that what the man wants to hear, reasons to keep pouring money in to our new Space Force. Personally, I think our Jinn are the remnants of an older race that has faded with time. But I'm willing to ignore that opinion if it keeps our project going. Do you plan on countering my decision, Carlos, or are we still a team?"

"You're going to ask me that after you took off on your own today? If we weren't a team, I would have called the President even knowing I would have had my ass chewed off. Don't ever question if you and I are a team, Mike Sands. I'm not sure when it happened but somewhere along the line I decided that you were my boss not POTUS. You've never asked but I even moved my wife and kids here so we could feel like a family again. Do you know what that cost me in moving expenses? At least Alice took the time to make all of us feel welcome."

Carlos's voice had gotten louder the more he spoke so I decided to keep my mouth shut. I threw my hands up in surrender and offered my hand as an act of contrition. A glance around and all eyes were on me wanting to know what I was going to do next. Taking a deep breath, I took out my phone and called the President.

"No time to talk, Sands. All I need to know is if you enjoyed your little space odyssey today. A yes or no will suffice and you can fill in the details later."

"Yes," was all I was able to say before the President terminated the call.

"Seems the President already knew I had taken a little flying holiday. Any idea who could have ratted me out?"

All I received was a lot of blank stares. I was shaking my head as I went to the kitchen for a snack.

CHAPTER 37

THE ONLY WORDS OF REBUKE I got from the President, when I spoke to him later that night, were, "A man needs a little time to himself, every once in a while. Just remember the courtesy of letting someone know where you might be going." He took the suggestion of an older Jinn race fairly well, promising to push through a larger appropriation to meet the probable threat. I kept quiet about my own suspicions.

The next weeks were busy. Roz kept locating more files buried deep in the shuttle's memory. He had worked out a method to record what he found using common Earth electronics. He made it easier by completing an intensive study course of the Ancient's language. He was amazed at the Ancient's ability to verbalize words and must have played the last log hundreds of times. Personally, I was amazed at Roz's ability to grasp advanced concepts which made me think Queen had deliberately kept her subjects at a diminished technical level.

Having only vestigial vocal chords, Roz also went on the hunt for an artificial larynx to help him articulate what he was thinking. He and the five other Jinn on my team seemed to pull away from the rest of us for a while, not even throwing items at me that needed translating. It came as a surprise when all of them showed up at my work station in the Council House and Minister stood in front of me.

"Okay, gentlemen, what can I do for you this morning?"

All of them began to smile as Minister reached up to his neck holding a small metal cylinder. The sound that came from him was tinny and shrill but understandable.

"We wish to show you what we have been able to do, Mike Sands. Roz has done a marvelous thing in finding a way for us to communicate with the rest of the human team. Is this not a good thing?"

"You guys continue to surprise me. I suppose it's stupid to ask why no one on the Queen's ship thought to do this a long time ago."

"We were always told it was impossible to speak like the humans and that to endeavor to do so would be contrary to the Queen's wishes. To disobey her was to court death so we continued to communicate internally. My team has actually begun to use these devices all the time except when we want to discuss private matters."

"Whoa, Minister, I thought Jinn were supposed to be very open minded and never kept secrets, at least that's what Queen said."

"She would have you believe a lot of things that were not entirely true. You are much the same; humans are, I mean." Minister was making a strange laughing sound as he watched my face.

"I suppose the same could be said of Queen's desire to keep the Jinn feeling less capable than humans," I commented.

Minister seemed to ponder that for a moment.

"We have been watching Roz for some time as he assisted you, Mike Sands, and have come to believe you are correct. He has begun instructing us in the Ancient's language. While we still are unable to understand or capably read the language, we are finding that it somehow feels familiar. How is that possible?"

"Can't you see the resemblance between you and the man in the video?' I asked "To my eye he looks more human than current Jinn but you still have many vestiges of the same human attributes. Why would language be so much different? If the Jinn were more human back then, what could have happened to change your genetic characteristics? I think Queen had the same question and has been trying to find a way to return your people to an older version of the Jinn. Her knowledge of the Ancient's may be her biggest secret of all."

"Roz has shown us that we are capable of more advanced learning which presumes that Queen kept that a secret as well," Minister said with a hint of disdain. "It leads me to the conclusion that there are many more like Roz on her ship."

My mind began to drift as Minister, Roz and the other Jinn kept up a continuing conversation among themselves even after they realized I was not paying attention. What the Queen knew or didn't know was primary in my thoughts until a new idea began to formulate. Just how old was Queen and how many previous Queens had there been? The absence of any ancestral pictorial archive seemed strange since every human culture, at least to my knowledge, had some sort of memorial tribute to those who had come before. 'What was I missing?' kept running through my head.

My musing led to wandering which took me out of the Council building and out to the desert. The crunching of an extra pair of shoes jerked me awake only to realize Carlos was right next to me.

"I hope you didn't think I was running away again?"

"Nope, just doing what I do to keep you in sight and out of trouble. Is there anything I can help you with?"

"If you can figure out why the Jinn Queen is so eager to arm and equip us when there is no apparent threat, I'd like to hear your thoughts."

"Damn, boss, this might be the only time you have asked for my help, other than when you have women problems. I thought you have been postulating that the Jinn had little technical skills. If that's the case, how does the Queen know what's good tech from bad? She hasn't given you one file that has useless data, at least that's what I get from Helen."

"You keep in touch with Helen, why is that?"

"Direct orders from Lillian. Since you seem to be spending more time here in Roswell, your wife number three, or is it number one, is trying to keep abreast of what you are doing without making a nuisance of herself. Hence, Helen and I relay observations. It also helps me keep in touch with the other members of my security detail."

"I hope you're not getting messages from Alice or Lee Anne that they wish I was spending more time at Edwards."

"Hell no. Both of them are happy to have you here. Besides, most of the team isn't at Edwards. They are at the various companies keeping an eye on all the new space craft being manufactured. The first ten attack craft are due off the assembly lines next week and field tests of the engines and weapons packages will happen soon after. You did know that, didn't you?"

"My head has been up Queen's ass trying to figure what her angle is. And, no, I've been letting Lillian handle anything tech related. Are you going to tell me I need to be spending more quality time with her or the space craft?"

"That's up to you, boss. You know I'd rather spend the time here where my family is now based than traipse all over the country following you around…that is when you let me. With the election happening in a few months your whole project could change."

"Is that something you heard from the President or is it conjecture?"

"President Phillips has been somewhat uncommunicative of late. Perhaps it's because of the campaign or maybe he is just tired of waiting for the purported Marauders to arrive. Either way, he's getting a lot of flak from his party and from the opposition regarding the amount of money going to you. A successful demonstration of the new ships may go a long way to keeping you in business."

"I'm not sure I want to be in business any longer. I miss my old life before the damn Jinn planted the fields of Dora on my doorstep. Why, at my age, did I need to do more than meet Alice and Jeannie and then retire to a comfortable living out here in the desert? Maybe I should blame Crazy Joe Farris along with the Jinn for starting something that was really way above my pay grade. Look at me Carlos, a middle-aged man with three wives and twenty-five more pregnant females, whatever you want to call them, all calling me daddy and expecting something that I don't know if I'm able to give."

"True, you've had a lot on your plate but in reality, you are the smartest one in the bunch even if you don't think you are. No one else could have kept such a disparate group together and have taken so much on yourself at the same time. You and Lawrence are the only two on the Project who have had extensive personal contact with an alien leader, no matter that she may actually be the enemy. Damn it, Mike, do you know how many people envy you because of your courage and insights?"

"Damn good pep talk, Agent Cortez. So, what do I do now?"

"Just what you've been doing. No one knows the Jinn or their history better than you; better than they do themselves, I'll bet. You may not realize how many people are listening to you when you reveal another of the nuggets you've dug out of the alien shuttle archives. You speak a language no one else on this planet has even heard of, partner, and created the only dictionary that can translate the ancient words. What do you do next, you dumb shit? You finish things and clean up the mess."

That was all Carlos had to say. He remained silent as I continued to walk eventually ending up at the side of the shuttle.

"Would you like to see where I find some of those nuggets you referred to?" I said as I ascended the ramp to the main cabin.

Carlos followed along and was surprised when I had him sit in the pilot's seat. The head set snuggled on his head I threw a switch and the alien archive appeared on the monitor.

"Christ, Mike, are all of those symbols what you have to search through? There have to be thousands of files stored here."

"I had Roz do a count and there are closer to one million files, some of them nested twenty or thirty deep. Roz and I take turns burning our eyeballs out looking through the data. Once every thousand or so of the files we find something useful. Would you care to give it a try?"

"You know I can't read this hen scratching. I don't know what to look for."

"Exactly my point, Carlos. Roz and I are the only two who appear to have the skill set needed to translate these files. I have to translate the information before I can give it to the team for review and implementation. It's a relief when I get a schematic for a new weapon or ship design because a schematic is a picture with very few words. What you see in front of you are the files that haven't been accessed yet. Click on one for shits and giggles and let's see if you get lucky."

The screen was touch sensitive so Carlos hesitated a long while before pointing to a file sitting in the upper corner of the monitor. My eyes practically popped out when a ship's design I had never encountered filled the screen. My hands were shaking as I leaned over Carlos, who seemed confused, as I began to move the schematic around on the screen.

"That has to be one of the luckiest selections I have ever seen," I whispered, still staring at the brilliant design in front of me.

"What am I looking at?" Carlos wanted to know. "Why are you so awe struck by the diagram?"

"This is a ship design that makes everything I've ever seen look like a peddle car. Jesus, Carlos, this is an interstellar ship that, if I read this right, will take us past light speed, maybe to hyperdrive." I began going to the sub folders and felt my blood pressure rising as I found new data after new data that was beyond exhilarating. "Look at that," I practically screamed. "This shows a way to increase interior protection for the crew from all the damaging exposure Queen says her people suffered while traveling in space. And this file explains how to change or fold space behind a ship to push it to increased velocity. My god, Carlos, you are a genius."

My guardian had to duck as I kept pounding him on the back in all of my excitement.

"So I guess you found a reason to keep on with the Project?" Carlos asked while evading my blows.

"All that we found or were given before was extraordinary, even the file of the ship Queen left for me. This surpasses everything else and is truly the game changer that makes me wonder if it was what Queen was really after. The problem, just like with the last big ship, is that there is no way to build it on the planet."

"That sounds like more science fiction than fact, boss. Can we even build anything out in space? We've never built anything larger than the space station, have we?"

"Not yet, but with the assistance of our new space fleet it might be easier than previously thought. We're going past baby steps and moving right on to giant leaps. So, do you think this find might be of interest to John Phillips?"

"Oh yeah, so long as you are the one to let him know. He'll most definitely want his own advisors to look at the data, too. Are you able to download this data? I'll bet the files are larger than any common storage devices I know about."

"Roz and I have solved that problem. Now here's another thought. Why were you able to spontaneously choose that file? Roz, with everything I've taught him, always seemed to avoid it. Seems time for another discussion with my Jinn assistant."

While Carlos watched, I pulled a drive out of a storage compartment and connected a home manufactured cable to both the main console and the drive. Using hand motions, I directed the file to the drive and sat back to wait for the transfer to end.

"This is going to take more than an hour, Carlos, if you want to go back to your family. Deciphering all the language will take several days but you are welcome to be my good luck charm while I work on that over the next week. I'll need to have a fairly clean copy to present to the President with certain important features withheld as a safe guard. I know I am really poor at saying it but thank you for keeping me on point."

"I should be thanking you for letting me be so close to all this shit. I'm your number one fan, Mike Sands, and that's what I'll say to anyone who asks."

The download took closer to two hours. Carlos and I sat mostly in silence with one or the other of us making a trip to use the rest room or to bring back some coffee. It was late when the file beeped done so I disconnected the drive to keep it safe on the drive home. It was the best I had felt in weeks.

CHAPTER 38

THE FILE WAS DECIPHERED AND translated after three long days, days in which I ignored my family and my coworkers. I had locked myself in my office in the Council building, not coming out unless my bladder was bursting. My father-in-law kept me supplied with nourishment and kept a watch on the room so that no one bothered me.

I could feel Roz and the Minister at the fringes of my mind but I didn't open up to them. The truth was I wasn't sure who I could trust and definitely didn't want any knowledge of the newly discovered ship's plans to be passed on to Queen.

Lawrence had gone back to Edwards to await the arrival of Earth's newly completed space craft and to prepare them for the test fights. With him gone Cassie had been coming to the Reservation to spend time with Roz. That situation had rectified itself with Cassie spending equal time with both men, often at the same time. I say men because she didn't seem to differentiate between human and alien.

My call to President Phillips bearing news of an important discovery was met with less enthusiasm than I had expected. I was granted time for an interview on the following weekend while he was staying at a remote hunting lodge on an outing in Wyoming. The location worked for me as I didn't want any of the big eyes in DC to have a close look at the Jinn shuttle.

Roz was surprised when I told him he was going with me and that he was going to meet the President. The reality was that I wanted time alone with the Jinn without Minister or the other Jinn nearby. On a whim I asked Alice to accompany me. It was more of a thank you for being so patient with me but I also knew she would enjoy seeing John Phillips.

Early Friday afternoon we were loaded up and ready to depart. I had made arrangements to fly to Edwards to confer with whatever team members were present and to leave a copy of the plans for the new discovery with Lillian.

Lillian practically climbed inside my skin when we arrived making Alice laugh and join in a group hug. I left Roz with Lawrence and took both women to Lillian's quarters; well, actually, my assigned quarters, for a little personal time. I did manage to find a moment to explain what Carlos and I had found but that was near the end of our visit. I'm not sure which event made Lillian more excited. I had to promise to stop at Edwards on our way back to Roswell so Lillian could get a better picture of the discovery and learn how President Phillips received the information.

Once we were airborne and Alice was comfortably seated in one of the passenger seats, I confronted Roz with my suspicions.

"Somehow, my alien friend, Queen seems to know things about everything we discover almost as soon as we do. How do you think she does that?"

Alice, hearing the hardness in my voice as I asked the question, moved farther to the rear of the shuttle fearing that the discussion might get ugly.

"I have no idea, Mike, but rest assured I have not been in contact with Queen."

"How can I be certain of that, Roz?"

"My mind has always been open to you. Would you have me swear my loyalty to you? Minister and I, as well as our Jinn brothers living here, have discussed that among ourselves. But since you didn't request it of us, we were not sure you required it. Now I believe it is necessary so you can maintain your trust in us. You also need to know that Queen is aware that we have shifted our allegiance to you."

"I've never asked anyone to swear allegiance to me, Roz, and see no reason to start now."

"You claim you know about us but you need to understand how we are bred. From our birth it is made mandatory that our only loyalty is to Queen. There is no other choice, Mike Sands. You have allowed us to work among you and have asked for a positive relationship, never a demand to serve only you. That has caused us to feel incomplete. We have discussed this change and, as a choice, wish to pledge our loyalty to you. It would honor us if you were to accept our offer."

This was delivered so strongly that I worried I would have to accept to keep them with me.

"Roz, that is very noble but will that change our working relationship?"

"It will only change how you are perceived by the Jinn, especially if we are to encourage other Jinn on the Queen's ship to join us."

If one can feel like an ass when he thought he was the superior being in the room, that moment had arrived. My perception that the Jinn were less intelligent than humans had colored my opinions and actions. Now I had to make a difficult adjustment and change my way of thinking.

"I'll accept your offer, however uncomfortable it makes me feel, but I still need to know how Queen gets her information."

"Have you considered that the one providing the information might be human?"

That thought made me stop and consider whether it could be true. It took a couple of minutes before I was able to answer the Jinn.

"I owe you and all the Jinn an apology, Roz. You have proven to be just as perceptive as humans. And you are right, my friend, the traitor could very well be human."

"You must look in the minds of all the Jinn, Mike, and satisfy yourself that we are true only to you. I would also suggest you look to all of the females who were returned to you from the Jinn ship as well as Lawrence Davis. We know he is your friend but he is the one human most influenced by Queen during his stay on her ship."

"I was already in Lawrence's head, as I was in yours and Cassie's and didn't see anything like that."

"I must point out that you were looking for files specifically left for you and not directives on how to behave while we work with you. Perhaps you need to go deeper in all of our minds."

"That would mean I'd have to look at every person assigned to the Project."

"Of course, Mike. That is what Queen would do."

Alice had moved closer when she realized I was not going to go ballistic.

"You'll have to include all of us who are close to the Project but not directly involved," she remarked sadly. "It's the only way to be sure of who is loyal to you."

"Why does all of this make me feel like I am going to have to act more like Queen? Every chance I have to step back I get drawn in tighter."

"No other human has your abilities, Mike," Roz remarked, as if I was the only one not to know this. "Queen told us as much when she first noticed you at the field of Dora. She said then you would either be our salvation or our ruination. I prefer to think the former, don't you?"

"I don't know what to think. I hope I won't be expected to peek in the mind of everyone I come in contact with, including the President, to see if they are loyal."

That discussion was over for the moment as we approached the secluded lodge where the meeting was to take place. Roz payed attention to finding us a secure landing zone behind the building while Alice held on to me trying to ease my mental turbulence.

The shuttle caused a large and expected commotion as it quietly landed. The lodge was a log structure, three stories tall and appeared to have a large number of guest bedrooms. A huge contingent of Secret Service agents flowed out of the building obviously not expecting to see the arrival of the Jinn craft. John Phillips followed the team out of the building and stood to the side, looking amazed at the size of the ship. When the side hatch ramp descended the President pushed past his security team and was the first one to enter the main cabin.

"God Damn, Mike," John said, acting like this was the best Christmas toy he had ever received, "you should have said you were flying up in this beauty. Shocked the shit out of my security boys," he said as he swept his gaze around the cabin, stopping when he got to Roz. "Is that one of the Aliens?"

"Mister President, this is Roz, one of the Jinn working on the Project and one of my most capable associates."

"Can I trust that he's not reading my mind like that fucking Queen?"

"I am not able to read your mind, Mister President, only respond to a communication when asked," Roz said indignantly. "I am quite capable of speaking to you."

"Fuck me, Mike, I thought you said the Jinn only use that mental telepathy shit?"

"The Jinn have vocal abilities but Queen never allowed them to be developed. As a result, their vocal chords have become stunted. We're working on strengthening their larynx so they won't have to use those tinny sounding prosthetic voice devices."

"So, you trust these guys now, even after everything they've done?"

"Not every member of the Jinn is loyal to the Queen, John." I decided not to inform him of the Jinn change of loyalty plans. "Some are as angry with her as we are, more so now that they know how they've been held back intellectually. Roz has proven that he is a match for any of my Project members."

John took a step back and looked around the cabin again, this time stopping when he realized Alice was standing patiently behind me.

"Have you been holding out on me, Mike? Can I assume this lovely lady is Missus Sands?"

"Yes, sir, she most certainly is. John, Mister President, this is Alice. She is the Genetic Botanist who has worked with Doctor Farris since the first time we saw the Jinn's Dora field."

"Well, Alice, I'll bet you never expected to be so ass deep in all this shit when you met Mike, did you? That had to have been some kind of first date, I'll bet."

"He was the right person at the right time, Mister President. And with him I've had the most exciting experiences of my life. My daughter feels the same way. I mean, how many other wives get to fly to an appointment with the President of the United States on an alien shuttle?"

"I like your attitude, Alice. I wish I had more of that in my cabinet appointees. You wouldn't be interested in joining me, would you?"

"I hope you're talking about a job, John," I grumbled. That comment elicited a laugh from everyone but Roz who merely looked confused.

"Okay, Mike, you're cutting in on my relaxation time, so spit out what was so important."

"This is for your ears only, Mister President. We need a secure location."

The President looked exasperated as he grabbed my arm and had me exit the shuttle. He had me follow him up a trail behind the lodge until we were at the edge of the woods, several hundred feet from his security team. I hadn't noticed him warning the team to stay away but we were alone.

"Your turn, Sands, let's have it."

"First, we have a mole attached to the project. Someone is keeping Queen apprised of our progress and I have a feeling that it is one of the human members of the team. I have a plan to root out the asshole but I need to know if there is anyone other than you who gets briefed."

"Do you think I would do such a thing?" President Phillips said in a tightly controlled voice.

"I doubt it, John, but I can't overlook anyone. There is only one way to be sure."

"You want to look inside my head? Do you realize how many secrets I have that you are most definitely not authorized to see? You are treading on some very slippery ground, Sands, very slippery indeed." He paused for a moment and any signs of friendship disappeared. "How is it you can do what that Queen bitch is able to do? Maybe I should think about whether you might be the Queen's spy."

"Other than Queen, I've never had anyone try to read my mind, John, but I would gladly let you snoop around in my head. My thinking is that we are the two least likely suspects, both of us having way too much to lose. If I told you that my intrusion would be like trying to locate a file in a computer, kind of like using the search function to look for a specific word or document, would that make things more agreeable. It's really all about trust, John. So I need to know, do you trust me?"

"Fuck you, Mike Sands, for questioning my loyalty. So, you can limit your search to…what?"

"I'd look for anything to do with Queen, nothing more."

"This is really hard for me but I'll agree if you let me return the favor."

The way John was staring at me made me worry that his security team would think something bad was going on. That lasted for a minute until John let out a loud guffaw.

"We are quite the pair, aren't we Sands. So, was there more to this meeting or was that enough?"

The release of tension caused me to draw in a huge breath.

"There's more. I was showing Carlos Cortez the control panel on the shuttle, explaining how we searched for any information regarding the Ancient's. He was playing around and activated a file that exposed something amazing. It was a series of files giving the specifications for an interstellar spacecraft that may be able to travel at light speeds and maybe more. Carlos, Lillian, and now you, are the only people I've told about this."

I handed a thumb drive to the President.

"The only problem is the ship is so huge, much larger than the last one we discussed, that I don't believe it could be built on Earth, John, only out in space."

"That had better be the last of your news, partner, because I'm not sure I can handle any more revelations. Okay, I need to do some thinking so you are all my guests until I come to a decision on my next move. You said you gave this information to Lillian? Isn't she another one of your wives? Wasn't there an Apache wife, as well? Maybe I should be looking at you for Secretary of State seeing as how you seem able to keep a lot of balls juggling at one time."

John grabbed my arm and walked me back to the lodge, stopping at the shuttle long enough to collect Alice and Roz.

CHAPTER 39

DINNER WITH THE PRESIDENT WAS a mostly informal affair, not anything like images I had seen of stately White House dinners. Everyone in the President's party, including all of the security team and my small group, were seated on both sides of a long trestle table. The lodge hosts brought out bowls of salad, platters of venison steaks and steamed vegetables and fresh baked sour dough rolls. It was served family style and after the initial rush it was evident that there was more than enough fare on the table for everyone.

Roz looked at all of the food before gingerly picking at the veggie platter and the rolls, reminding me that the Jinn were mostly vegetarians. Once he started on the veggies he smiled, enthusiastically filled his plate several times and looked completely satisfied. All through the meal it was evident that at least one of the agents was assigned to keep an eye on the Jinn. For his part Roz seemed oblivious and that was okay with me.

After dinner, when all the plates had been cleared to the kitchen and the table moved to a far wall, we all gathered around a roaring fire in one of the largest fireplaces I had ever seen. A coffee-and-bourbon mix was served in generously filled glassware and a sense of ease and comfort filled the room.

"So, Sands, can you see why I wanted to meet you here instead of my office?" John swept his arms around making me follow and look at the rustic charm. "My family built and has owned this camp for more than a hundred years. Only a select group of outsiders have ever been invited to join me here. You can now consider yourself and your family a part of that select company."

What was left unsaid was that John Phillips trusted me and was agreeing to let me trespass in his head. My response was a nod and a silent toast with my raised glass of bourbon. He smiled back and uttered one word, "Tomorrow."

I gathered that we were now overnight guests. What I didn't know until the next day was that Roz had been escorted back to the shuttle and told to spend the night there. Coffee laced with bourbon made both Alice and me ready for bed much earlier than our host. That was beneficial since I was awakened by a knock on our bedroom door at six in the morning.

"POTUS is requesting you down at breakfast, Chief Sands," came through the door. Whoever was outside did not wait for an answer since a request was more likely a command.

I took a five-minute shower using toiletries left for us on the bathroom counter and then dressed in yesterday's clothes. Alice was still asleep so I left her wrapped in a blanket as I went to meet the President.

"Do you always sleep so late, Sands, or is it the clean air up in this neck of the woods?"

"More like the amount of bourbon, John. And, yes, I always try to sleep until after the sun rises."

Much like at dinner the night before, the lodge chef served me a platter with three eggs, hash browns, both sausage and bacon and a side of three pancakes.

"Don't just stare at the plate, Mike, it's all meant to be eaten."

I ate and John drank from a seemingly never empty cup of coffee.

"You and I are going on a little hike after your meal settles down. I'd like to show you my favorite spot, a place I find I can truly relax. Perhaps we can have an exchange of minds while we are there. Are you good with that?"

Still having a mouthful of pancakes all I was able to do was nod my head. John returned the nod and walked to a room next to the stairway. Two security agents stood to either side of the door so I assumed he was not to be disturbed. After eating I asked after the Jinn and was directed outside. Roz was seated at a picnic table with his own breakfast plate, only missing the bacon and sausage. He looked up at me and smiled.

"This is a most wonderful place, Mike. Somehow this feels like a land the Jinn would love to call their home. Do you find it strange that there has been no mention of a home world for the Ancient's or the Jinn in any of the files we have inspected?"

"Perhaps the Ancient Ones had been in space for a very long time, Roz, and could not remember how to get back to their home. I imagine the Jinn think of a ship as their home."

"I could not go back and live on a ship, Mike, not after having experienced life on Earth. Promise me that you will not make us return to Queen, especially now that we know the meaning of being free."

"Can I assume you are speaking for all the Jinn on Earth? It sounds like you have become their spokesperson."

"We are of one mind as we have always been. The strongest of us leads and the others follow. You must have seen that on the Jinn ship."

"I was distracted by Queen much of the time including when she used me as a genetic experiment."

"My team was not involved with that, Mike; even though I can sense you wondering if that is true."

Before I could frame a response John came bustling out of the lodge and handed me a jacket.

"Nice as it is down here, a little elevation can make things a bit nippy. If you're done jawing with your pal, we need to get a move on."

Not waiting for me John started walking, more like a slow run, up a path that led to the tree line. I managed to get the jacket on and caught up just as we entered the forest.

"You need to look out for bears and mountain lions. I've only got my forty-four mag with me but would rather not have to kill any of the predators. This is their land and I kind of like being tolerated as a good neighbor."

The President set a rapid uphill pace that he managed to maintain until we broke through the trees. We were on a flat stretch of meadow that overlooked a deep chasm, dropping nearly a thousand feet or more. John walked towards the edge and sat on a wide flat rock, his feet not more than five feet from the drop off.

"Grab a spot, Chief Sands, and enjoy the view." John patted the rock next to him and then turned to stare out across the rift.

The rock had been warmed by the sun even though the air was cool. When I made like I was about to speak, John held his hand up as if to make me remain quiet. The two of us sat and looked out for nearly thirty minutes, hearing only the sound of the wind and the voices of numerous small animals who didn't seem intimidated by our presence.

"Can you feel why I like this spot?" John spoke so softly I almost missed what he said.

"It is a special place, John. It's like I was empty of everything. I can't even begin to tell you what I was thinking. Maybe it was nothing at all."

"Now is the right time to look inside me, Mike, while my mind is at its quietest."

The effort to reengage my own mind was made more difficult due to my sense of peace but eventually I was able to do my probe. What I saw both surprised me and seemed typical. I shifted in my seat and touched the Presidents arm.

"You told me when we first met that Queen had only contacted you the one time. Why did I see several conversations that occurred a month or more prior to our meeting?"

"God's truth, Mike, I only remember the one time. Can you see what she said to me?"

"They were mostly cautions that the Jinn were going to return to Earth. My name was mentioned each time but not why I was important, not until the final message. That one she left for me, somehow knowing that I would be traipsing around in your gray matter."

"A message for you, in my head. What kind of a sick joke is that?"

"Queen likes to play games and leaves me clues in the minds of people I am likely to visit."

"Well, what the fuck did she say?"

"It's kind of cryptic. Like most of her messages what it says is that I am close to the answer and she is surprised I made it this far."

"Answer to what? What kind of game is she playing?"

"Everything she has given us, the Dora, the plans for weapons, the shuttles, all of it required modifications or improvements, things her Jinn were unable to do. She engineered a threat by introducing the evil Marauders which caused us to create a better defensive grid and develop even better weapons. All I can surmise is that she thinks she will be able to take possession of all of it. She has underestimated us, John, at almost every turn but still keeps on playing. I should be elated by that but I keep asking myself what am I missing?"

"Didn't she tell you at one time she wanted you as her consort? Maybe she thinks you will hand it all to her as a wedding gift. I mean, what can one more wife mean to you?"

That was a question I was not about to address. My eyes were drawn back to the chasm and suddenly it was if a curtain was being lifted in my head. A cascade of memories began unfolding, one after another, faster than I was able to isolate but still just as clear as if they had just occurred. Every move I had made in my life, from the time I was an infant, to my education, time on the police department, the disintegration of my marriage to Lillian, my move to Roswell and my introduction to Alice, all flashed by only slowing when I saw the field of Dora and met the Jinn. Eidetic memory is what it is called, something that I had never known to have had in my toolbox. It allowed me to piece together every meeting with the Jinn, including all the times I now realized I had been under the control of Queen.

Anger was building up inside me, not hot and blazing but cold as an Arctic winter, making me determined to end this whole charade.

"Are you okay, Mike? You went away for a few minutes and got a look on your face that I hope is not meant to scare me. Does it have to do with the bitch?"

"Have you ever had a moment of clarity that is so rare that things seem to fall in place? Your special mountain top allowed that to happen and I am not sure I like what I found out."

"You're not getting off with that comment. What did you find out?"

"I'm not so sure about the consort part, John. I think she wants me to replace her."

"Right, she wants you to become a Queen? Isn't that a little out of the question since you don't have the physical equipment for the job?"

"Of all the humans on this planet she feels that I am the most like her, mentally at least. Roz claims Queen is afraid of me because she thinks I am stronger than her. She was only able to take control because she drugged me, something I would never allow again. The strange part of the puzzle was that Queen can talk to her Jinn, other aliens and humans using her ability to telepathically conduct a conversation. She can also leave messages for anyone who can go into the recipient's mind, that would be me, but she can't go in to retrieve anything left for her by a third party. It has to be driving her crazy knowing that I locked her out of my head and she can't get a read on how far along I am in figuring out her motives."

"You lost me when you said you might be stronger than Queen and that she was leaving messages in people's heads. If you're so worried about her why not blast her out of the sky?"

"My children are on the ship, Lawrence's children, too. That's Queen's advantage. We need to out think her and right now I am out of suggestions. Do you mind if we head back? I need to have a discussion with my family and my Jinn."

"Did you just say *your* Jinn? Is that what you meant to say, Sands?"

"I don't know, Mister President. Don't you call the citizens of this country your people? Maybe the Jinn are beginning to feel like they are mine."

CHAPTER 40

ALICE WAS ENSCONCED ON A BIG leather sofa in front of a roaring fire, drinking a cup of hot chocolate, when John and I returned.

"We need to head back, babe. Where is Roz hiding?"

"He was out on the patio. The cool air seems to suit him very well. Was your walk productive?"

"We can talk about it on the flight back to Roswell. Let's say our thank-yous and head for the shuttle."

While Alice was taking her cup back to the kitchen I turned back to John.

"We've been pretty lax in keeping in touch so I would appreciate a return to our old schedule, at least for the time being. I hope you will see it clear to give me some feedback on the things we talked about."

The President, smiled, slapped me on the back and walked away without saying whether he would or would not honor my request.

Roz was reluctant to leave the mountains but knew that we had important things to do. I tried to get him to say more about why some of the Jinn, those on Earth at least, were willing to challenge Queen by supporting me. He merely looked at me in a strange Jinn way and remained silent. I refrained from going in his mind and remained frustrated that he was not giving me an answer.

Alice pestered me with questions throughout the return trip. Per our agreement to never hide things from each other I gave her a general outline of my time with the President.

"I know Roz suggested that the person relaying information to Queen was a human but what if it was more than one person?" Alice theorized. "Taking that further, what if both humans and Jinn were feeding her tidbits of information, kind of like your bread crumb theory? How would you ever find the one guilty party if the guilt was so spread out?"

"I just managed to wrap my head around a human as the conspirator and now you throw another perfectly valid suggestion at me. What do you propose I do about that possibility?"

"First you need to figure out what the directive looks like, the one that causes someone to relay info to Queen. If you can identify it in one person it would shorten the amount of time to locate it in others, don't you think?"

"And then what? That might be a solution if I could reach several people at a time. Just thinking about it makes me exhausted."

"There is a way," Roz chimed in.

"Were you eavesdropping on our conversation, Roz?" I wasn't too upset since it did get him to talk to us.

"Queen can reach out to numerous Jinn at one time. We know you are at least as gifted as Queen, if not more so, and will have the advantage of using Minister and the other Jinn to assist in the search."

"You keep telling me that other than communicating telepathically you aren't able to do much else."

"Our Jinn would ride on your back, using your power, to look for the directive. You are probably capable of reaching several people at one time but with the additional Jinn providing support you could encompass far greater numbers. A secondary advantage, while you conduct the search, would be to deactivate and block Queen from reestablishing a connection to her targets. Isn't that what you have done to yourself?"

"Alright, so we work as a team to shorten the time needed to identify the spy or spies. Can we keep that from Queen?"

"She will probably figure it out in time but by then we should have eliminated her access."

Roz seemed fairly confident that his suggestion was valid and I had to agree that it was more than I had come up with.

"There is one more thing, Mike Sands." Roz appeared hesitant to go on.

"Am I going to like it?" Now that he was talking Roz just kept on going.

Alice was snickering and I had to poke her on the arm to get her to shut up.

"We need to make contact with some of my Jinn team on the Queen's ship."

"How are we going to know if the ship is inside or out of this galaxy? And then, pray tell, how are we supposed to connect with your friendly Jinn when we don't know where the fuck they are?" My attitude had gone from light to agitated in a matter of heartbeats.

"Queen has always had unlimited power and has used that power to connect with Jinn or humans who were some distance from us. You are just as strong and could use that strength to help us locate the ship and deliver a message."

"Right and walk right in to a trap set by Queen. It's not your brightest idea, Roz."

"You don't understand, Mike, you would just be locating the ship. Minister or I would deliver the message."

"You're right, I don't understand. Is this another case where I'm supposed to carry you on my back, fly the shuttle willy-nilly around in space until we find the Jinn ship or what?"

"I've upset you." Roz looked like he was ready to get on his knees and beg for forgiveness. "There has been a loss of understanding. You need do nothing but allow either Minister or me to access your power. We are still linked to our brothers on the Jinn ship but are not strong enough to reach them. We require someone like you or Queen to reach out and allow us to complete the connection. Once reconnected we can find out where Queen has parked the ship. Queen will not know since she is not part of that linking. Do you see that?"

I knew what the Jinn wanted but was too tired to know what to do. Alice was not saying a word but I knew she wanted to add her input.

"Look Roz, I'm too tired to deal with that right now. We'll discuss it again tomorrow or the next day. Can you live with that?"

Roz nodded and turned back to piloting the shuttle. I was hoping that Queen had finally gotten smart and had decided to go to some other galaxy, like Centauri Proxima. The thought of Queen moving almost four and a half light years from Earth while traveling at much less than light speed made me smile. My mind began pulling up information I didn't know I had accumulated; such as a ship traveling at one percent of the speed of light would still take over four hundred years to make the journey. That meant Queen would be gone a very long time. All I had to do was convince her to make the trip

.

CHAPTER 41

ONCE BACK AT THE APACHE reservation I was besieged by Carlos and the Jinn wanting to know what had transpired at the President's chalet. I was vague but did say that the President and I were of the same mind and that he had agreed to work with me. Carlos looked like he wanted to talk so we took a short walk away from the Council House. Once clear of anyone wanting to eavesdrop, Carlos started in.

"You know damn well you were supposed to have me with you. Did the President comment about my absence?"

"He never said anything. I pretty much had his attention the whole time, except when he was flirting with Alice. You're not in any trouble, Carlos, so relax."

"If you say so. Look, the Jinn have been acting crazy the last two days. Minister made me promise to arrange some private time with you and his crew. Do you have any idea what that is about? Do I need to have the security team on standby?"

"That must have been some request. Yes, I have a fairly good idea what's going on with the Jinn and it's probably due to something Roz mentioned on the flight home. Have your people stand down. I'll be in no physical danger; quite the opposite actually."

Carlos was looking puzzled as I walked away without explaining. I was still trying to come to terms with having a group of aliens declaring their loyalty to me.

Minister and Roz were waiting for me at the rear entrance to the Council building. It did not look like I was going to be able to grab Alice and make an escape from a meeting. Minister took the advantage and herded me in to the building surrounded by the Jinn.

"Roz has informed us that you are aware of our pledge of loyalty. All forty Jinn on this world have agreed to it and it is now up to you to accept it. This is important to us, Mike Sands, so I recommend that you honor our offer."

It didn't seem like I was going to be given a choice in the matter as none of the Jinn had ever acted with such determination.

"You already know I would be loyal to each of you without requiring a pledge of allegiance. But, since it is so important to you, and only for that reason, I reluctantly accept."

The Jinn began to smile, something they had begun doing more often the longer they were on Earth. Smiles, or any signs of happiness, were never present during my trips to the Jinn ship. My hope was that nothing would happen to change the Jinn's attitude.

"We can sense that you are tired," Minister pronounced, "but since we are all here, we wish to have you search us to remove any link to Queen. The first one of us that you examine will give you a location to search in all the rest. We can all connect once you have finished with us and that will allow you to do the same for all the Jinn staying elsewhere on the planet. That should save you time and make all of us more confident. It should also be true for any humans that will be examined. I wish to go first."

Having examined the President, I was quickly able to determine Minister's innocence and remove his connection to Queen. Roz was next and then all of the other Jinn were scrutinized in one sweep. The ease with which I accomplished the feat stunned me but none of the Jinn appeared to think it was unusual. All of them were innocent and now free of the former Jinn mistress. My surprise was that it didn't matter how far from me the Jinn were located; they all appeared as if they were as close to me as Minister or Roz.

"Is this going to be just as easy accessing all of the humans that need testing?"

"There is no reason that it would be more difficult," Roz explained. "You already have a connection to all that need testing and we will support you if you find it too difficult to handle everyone at one time. I am confident you won't need our help."

Before I could change my mind, I reached out and first felt the minds of every person on the Project. Every one of them had been approached by Queen and had divulged a small amount of information. I severed all the connections, most of them being very tenuous, and installed a block to keep Queen out.

Next, I made contact with all twenty-five women returned to Earth and found much stronger links to Queen. Each of them had directives that required them to pass along any information regarding the Project and specifically anything to do with me. Those links were disconnected and, on a whim, I directed each to notify me if Queen attempted to contact them. To that point none of the information given to Queen impacted the security of the Project.

My third foray was to examine each of the Security Agents assigned to the team. Except for Carlos, Helen and one or two others, no one had access to any information other than what they could overhear. Once again, I found that Queen had touched every single person on the team. Removing her from their heads was easily done and more blocks put in place.

Lastly, I connected to my family, Lillian, Joe Farris and Lawrence. That's where the shocks began. I was not surprised to find Lawrence strongly connected to Queen since he had been under her control for a long time. Interestingly, he had been trying to disengage himself and had actually prevented a lot of privileged information from being transmitted. The same was true of Joe Farris but he was more successful in denying Queen. Alice, Jeannie and Lee Anne had been contacted, repeatedly it appeared, but had little to pass along. Anger was my response as I installed stricter blocks meant to keep Queen away from all of them.

All I could think of was how to make Queen suffer rather than merely chasing her out of the galaxy. It dawned on me that Queen was doing a very good job of trying to make me become a Marauder. Was that the end game or was there still more to come?

Coming back to myself I found that none of the Jinn had left. I must have looked confused because Roz put a hand on my shoulder.

"Are you well, Mike? We are still waiting to assist you in connecting with the others."

My laugh must have shocked them.

"You were right, Roz, I didn't need your help. I got what I needed and know that there was more than one source. It was all too easy and could become addictive if I don't watch myself. Now, if you'll excuse me, I am going home."

Roz got a distressed look on his face as did Minister.

"We still need you to search out our brothers, Mike. You said you would help."

"Not today, Roz. Perhaps tomorrow if I feel up to it."

Everyone backed away from me as I stood and walked back outside.

Alice was seated in one of the lounge chairs with Carlos hovering close by.

"Were you just in our heads?" Alice demanded to know.

"I was and made sure Queen could not get in there again."

"You could have let us know and gotten permission," Carlos shouted. As soon as he realized he had stepped out of bounds he looked contrite. "Has she been in my head?"

"She was in everybody's head. Not one of the people I made contact with was clear of her interference and that included Jeannie. It was far easier just getting rid of her than waiting for all of you to give me a yea or nay. If that sounded harsh, so be it."

Every action that I took seemed to anger or distress someone. I was getting tired of hearing about all the gripes.

"Now, I want to go home. Am I driving myself or are you back in the driver's seat?" I said pointing a finger at Carlos.

The three of us trudged to the Suburban. Alice and I got in the back and let Carlos pilot us back home. Alice had her head on my shoulder and was holding my hand as if she was never going to let go. I finally began to relax and wondered when the next calamity would strike.

By the next morning I was feeling more like my old self. I avoided going back to the Reservation and instead contemplated flying back to Edwards. My phone had over a dozen messages that

I knew had to be from people who were indignant over my un-authorized intrusion. None of them were opened or answered but none were deleted. I did take Lillian's call later that morning.

"Did you find her in my head and is she gone now?" was her almost frantic demand.

"She was and now she's not. Did I disturb you too much?"

"Yes and no. I was spitting bullets at first but then knew you must have had a good reason. That's when I felt it had to do with the Bitch. Was I guilty of divulging anything important?"

"Surprisingly, no. Either you didn't have whatever Queen was looking for or you hid it away from her prying eyes. You have always been too analytical for most people and that had to include our Alien spy."

"What about the rest of the team, did you check them out, too?"

"I did and you can be assured we can continue on safely."

"Can you come back to Edwards, Mike? I think I need some personal reassurances."

"He'll return tomorrow, Lill, after I make sure he's fit to travel," Alice promised.

"Have I been on speaker this whole time?"

"You know the rules, Lillian. I keep no secrets from my wives. Are you objecting?"

There was a pause and a long sigh.

"I keep wishing you were like that when we first got married. We kept so much from each other over the years. It'll be nice to see you, the new you, tomorrow. Maybe you should bring Alice with you." Lillian did not sound as if she meant the suggestion.

"Not this time," Alice said wistfully. "I have to work. You can have him all to yourself."

CHAPTER 42

GETTING BACK TO EDWARDS DID not seem so urgent the next morning. By my third cup of coffee Carlos had come inside the kitchen to try to figure out my schedule.

"I thought your text said you were going back to Edwards this morning. Did I misread something?" Carlos said between sips of his own cup of coffee.

"You don't look any more enthused about flying back than I do. Lawrence is supposed to do his first test flight today so I really should be there. Has Roz prepped the shuttle?"

"I think he slept on top of it last night so he would be ready when you arrived. Did something happen on your trip to see the President that made the Jinn act like puppy dogs around you?"

"What do you mean, did something happen?"

"Well, all the Jinn are usually kind of standoffish but when you got back it was almost as if you became their favorite uncle or something."

"We came to an understanding is all, nothing too serious."

Carlos stared over his coffee cup at me, not saying a word, but looked like he didn't think that was all that had happened.

"We need to go," I said and pushed away from the table.

Our drive to the Reservation was done in near silence, broken only when Carlos had to stop and shout at several steers blocking the road.

All of my Jinn were waiting by the shuttle when we walked up which seemed to reinforce Carlos's opinion I had gained some status with the Aliens.

"Why the Honor Guard, Minister? You guys don't usually come outside when I have to travel."

"We wondered if you had thought more about contacting our friends. It is best to be done before Queen gets some sense of our plans."

"Give it a rest, would you. I'm only going to be gone for a day or two and we can discuss it some more when we get back. Queen is blocked from any contact with us so we should have plenty of opportunity to make the call."

Minister and the other Jinn were looking subdued as I pushed Carlos and Roz up the ramp.

"Don't say a word, Carlos. You'll know what that was all about in due time."

Roz took the controls and the shuttle quietly lifted off the ground.

"Take us out past the gravity well, Roz and plot a slow ride to Edwards. I need time to think."

Now I had both Roz and Carlos watching to see if I had gone crazy but I ignored them.

"Exactly how far is that, Mike?" Carlos asked not looking very confident.

"It's about four thousand miles. Far enough to stay out of contact with the planet and maybe close enough to sense if Queen is somewhere close by. Are you nervous about something?"

"I've only flown in atmosphere and this is a little unnerving. I mean, what if something goes wrong? And, yeah, what if Queen is close by?"

"This is like sitting in your mother's lap, totally safe. And if something did go wrong, and it won't, Lawrence has the other shuttle and ten brand new space-worthy fighters ready to make a test flight. Maybe you can use the other monitor and help Roz look for new files. You did pretty well last time."

Roz was trying to ignore us. He had the video of the Ancient's Medical Officer on his monitor and had scrunched up his face while looking at the image.

"Staring at the Doctor is not going to make anything clearer, Roz. You'd be better off trying to figure why he was in charge of a vessel that size. Why not look for his medical files? That might give us some clues to the composition of the crew."

Another light went off in my head. Why would a medical officer be in charge of a ship? Was it because the ship was a test facility? If Queen was comfortable working with genetics to improve her next generation, why wouldn't the same be true of the Ancient's?

"This is important, Roz; I need anything with the Medical Officers name on it. Medical records are best but any other document you can find will be important."

"What just happened, Mike?" Carlos demanded to know.

"If I'm right, the ancient ship was designed to do in larger scale what Queen did by stealing Lawrence's and my sperm. I have no proof except for a gut feeling but I know I'm right. What if one of the Ancient's experiments went wrong and the end product was the reason the Ancient's were attacked. If we find something I only hope I am able to read what they documented. I'm still not as fluent in their language as I need to be."

Roz's shriek had me running and peering over his shoulder as file after file filled the screen.

"What the hell is all that?"

"I don't know, Mike. I located a section that had a word I'd never seen before and when I activated it all of these files came pouring out. They lined up in some kind of a sequence but none of the titles are familiar to me."

"Fuck me, Roz, the word on that first file translates as experiment. Open that one and then scroll to the very last one and open it, too."

While Roz worked at his console and Carlos hovered not knowing what we were doing, I pulled the first file over to the console at the second seat. The author had the same name as the officer in the video. There were a lot of definitions and some descriptions of what the first experiments were designed to do. Putting most of the words together I still had to infer meanings for the words I couldn't decipher.

At one point my head was ready to explode as I figured out the word that we had been missing since finding the very first file in this shuttle's memory. My head went from blisteringly hot to very cold when the person writing this log referred to each failed test subject as 'Jinn.' Right at that moment I wished that I had a linguistics expert who was fluent in the Ancient's language. What if I was wrong and the translation meant something completely different, except I knew it didn't.

"Did you get to the last file yet, Roz?"

"There are over four thousand files here, Mike. The last one seems to be dated almost at the same time as the ship's log. That would appear to be fairly significant."

The file was not very long. It described another failed attempt to reverse the effects of the earlier tests. The gist of the file was that the 'Jinn' were out of control and posed a threat to the entire ship's company.

When I looked up both Roz and Carlos were staring at me as if I was about to do something crazy.

"You don't get to keep us in suspense, Sands." Carlos had his fierce security agent look on his face and was not going to back down. "What was so awful that caused you to turn ten shades of white?"

"Back off a minute and let me get my head around this. Okay, first, the initial file described the protocol for a series of experiments, obviously using live subjects. Each failed experiment was classified as 'Jinn.' I don't know if that is the genealogy of the name of your people, Roz, but that's what the document seems to indicate. I did have to interpret a bit but I'm fairly sure that's accurate."

Roz had a strange look on his face, an expression I had never seen before.

"What else did you see, Mike?" Roz said so quietly he was hard to hear, even in the close confines of the shuttle bridge. "There was something bad in the last document, wasn't there?"

"The report was fairly brief, as if it was written in a hurry. While I'm not sure of the subtext, the writer claims the ship was under attack by the 'Jinn'. The problem as I see it is that as violent as the 'Jinn" are purported to be, how can that explain how docile your people are, Roz? Every time I make some kind of connection, something seems to be missing. Are there any images of the test subjects in the rest of the files? If you could find something that would clarify a whole lot of wrong thoughts going through my head."

Roz went back to work on the files while Carlos and I went to the rear of the cabin.

"What you found, Boss, that wasn't very good, was it? Why would there be such a difference in personality in what, a couple thousand years?"

"Look around the planet, Carlos, and tell me how some people are peaceful and productive yet others are vicious and have no respect for almost anything. It scares the shit out of me that Queen wants to take her people back to the animal state. Her whole objective is to create more aggressive Jinn."

"So, what do we do?"

"I don't know. There has to be a causal factor as to why the Jinn went from tiger to pussy cat and the people we need to help figure it out committed suicide. This is a problem that requires a more scientific approach. I think Alice and Doctor Farris are about to get a new project."

We were interrupted when Roz jumped out of his seat and sat down next to us. He pointed at the screen but would not say anything. I walked to the pilot's position and stared at an image labeled test subject. It was a near perfect photo of any one of the Jinn I had met. Under it was a label that said "Jinn."

CHAPTER 43

"I DON'T UNDERSTAND," ROZ CRIED. "How can that thing be called a Jinn? None of my brothers nor even the working females has ever acted like that."

We landed at Edwards and had been joined in the conference room by Lillian, Lawrence and whoever of the Project members that were not out in the field. Roz had transferred the files to a hard drive and we were going through them, one by one, all being projected on the large screen monitor. Roz was too frazzled to help me translate so I got the largest share of the workload. Others on the team who had been studying the Ancient's language jumped in when they saw something they recognized but the terms were too technical for them to contribute very much.

It was past ten o'clock that night when Lillian dragged me off to bed. As with the other files I had read, the newest ones remained in my mind long after Lillian was done abusing my body. She was snoring softly as I lay awake having random files cascade across my consciousness until one particular file hit home.

Even back to the time of the Ancient's the main food source for both the Ancient's and their test subjects was Dora. It was one notation, buried within some untranslatable language, which seemed important. The Dora fed to the test subjects had been altered to promote a faster response to stimuli. No reference was made to what changes were made. It made me question if Queen was conducting her own experiments. Was she looking for a planet that would alter the Dora's genetic structure to replicate what was given to the test Jinn?

Perhaps it was a secondary plan to using my sperm to create the new version of the Jinn. Worse yet was the thought that the improved Dora that Doctor Farris and Alice had created had removed an ingredient in Dora that could have been what was keeping the Jinn docile.

Sleep was gone so I dressed and left Lillian breathing heavily. I headed out to the larger shuttle thinking I would do some more digging in the stored files. Roz had beaten me to it and was opening and closing files faster than I could.

"What in the hell are you doing, Roz? Aren't you supposed to be sleeping?"

The Jinn practically fell out of his seat when he realized he was no longer alone. Stranger still, he looked embarrassed, a rare appearance for the normally stoic Jinn.

"I needed to find something that would explain why the Ancient's and the test subjects were so different and why their Jinn were so different from me and my brothers," came out in a rush with no breaks for air.

"Did you see anything in the files you were rushing through? The question you are attempting to answer kept me awake, too. I might have a possible explanation but it would help to have some corroboration to give to Joe and Alice."

"I have not found anything, Mike. With so many files and my limited ability to read the language I feel like I am overlooking important information."

"Something I read earlier floated to the surface as I tried to sleep. It had to do with Dora and a possible alteration to its structure. It's too early to try and run it by Joe or Alice so I thought I'd dig around some more, much like you are doing, I guess."

Roz spun around and started going through files he had already perused.

"I saw a file on dietary necessities a while ago. Perhaps I was going too fast and didn't pay enough attention to what it said. Now I can't remember if the file was a main one or nested somewhere inside. Why did the Ancient's have to store their data with no master names?"

Roz was retracing his steps as quickly as before, opening and closing files faster than I could read the headings. His motions were so hypnotic that I began to doze off. When he stopped it was so sudden that the lack of motion snapped me out of a light sleep.

"This is the one. I recognize that the word for Dora is mentioned many times and the symbol for the Jinn is also in the text."

"Push it to my terminal, Roz, but keep looking for anything else that might be pertinent."

How the Ancient's could accumulate such a massive data base with no apparent way to do a search puzzled me. That had to be another thing I was missing, more than one something no doubt, but until I had a better understanding of the language of the Ancient's it was strictly hunt and peck.

The file opened up to a graphic of a Dora plant and a whole lot of verbiage that I had trouble deciphering. Symbols abounded and made me dizzy looking at them. One page down was another graphic of a slightly different Dora plant and a third page down another version. Not having Alice or Joe close by meant I was going to have to wait to get a better understanding of what I was looking at. Not knowing why, I had a bad feeling about the contents of the file and what it meant to the Jinn.

Light coming in the open hatch of the shuttle reminded me that I hadn't slept all night. Roz was passed out at his seat. I had another first when I realized it was the first time I had seen a Jinn sleeping. I shook myself awake and dropped a copy of the Dora file on a thumb drive before wandering to the mess hall for coffee and some breakfast. Lillian was already there and poured me a cup while I was putting food on my tray.

"You look like shit, Chief Sands. Did you sleep at all?"

"Too much in my head, babe. What time is the first test flight? I might need a nap before Lawrence starts in on how great a pilot he is."

"Not until eleven. Grab a couple of hours. I'll come and wake you up."

"I think I'll set my alarm. Your way of waking me up will either kill me or cause me to fall back to sleep after you're done."

"Have it your way. I have plenty of work to do so I'll see you later."

Before I could make my way to my quarters Lawrence walked in to the mess hall and sat down across from me.

"Are we okay, Mike, I mean did I do something that you thought was wrong?"

"No, we're okay. I'm a little out of sorts with everyone it seems. It probably has to do with trying to figure out what Queen's game is. I keep hoping that once we figure her out things will go back to whatever normal is going to be."

"Good, because I need a favor."

"I hope it doesn't involve any serious thinking because I'm kind of wiped out."

"You know the design of the new fighters has two seats placed next to each other, right?"

"We are not going to change the design at this late date…"

"Stop rambling, goddamn it. I'm not changing the design. I want you to be in the copilot's seat when I do the flight today."

"Are you insane? Lillian, then Alice and maybe Lee Anne will cut your nuts off if anything happens during the flight. Why do I qualify as a copilot? There are several engineers who probably deserve the ride before I would."

"It's because you're my friend and I trust you to catch anything I might miss." There was a long pause. "You can also get inside my head and keep Queen out. None of the engineers can do that."

Lawrence's intense look made me look away as I tried to run all the pros and cons of taking the test flight. The thing that won me over was the excitement I felt when I knew I was going to be one of the first to fly in a space worthy hypersonic fighter built on Earth.

"Won't I be a handicap if things go south?"

"Jesus, Sands, you flew the Golden Eagle, you've had time flying both of the Jinn shuttles and you know damn well you'll be an asset in the second seat. How many other people do you know who have flown that far in deep space?"

"What about a flight suit? Nobody's fitted me for one since we flew to meet the Jinn ship."

"That same suit has been modified for the test flight. All you have to do is make sure you empty your bowels before we lift off."

"You had this all planned out, didn't you, you dumb son-of-a-bitch? What if I'd said no?"

"Trust me; there was no chance of that happening. Lillian said the same thing when we discussed it a little while ago."

All I could do was nod and start to walk away.

"I'm going to take a nap. Make sure it's you who wakes me up and not Lillian. I'll see you in a couple of hours."

CHAPTER 44

THE FIRST PART OF THE FLIGHT was anticlimactic. Like the Jinn shuttles, we used the ships antigravity engines to lift us clear of the airfield. At five thousand feet we started the rocket engines and began to boost our speed. The digital altimeter spun upwards too fast to see the numbers and before we knew it we were beyond the atmosphere. Our course was much the same as the one Roz and I had taken in the shuttle, keeping us opposed to the moon and other planets and in the Earth's shadow. We were traveling far north of Mach Ten but felt little acceleration pressure in the cabin. Lawrence felt so comfortable that he passed me the controls and watched me sweat as I guided the ship deeper in space.

We slowed our rate of acceleration and used the thrusters to maneuver finally coming to a stop.

"Damn, that was fun," was all I could say. "Do you see anything out there that needs blowing up?"

Lawrence began to laugh and just pointed outside.

"Pick a piece of rock and I'll set the coordinates for the cannon. I'll let you take the first shot since you're so blood thirsty."

The first blast of the plasma cannon took our breath away. It made the test fire of the original cannon used on Earth appear weak in comparison. Our target, a rock the size of a small mountain more than ten miles away, was completely disintegrated after one blast. It was so impressive it left both Lawrence and me slack jawed.

"Have you ever seen anything like that, Sands?"

"Never saw anything like it, partner. Do you suppose that rock was anywhere near the size of Queen's ship?"

All we could do was stare at each other and then look outside at the small particles of rock still spinning away from the blast site.

"I forgot to ask, did you get everything recorded?"

Lawrence smiled and pointed to the monitor on my right side. The white flash of the plasma blast leaving the ship was fascinating as was the moment it struck the rock. Lawrence slowed the sequence down so we could see the rock turn a dull red before exploding.

It was time to turn around and head home. We reentered the atmosphere, feeling none of the heat, and descended using the antigravity engine. The only failure was to the communications array. Once we were behind the Earth and flying in the shadow our radios conked out. The tower at Edwards finally reached us on my cell phone as we were on our return approach.

The commotion on the ground once we arrived kept us busy explaining all that we had experienced.

"Did Lawrence really let you fly that thing?" Lillian wanted to know.

That caused a fury of other questions and enough noise to give me a headache.

The noise diminished as Lawrence replayed the plasma cannon test fire on the conference room monitor. Excitement in the room completely disappeared at the same moment the rock disintegrated. It was as if the devastating power of the cannon brought to clear focus the reality of why the small ship had been built.

Someone in the back of the room called out, "Was that what you were expecting, the total annihilation of that rock? Could that be used against us?"

It was Lawrence who replied with some rancor a more obvious answer.

"It's a weapon that can be better used against the Queen."

The room was now deadly quiet. The only sounds were the occasional word "Oh" coming from the group as they finally realized why we had contracted for the manufacture of the new ship.

"I suppose all of you thought we were given a gift and an exciting new toy to play with," he said. "We are under a threat. Before she gave us all the new 'Toys,' that threat would have been enough to defeat us. We're still trying to figure out why

Queen was so generous but it's certainly not a noble gesture on her part. She usually takes what she wants. You can bet your sweet asses that she wants all the upgraded technology you develop."

Lawrence's vehemence surprised me. He had been acting submissive ever since he was allowed off of Queen's ship. It suddenly dawned on me that the only time he had truly seemed happy was when we blew up the piece of space rock. Maybe happy wasn't the right word. It was more maniacal, as if he finally had the means to repay Queen for her treachery.

I wasn't the only one stunned as Lawrence stormed out of the room. It took a second before I followed him out to the hanger where our first test bird was being inspected.

"I suppose you are thinking of taking this baby out and blowing Queen out of the sky," I remarked as I came up behind my friend.

"Don't you think she deserves it? She hijacked you, too, didn't she? Well, she wanted more aggressive and I want to show her what human aggression looks like."

"I have no problem showing Queen what we can do but what about all of the other folks on that ship? Roz and Minister believe the Jinn are coming to their own conclusion that they have been ill-served by their monarch. And what of all our children that are due to hatch? They don't deserve to die because of your need for revenge."

"How can you have been a cop for so many years and not want a little pay-back? Every cop show has at least one guy who needs to get his rocks off fucking with people. Why couldn't you be that guy?"

"I probably had a few partners who thought the same thing. Not in my nature, I guess. My preference would be to separate Queen from her ship and her people and send her floating in to the sun minus a space suit, of course. If that's not possible, we try to rescue as many of the Jinn that want to emigrate off of the ship, and that includes the children."

"What does your buddy, the President, think of option number two? That sure would create a shit storm in Congress. As to the fucking eggs, I had no idea Queen was going to use me as a sperm factory. All I wanted was a piece of exotic alien ass. What proof do we have that Queen really inseminated one hundred eggs with my sperm? It's an abomination, Sands, and morally bankrupt. It makes me want to cut my nuts off."

"You forget that there are another hundred eggs inseminated with my sperm ready to be born. I can't sentence them to death and I sure don't want them to be raised by Queen. So, now you know what I think. How are we going to solve this conundrum short of mass murder?"

Lawrence's face was a picture of torture. He was shaking his head as he walked away, turning every so often to see if I was going to follow him. I didn't. My feet were rooted to the concrete as his footsteps drifted away.

Needing a friendly voice, I called Alice, hoping she was between classes.

"It's about time you called. How was the test flight?"

"It was awesome, babe, but the after effects not so good."

I related the joy of the flight and then Lawrence's reaction to a question of how the ship and weapon were going to be used.

"He's acting like a real nut case at the moment. I think I need to get him back to Roswell so Cassie can work some magic on him."

"She's really starting to show, Mike. With how he's feeling, is it a good idea to shove the fact that she's carrying your children in his face?"

"That's all Queen's doing, not mine."

"That makes it all the worse. He might end up hating both you and Queen."

"Maybe Lawrence is right. Maybe we should blow Queen out of the sky."

"Wouldn't that be fulfilling Queen's wish that you become the Marauder? It's not a good option."

"You always see the logic in things. It's one of the reasons I love being close to you. Taking a step back from being lovey dovey, before Lawrence and I took the new ship on its maiden flight, Roz and I discovered some new information relating to Dora and how it affects the Jinn. You and Doc Farris need to give the information a thorough going over before we make any decisions on what to do with any of the Jinn. I'll be home in a couple of hours."

CHAPTER 45

LAWRENCE GRUMBLED SOME WHEN I suggested he return to Roswell with me but boarded the shuttle without further complaint, especially since Carlos was behind him with a hand in his back. Roz had us off of the ground and on the way within twenty minutes of my making the decision to leave.

Alice, Jeannie and Joe Farris were waiting for us when we landed. Both Roz and Lawrence were searching the other faces hoping to see Cassie but she wasn't there. Alice noticed me looking at her baby bump and pulled me aside.

"Cassie moved back to the dorm to be with the other pregnant women. She didn't say why but I got a sense it had to do with the tension of having two men in her life. I guess she isn't as understanding about a poly family as we are."

"Maybe it's Lawrence and Roz who have the issue. They're both supposed to be adults so let them work it out. Right now, we need to deal with a more pressing problem. Let's grab Carlos, Jeannie and Joe and head to his lab."

I wouldn't answer any questions until the two botanists had loaded the file in Joe's computer. Jeannie surprised me when she stood over my shoulder as I began to explain what I found on the file and then corrected some of my translations.

"Uncle Joe, Minister and I have been studying by using your translation program, Pops. We wanted to help you figure things out," she finished by wrapping her arms around my neck.

All I could do was smile when I realized she might be better at this than I was.

"Okay, little girl, you take over while I sit on the couch and watch."

The two botanists and Jeannie pored over the file for two hours before realizing I had dozed off. I awoke to Joe poking my arm.

"I need your take on this file, Sands, and don't try to sugar it up."

All three of them were gathered around me and waited while my sleep deprived mind cleared.

"Okay, here's what I think. It was my impression that the Ancient scientists had tested the Jinn with several different variations of Dora. It is much as you did, Joe, when you refined the addictive properties out and set the standard for new crops. How close is that to your assumptions?"

"Close enough for now. My question is what was the normal Jinn disposition before all the testing began? Minister and his chums have been on my modified Dora for months and they don't seem to be ready to kill anyone. Do you think if Queen had knowledge of this information, and had someone who could read this gibberish, that she would have needed you or Lawrence to propagate her next generation of Jinn?"

"Roz said he didn't think that the files in the larger shuttle had been viewed until we did when on one of our flights. I have to believe that must be true based on your last conjecture. So, what do we do now? Just so you know I'm against replicating any of the testing done by the Ancient's."

"No one is suggesting that," Alice said. "Breaking down the chemical composition of the samples shown in the graphics might aid us in determining if we were ingesting an adulterated product. We really have very little background on what Dora is and this might shed some light on where it came from."

"So, bringing the files here was a good thing?"

"You know damn well it was good," Joe shouted. "You've gotten a damn sight smarter since you took up with Alice so don't act like you don't know shit. What we need to discover is which of the samples led to the Jinn becoming violent and ensuring that whatever it might be is not inside any of the product grown on Earth. Now, I want Carlos to take you and your family home so I can get some real work done."

Alice made me sit down for a meal before escorting me off to bed. I was asleep before my head hit the pillow so I don't know if she was disappointed in my lack of attention. I was awake by six the next morning. Alice was already in the kitchen and looked like she hadn't had much sleep.

"Sorry I crapped out on you last night, babe. Why does it look like you didn't get much sleep?"

"I was on the phone with Joe half the night discussing his findings and then couldn't fall asleep. He thinks he found the compound that caused the Jinn to go psycho. None of it is in any of the Dora we have on Earth. We're not sure what variety Queen has in her larder or what she feeds her consortium of ships to keep everyone loyal."

"It still doesn't answer the question of where the Jinn came from or whether they were another variation of the same race as the scientist. Personally, I like the Jinn we have here and would not want to run up against the crazy ones noted in the files."

Alice kept dozing off as she sat contemplating her cup of coffee, so I suggested she get a couple hours of sleep.

"I'll do that but I want a favor from you," my wife remarked as she kept her head propped up with one hand. "You need to go to the dorm and visit your baby mommas. I kind of promised them you would do that when you got back to town. I'd go with you but I'm too tired."

"You know how that freaks me out, Alice." The look I got needed no words. "Okay, I'll stop by but only for a little while. Meanwhile, before I go, why haven't I seen Lee Anne?"

"She's been attending to some Reservation business. She didn't say much but she looked concerned. Give her a call. Maybe she'll talk to you."

Since it was too early to visit the dorms, and Alice had gone to bed, I risked waking Lee Anne if she had been staying with her father on the Reservation. She answered on the first ring.

"God damn it, Mike, I'd hoped you would call last night. Are you okay, no injuries or mishaps from flying the new ship?"

"The ship was fine and everyone was excited. I was too tired to do more than fall in bed. I'm sorry if you were worried. You could have called Alice or Lillian for any news."

"Alice maybe but Lillian is too clingy to suit me. So, I need to know if you are coming out to the Res today. Abraham and the Council need some answers and they are not listening to me for some reason. They insist on speaking to you. That pisses me off, being the Chief's daughter and you…"

Lee Anne stopped before saying that she thought that I was not really an Apache.

"I'll be out in a while. I promised Alice I'd visit with my twenty-five other wives first. How's my Apache bride doing with her pregnancy?"

"You'll see when you get here. Now go visit with all the little women and keep your pants on. Pregnant girls get hornier, you know."

"Why does everyone forget that I had nothing to do with physically making those women pregnant? Sorry if I shouted but everything about this makes me sorry I ever met the Jinn."

"I'm not. Whatever Queen did to you has made you a far more interesting man. You should ask her if you don't believe me."

Lee Anne ended the call before I could think of a smart retort. The only thing left to do was to find Carlos and head to the university.

Cassie and Chrystal were waiting for me in the dorm lobby. Alice must have given them a heads up about my pending arrival. Cassie gave me a very tight hug making her baby bump press in to my stomach. Chrystal did the same and tried to give me a kiss to match. I turned my head at the last second which earned me a disappointed look. All I could think of was Lee Anne's warning about horny pregnant women.

Chrystal grabbed my arm and led me to the cafeteria where the rest of the women were waiting. For not having given any of them much attention all wanted me to feel their bellies and listen to how much they loved carrying my babies. Lillian was never that into the idea; too busy; "Maybe later," she'd say.

I gave it an hour and a half before I had to get away from the smothering I was receiving. All twenty-five women walked me out to my car which must have caused a lot of eyebrows to raise and fingers to point and waggle. All Carlos could do was laugh. We were half way to the Res before my heart stopped pounding and I was able to take a normal breath. As soon as we parked at the Council Building Lee Anne came out to greet me.

"You look like you've been through a war, babe. Was it too much to handle all twenty-five preggy women at once?" Lee said snidely as she started to laugh while at the same time giving me a hug and moving my hand to her growing belly.

I don't know what it is with my women. All of them seem to enjoy my uncomfortable moments and are not hesitant about setting me up for more of them.

"Am I going to get ambushed inside or is this just a Q & A session?"

"The Council is concerned about all of the government traffic," she said while looking at Carlos. "Having one or both Jinn shuttle's parked here makes for a lot of curiosity of the official kind," another look at my security partner, "and from the locals who can't seem to keep their mouths shut. In the last few months Tribal Police have had to shoo a bunch of yahoos off of our lands. Who knows where they came from? The numbers keep growing and that worries the Council."

"I suppose it's time to move the Jinn and our offices to a location that won't draw as much attention. It would be nice to have a hanger or warehouse where we could hide the shuttles when they're in town even if it's a little way out of Roswell."

"I'll get on that while you go in and placate the Mescalero. Be especially nice to Abraham. He's been defending you all morning."

"Your father is the one person on the Council that I am always nice to."

The meeting with the elders of the tribe went as expected. Once I volunteered to move my collection of Jinn to new quarters, they decided it was time for a small celebration. Abraham, my father-in-law and the tribal Chief, passed around a bottle of twenty-year old scotch and announced that he was the one who had made me decide to move out. One toast later and I was on the way to the basement to inform Minister and the other Jinn that they were going to be moving.

Ten minutes later, on our drive back to Roswell, I received a text to call POTUS. Carlos shrugged his shoulders letting me know he hadn't caused that to happen. The President answered on the first ring.

"What happened to your calling me every day, Sands? Is our bargain so unimportant you can blow me off?"

"All I can say is I'm sorry, John. By the time the flight was completed and we were on the ground I was a little busy with the engineers who needed my feedback. I was running on short sleep and then had to restrain the blood lust in my partner."

"Forgive me if I'm a little blunt but who the fuck gave you permission to fly that plane? Your job is to be the boss, not someone who flies off whenever he damn well feels like it." There was a pause and then, "Now that I got that out of my system," there was another pause, "tell me how it was flying that thing. The video of you blowing up that rock would have made me wet my trousers had I had been there. Where the fuck was Carlos while you were gallivanting all over space?"

"There are only two seats in the plane and I don't think Carlos would have done too well strapped to the fuselage. But the ride in that ship was awesome. The video of the first use of the plasma cannon did not do it justice. Watching that huge rock come apart was one of the most devastating and yet thrilling things I have seen."

"One of these days, Sands, I am going to have to see that for myself. Was the blast strong enough, do you think, to disable the Bitch's ship?"

"There are ten of the new ships nearly completed so, yeah, they could do the job. But there are some considerations before we go that far."

"You're not going soft on that big insect, are you? I won't stand for any talk that spares that thing."

"Queen is too devious and dangerous to be let off. However, there are a lot of Jinn who would welcome getting out from under her thumb. There are also the children to consider."

"God damn you, Mike; I hope you're not thinking about all of those bugs moving to Earth and taking up residence. We've got enough trouble with finding space for folks on Earth who want to cross our borders. No damn way you'll be able to get Congress to approve that plan unless you convince them it was their idea. Fat fucking chance of that happening."

There was a lull as I could feel the President thinking.

"Here's another thought for you. You've said there are one hundred little cross bred eggs on that ship that have your DNA, is that right?"

"One hundred of mine and another one hundred of Lawrence's."

"Did Queen assume that you were married to her?"

"She referred to me and Lawrence as her consorts. I don't believe there is such a thing as marriage on a Jinn ship. Why is that important?"

"Section 301 of the Immigration and Nationality Act says that if one of the parents has had a residence in the United States or one of its outlying possessions prior to the child's birth, that child would be a U.S. citizen at their birth. I have no idea how the Supreme Court would look at a bunch of half insect alien births fathered by a U.S. citizen in outer space. God, I'm going to get hammered if this gets out prior to the election next month. You owe me the courtesy of keeping this all under wraps for a while. Can I count on you, Mike?"

"What's your position going to be on the Jinn and the children once you are reelected?"

"I don't know. There's a lot to consider. I'll try to do what's right for both you and Lawrence but I won't go against U.S. law or the Constitution. My conscience and my party won't let me. Do you understand me?"

"I get it. I also get that I might have to make plans to get things done on my own. Do you understand me, Mister President?"

"I do, Mike. Just make sure you come out of things alive. You've got a real nice family that needs you and, although it's hard to admit, I'd like to think I'll have you as a friend for a long time when this is all over."

CHAPTER 46

A FEW DAYS WENT BY WITH no new calamities to occupy my time. With Carlos attending to some family matter, it allowed me time to drive my old pickup around the area looking for vacant property. Edith Murray, my real estate broker, called saying she had some news.

"Edith, I hope you've something good to tell me. I think I've covered Roswell three times over."

"It may be good news if you don't care what the property looks like."

"Almost anything will be okay so long as it is accessible and large."

"Well, there's an abandoned warehouse west of the airport that's been empty for a number of years. It's about to be put up for auction by the bank but I asked them if a cash offer could get them to forestall things. We have two days to make a decision. I hope this property is a good choice as there is absolutely nothing else in the city that meets your needs."

"You always come through for me, Edith. Thanks."

Her next test message identified the address as 1201 South Nevada Road, in an almost desolate area southwest of the airport. There was no vehicle traffic on the road as I made my way to the abandoned building. The west end of the airport was an airplane grave yard, something that would mask any sightings of my two shuttles. One private residence was across the road but no other buildings were close enough to see anything that might happen at the property. The warehouse was in rough shape, needing new roll up doors and some high security fences, but it might serve our purpose. The neighboring residence might make a good home for the Jinn, giving them a sense of independence, so long as that didn't come back to bite me in the ass. All I needed was an okay from the President and a promise of some additional funding.

Edith seemed to be waiting for my call.

"Get me a good discounted price on the warehouse, Edith. Make those bankers squirm. And while you're at it, see who owns the house across the road and see if they want to sell."

"Is this another of your impetuous purchases or do you actually have use for that worthless piece of property?"

"Eye of the beholder, old friend, and yes, I do have a use for both properties."

"You're always fun to deal with, Chief Sands. I'll call you back."

Edith was always very cooperative especially if it meant she was going to get both ends of the sales commission.

Pictures of how I was going to improve the warehouse so it could provide shelter and a secure location occupied me as I worked on a design on my tablet. Expecting Edith to call me back I was surprised when the phone ID identified the caller as Joe Farris.

"Hey, Joe what's…"

"Stop talking and listen. I need you out here to my place. Alice is on her way from the college so get your ass in gear and get over here."

"What's this all…" was all I got out when the line went dead.

Joe was always abrupt but he usually allowed me to finish a sentence. The fact that he had Alice on the way had my nerve endings jangling. Putting thoughts of the warehouse aside I spent the next twenty minutes driving and trying to figure out what calamity Joe had uncovered.

It seemed like a convention was taking place based on the number of vehicles parked in front of Joe's house. Alice's SUV was parked next to Carlos's Suburban and a couple of other cars I couldn't identify were behind them. Carlos was on the front porch waiting for me and walked to my truck.

"Joe is in some kind of a mood, boss. He's got Roz and Minister in there and Lawrence and Cassie just showed up. What's going on or are you just as mystified as I am?"

"Joe's always full of drama but this is over the top, even for him. Best thing to do is to let him play his game and maybe we'll find out."

Everyone in the room, including several security personnel, turned to stare at me as I walked inside. Joe came bustling up and grabbed my arm.

"You're not going to believe this, Sands, but I might have figured out Queen's game," he said as I was pulled over to his lab.

"You remember when we were all concerned about the design of the Dora and its genetic structure? Well, I've been doing some correlations between the Dora, the Jinn, the pregnant women, and that includes Alice and Lee Anne, Lawrence and finally you. I was wondering what Dora was doing to us especially after you showed us the video of the Ancient medical officer and then the file showing the variations in Dora. Guess what I found?"

"Am I going to get a chance to answer or are you going to interrupt me again?" Joe just grunted. "Okay, so tell me."

"I got to thinking back to when we all went out to that first field of Dora and all of the plants kept shying away from me. I thought they were sentient at first but their actions always bothered me. When you came back from the Jinn ship and figured out that you had become a sperm donor something clicked so I started to research anyone who had been in contact with the Jinn. I retrieved DNA samples from all of you, Jinn and human, looking for a connection. I added all the pregnant women, including your wives, to donate a sample. Don't get your panties in a bunch, I'm getting to the point of all this. Now, consider this fact. Eating food products native to this planet has no effect on the genetic structure of the human body absorbing it. Dora, as evidenced by the files you gave me, would appear to do the opposite. Comparing the genetic structure of everything I have mentioned I assumed there would be wide variations due to ethnicity, diet, blah...blah...blah. What I got was very strange. All of you, including me, have extra sets of genetic pairs that, in humans at least, should not be there. I had to round up some folks who have not been exposed to Dora and found they didn't have the markers. Your markers, Mike, are similar but different and appear to have been a part of your genome for most of your life. All the outsiders disavow having eaten anything with Dora so why aren't their markers identical to yours. Can you explain that?"

I was at a loss to understand what Joe was saying. It had been the longest string of words the old scientist had ever uttered in my presence. Looking at the glazed over eyes of most of the people in the room I felt they also wondered where this was going. I suddenly made the connection.

"You think I've had contact with the Jinn at some other time in my life, before I met Lillian, is that it? Is that why the Dora seemed to accept me?"

Joe ignored my comments and went on with his story.

"I called in some favors and had a colleague round up some old blood samples of yours, from medical exams both here in Roswell and in Los Angeles. I compared them to the latest samples all of us took in the last year. There was no Dora on Earth back when your early samples were taken so your suggestion is probably the correct one."

"That's insane, Joe. I would have remembered something that traumatic, don't you think?"

"Didn't you say you lost a bunch of days on the Jinn ship?"

"Yes, but I did manage to get those memories back, after a fashion. I've got nothing that tells me I was visited or abducted."

"That's why I have Minister and Roz here. Both have been part of the Jinn scientific team that I assume was responsible for the abductions of the women living on the Jinn ship. Cassie, can you tell us how long it took before you realized you had been kidnapped?"

"It was different for all the girls but most of us felt we had lost a month or more. It was one of the older girls who told us that we had been on the ship for a while. None of us can recall the missing time."

"And you, Minister," Joe continued, "wasn't it you and your cohorts who caused this memory loss on your captives?"

That caused all eyes to move to the Jinn.

"There is much you do not know, Doctor Joe. It is true that the Jinn have been to your planet more than once, more times since this Queen became our leader."

"And each time you kidnapped more of our people. What was the purpose?" Joe was on a roll but agitated, his fists held tightly at his side.

Minister was squirming and I heard him throwing thoughts out asking his fellow Earthbound Jinn for support. None responded. He finally looked to me for help.

"Queen told you, Mike, that she wanted you as a consort. Did she hurt you or Lawrence? None of the guests on our ship have ever been injured and all were eventually returned to this planet in better health than when they left."

"You keep avoiding the question, Minister," I threw at him. "Sure, I wasn't injured, as far as I can remember, but why put me in a coma and then steal my reproductive material. Wouldn't a simple request have been appropriate? And what of all the women being forced to become sex slaves for you and the rest of the males and then get impregnated against their will? None of that sounds much like being a guest. It is much more like being a prisoner and a test subject."

"Would a prisoner have been given as many gifts as Queen gave you?" Minister whimpered. "What did you offer in return? You provided the Queen samples of material easily replaced. Lawrence did the same and had the comfort of Queen's body as his prize. The Jinn do not give things away without payment even if there is no verbal agreement as to an exchange."

"Why does it sound as if you still remain loyal to Queen? It's not been more than a couple of days since you and your brothers claimed you needed to shift loyalties to me. I guess that was just joke, am I right? What about you, Roz, is that how you feel?"

"No, No, No, Mike. You are only hearing from Minister. My brothers and I have sworn ourselves to you. I don't know what Minister is talking about."

"You misunderstand, Mike Sands," Minister cried out. "As before, I was explaining the Jinn philosophy not where my allegiance was pledged. I am still a Jinn, after all, even if my ideas are different from Queen's. The fact that you were drugged was not done on my order nor any of my team. That was all done on the order of Queen."

CHAPTER 47

"WHY IS THIS THE FIRST TIME we've heard about this?" I was getting very pissed and Minister was my target.

"You never asked that question before. I have always answered you with honesty, unlike others on the Jinn ship."

The conversation with Minister was bringing up other thoughts, some new and some as if dredged up from deep in the muck in my head.

"Let's go about this a different way. Joe, you can jump in any time you want with more specific questions."

The room was quiet as if everyone was waiting to hear where I was going. Minister was bouncing on the balls of his feet as if he was preparing to run out of the door. Even Roz was getting nervous, probably thinking that if Minister didn't have the answers, I wanted that he would be next on the hot seat.

"You said that Queen used the Maloi to carry out specific instructions. What kind of things did they do?"

"They worked with modifications to the Dora genome. They also were used to obtain the subjects that were used for our examinations."

"What kind of modifications?" Joe demanded to know. "How would they know what to look for?"

"They were given specific information by Queen. Dora has always been fed to all of the people of the Consortium but some needed to be modified to meet their dietary needs. There were at least six different formulations, most for food and others for the creation of materials to make things like clothing. There was also the structure change needed to use the Dora as fuel for the ships. That was one reason why we needed so many garden locations to raise the various versions of the crops, like the one where we first met. Raising Dora is my specialty."

"I've developed over a hundred different variations for the use of Dora," Joe boasted, "and the Maloi only managed six or seven. How is that possible?"

"That was all the information Queen had managed to uncover."

"She managed to uncover," I all but shouted, "uncovered from where? According to Her Highness none of the Jinn or her associates could understand much science or engineering concepts. Supposedly, that's why she handed that stuff to me, including all the untranslatable files from the Ancients. It's very convenient that she gave the Maloi information that was in the Ancient's files, don't you think? How about you, Roz, does any of this seem unusual?"

Roz's eyes got large when put on the spot. All he could do was shake his head.

"What are you suggesting, Sands?" Joe wanted to know. "Did the bitch actually have access to the same information you found on the shuttle and managed to understand it?"

"That's not possible," Minister cried. "Queen always said the texts were indecipherable. We would have felt it if she had been untruthful."

"We call that sort of thing lying or acting like a politician," Joe threw out.

"It's already been shown that Queen is able to hide the truth so lying is not that far a stretch," I mused. "It does beg the question that if she had the Ancient scientist's notes why make it seem as if she needed us to translate them."

"I believe it was you, specifically, that was needed, Mike," Minister managed to squeak out while staring at the floor. "Queen spoke of you often while we were on the return to your world to plant the Dora crop. That desert site was opportune because she knew you were close by. She claimed that you had been a favorite and constant topic of her predecessor. Queen's way of mentioning you was not very complimentary. She had been sworn to continue surveillance of you before the old Queen died and our Queen ascended the throne."

My head was spinning as I tried to connect all the dots.

"Joe, what was the chemical composition of the first batch of Dora you found? I mean, what was it supposed to do and, if you altered it, what did you change?"

Joe went to his desk and rummaged through his notes. That was the only action in the room as everyone watched the old scientist moving stacks of paper from one pile to another. Alice moved over to assist him as it was her analysis that confirmed the plants alien nature. Five minutes later both scientists smiled.

"The original plant we examined," Alice said while looking at Joe, "contained compounds that were shown to improve health and vision. One of the smaller components, not identified at first, proved to be some kind of a sedative like drug. We initially discounted its purpose until we noticed that people ingesting the early Dora enhanced foods had a tendency to be extremely relaxed and easily directed. When the compound was removed the normal human condition returned. We found the same compound listed in the notes you brought back from the shuttle, Mike."

"Which version of Dora was fed to the Jinn and the Consortium?" I wondered out loud.

"Since there was never a moment when any of the members of the Consortium acted as if they were unhappy with the manner in which Queen ruled, I would assume that a version of the Dora you first experienced was given to everyone," Minister admitted reservedly. He sounded very respectful as if trying to work his way back to my good graces.

"You have to know that someone was able to concentrate that shit," Lawrence jumped in for the first time. "I mean everyone involved in Queen's fuck fest had to drink a small bottle of it before we were compelled to perform. That included all of the women, too. That sure didn't make us feel mellow and unenergetic. Very much the opposite considering the length of time we spent copulating."

"But you didn't feel angry or ready to do battle," I remarked, "at least I didn't when I was using it to generate more energy while transcribing the Ancient's text."

"So that's two versions," Joe stated, "plus whatever was used for fuel makes three."

"And none of the alternative uses was ever explained to us," I spat out. "She wanted us compliant but made no effort to take advantage. I wonder, was it all a test?"

"She's playing us again," Lawrence said, "just like she does everything. It's all one big game and we were supposed to be the prize."

"She has to know by now that Earth won't roll over and let her take over," came from Carlos who had always been my silent partner and advocate. "Everything we've seen and learned was that Queen has spies on the planet and must know that our defense systems can blow her out of the water, so to speak."

"Sure, she has to know that but she also must know we can't do that with all the innocents on board her ship. Lawrence and I might disagree on what to do about liberating those Jinn that want off her ship, and that includes the babies, down here but I, for damn sure, won't let them die."

"Queen's experiment with cross breeding was to be a temporary measure. I think she always intended for you to try to save them," Minister offered. "Her other option was to feed them, especially the females, to her workers."

"Please explain what that means," Alice said, moving to glare up at the taller Jinn.

"Unlike humans, we honor our dead by devouring them. Unwanted females and the disgraced are punished by being given to the workers. It is considered penance for the guilty but the workers consider receiving the dead a reward. Mike's children, and Lawrence's, were most likely to be studied and then given to the workers in a ritual ceremony. On the other hand, should you rescue all two hundred, you would be forced to find homes for all of them. My question is with both yours and Queen's genetic material, who would be the one to earn their allegiance? Do you think you could trust that they would not spy for Queen?"

"So, I can't abandon them and it might not be prudent to bring them here, is that what you're saying?"

"We are not leaving them out there with that evil woman," Alice threatened. "You need to save them, Mike Sands, and give them a home."

"Here, in Roswell, the home of alien invasions? How do we care for two hundred half alien beings? No, make that two hundred plus however many babies are close to being born in the dorm. Christ, I can already feel the heat the President is going to throw our way. What if our only ally doesn't get reelected, and then what do we do? Depose Queen and I take her place as the monarch of her consortium?"

Everyone was now staring at me. Minister, Roz and Cassie were all nodding yes while the rest were in shock.

"All of the girls at the college would like that, Mike," Cassie commented with a smile. "No one on Earth would understand us having half alien babies and wanting to keep them."

Lawrence spun around and stared at the diminutive woman who was holding her very large belly.

"You'd go back to that ship with Mike rather than stay here with me or even Roz?"

"I'd go to space in a heartbeat," I said forcefully before Cassie could answer. "But only if I was allowed to build one of the behemoths whose designs we found, and only if my Earthly family would agree to go along."

Alice had been ready to punch me but instead grabbed my arm and held tight.

No one was saying anything so I sat down on the couch waiting for another shoe to drop. Before I could utter a word, my head spun as more long forgotten memories flooded my head.

I was taken back to a time when I was no more than five or six. I was in a near state of delirium suffering from viral pneumonia and laying in a bed in a children's hospital. A plastic tent, the side puffed out, covered my body. All I could feel was the thrum of a motor and a slight breath of cool air flowing across my face. I was the only one in the room as far as I could see. Turning my head or moving my body was painful and disorienting so I was limited to what I could see from the corners of my eyes or a view of the ceiling through the plastic.

At one point a shadow filled my vision. A warm hand reached in under the side flap and brushed the hair from my forehead. That was my last thought as I fell asleep. When I woke I felt better and wasn't in any pain. It didn't seem as if any time had passed, but by the shadows in the room I knew it must have been a different day.

A nurse, sounding excited, was at the foot of my bed speaking to my mother.

"It's not normal for a child to recover so quickly Missus Sands. Three days ago, he was in a severely weakened state and close to…I'm sorry, I almost said the wrong thing. He was very ill and today he is almost ready to get up and walk out of here."

"How's that possible?" my mother was shouting, not believing the nurse. "Doctor Ryan told us to prepare for the worst and now you're saying the doctor was wrong?"

"You make it sound like you're disappointed the boy is going to be okay, missus. You should be overjoyed that whatever we did, or God did, he is on the way to recovery."

My mother looked over at me and then turned and walked from the room.

"Aren't you even going to say hello to your boy, Mary Sands," she said to my mother's disappearing back. "Damn stupid woman, you should be happy."

That night, with the tent gone, I was again awakened by a hand on my forehead. The smile on the face of the woman standing over me made me feel loved, something I rarely experienced with my mother. It was as if I could hear the woman talking to me but she never said a word out loud.

"There will come a day when we will meet again young Mike Sands and you will prove your worth. This is the last treatment so drink up and go back to sleep."

She moved the vial of blue liquid to my lips and held it as I drank. As my eyes closed, she was moving away from the bed and then she was gone. I never saw her again.

"Are you okay, Baby?" Alice said worriedly. "You had another one of your fade outs. Either that or you needed a nap."

Alice was sweeping her hand across my brow, an act that felt so familiar and caused me to shiver.

"I was remembering when I met the old Queen."

"What?" Alice exclaimed.

"When did that happen?" Minister shouted. "She's been dead for a long time."

"I was a very sick young kid and she paid me a visit in the hospital. She fed me vials of liquid Dora and cured me. Minister, what can you tell me about the previous Queen?"

"She was loved and thought of as the greatest Queen of all. As you know, the Jinn do not feel emotions as do humans. When the current Queen killed her and usurped the old one's seat, I am told that the entire ship was in tears. I was too young to know why but I still cried with the older ones. The only one not to shed tears was the new Queen. If the old one had truly visited you, Mike Sands, it means you had to be special and justifies our decision to pledge loyalty to you."

"Well, Sands," Joe said sarcastically, "I guess that might explain why your DNA markers are different than the rest of us but not what the old Queen was looking for when you got the surprise visit. It also proves that liquid Dora, in one form or another, was in use long before the bitch came to power."

"This is the first time I can remember thinking about her and no one, alien or human, has ever mentioned the old one's visit to me. I might have been sick back then but I still know I lost three days while I was recovering. Why do I get the feeling that I'll only get the answers I want by paying a visit to Queen?"

There was a chorus of 'No's' and 'What are you thinking?' surrounding me but I knew Queen had been waiting for me to come to that conclusion.

CHAPTER 48

NOT WAITING FOR WORD TO get back to the President about the meeting at Joe's house I made the required call. "What news do you have for me, Sands? You have to know I get very anxious waiting for you to tell me something I'm going to like."

"I'd love nothing more than to do just that. Okay, so there are a couple of things. Doctor Farris called a meeting out at his place today to discuss genetic changes in those of us that had consumed Dora. All of us had extra DNA pairs that are not present in those who hadn't ingested Dora. We also discovered that Queen was using one of her Consortium alien members, the Maloi, to do a lot of her dirty work. Queen seemed to have some knowledge of the files we uncovered but not enough to give her an advantage over us. She appears to have passed that information to the Maloi."

"So, what does that do for us? Sounds like Queen has her own agenda and doesn't care what we do."

"That's the trap, John. I seem to be right in the middle of things. The children are the bait and I, for a reason I still haven't figured out, am the prize. We all agree that she wants me back on her ship but I'm not about to fall for that until we have all ten of our new planes ready to give me some support."

"Under no conditions are you to go near that bitch, Chief Sands. That is a direct order from your Commander in Chief. Is that understood?"

"I got it, boss. I wouldn't know where to look for her ship so that's a moot point. Anyway, my other news is that I need another appropriation. The Apache want us off of the

Reservation and I'll need a place to house my team and the shuttles when they are in Roswell. I found a warehouse near the airport graveyard that suits our purpose but it needs a bunch of work. I should have an estimate of what we need to spend once the bank holding the property gets back with the sale price."

"What the fuck, Sands? The election is in three weeks and you keep coming up with dumb shit ideas that could derail the thin margin I'm riding on. A building near a graveyard is very appropriate since both of us might end up there. This had better be a sound investment or we're all fucked. You know, you're a hard man to keep as a friend. Keep me posted."

I was listening to more dead air which seemed to be the way most of my phone conversations with the President ended.

Another family counsel was waiting for me when I got home. Alice and Lee Anne never let me relax or grab a drink before they started in on me about making a trip to Queen's ship. Jeannie, Carlos and Lawrence were in the background to give my wives some support.

"Stop it, all of you. The President has given me an order to stay on Earth. You're wasting all that energy for nothing. Now, can I pour myself a drink or do you have more to say?"

Having stolen their thunder I was surrounded, once again, by my women.

"You're not planning on listening to him, are you Mike?" Lee Anne demanded to know.

I took her face in my hands, something that usually upset her.

"I promised the man I would stay home for the present. I never said it was forever."

Kissing Lee Anne was usually a good way to end things and that was what I did.

That first glass of bourbon led to a second and a third before Alice took the bottle away from me. My recliner felt so comfortable that I was asleep in a matter of minutes. That's when I saw the old Queen again. She was stroking my forehead and telling me a story, a story of how I came to be.

As I was remembering, her entire conversation was in my head. The hospital ward was dark, only one or two night lights were shining in the corners of the room. Even so, the beautiful face of the story teller was like its own shining light.

"You have no idea why you are special young man, so I'll tell you. Some time ago your mother was on my ship. She was not happy so we didn't make her stay. I gave her a gift before she left to go to her new home, something of me that she carried inside of her. Your father, one of our other guests also left a gift with your mother and that was you. You will not think of any of this conversation until a time when it becomes very important. Rest now my son and be well."

Jeannie shrieked as I jumped off of my recliner and stood staring at nothing. Alice and Lee Anne ran to me, each grabbing an arm as if afraid I might fall. Jeannie was hugging me around the middle.

"Was it another memory, baby?" Alice asked. She was looking at me as if I had gone crazy for a minute.

"What memories are you talking about?" Lee Anne wanted to know.

Since I was not answering Alice replied.

"He keeps getting flashes of memories, things that were repressed. He had one earlier today when he recalled having met this Queen's mother when he was a boy. Whatever's happening, it sure upsets him and makes him act all weird."

"I'm okay now, ladies, but I need to sit back down."

"Are you going to explain what just happened?" Alice demanded, not letting me move.

"I'm not sure I can, babe. It explains things that nobody ever discussed when I was around. They are things that I wanted to, no, make that needed, to know from when I was a kid. It explains why my mother never gave me the affection I saw other kids get from their parents. If the memory is true my whole life may have started on a lie."

"Damn, Mike, that sounds like a soap opera kind of story," Lee Anne said, trying to lighten up the mood.

"That's not the best part. We assumed that Queen was the first of the Jinn to infuse her DNA in a human genome in order to create a hybrid. What if her predecessor, her mother, had the idea first? What if an unwilling human visitor provided a gift that impregnated a female Jinn who, like all the women at the dorm, was allowed to go to Earth."

"When was all that supposed to have taken place?" Lee Anne asked, going along with her earlier soap opera theory.

Alice was standing quietly next to me and took my hand. She had figured it out.

"It was over fifty years ago," I said speaking a little louder than a whisper.

Lee Anne looked over to Alice ready to laugh until she saw her sister wife's face.

"Sweet Jesus," Lee Anne cried, "you're talking about your mother, aren't you?"

"It also means that Queen is his sister." Alice said as she buried her head on my chest so that I was supporting her.

"It's probably why the old Queen came to visit me in the hospital, to make sure her grand experiment didn't die out before reaching maturity. So the question is what the fuck do I do now?"

CHAPTER 49

SLEEP DIDN'T COME EASILY THAT night even with two very warm bodies curled up next to me on the king-sized bed. The thought kept running through my head that I didn't know who I was supposed to be. One repressed memory had seemingly changed everything. Queen had to know about our relationship but what of the other Jinn. Tempting as it was, I put off trying to contact Minister or Roz to put the question to them.

I gave up trying to sleep just before the first rays of sunlight hit the horizon. I squirmed out from between my wives and headed for the kitchen. While the coffee brewed, I scanned the internet for any new items that mentioned alien invasions or sightings of aliens in America. Every kook had an opinion of when an invasion might take place but it was all bad fiction. We were in the clear and better yet, so was the President. My big concern that morning was whether or not to inform the President of my discovery.

At seven Lee Anne came in already dressed for work.

"You look like shit," she said. "Trouble sleeping? Too many horny babes crowding you out? Personally, I slept fine, probably because of the bed warmer next to me." Lee Anne poured coffee in her travel cup and turned back to me. "I wish there was some way for me to help you decide how to go forward, baby, but I have no idea what you need to do. Call me if you think I can help with anything." One quick kiss and ten seconds later she was out of the door.

My e-mail announced a new message as I pondered my next move. It was from Edith Murray.

'The bank quoted a price of one hundred fifty thousand for the warehouse. It's a fire sale, Mike. They were so eager to unload the property that they finally settled for seventy-five thousand. Hope that works for you. The house across the way is supposed to be vacant. I contacted the owner, a Missus Wilcox, an elderly widow, who was just as eager to sell. She agreed to forty thousand for the five-acre parcel. Turns out both properties were going to be bulldozed as soon as they could be unloaded. Need to know soonest. Edith'

The President answered on the first ring.

"Please say something good, Sands. This has been a ball buster of a morning."

"Can we get one hundred and fifty thousand for the two properties is my first comment?"

"Yeah, we've got a slush fund for small amounts like that. If you need more just ask. You need to put those properties in your name and keep the government out of it. I'll have the money transferred to your account later this morning. What else do you have for me?"

"This part is kind of difficult, John. I had another recovered memory, actually two, yesterday, that are kind of important. You already know I pull facts and memories out of other people but these two go back to when I was a kid."

"Please make this the short version. I have people waiting for me."

"When I was a young boy, I was in the hospital and received a visit from Queen's mother, the old Queen. She told me a story of how my own mother had been one of the early females impregnated. While on the Jinn ship, she was somehow infused with the old Queen's DNA, impregnated by one of the male abductees and sent to Earth. Yesterday was the first time I knew about it."

"So, what does that mean to me?"

"It means that Queen is my sister, sort of."

"You're not fucking changing sides, are you?" blasted out of my ear piece.

"Christ almighty, John, are you paying attention? Not only was my mother basically raped by the Jinn, I ended up fertilizing my sister's eggs. Can my life get any more screwed up?"

"Wait, does that make you a part scum sucking Jinn?"

"I'm human; at least Joe Farris claims my DNA identifies me as human."

"Okay then, just keep your dreams or memories, whatever they are, to yourself. I'm rising in the polls so you make sure..."

"Yeah, I understand. We need each other." Once again, I was talking to dead air.

Feeling somewhat disassociated from things it felt like I needed to be away from everything. I grabbed Carlos and made him drive me to our soon-to-be new warehouse. While we were on the way I sent Edith an e-mail letting her know the money for the purchase of both properties would be in my business account that day and to close the deals. My mind was still trying to wrap itself around the facts of my birth so there was almost no conversation during the drive.

"I don't suppose we have a bolt cutter in the back?" Since we were agreeing to a purchase, I wasn't too worried about getting arrested for trespassing at a vacant and derelict building.

"If that's to cut the lock off of the chain link fence you won't need one. I scouted this place out last night and the gate probably hasn't had a lock on it for years. Insect repellant might be more appropriate."

The rest of the ride was made in silence. The gate to the parking lot was standing wide open when we arrived. Two old abandoned looking pickup trucks were parked next to the open largest cargo bay and country music was quietly coming from somewhere nearby.

"Do you think we have company today, boss? Maybe you should call for some extra help before going inside?"

"Not yet; let's see if they mind the extra company before we give them the old heave ho."

The inside was dim but light enough to make out that there were no people inside. There was the smoldering remains of a small fire out on the floor. It wasn't until we got closer that we were able to see what was left of what must have been a party, including the remains of a small stuffed animal in the fire.

Seeing the stuffed animal brought back images of wild parties my mother had taken me to when I was no older than seven or eight, parties where she was seeking out her next companion for the night or week. Pictures of mostly naked men and women drinking, smoking and playing grab ass before heading to the shadows to do things that a youngster shouldn't know about began overlapping the space around the fire in front of me. Some of the young partially dressed girls in my mental picture looked like they were scared to death.

Somehow, that image made me think of a ship full of kidnapped young women who were subjected to abuse by the males in the Queen's security team. Thinking about my mother being molested caused me to snap.

Several very bad things were going through my mind on how I wanted to confront my mother regarding the way she had treated me and the Queen for how she had treated her kidnapped females. The sound of squealing tires in the parking lot brought me back to the present. Lee Anne and two other officers came rushing in, all of them looking surprised to see me standing alone in the middle of the warehouse.

"What the fuck, Mike," Lee Anne shouted. "What did you find this time? Carlos said you might need help."

It was like a fog was clearing and I must have looked stupid as I was unable to answer at first.

"Something triggered a bad memory of my mother and it got me all riled up. I kind of lost myself for a minute."

It was Lee Anne's turn to give me a hard look.

"Do you think something bad happened here last night?"

"I'm not sure. I've seen debris like this at parties back in LA. I assumed the same thing was going on here. I didn't think this was a meeting about selling Girl Scout cookies."

"What do you want us to do?"

"Look around the area for obvious OD's and maybe any women who might have been molested." Saying that I turned away and walked out to the parking lot.

Carlos, seeing my sour expression, grabbed a fire extinguisher and a shovel from the back of the Suburban and walked back inside the warehouse.

Lee Anne followed me outside. She reached over and gave me a kiss on the cheek. "You're not having a very good couple of days, are you, Chief? Too bad I don't have time to make things all better for you. Keep your schedule open for tonight. I'll see you then."

Once the tow trucks had arrived to impound the two pickup trucks and the police units had departed, I walked back to watch Carlos preparing to douse the still burning fire. Most of the party debris had been scooped up but personal belongings that obviously belonged to some of those attending the party still littered the ground. Feeling the anger starting to return I grabbed the shovel and dumped it all in the fire. It was as if I was burning away something unhealthy that had been in my head. Looking over my shoulder I noticed Carlos standing quietly but still holding the fire extinguisher.

"Let it burn for a while and then put it out. I'm going to walk the perimeter of this place and see if any other trespassers are hanging around."

My last thought as I walked away was how I would like to have had Queen join all the detritus in that fire. By the time I had made a complete circuit Carlos was putting the shovel and fire extinguisher away. I pointed across the street and began a walk to the purportedly abandoned house I had purchased.

CHAPTER 50

MY FOOTSTEPS CRUNCHING THE GRAVEL on the driveway didn't do much to soothe me as I made the long walk to the front of the house. The sound of country rock pouring out of the front window disrupted the calm mood I was just starting to achieve. Carlos pulled up behind me in the Suburban before I could knock on the door.

"Hang on boss. We have no idea who's inside this place. Let's take it slow."

Carlos walked around the outside of the house and nodded when he came back down the driveway. Pounding on the door didn't seem to attract any attention. I was seconds away from kicking the door in when a voice from inside called out.

"We ain't wantin' anything, so go away."

I ignored that and began pounding on the door frame since the door looked like it was ready to fall down.

"What the fuck, man? You crazy? I said to go away." The door swung open at that last comment. A guy, no more than twenty and covered in tattoos and body piercings, stepped forward not expecting to see me on the doorstep and Carlos standing in the driveway, holding his service weapon. The man took two steps back, tripped on the ragged edge of the carpet and landed on his ass.

Because of the way my day had gone and the funny look on the man's face, I was unable to control the laugh that came out. It felt good having something to laugh at. Carlos was trying to hold a laugh in but he finally relented.

"Why you think this is funny?" the man on floor screamed.

"Sorry, it's been a rough day. Who are you and why are you in my house?" came out between chuckles.

"Name's Tyler and old man Frazier said we could kick here for a while."

"Who's this old man Frazier? The old owner before the bank took it was a lady named Wilcox."

"What's all that to you, anyway? I ain't movin, if that's what you think."

Movement at the back of the room caught Carlos's attention.

A young Apache girl, maybe twenty, was in the doorway to the hall. I froze in place because the girl looked like a younger version of Lee Anne. She reached over and turned the music off making the silence feel louder than the noise it replaced.

"Hello, Chief Sands," she said. "I'm surprised to see you here."

"Who the fuck is this guy?" Tyler started to say.

"Shut up, Ty, and don't interrupt again." She even sounded like Lee Anne. "Sorry about Ty, Chief. He's really kind of stupid but mostly harmless. Are you here to evict us?"

"What's your name, girl? Let's start with that and then we'll talk about evictions."

"It's Ellie Torrez. We met on the Res when you and Lee Anne had your commitment ceremony. She's my cousin and I guess now you are, too."

"You related to the pig, Ellie? That's not good, as far as I can see." Tyler was still on the floor. He suddenly shut up when he saw the look on Ellie's face. It was Lee Anne all over again.

I made a quick decision.

"Tyler, you need to gather up all of your gear and get the fuck out of my house. Any delay and my good friend, Carlos, will have to give you some assistance. Do we understand each other?"

"Ellie, you gonna let him do me like that?" Tyler said from his place on the floor.

"You better start packing, Ty, and don't bother to try to see me again after you're gone."

My phone going off distracted me. It didn't surprise me when I saw it was Lee Anne.

"Can't I leave you alone for one minute," assaulted me as soon as the line connected. "Carlos texted and said you were dealing with more trespassers. Do you need my help?"

"Not unless you want to help deal with your cousin Ellie. Seems she is one of the trespassers."

"Abraham is not going to like this. Did she do anything stupid? She's normally a good kid. Can I come get her?"

"She's okay. I'm kicking her boyfriend out but she's staying. Are you still looking for party survivors?"

"Yeah. We found a couple of young girls roaming around, still high but alive. I've got a female sex crimes detective with them. No telling what they were made to do. And what did you mean when you said Ellie's boyfriend? You better keep him around until I can get over there. That means Ellie, too."

Lee Anne must have been walking as she talked because I heard her car start up just as the phone disconnected. I was really getting tired of having people hang up on me.

Carlos walked up next to me and leaned in close.

"Not making any judgements, boss, but I can see the wheels turning in your head. You're worried that Lee Anne might want to have Ellie join in your house full of females, aren't you? You might be asking for a lot of trouble."

"Thanks for your concern, partner. You know how your advice about women has worked out for me in the past. My plan is to let Lee Anne handle things and for me to get far away for a while."

"Where are we going and when do we leave?"

"Roz and Minister need to come with us. It's time for another heart-to-heart chat about Jinn history, especially where it concerns me."

Ellie had snuck up on us as we discussed our plans.

"I know about the Jinn," she announced as if she was discussing her daily agenda. "Uncle Abraham had me delivering meals to them in the Council Hall basement and I got to talking to them. A couple of them are kind of cute and wanted to practice their vocal skills with me. Are you going to move them over here, is that why we're getting evicted?"

"You put two-and-two together pretty fast, young lady. Why are you so interested?"

"I like them is all. If they are moving in here, the place will need to be completely cleaned up. Those guys are very fastidious. Can I volunteer to make this place ready?"

"Jesus, how did we go from you trespassing to becoming the property manager? Do you think you're up to it?"

Carlos slapped me on the back and walked outside to hide his laughter. He was just in time to see Lee Anne careening in the drive, sliding to a halt alongside the Suburban. She bypassed me and Ellie and headed straight for Tyler.

"Is there one good reason I shouldn't throw you in jail?" was what she managed to sputter out. Her look of disgust was so palpable that I had to take a step away. "In fact, it might be better if you were not anywhere in New Mexico nor any closer than two states away from my cousin. Is that clear enough?"

Lee Anne kept an eye on Tyler as he put all his belongings, meager as they were, in the front yard. She turned her attention to Ellie who had moved behind me.

"I'm taking you home, Ellie, so don't give me any shit."

"I'm not going back to the Res, Lee. I'll run away first."

"Not the Res, dip shit, home, where I live. You're okay with that, aren't you Mike?"

I nodded and heard Carlos in the background saying "I told you so".

"The Chief said I could redo this place to make it ready for the Jinn. Are you okay with that, cousin?"

Ellie was looking back and forth between Lee Anne and me so I walked in the house to reduce the number of approvals needed. When my phone went off this time I was happy for the distraction.

"Chief, it's Edith. The money showed up five minutes ago. You'll need to sign the papers tomorrow morning. Anything else you need done?"

"Order a roll off trash container for the house and make sure all the utilities are on and changed to my name. Get hold of your engineer buddy and send him out to the warehouse. I'm out of pocket for the rest of the day. Call Alice or Lee Anne if you need something."

This time I cut the phone connection first.

CHAPTER 51

WITH LEE ANNE HAVING EVERYTHING under control, Carlos and I drove to the Res to collect Roz and Minister. As usual, Roz was excited to take the big shuttle out for a spin and Minister seemed eager to get back on a more positive footing with me. Both were waiting outside the Council building and made a rush for the shuttle as soon as we pulled up.

I let Carlos have the co-pilot's chair while Minister and I lounged in the passenger section.

"Here's the deal, Minister," I said as the shuttle lifted off. "Last night, after our somewhat chaotic meeting at Doctor Joe's place, I had another memory pop up. It seems my mother was taken before I was born and gifted with one of the Old Queen's eggs. Then my mother was impregnated by another abductee, a man also given the same gift, and then both returned to Earth. Does any of that sound familiar?"

Minister was smart enough not to speak and sat looking uncomfortable.

"So, nine months later out I came, loaded with the old Queen's DNA. Now, fifty years later more children are ready to be born but the loving, benevolent mother Queen is nowhere to be found. Instead, we get the devious and corrupted new Queen. My question to you, Minister old pal, is why was my mother chosen and why so much interest in me?"

"You ask me questions that I can only speculate on. You forget that I was very young when Queen replaced her mother. All I might know was what I heard my elders discuss after they stopped grieving."

"Just tell me what you know or who to contact that might know more."

"You would have to contact Queen's ship. That would probably alert Queen and put others in danger."

"Why are you being so obstinate? Five minutes ago, you wanted me to contact friends of yours on the ship. Do you think I'm worried about anything Queen might think? I can take care of all the Jinn if I need to."

Minister and Roz exchanged a brief look and both began to look despondent.

"Rumors went around the ship that the old Queen was slain because she planned to bring you to the ship to be raised as her son and the next ruler. That caused a disagreement among the Counselors over the propriety of bringing an outsider onboard, especially one they considered an alien, and changing the historic manner of succession. Now Queen is worried that you might still want to assume the position that the old Queen had intended for you."

"This is all bullshit, Minister. All Queen had to do was to stay away from Earth and plant her damn Dora on some other planet. You're not saying something. I can feel it sitting there."

"She thinks you tarnished her name by causing her to kill her mother instead of allowing her to die naturally. Part of her coming to Earth was to get her revenge by first earning your trust and then causing you to be disgraced."

"So, I get the earning trust part based on all the gifts I received but how does that become a disgrace?

"In Jinn society it is presumed that the return gift will be at least as magnificent as the gift given. She believes you will be dishonored by your failure to have done so."

"Taking my sperm was not enough of a gift?"

"She felt that was her right to take as she would the seed from any consort. To her mind you have not given anything as compensation."

"Has she forgotten about the aggressive nature of humans? What if I were to give her a few sonic blasts in her engine compartment, would that suffice?"

"You would destroy everything on the ship?" cried Roz. "That would be murder."

"There are numerous governments on this planet who would see Queen as an aggressor and gladly take the first shot. Why has Queen learned so little of human nature if she has been taking victims from our planet for who knows how long?"

"She listens to her Counselors, Chief Sands. I know this because I was one of them before deciding you were following the correct path."

"So now you choose to advise me, is that it? How do I know you aren't doing the Queen's bidding?"

"Look in my mind if you do not believe me. You are far stronger than Queen and can see everything that I say is true." Minister was almost in tears, a most un-Jinn like appearance.

Minister's mental keening was so loud in my head that it took a second to realize he had been joined by all the Jinn below us on Earth. My first reaction was to tell all of them to quiet down so I could think. The suddenness of quiet was so complete I worried that I had harmed them until I saw the peaceful look on Minister and Roz's faces.

"How were you able to do that?" Minister said in wonder. "Queen would have let us go on until we were all exhausted."

"You were hurting my head so I had to stop the noise. What was all that?"

"It was the community sharing my grief. It does not happen often but the Jinn experience it several times in their life cycle."

"Can you tell how far away you have to be to not be influenced?"

"Since you did not join in it was probably only felt locally. I'm not sure what would happen if you added your power to the grief."

"Does Queen get affected in the same way as the rest of the Jinn?"

"Of course she does. She is one of us. Is there a reason why you asked that question?"

"I am looking for a way to disable the Queen without killing her. It would be good to have her somewhat incapacitated when we have a conversation."

"If you are able to incapacitate the Queen it would also incapacitate all of the Jinn on the ship. That would leave us vulnerable to the more aggressive members of the Consortium."

My mind was turning over trying to understand what Minister was talking about. I thought the Jinn screaming in my head had disoriented me but realized that he had gotten very worried.

"What does the Consortium have to do with my talking to Queen? She gave me the impression that they were all her lap dogs; that she had saved them from worse elements out in space."

"There are over eighty Consortium ships that rely on the Jinn for food and fuel. They gladly accept what Queen gives them but it does not mean they enjoy being dependent on her generosity. If they were ever to join forces instead of distrusting each other they would become a major problem for the Jinn. If you disable all the Jinn while trying to control Queen you would endanger not only them but your world as well. Queen is the one who keeps the Consortium from pillaging your planet."

"I suppose Queen is aware of that and depends on you to advise me of her reality."

"It is why she didn't oppose me when I said I was going to join with you, Mike Sands."

"Ten war ships aren't going to be enough, are they?"

"If the Jinn are not able to provide food and fuel to the Consortium, they will go to Earth to obtain it. Most of the races are not nearly as civilized as humans or the Jinn. Do you understand the difficulty you face? Queen will allow all the new children to go to Earth with you as their master if you allow her to leave with the Consortium," Minister said as if he was reciting something he had memorized. He went very quiet and had a hard time looking at me. "You have to forgive me, Mike. I had no idea Queen had left that message in my head to deliver to you."

"Damn that woman, she's played me again. I can't shoot her down or disable the ship without putting all of Earth and the Jinn at risk. Dig around in your head and see if there is a message that suggests what I do next."

Minister looked upset but he had no answer.

"What about you, Roz, do you have anything to say?"

"I was never close enough to Queen to receive anything. I'm not even sure she realizes that I never returned to the ship."

"Next question, how long do you think I can delay before having to make a decision on what to do about Queen?"

"Isn't that a concern for your friend the President?" Minister asked. "Much seems to depend on his support."

"Good observation. He's the one who provides us with the money to keep our project going. If he does not get reelected, we might not have a friend in that office. Funds could get cut off, additional ships would not get ordered, the children, mine and Lawrence's, left for the Consortium to deal with and Earth under a threat of invasion. I'm dependent on my relationships with a friend and an alien. John Philips is not going to be happy when I tell him about this discussion. I don't suppose you could find me a bar located this far from Earth?"

It shouldn't have surprised me when Carlos pulled a flask out of his jacket pocket and passed it over to me. He looked pretty smug as I took a hefty drink of the boze that I realized he had taken from my bar in Roswell.

"Take us to Edwards, Roz. I need to make plans and discuss things with Lawrence and Lillian before I make a complete ass of myself."

CHAPTER 52

LAWRENCE'S PLAN WAS TO WAIT for the rest of the first order of space planes to arrive and then blow every Consortium ship we could find out of existence. His was the only plan that was so drastic and never addressed the overwhelming odds he would face. Lillian's suggestion was to take me to bed and think of something while we relax. I knew there would be no thinking done if I took her suggestion. In fact, no one had any ideas that were any better than me having a heart to heart with Queen. An afternoon of discussion gave me nothing useful to tell the President.

The President's aide answered the private line on the first ring.

"He's up to his ass in alligators, Chief Sands. He'll call when he is able." More dead air.

I took Lillian up on her offer, figuring that some stress relief might clear my head. My ex-wife was more than happy to oblige.

Six hours later the President's call arrived.

"Have I ever expressed what a fucked-up job it is being President, Sands? So, if you tell me that the only way to deal with the bitch is to go to war, well, I don't want to hear it."

"That was Lawrence's suggestion but it would really put us in a bad spot." I went on to give him the various scenarios ending with my plan to talk to Queen rather than kill her.

"If she's so strong," John declared loudly, "that she can control so many alien ships, why hasn't she tried to control us?"

"She needs me as an ally, even if she truly hates that she does. So, she plays head games and makes me work for answers and suggestions that satisfies her and makes me feel dependent. That, of course, is her point of view. Mine is to play her game and beat her. Doing so is still going to cause us to do just what she wants us to do. That, by the way, is the opinion of my Jinn advisors."

"You see, Sands, you have in fact become my first intergalactic ambassador. I wonder what Congress is going to think when I announce that appointment after the election. In case you haven't been paying attention I'm up in the polls by almost eight percentage points. Not dead bang but it's getting there. But, just to be sure, make no obvious moves that can hurt me until the final votes are in. The Electoral College shouldn't be a problem. If you decide you need to make a move, be sure to give the bitch my regards."

With the sudden end of the call the feeling that the President had given me tacit approval to move forward made me smile. Now I had to figure a way to find Queen's ship and get on board without getting killed.

Lawrence thought I was crazy right up until I told him I needed as many of the new ships ready for flight before I tried to find Queen. Finding qualified pilots was another matter.

"It's already taken care of," Lawrence remarked, a snarky smile on his face. "I contacted some of my old squad mates and maintenance crew personnel so we could be ready for our next adventure when you give us the go ahead. The next five ships are due here within a week."

"How long do you need to train the pilots and flight crew?" I asked hoping it would not be too long.

"Less than two weeks should be enough. Those birds practically fly themselves. On that subject, what about coming up with a name for the planes? Calling it a space plane or something like that is not to the teams liking."

"I suppose you already have a suggestion."

"Do you have any objection to calling them Scorpions? It has a nice ring to it and everyone I asked seemed to like it."

"Seems like there was a military jet being developed by that name."

"So, make them Interstellar Scorpions if you're worried about copyright infringement. We built these things to protect Earth and kill invaders. Scorpions are good at that."

"Fuck it, Lawrence, call them what you want. Just make sure your team is ready to go after the election."

Lawrence turned and began walking away but I caught his parting remark.

"We'll be ready and I trust Queen enjoys what we are about to do to her."

My thought was that I hoped Lawrence was not going to be too disappointed when I ended things with Queen without a shot being fired.

The next week was chaotic with two Interstellar Scorpions arriving every other day until the first six were lined up on the pad in front of the hanger. Not wanting to get in the way of the training, I had Roz fly my little band back to Roswell.

By the time we landed Ellie had cleaned up the new residence and moved the Jinn to their new quarters. Edith had her architect draw up plans based on my design for the warehouse and presented them to the city for approval. Since everyone else was handling things, I took the opportunity to sit back at home and run ideas through my mind on how to deal with Queen.

A new problem presented itself on an evening when I had consumed more than a fair share of thinking sauce, a bottle of Maker's Mark.

"You realize that all of us women are getting pretty far along in our pregnancies, don't you?" Alice threw out at me.

I smiled and looked bleary eyed at my wife's expanding belly. Since she was so close, I reached out and lovingly placed my hand on top of our child. Alice smiled back at me and held my hand in place.

"Have you given any thoughts on how we were going to care for all of the babies being born so close together? We'll probably need more than two neonatal doctors and several nurses to handle the daily needs of mothers having multiple births. Luckily, none of the mothers look like they are going to deliver early so we have over a month to get organized."

Something about the manner in which Alice delivered her announcement dragged me back from my state of intoxication.

"Why does it sound like you have already put a plan in motion? Is there something I should be doing?"

"Don't worry, baby, Doctor Joe and I have got it handled. We've both called on people we've worked with who would enjoy conducting a project dealing with multiple women giving birth at the same time, all of them having no family connection and no support structure, except for us, of course. We are getting donations of equipment, most of it used, and staff from all over the country. Everyone is excited and just waiting for a call announcing the first impending birth. The only thing they don't know is that there is only one father for all the babies."

"And let that be our secret, other than talking about you and Lee Anne." My mind cleared even further, ruining a good buzz. "How does that work, both you and Lee Anne ready to deliver at the same time as the others?"

"We become a control group of sorts. Neither of us is having a multiple birth so we should recover faster. The whole plan was to have our two babies measured against the babies carrying the Queen's DNA."

"Might there be a conflict since the children of the twenty-five will have the DNA of both the old Queen and the current one? I'd want to see what the genetic code on those kids looked like before your team discovers the extra pairs of DNA."

"Are you worried that having input from two Queen's might cause problems?"

"You mean four of us, don't you? Each woman, two Queens and me."

"Damn, Joe never phrased it like that. I wonder if he considered that factoid."

Alice plopped down on my lap and nestled against my neck.

"This is going to be so much work, baby. Just make sure you don't go flying off to challenge Queen and then forget to come home."

"I have a feeling everything is going to end up all right. Just keep my place warm until I get back."

CHAPTER 53

R oz, Carlos and I made another trip back to Edwards to see how things were progressing. The President had been correct in his assessment and had been reelected by a comfortable majority of the popular vote. Now it was up to me and the team to ensure that the Earth remained safe.

Lawrence was strutting around like a peacock as he proudly showed off his fleet of Interstellar Scorpions. There was a little confusion when I called for a team meeting and Lawrence had to take a back seat.

"Everyone here knows who I am but I'll give an update for the new pilots and crew members. My name is Mike Sands and I am the Director of Project Roswell. My boss is the President and I am the only one who has the responsibility to keep the man informed and receive his orders. Lawrence, at my request, made sure that all of the Scorpions were flight and fight ready. It is my job to ensure that everyone here, pilots, crew, engineers and other support staff, are ready to assist me in delivering a message to our presumed enemy that will avoid putting us in an unwanted conflict."

As I looked around the room, I could see agreement on all but the pilots. They were trying to get Lawrence's attention as if to ask why he had said he was in charge. Lawrence was slouched down in his chair and was not looking at anyone.

"Just so we are all clear, if there are any doubts as to the chain of command on this project you are free to come to me, Lillian Sands, Lawrence Davis or anyone who has been with us since the inception of Project Roswell. Are there any questions so far?"

The room was quiet except for a few of the older engineers telling me to get on with things.

"Our mission is pretty evident, to find the Jinn ship and contact the Queen. Once we locate her vessel, a very large interstellar ship, I am going to initiate contact with Queen and travel to her ship for a face-to-face meeting. Roz will fly me there in the larger shuttle and Lawrence and the Scorpions will ensure my safety from a safe but still lethal distance. There is some very valuable cargo on that Jinn ship that I demand be kept safe. Armed conflict is to be a threat only unless you are fired upon. Do I make myself clear?"

One of the new pilots shouted out, "I thought we were here to eliminate an enemy not coddle them."

This had to be some of Lawrence's rhetoric that was being thrown out.

"Queen has eighty ships in her fleet, eighty ships that are somewhere outside of our galaxy. I have no idea what kind of armament those ships have on board nor what their attitude might be if their fuel and food supply is destroyed along with the Jinn ship."

The murmuring in the room got louder as people began to realize that Earth could be in line for an invasion or worse.

"Everything Queen has done to get us to this point was self-serving. Earth is fertile ground for production of Dora, the source of most of the Jinn's food and fuel supplies. We can either be her ally or her enemy. Since she controls her Consortium, it seems appropriate to keep Queen on a leash since she has no idea what we can do to her and her fleet. It is important to remember that most of the advanced equipment we are able to use against the Jinn came from them. Our advantage is that they don't realize how good we are at improving on the technology. It's a close game of chess and we are at the end game. Let's make sure we have her at check mate. Any other questions? If not, let's go to work."

Once everyone had cleared the room Lawrence came stomping up to me.

"You made me look like a fool to my pilots, Mike. They need to have the utmost confidence in me as a leader and you might have put that in jeopardy."

"When did you forget who was in charge of the project? All of your team should have been given that information. All I did was reinforce what needed to be said. You still lead the flight team and I am relying on you to keep me safe. Fail to do that," I said and then paused, "and there are a whole lot of women who will want your scalp."

My smile at the end seemed to ease the tension and I could see Lawrence's shoulders relax. He was nodding his head as he grabbed my hand.

"My biggest problem in the military was my inability to follow the directions of my superiors. It's the prime reason I never promoted past Captain. My anger at Queen and my old superiors somehow got transferred to you and that was wrong. All I ask is that you get your ass off of that Jinn ship before giving me the order to knock it out of the sky. I will do everything in my power to make sure you get back to Roswell...alive."

"You need to keep your finger off of the trigger and all will be well, partner. I've got a hunch that I'm going to come out of this smelling sweet. Seventy-five babies are counting on me."

"You mean the ones on Earth, don't you? What about all of the others on the Jinn ship?"

"That's all part of the discussion, isn't it?"

"Did Queen ever tell you when they were supposed to hatch?"

"No, but Minister thought it should be about the same time as the girls at the university. He seemed to think there was some kind of a connection between the girls on Earth and the eggs on the ship. Normally all the Queen's eggs hatched within a day or so of each other but that time was long past. Are you worried about the eggs you fertilized?"

"I'm not sure how I'm supposed to feel. They're mine and not mine. How are you feeling about the ones you, I mean, Queen fertilized using your junk?"

"Same with me, I'm not sure what to feel. Curiosity is probably close. I'm still trying to get over being the father of all the babies about to be born in Roswell, other than the two I had direct participation in making."

"Is there any chance I could go with you to talk to Queen?"

"Not this time; especially not this time."

Lawrence was quiet for a long moment before he looked up.

"When do we go? My guys are ready and I know you are so let's do this thing."

"Let's plan for the day after tomorrow. I need to get back to Roswell for some personal time. You could do the same with Cassie."

"Don't take this wrong but she's having your babies, not mine. It makes things kind of awkward."

"You don't know it's not yours. Whether you recall it or not she claims that you were with her on the ship and for some long encounters in my house, if embarrassed smiles mean anything. Come with me so you can talk to her. We'll leave in a couple of hours."

There was no surprise when we found Lawrence on the shuttle when Roz, Carlos and I came onboard. Roz allowed Lawrence to take the controls as we headed east. Carlos and I took seats in the back not wanting to overhear anything the two rivals for Cassie's attention had to say. It ended up being a quiet trip.

Alice and Lee Anne were waiting for me when Carlos dropped us off at the house. One of the girls had convinced Cassie to be there, too. Her greeting Lawrence in the living room was very brief as she quickly dragged him back to their bedroom. Alice and Lee Anne liked that idea and we soon followed to our room.

We spent the next day together, adding Jeannie, by going on a picnic. I was surprised when the girls wanted to go to the same field where the first crop of Dora had been found. We parked on the rocky rise above the field, amazed that a new crop was already chest high. Minister and two Jinn that I didn't recognize were in the middle of the field. When I looked down after a while Minister was walking near the edge of the crop on his way to where we had spread our blanket.

"Mike Sands, I am surprised to see you out here. Have you come to reminisce?"

"It's more of a farewell lunch. Can we offer you something to eat?"

"No, I have already eaten." Minister looked at my family and seemed to hesitate before he spoke again. "Would you accompany me to examine the crop? It's the newest variety designed by Doctor Joe."

Not knowing what was on his mind, I followed. As we walked down the hill I reached over and touched Minister's arm, a sign of friendship to the Jinn.

"We haven't had much time to talk, old friend. I wanted you to know that I hold no hard feelings as a result of our last conversation."

"You need never worry about how I feel or how any of the Jinn feel. You are the one who we have chosen to follow and know you would not intentionally do us any harm."

We kept up the discussion as we were walking.

"You can see how the Dora has chosen you as well," Minister gloated.

"It's kind of unnerving, if you ask me. Why does it do that?"

"It recognizes your genetic composition and knows that it comes from the old Queen. A secret I have only told Doctor Joe is that I took skin samples off of the branches from your first visit to these fields, collected DNA from the cells and imbued the master plant on the Jinn ship with it. Every Dora plant knows who you are and that they are related to you."

"I don't suppose Queen knows about that, does she?"

"Of course not. She would see it as an act of treason. But in the years since that visit every Jinn, and even those of the Consortium who use Dora, has been eating Dora with your essence inside. Even Queen now has a part of you inside. Do you not find that ironic?"

"Ironic isn't what I was thinking. I need the opportunity to defeat her, if we can manage to find out where her ship is located. And now I might be fighting myself when we meet."

"Your genome is so much stronger than hers, especially with the additional essence of the old Queen, that you should have a decided edge." There was another brief silence. "My reason for taking you away from your family is to ask if I might join you when you meet with Queen."

That request caused me to stop and stare at the Jinn.

"Won't that be dangerous for you? You did switch loyalties and abandon the Jinn ship."

"If there are other Jinn on the ship who feel as I do the only way to verify it would be for me to appear by your side. We would each gain stature and I would be able to receive the pleas of those who wish to follow us."

"And Queen is just going to sit back and allow that to happen? She's a tricky and conniving witch who had no hesitation in killing her own mother. I don't think she would hesitate doing the same to us, given half a chance."

"You must not express that kind of weakness, Mike. That will surely be our end."

"In the game of chess, you only show weakness when it opens the door for a trap. Okay, you can come along. It might actually be the distraction I need to pull out a win."

By the time I got back to the picnic Lee Anne was looking angry.

"What did that traitor want with you? I hope you gave him a good tongue lashing."

"Why does everyone assume that because a person looks human that they will react like one? Minister is a Jinn and sees things from a Jinn perspective. We had a good talk and I received some important information on my handling of Queen."

"So now you're best buddies again?"

"I trust that he is loyal to me, at least until he proves he's not."

"Why does that sound like you're going to take him with you? That could be a major mistake. I don't want you to do anything that will jeopardize your safe return, husband of mine. I know Alice thinks the same way."

"I promise to be back before the babies arrive. Now, can we just enjoy the afternoon and not think about the Jinn?"

That last statement sounded hollow since we were sitting not one hundred yards from a field of blue vegetation planted by the Jinn.

PART IV

BUILDING A COLONY

CHAPTER 54

CARLOS WAS IRATE WHEN I told him he was not invited to the Jinn confab. My reasoning was that he had his family in Roswell and I didn't want to see them devastated if my mission failed.

"That's utter bullshit, Sands. You have a bigger family than I do and that's not stopping you from risking your neck. My orders from the President are to keep you safe and I can't do that if I'm still on Earth."

"That's a very compelling argument but the answer is still that you are not going. Much as I hate it the responsibility to see an end to this whole fiasco is mine. I'm not even sure that Queen would allow you on her ship. It might be difficult enough getting Minister and Roz on board and I'll need them to guide me away from any potential land mines. Do me a favor and look after my family if you insist on providing protection to someone."

And that was how we left things as Roz took control of the shuttle and flew Lawrence, Minister and me back to Edwards to meet up with the Scorpion Wing.

It took another two days to make sure that all the ships were fueled and equipped with enough food and miscellaneous supplies to last for several weeks.

The game plan was for the shuttle to lift off first and get some distance from Earth. A search to locate Queen would be initiated and once contact was established the Scorpion Wing would follow. Somehow, I was not surprised to sense Queen and the Jinn ship parked in an orbit less than eight million miles from Earth.

"So, what do we need to do to connect with your people, Minister? I assume they will still be ready to assist us if we need them."

"I will have one of my friends in my head and all you need to do is call out to him. If it is safe he will answer."

"Who is going to have the conversation, me or you?"

"I will speak to him first and then you can address any questions he might have. This one has been unhappy with our Queen for a long time but never had a way to express himself without placing himself in danger."

"You're sure Queen will not be able to intercept our conversation?"

"There is always a chance for that, especially if my friend has already been compromised."

"What a nice time to mention that, Minister. How likely is it that we've already been found out?"

"Connect me and we will soon find out."

All the worry and tension seemed to be for naught as Minister's friend was ecstatic that we were on the way. We were told that Queen had been busy preparing for her newest broods to hatch and was often not seen for long periods of time.

At our maximum speed of just under one hundred fifty thousand miles an hour, which didn't include the time needed for acceleration and deceleration, we were still almost three days away from the ship. Lawrence and his crew had departed Edwards not long after we had contacted the Jinn ship. Even with a higher top speed, he and the Scorpions were still going to be at least a half day behind us.

Minister and I used the time to run various scenarios but every ten minutes he would shake his head.

"You over think everything, Mike. React to the moment and don't let Queen intimidate you."

I was jumpy as a cat on hot asphalt right up until the minute the Jinn ship came in to view. A momentary sense of calm came over me, the same calm I had felt when the old Queen came to visit me in the hospital. We had come to a stop waiting for the Scorpions to get close; enough time for Minister to contact his friend to let him know we were near the Jinn ship and enough time for my nerves to begin to fray.

Roz began a slow approach to the Jinn ship, the first time I was able to truly see how enormous the vessel was. There were no alarm bells going off as we settled in at a bay deep inside the ship nor did we encounter a welcoming committee. We secured the shuttle and had Minister lead the way to the Queen's quarters.

Every Jinn we met on the way accepted our being there as if we had always belonged. The sense of normalcy caused my skin to crawl, barely accepting the feeling that there was a trap waiting for us just a little further up the way. By the time we made it to the Queen's chamber I was even more nervous than on our approach to the Jinn ship. All of that anxiety crashed when we walked in to an empty room.

A female attendant rushed by us, stopping to stare at Minister but then smiling at me.

"Queen is with your children, Mike Sands. She is aware that you are here," came in my head as she rushed out. With the Jinn on Earth now speaking aloud it suddenly seemed strange to return to silent conversation.

"How do we get to where ever the eggs are kept?" I threw out uneasily, hoping someone would lead me to the Queen.

"Only women are allowed to be in there," Minister answered, acting shocked and almost as nervous as I was. "You will not be able to get past the guards."

"Just point me in the right direction and let me worry about that."

Minister walked to a hallway behind the Queen's couch and pointed to two females of a type I had not seen before. They were stationed at both sides of an ornate doorway and were already looking at Minister and me with evil intent. Minister scrambled back to the Queen's chamber where Roz still waited, leaving me to face the guards on my own.

With Minister gone the two guards relaxed and actually smiled as I approached. The first one put her hand on my arm, a sign of respect, and reached to open the door.

"Queen is waiting for you. She instructed us to allow you inside. It is a great honor, Mike Sands."

"Thank you, but why is everyone being so cordial to me? Hasn't Queen said that I am an enemy?"

"To the contrary. She has boasted about how you were going to release us from our connection to the Consortium. You are our savior."

My mind was in turmoil as I was led through the first door and to a hall with doors opening to two chambers. For another first, each door had writing on it, nothing I could decipher but similarly close to the Ancient's language. My guard opened the first door and gently ushered me inside. The air was warm and very humid causing sweat to form on my face and all over my body. Queen was standing across the room and smiling. In front of me were small beds, each holding what I thought looked like pupae. I could see forms inside squirming, each form looking like a human baby.

"These are all your children, Mike Sands. Are they not beautiful?"

I don't know what shocked me more, that the children were all mine or that Queen had spoken aloud.

"How is it you can speak when all you ever did was put stuff in my head?"

"You are to blame, my beloved consort. When I became aware that you encouraged my Jinn on Earth to strengthen their vocal muscles, I decided that I should do the same. Even with the stress and discomfort I grew to love the sound of my voice. In fact, many of my people are now following my decision and making such lovely sounds. Is it true the Ancient's spoke as you and I do?"

"The history we uncovered would make it seem so, Queen."

"You should speak to your children, Mike, so they will know who you are when they emerge from their chrysalis. Most are very close. Have you decided how you will care for them when they have been born?"

"I thought you wanted them to be raised as Jinn but develop some human characteristics."

"These children are mostly human and need to be among their own kind. You need to take them to Earth and raise them as your own. Your wives should be close to having their babies and it would be good for these to know their siblings."

"You mean Alice and Lee Anne but what of my other children, those of the women you impregnated with my seed? How am I supposed to care for almost two hundred children? How do I really know that any of them are really mine?"

"So many questions. Of course, they are yours. You mated with me to make this brood and were very energetic about it. It is true I used some of your seed on the human women but that was really something I thought of after I had my way with you."

"What do you mean we mated? I was told that my sperm was taken in a laboratory."

"Only what was needed for the Earth women. Our special blend of Dora gave you a tremendous amount of seed. It was probably still in your system when you mated with your wives. If you can hold your questions let's go to the other room and view the remaining children."

"Right, those that Lawrence gave you."

"Perhaps some of them are from Lawrence. Most of them are yours."

The second room was much like the other, just as warm and humid, and containing beds holding squirming shell covered babies.

The heat and the reality of having to care for so many children was making me light headed. Leaning against the wall I tried but failed to come up with much to say.

"You haven't answered me on how you expect me to care for so many children. The President is worried about the public perception when he has to explain where the children came from and that one man was responsible for their conception, with some help from Lawrence. He's trying to bend the law to show that all of them are citizens of our country but what if he can't get Congress or the Supreme Court to go along with his thinking? Did any of that even cross your mind?"

"Let's go back to my chambers where we can relax and talk more comfortably. I'll try to explain my reasoning."

CHAPTER 55

THE GUARD WHO HAD ESCORTED me to the birthing room was suddenly by my side and assisted me in walking out of the room. She gently placed me on the Queen's couch, really a very large love seat and used for that purpose. Minister and Roz looked shocked at my appearance but never moved as the Queen came in and sat next to me.

"You two have been very helpful but it is time for you to be elsewhere. Go talk to your followers if you wish while Mike and I continue our conversation."

"Did you hear that, Minister," Roz said excitedly, "she can speak?"

Minister, looking worried, pushed Roz out of the chamber while glancing over his shoulder at Queen and me sitting close together.

"You appear to have gathered quite a following among the Jinn, my consort. That is as it should be. My mother was correct when she declared that you would be an impressive leader. I'm sorry that she isn't here to see her plan fulfilled."

"According to Minister, she isn't here because you killed her. I'd like to believe she might have done things a little differently."

"Still so naïve and so brilliant. A strange combination. My mother ordered her own death, Mike, just as all of the Queens before her. She also knew that the Jinn needed an infusion of new genetic material or we would become extinct in a few generations. She was the one who decided to include human genetic material in our future births but wanted one specific person to provide it. I don't know how she selected you or your mother only that I was duty bound to follow her wishes."

For the first time since I arrived, I sensed some hostility.

"I know that your mother infused Jinn DNA in both my mother and the human male she had selected," I said as I tried to make my feelings clear. "She caused them to mate and then returned them to Earth. I never met my father, only a succession of men my mother brought home. When I was deathly ill and dying your mother visited me. I'm sure she cured me and, like you've done, left messages in my head. I recently recovered some of those memories but nothing was said about my being a father to three hundred kids."

"My mother loved her games. It's one of the things we both inherited from her as you well know. Another thing was that she felt an obligation to continue the Jinn bloodline. Your mother was a test to see if that could be done. The egg in your mother's belly was one of our own Mother's, planted by her and fertilized by the mate she had selected. There is none of your birth-mother's genetic material in you, just Jinn and a random male human. You are the proof that the Jinn line can continue."

My mind went crazy until I looked in Queen's head and saw that everything she was saying was true. A memory from the old Queen ignited another stored memory and confirmed what Queen had said. Queen was my biological sister. Watching me trying to make sense of my new history, Queen patiently waited until she knew I would hear her as she continued to speak.

"In order to ensure the continuation of the Jinn I am going to allow as many of my people, male and female, to accompany you to your world. All of them have been directed to assist you in caring for the children. You must raise our babies as if they were bred on Earth and encourage them to mate with true humans. The Jinn genetic material will be carried on and in that way the Jinn will not have died."

"Why go through all of the games when that was what you wanted, to protect your line?"

"Our line, Mike, ours. It was also to prepare you for what comes next. I never lied about the Marauders. They are coming but they are not who I said they were."

"Are we still playing games or do you have a point to make?"

"Can I give you some history since you seem to enjoy that part of our interactions?"

"If it will explain things more quickly then go ahead." I was hoping that Lawrence was not going to have an itchy trigger finger while Queen took her time educating me.

"After we tried to deceive you by referring to the Masters as our leaders, they and some of the other more hostile Consortium members decided they would all like a turn at becoming the leader. I was able to hold them off by denying them food and fuel. When our own supplies began to run low and we were unable to find another world that was conducive to growing Dora, the Consortium became angry. We were forced to break away from them and head back to your planet. I didn't lie when I said their ships were much slower than the Jinn ship but it has not prevented them from coming after us. They will eventually arrive at this system. When they find we still have no supplies or have fled to some other system they will go on to your planet. You had to be prepared."

"What of you and your people, what happens to you?"

"We will fight and probably be destroyed. My mother's worst vision will then become fact. We will be gone, much like the Ancient ones you are always speaking of."

"Why wait for the marauders. My government is ready to destroy you now. In fact, Lawrence has a team of ships surrounding this vessel, ready to open fire. Before I can prevent that from happening, I need some assurances from you."

"Of course, whatever you require. Most of my Jinn already look to you as their leader. My final acts should be to ensure the safety of my people and then you can complete the ritual."

"Okay, Queen, now I'm confused. What ritual are you talking about?"

"Once my people are safe you must take my life and assume complete leadership of the Jinn."

"Jesus fucking Christ, Queen, I am not about to kill you. I am trying everything I know how to do to keep you and your people alive."

"How would that look to your President? Wouldn't you be shirking your duty? Lawrence would do it for me but he is not the preselected leader, you are."

"You really don't understand me, do you? In all my life I've never had to kill anyone. I will not allow you or any of the Jinn to sacrifice themselves like the Ancient's on the video nor will I allow you to die. As contrary as you are you still intrigue me, sister or not. I would prefer to keep matching wits with you and offer you any protection my world can provide." Queen smiled and sat back. "Damn you, woman, did you just play me again?"

"That was never my intention, Mike, but it appears as if you continue to play after I have capitulated. How can we make your suggestions work if I am not to die?"

"I'm not sure. There has to be an agreement by my government and probably the governments of the rest of the planet's countries. First, we need to be closer to Earth so I can contact my President."

"Why not do it from here? You've blocked me from contacting him but you still have the ability to have him receive your message."

"That feels so intrusive, Queen. The man has some strong feelings about having people in his head."

"More so than waiting to relay an important piece of information that can forestall a war?"

"Point taken. I'll give it a shot."

My first try had me too nervous to complete a successful connection. The second try went better.

"Mister President, it's Mike Sands, can we talk?"

"Fuck you, Sands; you know how I feel about this. Where are you and why can't you call me on the phone like a normal person would?"

"I'm eight million miles from Earth, John, in a meeting with Queen. My cell doesn't seem to have service out here."

"Always a smart ass. Okay, make this short so you can get out of my head."

"First off, I need a home on Earth for all of my soon to be born children. I would recommend a place that is out of the public eye and in a reasonably comfortable zone, kind of like your vacation home."

"You mean the children you are about to have at the university, I assume."

"You know I also mean the ones on the Jinn ship. They are going to need housing, food and medical attention and room for the attendants who will care for them. I know it's a lot to ask for but it's a humanitarian act to save a dying race."

"Now you've jumped in to a totally different problem. What makes you so sure the Jinn are dying? Was that something the bitch told you or do you have evidence?"

"Both, I guess. Until Lawrence and I came on board the Jinn ship Queen had not had a clutch of eggs for a long time. It seems the Jinn genome had gone infertile and required someone new, humans being that one, to regenerate Queen's ability to lay eggs."

"And you know this to be true? How can you be sure when the bitch has lied before?"

"She's my sister, damn it, and I verified what she said."

"Is that some kind of a euphemism or are you seriously telling me that you now believe that you are, in fact, part Jinn?"

"It's the truth as of a few minutes ago. When Doctor Joe ran our DNA months back, I came back as human with a couple of strange Jinn DNA strands. We passed it off to consuming Dora. I guess he didn't have enough information to see the truth. The Jinn genome is very close to human."

"You're giving me a headache, Sands, a high-grade migraine."

The President went silent but I could sense he had all kinds of thoughts going through his mind. As a courtesy I refrained from peeking.

"Okay, here's my plan. There are ten thousand acres for sale next to my property in Wyoming that I had planned on buying. We use some slush fund money, in your name of course, and buy the property. We can construct what you need and use temporary housing until everything is ready. Who do you have to look after all of those eggs?"

"Queen is allowing Jinn volunteers, some with experience dealing with this current batch of eggs, and I hoped to get some of the Mescalero midwives to help out."

"Not the Apache's, Mike, we will ask my Osage family to help out. If I am going to be a party to this, I want to have a say in how the children are raised. The Osage believe children belong to the entire village and I like that philosophy. I just hope this doesn't get me impeached if we're found out."

"You are a man of many surprises, Mister President."

"Save your sarcasm and sympathy for later. What else do you have to tell me?"

"Queen didn't lie when she told us about the Marauders. What she didn't say was that they were the other members of her Consortium, upset because she wouldn't give them a shot at being the leader. When they insisted, she ran. That means that about eighty ships are on the way but probably won't be here, according to my calculations, for several years at the soonest."

"What makes you so sure of your calculations? Are you a fucking mathematical genius now, too?"

"Something like that. Anyway, the Consortium, according to Queen, is short on food and fuel so they are most likely trying to conserve unless they find a new food source. They might scavenge some of their members, also likely, which will reduce the number of attack ships. The longer they take the fewer ships show up. The upshot is that after Queen delivers the children to Earth, she will refuel, build up her food reserves and then stand guard somewhere north of Mars to act as an early warning system."

"Is that all?" The internal sounds of my friend making decisions filled the otherwise quiet air. *"I guess we have our work cut out for us. When can I assume you will be back home?"*

"Once my discussions with Queen are completed, I will be on my way."

As upset as I get by people terminating a phone call without saying goodbye, it was just as upsetting when the President did the same when he kicked me out of his head.

CHAPTER 56

QUEEN HAD BEEN WAITING PATIENTLY while I conversed with the President.

"Can I assume that your President has come to your way of thinking?" Queen had a smirk on her face as if she had known all along what decisions had already been made. "I have a transport vessel waiting in the docking bay equipped and ready for transporting your children and any Jinn who wish to follow you. All you need is to tell me that you are ready to go."

"You were pretty confident the President would give in. Did you leave a suggestion in his mind to make that happen?"

"You are the one who convinced him. He just sensed the goodness in you, much as I have learned to do."

"What is that supposed to mean, Queen? Did you think of me as someone evil?"

"It has more to do with my mother doing what she thought best for the Jinn."

"I suppose you mean planting one of her eggs in my mother. Other than saving my life I've not received much from her or you and most certainly being an heir wasn't mentioned."

"Do you believe your mother was the only female to receive one of her eggs? My mother must have planted a hundred eggs hoping for one of them to be able to keep the Jinn from disappearing. If you think it was so successful, why were you the only one to survive? After mother spent so much time fawning over you and keeping you alive, instead of embracing what she wanted, I wanted you to die."

Queen stopped talking and looked as if she still hated me. That look passed and one of resignation replaced it. For the first time I began to feel that my mission might be a success.

"It took me a long time to change my way of thinking, Mike. I had replaced my Mother and had nurtured smaller and smaller clutches of eggs when I realized there were fewer Jinn each cycle. I was never able to increase what was needed to maintain a healthy number of followers. Before you and Lawrence spent time with me, I thought I had become barren. Worse was that there was no young Queen available to take my place. It was never on a whim that I chose you and later Lawrence as consorts. I was desperate to find a way to save my people. That was when I learned that my mother had been correct, that you, and to a lesser degree Lawrence, would father the next generation of our people."

Queen stood and took my arm, pulling me back towards the nursery. Once inside she stood me between two rows of near full-term babies.

"These are the legacy, Mike Sands. Look at them and imagine the babies in a human woman, wrapped in an embryonic sack, much like these little ones. Human and Jinn babies develop almost identically although Jinn young usually progress much faster than those in these rooms. Feel the outside of the sack, Mike, and see how these young ones appear to reach for you. Now move along the rows and touch each one. See how they are already bonding with you, sensing that you are the sire to all of these precious beings."

Walking along each row and moving my hands over the soft but tough outer membrane I felt as if I belonged to each of them and that they belonged to me. Finishing in the first nursery I went to the second and repeated acquainting myself with my children. I was surprised when the smaller clutch fathered by Lawrence responded to me much the same as those that I had fathered. I looked up in surprise.

"Why are these children reacting to me like that? Shouldn't they be doing that with Lawrence?"

"These are Jinn babies, Mike. They sense who has their best interests at heart. When you and I mated, even if you had not done so with total knowledge, there was a feeling of affection involved. Perhaps not the same as you have with your human wives but enough to satisfy the Jinn. With Lawrence, there was none of that. He was a tool and I was a ready vessel. These children already know the difference."

"If you feel so close to your offspring why not join them and come down to Earth with us? I know that in time even the President will get used to the idea of a Jinn Queen living close by."

"He will not change his opinion nor do I wish to live where I am subjected to time being broken up in small increments. Life on board my ship is more to my liking."

"But you'll disappear in time without new clutches. That doesn't seem right."

"I have a plan for that but you must be willing to help."

"Am I going to like what you are going to suggest?"

"You seemed to like it the last times. I know that I did."

"You want me to fertilize more eggs, is that it? I had no knowledge then that you were my sister or that I was a willing participant."

"You will be saving an entire race, both on your planet and in space. I will guarantee that one of the brood will be the next Queen so that the space going race of Jinn will continue, but only if you agree to be the sire. What if I told you that I had contacted Alice and she has agreed to you being my consort one more time? She didn't even sound surprised when I told her you were now expressing the pheromones that all Jinn leaders needed to attract new mates. A picture of all your wives came in to her mind and then laughter. She said she already knew."

"This is crazy. You keep making out like I'm more Jinn than human and then organizing things so that no matter what I decide, thinking I was in control, you still get what you want. The games need to stop, Queen, and honest dialogue has to take their place."

"As you wish. So, to be truthful, is Lawrence really close by and ready to damage my ship?"

"He is and I guess I should let him know I will be staying on your ship to prepare the children for transport. Is one day going to be enough time?"

"If you are referring to the manner in which humans determine time then better make it at least two of your days. There are a lot of babies to create in addition to the ones we need to move to the transport."

Roz and Minister were selected to coordinate moving the nurseries to the transport and for arranging quarters for the Jinn moving to Earth. Every so often I checked in to make sure that everything was going smoothly and then returned to Queen's private quarters.

By the time the transport was ready to depart I was exhausted and eager to be on the way home. Roz was chosen to pilot the transport and I demanded to pilot the shuttle. Lawrence agreed only if I kept in continual communication with him so that I didn't make any rookie piloting mistakes. My business partner was not totally happy about not being able to test the firing capacity of his new ships cannons but I guaranteed him the opportunity would come much sooner than anyone wanted.

CHAPTER 57

FIVE DAYS LATER WE WERE back on Earth. The transport was much slower and less nimble than the shuttle. I waited until we were approaching our re-entry window and made a fast descent to our new home letting Roz bring the big ship down at its own pace.

The welcoming committee at our new Wyoming home was more than I expected. I knew John Phillips would be there and more than half hoped Alice, Jeannie, Lee Anne and Lillian had been included but I didn't expect to see an entire MASH unit set up ready to receive and examine all of the new arrivals. I had landed several hours sooner than the transport knowing Roz was still figuring out how to navigate reentry in the ungainly ship. My wives and daughter were in fact waiting and the first to surround me, ensuring I was still the same person who had departed days earlier. We stayed like that until John forced his way to the front and wrapped me in a bear hug.

"Glad you made it back in one piece, Ambassador Sands. I know you want to spend some time with your ladies but there are some people you need to meet."

We walked towards the medical pavilions and stopped outside a unit that looked different than the military tents. Five women, all over six feet tall, followed by three men even taller, came out to introduce themselves. All of them, both men and women, gave me a warm hug instead of a handshake and stood smiling and watching me closely as John introduced them.

"These folks are members of my Osage family. You can see that I am the runt of the litter but all of us are here to make sure your children receive first class care. The medics will do the initial examination and then my people will assist you, or your Jinn attendants, in preparing the young ones for their first days on Earth."

"Are your people always so affectionate? They make me feel like I'm under a microscope."

That made all of them laugh and a babble of happy words surrounded me until they went back to whatever preparations they were doing before I interrupted them.

"You made quite a hit, Sands" John said somewhat enviously. "The women are already hoping to share blankets with you."

Carlos was standing behind the President. I could hear him laughing and telling Alice that I was incorrigible. She just laughed with him and said it was in my nature. She was still smiling as she took me in her arms and led me away.

"We were given a tent a bit apart from the others, just a little alone space for you, me and Lee Anne," Alice cooed. "Lillian and Jeannie are sharing quarters with the Osage women. I hope Lillian doesn't corrupt all of them."

Landing space for the transport had been cleared outside of camp. I hadn't fully realized how huge a ship it was when seen in outer space but when compared to my shuttle and all of the equipment on the ground it was massive. When the door to the cargo bay opened and the ramp descended, I recognized the ship's hold as the same one where I had first met the ones who called themselves the Masters. Roz, unlike the trip to Queen's ship, was all smiles as he walked down the ramp surrounded by three very happy Jinn women. I wondered how that was going to go over with Cassie.

Each day was a matter of anticipation and education. My twice daily connection to the beds of fetuses went from being a chore to an eagerly anticipated series of moments. Each pass of my hands over a Jinn fetus bonded us more strongly, even getting to a point where it seemed that they were trying to tell me when they would be born. The same feeling occurred when I placed my hands on Alice's or Lee Anne's bellies. It was surprising when an occasional shuttle would arrive from space that disgorged more of the Jinn from Queen's ship. They had not been expected but were none the less welcomed. Equally surprising were the arrivals of members of the Mescalero who insisted it was tradition to have tribal members present at the birth of one of their own, pointing to Lee Anne and Alice, both of whom had taken maternity leave.

My wives were going to be staying at the colony for the foreseeable future and should be well attended to. Lee Anne's cousin, Ellie, was one of the first Mescalero to arrive and pointedly told me it was at her cousin's request. There was more behind that arrival, or so said my friend Carlos, but I chose not to look at the reasoning too closely. John Phillips even began to take longer weekends away from his duties to spend time with us, or more practically, with the female members of the Osage.

When not bonding with my future children I probably micromanaged, or tried not to interfere with, the construction of housing units for the growing number of people who were living within our new Jinn colony. The contractor who built my Roswell home brought in a crew to construct an even larger version of the house, meaning more bedrooms and recreational space. Since both of my ladies were nearing the end of their term, I was eager to have the house finished and ready for the arrival of new little ones. It became a race to see who would be done first.

When the turmoil became too great, I began to wander the expanse of the property. I made my way through the recently planted field of Dora and through the forest on the western edges of the property that led to the same canyon that backed up to the President's family lodge. I found my own rock to sit on and let my mind go free of everything that had occupied my time. I didn't think about babies, or wives, or even of the fate of the Jinn. I sat in the sun and listened to the sounds of the creatures that inhabited this land. And once in a while, I even caught an image of my sister, the Queen, sitting in space in a nearly empty ship, staring to the far reaches of the solar system, neither of us seeing anything.

ABOUT THE AUTHOR

P.N. Haberman

Once, in Junior High School, I wrote a skit for a school talent show that was based on something Red Skelton had performed on his television show. The look of shock and disbelief on the faces of those charged with approving my act, and their subsequent rejection without a word as to why I was disqualified, left me with the idea that whatever story I wrote was going to be only for me. Instead, I began to research and expand on required essays in public schools and university all of which were received with praise. I began to write to receive the accolades.

Later, as an officer with the Los Angeles Police Department, my reports were embellished with far more information than my peers. Supervisors would roll their eyes when I appeared in front of them needing report approval but the follow up detectives were appreciative. Later, as a supervisor and investigator, I was allowed to write as many long and informative entries as I wished. That included articles written for local publications as a representation of the LAPD. It gave me encouragement to return to college to study writing and communications.

Some of my earliest efforts at more sophisticated fiction were done at that time. That led to my involvement with writers from the Independent Writers of Southern California (IWOSC) and then a writing coach, Joel Saltzman, who published my story written for his seminar.

Encouragement was all I needed. Marilyn, my wife of over fifty years, has been extremely tolerant of my need to flush stories from my brain and acts as one of my readers. She, our two adult sons and other readers keep me filling up pages of notes and mostly finished fiction. 'It Started in Roswell' may be the first novel to be published but there are over eighty stories in a queue waiting for their turn to come to life.

So, I guess you could say that I have always thought of myself as a writer and continue to do so. It did not matter what education or occupation I followed. The important thing was that within each realm was the means to express myself in print. I have always written the truth as I saw it and fiction as I wish it to be. Point of view for both has always been up to the reader to discern.

AUTHOR REQUEST

How to Write a Comment on Amazon

If you enjoyed *IT STARTED IN ROSWELL* and would like to post a comment on my Amazon book page, here's how to do it: Type *Amazon.com* in your search bar and then click on "Books" in the drop-down menu — then type in my book title in the search window.

When you get to my book page (you'll see the book cover), click on *Customer Reviews*. When a box opens, type in your comment or brief review. You don't need to write a whole book report! Just write down something that made the book interesting to you, or something you particularly liked or identified with. (Note: The main rule is you have to be an existing Amazon member to submit a review; you can use the password that goes with your account).

Why is this important? Statistically, customer reviews sell books! Book-buyers want to read reviews and comments before deciding to buy a book. If an author has no reviews, that discourages customers from buying and THAT means the author gets no royalties. Thank you so much.

P. N. Haberman

Made in the USA
Middletown, DE
11 June 2021